A LOST KINGS M

MORE THAN
Miles

AUTUMN JONES LAKE

More Than Miles (Lost Kings MC #6)
ISBN# 978-1-943950-04-1

Edited by: Vanessa Bridges, PREMA
Edited by: Tricia Harden and Jessica Descent
Proofreading by: Sue Banner
Cover Design by Sarah Hansen, Okay Creations www.okaycreations.com
Image by: Wander Aguiar
Cover Model: Jacob Rodney
Formatted by: Stacey Blake, Champagne Formats

About *More Than Miles* (Lost Kings MC #6)
by Autumn Jones Lake

Blake "Murphy" O'Callaghan, Road Captain of the Lost Kings MC, has the world by the balls. Money. Women. The wide-open road. It's all his, everything he wants…except the one girl he loves, the one girl who's off limits. His best friend's little sister, Heidi.

Abandoned by her mother when she was only eight, Heidi Whelan's familiar with heartbreak. Especially the heartbreak of falling in love with her big brother's best friend. When Murphy pushed her away, it broke her heart. Now, on her eighteenth birthday, he claims he loves her? Growing up around the Lost Kings MC, Heidi's witnessed his manwhoring ways. He'll never give that up for her. Besides, he's too late: Heidi's in love with her high-school boyfriend Axel.

Axel Ryan loves two things—motorcycles and Heidi. He signed up to be a prospect for the Lost Kings MC because it seemed like a fun way to get closer to her. Now that he's gotten a taste of MC life, he's not so sure this is where he belongs. He's confident Heidi shares his dreams for the future, so even if he chooses another road, their relationship will survive the detour.

With more than miles between them, will the deceptions they've lived with for so long be too much to overcome? Can Murphy convince Heidi that the hard roads they've traveled will lead to the most beautiful destination of all, or is he destined to ride the open road alone?

Acknowledgments

The number of people who need to be thanked for making More Than Miles come to life might be longer than the actual book! I hope I don't forget anyone, but if I do it's not that I don't appreciate you.

First, thank you to my readers. Your love of my characters continued support, and eagerness for each new book continues to amaze me. As a life-long reader, I know how many choices you have when you pick up a book. That you choose to read—sometimes re-read—my stories is beyond flattering. Thank you.

My critique partners, Cara Connelly, Kari W. Cole, and Virginia Frost. I don't think I thank you enough for all of your support, encouragement, and help. You make Wednesday my favorite day of the week.

K.A. Mitchell, my friend, and mentor. You're one of my favorite people in the whole world. Thank you for everything you've done and continue to do to help me become a better writer.

Lili Saint Germain, thank you for your cover advice and helping me focus on the why.

Angi J., Amanda, Brandy, Chris, Clarisse, Elizabeth, Iveta, Tamra, and Shelly. Thank you from the bottom of my heart for sticking with me for another Lost Kings book. Andrea F., thanks for jumping in for Murphy's book!

Vanessa Bridges, my patient editor, thank you again for your dedication to helping me refine and shape Murphy's story. Thank you for continuing to go beyond what's required. Even if I'm a little prickly at first, your advice and guidance is always appreciated.

Lisa Miller, thank you for helping me with my research and allowing me to pick your brain. Also, thank you for taking the time to create the More Than Miles playlist for me on Spotify!

Johnnie-Marie, Tanya S., and Terra, thank you for the time you spend promoting my books. Elizabeth, thank you for "getting me" and shouting your love of LOKI from the rooftops.

My Lost Kings MC Ladies Facebook group, thank you for being there. Thanks for loving LOKI so much and laughing at my Mr. Lake stories.

Iza thank you for your continued #WrathLove and all the hot, bearded man photos.

Thank you to my readers old and new that I've met this year. It's been wonderful getting to know you. If you see me at a signing, don't be afraid to say hello—I'm more scared of you, than you are of me!

Ah, and finally, my own personal romance hero, Mr. Lake. My fiercest supporter, who is always ready to kick the ass of anyone who sneers at romance writers.

Dedication

To Bub. It isn't the same without you.

Glossary

I first used a glossary in the *Road to Royalty* Limited Edition boxed set and again in *Tattered on My Sleeve* and *White Heat*. I've made a few small updates and changes here. If you're new to the Lost Kings MC series, this is a good place to start!

The Lost Kings MC Organizational Structure

President: *Rochlan "Rock" North.* Leader of the Upstate NY charter of the Lost Kings MC. His word is law within the club. He takes advice from senior club members. He is the public "face" of the MC. Much to his annoyance, Rock is seen as the "father figure" in the club, especially by the younger members.

Sergeant-at-Arms: *Wyatt "Wrath" Ramsey.* Responsible for the security of the club. Keeps order at club events. Responsible for the safety and protection of the president, the club, its members and its women. Disciplines club members who violate the rules. Keeps track of club by-laws. In charge of the club's weapons and weapons training. Will challenge Rock when he deems it necessary. Outside of the MC, Wrath owns a gym, Furious Fitness. He is experienced in underground MMA style fighting.

Vice President: *Angus "Zero" or "Z" Frazier.* In most clubs, I think the VP would be considered the second-in-command. In mine, I see the VP and SAA as being on equal footing within the club. Carries out the orders of the President. Communicates with other chapters of the club. Assumes the responsibilities of the President in his absence. Keeps records of club patches and colors issued. Z also co-manages the MC's strip club, Crystal Ball.

Treasurer: *Marcel "Teller" Whelan.* Keeps records of income, expenses and investments.

Road Captain: *Blake "Murphy" O'Callaghan.* Responsible for researching, planning and organizing club runs. Responsible for obtaining and maintaining club vehicles.

Prospect: A prospect is someone who has stated a clear intention of being a full patch member of the Lost Kings MC. The Lost Kings vet their prospects for two or more years. To vote a prospect in as a full patch member, the vote must be unanimous. Not all prospects will become full patch members. Some will realize the club is not for them. For others, the club will realize that the prospect is not a good fit for the club. Prospects are expected to show respect to all full patch members and do whatever is asked of them.

The Lost Kings MC has three prospects that we've seen so far. **Hoot** and **Birch** have been around since *Slow Burn (Lost Kings MC #1)*. We first met **Axel Ryan** in *Corrupting Cinderella (Lost Kings MC #2)* and got to know him better in *Three Kings, One Night (Lost Kings MC #2.5)* and *Strength From Loyalty (Lost Kings MC #3)*. He is a main character in *More Than Miles (Lost Kings MC #6)*.

Other members

Cronin "Sparky" Petek: Sparky is the mad genius behind the Lost Kings MC's pot-growing business. He is rarely seen outside of the basement, as he prefers the company of his plants.

Elias "Bricks" Serrano: We saw Bricks and his girlfriend Winter in *Slow Burn* and *Corrupting Cinderella*. One of the few members who does not live at the clubhouse, he performs a lot of general tasks for the club.

Dixon "Dex" Watts: We've also seen Dex throughout the series and gotten to know him better in *Strength From Loyalty (Lost Kings MC #3)*. He co-manages Crystal Ball.

Sam "Stash" Black: Lives in the basement with Sparky and helps with the plants. We got to know him a little bit in *Tattered on My Sleeve (Lost Kings MC #4)*. Otherwise, we're not really sure what he's up to downstairs.

Thomas "Ravage" Kane: We got to know him a little better in *Tattered on My Sleeve*. Ravage is a general member who helps out wherever he is needed.

The Lost Kings MC Ladies

Hope Kendall, Esq.: Nick-named *First Lady* by Murphy in *Corrupting Cinderella (Lost Kings MC #2)*, Hope is the object of Rock's love and obsession. Their epic love story spans four books; *Slow Burn, Corrupting Cinderella, Strength From Loyalty*, and *White Heat*.

Trinity Hurst: Caretaker of the Lost Kings MC clubhouse and the brothers. She and Wrath have a long, tattered love story full of lust, fury, and forgiveness in *Tattered on My Sleeve (Lost Kings MC #4)*. She and Wrath are also featured in *White Heat (Lost Kings MC #5)*.

Heidi Whelan: Teller's little sister. You have seen glimpses of Heidi through *Corrupting Cinderella, Strength From Loyalty, Tattered on My Sleeve*, and *White Heat*. She is also featured in a short story in *Three Kings, One Night (Lost Kings MC #2.5)*.

Lilly Volkov: One of Hope's best friends and frequent "booty call" of Z. You've met her in *Slow Burn, Corrupting Cinderella, Strength From Loyalty, Tattered on My Sleeve, White Heat* and two short stories, "Z and Lilly" in *Three Kings, One Night* and "Infatuated" from the *Pink: Hot 'n Sexy for a Cure anthology*. She will be featured in *Zero Tolerance (Lost Kings MC #8)*.

Mara Oak: Friend of Hope. Also an attorney. She's appeared in *Slow Burn, Corrupting Cinderella, Strength From Loyalty, Tattered on My Sleeve,* and *White Heat*. She's married to Empire city court judge, Damon Oak. Their story, *Objection*, will be available soon.

Lost Kings MC Terminology

Crystal Ball – The strip club owned by the Lost Kings MC and one of their legitimate businesses. They often refer to it as "CB."

"Conference Center" – The clubhouse of the Lost Kings MC. It was previously used as a high-end religious retreat and is sometimes still jokingly referred to as the "Conference Center" or "Hippie Compound."

Empire – The fictional city in Upstate NY, run by the Lost Kings.

Furious Fitness—The gym Wrath owns, often just referred to as "Furious."

Green Street Crew – Street gang the Lost Kings do business with. Often referred to as "GSC." "Loco" is their leader and frequent nuisance to Rock.

LOKI – Short for Lost Kings.

Vipers MC – Rival and frequent enemy MC. Runs Ironworks which borders the Lost Kings' territory. Their president Ransom and his SAA Killa appeared in *Tattered on My Sleeve* and *White Heat*.

Wolf Knights MC – Rival and sometimes ally of the Lost Kings. Their president Ulfric appeared in *Slow Burn*. Their SAA Whisper is a partner in Wrath's gym and appeared in *Tattered on My Sleeve* as well as *Slow Burn*. Actions taken by the Wolf Knights have seriously impacted the Lost Kings in recent times.

Other MC Terminology

Most terminology was obtained through research. However, I have also used some artistic license in applying these terms to my romanticized, fictional version of an Outlaw Motorcycle Club.

Cage – A car, truck, van, basically anything other than a motorcycle.

Church – Club meetings all full patch members must attend. Led by the President of the club, but officers will update the members on the areas they oversee.

Citizen – Anyone not a hardcore biker or belonging to an outlaw club. "Citizen Wife" would refer to a spouse kept entirely separate from the club.

Cut – Leather vest worn by outlaw bikers. Adorned with patches and artwork displaying the club's unique colors. The Lost Kings' colors are blue and gray. Their logo is a skull with a crown.

Colors – The "uniform" of an outlaw motorcycle gang. A leather vest, with the three-piece club patch on the back, and various other patches relating to their role in the club. Colors belong to the club, and are held sacred by all members.

Dressers – Slang for a motorcycle "dressed up" with hard saddle bags and other accessories. It's designed for long-distance riding.

Fly Colors – To ride on a motorcycle wearing colors.

Mother – First chapter of the club.

Muffler Bunny – Club girl, who hangs around to provide sexual favors to members.

Nomad – A club member who does not belong to any specific charter, yet has privileges in all charters. Nomads go anywhere to take care of business usually at the request of the club president.

Old Lady/Ol' Lady – Wife or steady girlfriend of a club member. Has nothing to do with her age.

Patched In – When a new member is approved for full membership.

Patch Holder – A member who has been vetted through performing duties for the club as a prospect or probate and has earned his three-piece patch.

Prospect – A prospective member of the club. The club needs to unanimously vote him in to become a full member.

Property Patch – When a member takes a woman as his Old Lady (wife status), he gives her a vest with a property patch. In my series, the vest has a "Property of Lost Kings MC" patch and the member's road name on the back. The officers also place their patches on the ol' lady's vest as a sign they have agreed to always have her back. Her man's patch or club symbol is placed over the heart.

Road Name – Nickname. Usually given by the other members.

RUB: Slang for Rich Urban Biker. A term generally used by real bikers to describe a person who rides an expensive motorcycle on weekends, and never very far. A poser.

Run – A club sanctioned outing sometimes with other chapters and/or clubs. Can also refer to a club business run.

One

On the Edge

MURPHY

Been waiting for this day for what feels like forever.

My hand's in the air, ready to knock when the door swings open. Heidi's mouth drops in a surprised gasp. "What are you doing here? Axel was supposed to pick me up."

"They needed him at the clubhouse. Besides, it's your birthday, gonna take you for a ride."

Her lips twitch into a smile. "Okay."

She takes a step back to let me muscle my way inside. My arm brushes against her as I pass, and her sweet scent snaps something inside me.

My foot lashes out behind me, kicking the door shut.

"Happy eighteenth birthday, baby girl."

She takes a step back and crosses her arms over her chest. "Thanks."

Every step I take closer to her, she takes one away. Finally her back's to the wall and she's got nowhere else to go. She turns and I slap my hand against the wall to stop her.

"Heidi, look at me."

Her big brown eyes blink up at me. Words can't express what's inside my head or heart. Instead, I lower my mouth to hers. Capture her lips in a soft kiss. As soft as I'm capable of. I pull back just to breathe her in. My hands slide into her hair, holding her still so I can taste every inch of her sweet mouth.

I'm a bastard, because this isn't the first time I've kissed Heidi. We kissed two Christmases ago under the frigid night sky and last year on her birthday.

But it was nothing like this. I don't have to hold back now. She's mine and I'm ready to finally be hers.

Her hands settle on my shoulders. Not pushing me away. But not urging me closer, either. I pull back.

"What are you doing, Blake?" she whispers.

"Claiming my girl."

Her gaze skips away. "I'm not yours."

My arms wrap around her waist, tugging her against me. "Yeah, you are. You've been waiting for this day as much as I have."

One corner of her mouth twists down. It's an irresistible gesture she's done since she was a kid. I've always found it cute.

Now? It's fucking hot.

My lips seal over hers again. This time, she opens for me, slides her hands over my chest, twists her fingers in my flannel shirt, and pulls me closer. My hands slide from her waist to her ass, pulling her against me. She wraps her arms around my neck, holding on to me as I lift her off her feet and carry her to her bedroom.

I kick that door shut, too.

I've got fucking hornets buzzing in my stomach. I've thought about this for longer than is wise to admit. Yet I'm nervous.

We break our kiss.

"Marcel?" she asks.

"Your brother ain't comin' home any time soon." Now isn't the time to talk about my best friend. We'll deal with him later.

Reaching out, I rub my knuckles over her cheek, then cup her jaw and pull her to me for another kiss. I've never loved kissing anyone the way I love kissing Heidi. Even if that's all she lets me do today, I'll be a satisfied man.

One of us moves us to her bed. Probably me. She slips off my cut, carefully setting it on her desk, barely breaking our kiss. My hands run down her back, cupping her ass, pulling her against me. I twist us onto her bed, keeping her on top of me. My hands slip under her sweater and she freezes.

"Baby, I'll be gentle. I won't hurt you," I reassure her.

She snorts and rolls off me to the side. "I'm not a virgin, Blake."

With a growl, I roll on top of her, pinning her to the mattress. "Don't give a fuck, Heidi." But deep down I do. I'm furious. Not at her. I could never be mad at Heidi. She's the sweetest, brightest thing in my world. Always has been. It's the whole situation that pisses me off. And I know right this second, I'm never voting her boyfriend, Axel, into the club. No fucking way.

I have no right to be mad. She was never going to wait for me. Especially not after she caught me in a three-way in the middle of her brother's living room a couple years ago.

"We're even, baby," I whisper while kissing her neck.

She groans. "I doubt that."

Yeah, well I ain't been a saint. But that shit's over. I don't ever want another woman's hands on me again.

I draw back, peering into her eyes. "Axel?" I fucking hate saying his name here in her bed. Thinking of him in here with her is *royally* pissing me off. I haven't been with anyone in a while. It's not much, but it's all I have to offer her.

"None of your business," she shoots back.

"From today on, everything about you is my business."

She doesn't answer. Her hand reaches up and tickles over my beard. "This is scratchy."

I can't help laughing. "I'll shave it off right the fuck now, Heidi."

There's that little twist of her mouth again. "Don't," she whispers.

We keep kissing while I undress her. Slowly peeling off each bit of clothing. I'm fuckin' excited, happy, scared and hard as steel all at the same time. She helps me toss my shirt on the floor. Those little hands of hers skating over my back and shoulders send shock waves through me. I move down her body enough to run my tongue over one nipple and then the other. She gasps and arches her back. It's completely silent in here except for the sounds of us.

Her hands fiddle with my jeans. She gets the button undone, then runs her hands over my sides. I struggle to push and kick my jeans and boots off. I don't want to leave the warmth of her body for even a second.

"There're condoms in my desk," she says, while slipping her arm out and pointing.

Like fuck am I using Axel's goddamn condoms. "I got it," I grumble, and I swear she smirks at me.

Heidi's always had an independent—some might say *bratty*—streak. I love it. I need a woman who stands up to me.

I need *her.*

As I drag my fingertips down her belly, over her hip and down her thigh, she hums in my ear. This crazy sexy, humming-purring sound I've never heard from her before.

I want more.

My hand trails back up her thigh, between her legs. Her heat sears my skin. I hiss when my fingers brush against her. So fucking wet. I circle her clit, and her humming noises turn into moans. I bury my face against her neck. "Heidi."

My finger traces her slick pussy and teases inside. She lifts, pressing herself into my touch. Next time I want to draw this out. When we're in *my* bed. Or maybe I'll take her away where we can be alone. Where I can spend hours devouring her. Learning everything about her. But now? My dick's throbbing. I'm worried if I wait much longer, it won't be good for her.

Her hands shackle my wrist while she keeps me in place. Her forehead wrinkles and her lips part. "Oh, right there. Please, more." The words come out as breathless pants. She grinds herself against me faster, riding my hand while she comes hard and loud. She's more demanding and sure of herself than I expected.

I like it. A lot.

I need to be inside her. If it doesn't happen soon, I'm pretty sure

I'll die.

Heidi

I should feel guilty about this. Why don't I feel guilty?

Twelve-year-old me is doing cartwheels inside, that's why.

Future Heidi knows this is a horrible idea I'll regret.

I've wanted Blake to look at me this way for years. When I found him waiting for me on the other side of the door, I knew this was where we'd end up.

It was inevitable.

The Heidi in the here and now wants what's been denied for so long. I'll have to fix the many broken pieces afterward.

Blood thunders through my ears as I come down. My eyes flutter open and I find him watching me intently.

"Beautiful." To me, his low rough voice is both comforting and thrilling.

Between my legs, his fingers still gently trace circles against my sensitive flesh. "Are you all right?" he asks. I've known Blake my whole life, but never this version of him. Sweet, gentle, and determined.

"Blake, that was…" I can't finish the sentence. I have no words.

He leans down and kisses my nose, then my lips.

My heart pounds impossibly faster as he reaches into the pocket of his jeans and slips out a gold foil square. Was he carrying that in the hopes that we'd end up here? Or is it one of many he carries around on a regular basis, in case some chick wants to drop her panties for him?

Fascinated and conflicted, I watch as he rips into the wrapper, tugs out the rubber and expertly rolls—

From the floor, Blake's phone gives off a muffled buzz.

He hesitates. "Fuck."

I'm practically panting with anticipation. He's so close. The phone buzzes again, and I groan. He nips at my ear. "Ignore it, Bug."

Goddammit. Past Heidi remembers the dismissive way he's called me that for years. How insignificant it makes me feel. How much he knows I *hate* it and he calls me it anyway. To say it now, when everything's about to change. When we're about to…no. Just no. I can't.

I press my hands against his shoulders and push him back. "You should get that, *Murphy.*"

His eyebrows draw down and his gaze roams over my face. "What's wrong?"

A breeze from my open window drifts over me, and I close my eyes. "We should go." I don't wait for an answer. Instead, I shove my way out from under him and scoop my clothes up off the floor. I've been naked in front of one guy in my life—Axel, yet somehow that's not what's bothering me. I'm perfectly comfortable around Blake— and *that's* what bothers me.

"Um?" His hand reaches out, latching on to mine.

"I can't do this with you."

He sits up and I focus on my closed bedroom door so I won't drool all over his perfectly sculpted body. I swallow hard. I've fantasized about seeing Murphy like this for years. *Years.* And I can't even enjoy it.

I love Blake with all my heart. But I'm *in love* with my boyfriend, Axel.

Tugging my hand out of his grasp, I take a step back and slip my shirt on. With some fabric between my skin and Blake's hungry eyes, I can think straight.

"I'm going to…" I gesture at the bedroom door lamely and scurry out.

When I emerge from the bathroom, he's fully dressed and waiting for me by the front door. As I approach, he glances up and a pained smile curves his mouth. "You okay?"

No. I'm rattled right down to my bones. "Yeah, I just know people are probably wondering where we are."

I think he knows I mean *Axel* is wondering where I am because Murphy's mouth turns down. He twists the knob and holds the door open for me.

When we pull up the clubhouse driveway, butterflies dance in my stomach. Except for lockdown situations, I'm not supposed to hang out at my brother's motorcycle club. Most of that went out the window this past summer. The club president—Rock, who's the closest I've ever had to a father—gave his okay for my party to be held up here, since it's my eighteenth. That and I think since he's settled down with Hope—who's like a mother to me—the guys aren't allowed to have the wild parties they used to. Blake parks his bike way down the hill. When he shuts the engine down, I get off and shake out my hair.

"Why'd you park all the way down here?"

"I need to talk to you."

My gaze darts to the house. I know the layout of the clubhouse pretty well. There are no downstairs windows facing this way, but there are plenty of upstairs windows that do. Not that Axel should be in any of those rooms, but still.

"Can we walk while we talk?"

Blake shakes his head in an exasperated way that almost makes me feel sorry for him. I don't mean to be a brat. I hate disappointing Blake more than anything. Maybe more than anyone. But I'm so damn confused. I need to get away from him. Away from everyone. I don't even want to go to my party anymore. The thought of seeing Axel, while all the places Blake touched me are still tingling, twists my insides. In a few brief seconds, I lost control and turned into the kind of whore my grandmother always said I'd be.

Blake eases my helmet out of my hands and wraps his arm around my shoulders, guiding me up the driveway. "I meant what I said, Heidi. I want you to be my girl."

I stop dead in my tracks. "Are you fucking kidding?"

"No, I'm not fucking kidding," he says so low and determined my skin prickles. Using his bulky body, he pushes me off the driveway into a clump of trees. The emotions swirling in my belly scare me. I want him to do things to me that I have no business thinking about. Starting with ripping my clothes off and pinning me up against the nearest pine tree.

Why does it have to be wrong to have what I want? Why do I have to know that Murphy's bedded every willing girl in the tri-state area? I don't want to be one of hundreds.

With Axel, I know I'm special.

Two

AXEL

Something's wrong. My girlfriend can't look me in the eye and that's never a good sign. Murphy's glued to her back and that isn't a good sign, either. I'm not stupid enough to think it was an accident that I got called down to Crystal Ball right as I was supposed to leave to pick Heidi up.

This prospect gig is bullshit. I love to ride. Love Heidi. I even like most of the brothers. But giving up my life to the Lost Kings MC? Putting the club first? Every day it's clearer I'm not cut out for this life.

I don't trust Murphy.

The MC's president—Rock, a guy I actually like and respect—just spent the summer in jail for a crime he didn't even commit. Everyone had to be on lockdown in case a rival MC tried to hurt anyone associated with the club.

I don't want to end up in jail.

Rock's done a good job of keeping me out of serious club business. But I'd have to be an idiot not to know they're into all sorts of illegal activities.

What the heck did I get myself into?

All because of Heidi.

"Hey," she says softly as she approaches and wraps her hand around my forearm. "Where were you?"

"Hoot needed me to run something down to him." I don't mention the strip club, because I don't feel like fighting over it.

She doesn't even press me for details. Another bad sign.

"Why'd *he* come get you?"

Her shoulders nervously jiggle. "Birthday ride. Same old."

Yeah right.

"There's my baby sis!" Teller shouts as he picks Heidi up in a big hug. "You turning eighteen is bullshit." He sets her down and leans over, placing his fingertips at knee-level. "I swear, just yesterday you were this big."

Something sarcastic like, *Maybe if you'd paid more attention to your sister rather than fucking around, you'd realize she's been an adult for a while now* wants to come out of my mouth. But I hang on to the thought—for now.

Heidi's birthday party isn't the place to start listing my beefs with Teller.

MURPHY

I need a bucket of ice for my balls.

Two seconds from finally sinking inside Heidi and my phone ruined it.

Now instead of some after-sex cuddling with the only girl I've ever wanted, I'm being tortured by her scent still lingering on my skin. She came on my hand. It was fucking beautiful. Perfect. Better than I'd been fantasizing about for longer than I want to admit.

Then it got fucked up.

Motherfucking phone. Why didn't I turn that shit off the second I pulled into the parking lot?

Now, she's ignoring me. Pretending what happened between us doesn't mean anything. Hell, pretending it didn't happen at all. Heidi drives me crazy. She's good at it. Been doing it for years. She's been coming on to me since she was twelve. It killed me, but I rejected every one of her sweet-awkward-girlish advances because it was the right thing to do. Somewhere along the way, I crossed a line and hurt her feelings. I hated myself for it, but I didn't know what else to do. Looking at her now, I should applaud myself for my self-control. Heidi's a little sex kitten.

A sex kitten with a boyfriend.

Fucking Axel.

Confirming that Axel's had what I've wanted but couldn't have pisses me off. Thinking of them together makes me want to rip his arms off and beat him to death with them.

More than that, she's *my* girl. My little Heidi-bug. I'm just as hyper-protective of her as her older brother, my best friend, Marcel. Axel putting his grubby hands on Heidi bothers me for so many different reasons.

A good caveman would have declared her off-limits years ago. Then I should have wrapped my dick in a metal cage.

She glares at me from across the room, and even that turns me on. Shit. I've seen her naked now. Brings temptation to a whole new level. I can't stop thinking of us being together again. How the fuck do I make that happen?

"Are you okay, Murphy?" Hope's gentle voice knocks me out of the man-rage I'm working myself into. There's nothing I won't do for Hope. Not only because she's my president's wife, but because of the way she's unofficially adopted Heidi and been so good to her. For her I'll settle the fuck down and pull on a tired smile.

"I'm good, First Lady. How you doing?"

She tips her head toward Heidi and Axel. "Everything okay there? I saw you were the one she drove up with."

For one stupid second, I consider confiding the whole mess to Hope. But if I detect a hint of either pity or disappointment in her eyes, it'll shred me even more.

"Just the usual birthday ride."

Hope's not fooled one bit.

"You're looking nice and tan. Hawaii agreed with you."

She rolls her eyes at the clumsy way I changed the conversation. "You've already heard all our honeymoon stories. Well, the ones you're allowed to hear."

I chuckle and the corners of her mouth tip up. "At least I made you laugh." She squeezes my arm one last time before Rock hooks his fingers in her waistband and yanks her against him. She yelps and slaps his arms as they band around her middle. "Murphy and I were having a conversation." She's laughing too hard to sound stern.

He says something against her ear that turns her cheeks pink and includes the word *wife*, before lifting his gaze to me. "What's up, brother?"

"Nothing, prez. I'm good."

Rock glances at Heidi and shakes his head. "You talk to her?"

"Not exactly."

Hope raises an eyebrow with an expectant expression on her face. I've never figured out if she's on my side or Axel's. I think she's purely team Heidi and I love her for that. Heidi's needed a mother for as long as I've known her. Whether she meant to or not, Hope's stepped into that role. Sometimes I think she's the only one who understands Heidi.

Maybe I *should* confide in her.

Christ, when did I turn into such a pussy?

Over any other chick, I'd never be so stressed. But Heidi? She's everything.

"Hi, Serena," Hope says, looking past me.

Fuck.

I already feel like shit that I've been stringing Serena along for weeks now. Having her here at Heidi's birthday party is a whole new realm of fucked-up fuckery.

"Hey," she says as she joins us.

Hope responds with a warm smile. After hanging out at our downstate charter for a couple years, Serena's still not used to an ol' lady who's actually nice to her. I know she's probably uncomfortable and it's my fault she's here, so I grab her hand and pull her to my side.

Of course, that's when Heidi finally glances my way. Her nose wrinkles and she wraps her hand around Axel's arm even tighter.

Why does everything have to be so fucking complicated?

Someone turns down the lights and people start singing "Happy Birthday." Trinity and Mariella carry out the cake they'd been working on all day, and Heidi drops Axel's hand to race over and meet them at the bar. Everyone cheers as she purses her lips and blows out the candles. Christ, not two hours ago, I'd been kissing that mouth.

Confused, Serena squeezes my hand to get my attention. "Is she a club girl?"

"No," I snap and instantly regret it. "That's Teller's little sister."

"Oh. Sorry."

Not her fault. I'd been doing my best to keep Serena and Heidi far, far away from each other. It's why I'm real curious about her turning up here tonight.

"I'm glad you texted me to come up."

"What?" My gaze scans the room, landing on Axel. The dickhead smirks at me.

Well, I guess he got even with me for sending him to Crystal Ball. Surprised the little prick was so bold.

After everyone has cake, Heidi receives hugs from Rock and Hope. When an acceptable amount of time passes—approximately four seconds—Rock grabs Hope's hand and drags her to the door. She hits the brakes in front of me.

"Will you be okay?" she asks.

Rock sighs and turns, pushing a finger against my chest. "I know you have your hands…full." He flicks his gaze at Serena, who's chatting up Trinity by the birthday cake. "But keep these fuckers in line, please. I don't know where the fuck Z's at and you know Wrath will haul Trinity's ass out of here any minute now."

"Yeah. No problem, prez." I survey the room again and the corner of my mouth turns up. "Sure you don't want to stick around?"

He rolls his eyes at the stupid question. "Yeah, I'm good."

Hope hugs me tight and whispers, "Behave" in my ear.

Even though they made a quiet exit, it's as if everyone in the room knows Mom and Dad have left the building. The volume of the music increases, the clothing on the girls decreases.

And I'm *bored*. Tired of the whole thing. Right or wrong, I've been around this scene since I was twelve. Love my brothers and love my club. But sometimes I wish things were…quieter.

Heidi

My throat's so tight, it's a miracle I have any breath to blow out my candles. Murphy has a girl at my party? After we almost…?

I vaguely remember her from Hope and Rock's wedding, but she looks different tonight. Sluttier. Murphy brought her to my birthday party as his date?

I can't even comprehend it. After he spewed all that bullshit about wanting me to be his girl?

Squeezing my eyes shut, I say a quick thank you to whatever gods are above that I stuck to my guns and said *no*. I'd feel even stupider if we'd gone all the way.

"Are you okay?" Mariella's soft voice helps me tear my gaze away from Murphy.

"Who is that?"

"That's his downstate girl," Axel says as he approaches and slips an arm around me. "She moved up here to be near him. She goes to school with us. I'm surprised you haven't met."

Axel's tone seems calm, but I sense the *I-told-you-so* undertones. I realize I'm being ridiculous since my boyfriend's here. But in my mind, it's two completely separate things.

"I'll have to say hello later," I answer coolly. Even though I'm pissed Murphy invited her to my birthday party, I won't give Axel the satisfaction.

"We need to talk," Axel says against my ear.

"Want to go upstairs?"

Axel isn't the one who has a room here. I am. Hope and Trinity let me stay up here over the summer when the club went through a rocky time and I still have use of it when I want.

His lips press against my cheek. "Yeah. Your brother's gone."

Just because I turned eighteen and I have use of a room in the clubhouse, doesn't mean I want to flaunt sneaking my boyfriend into it. Hope and Rock already left. My brother disappeared but might return at any time. Wrath and Trinity won't care.

No, the only person who might have something to say about it is Murphy. And I'm not interested in his opinion.

I wrap my hand around Axel's and lead him through the crowd.

"Leaving your own party?" Wrath asks as I brush past him. His serious tone stops me in my tracks.

"Are you cockblocking me, Uncle Wrath?" It's a brash, obnoxious thing for me to say, but I think Wrath expects that of me from time to time and I hate to disappoint.

His usual stone-cold face breaks into a hint of a smile. "Not at all." His gaze swings to Axel. "Better disappear now, prospect, before *someone* finds work for you."

Yeah, by someone, he means Murphy.

Trinity winks and I feel a flutter of guilt. Jealous over her friendship with Murphy, I've acted like a snot to her for years, even though she's always been kind to me and tried to make my birthdays special. "Thank you for my beautiful cake, Trin."

Axel nudges me and we continue pushing through people to get to the staircase. I don't look behind us once.

When we're in my room, Axel pushes me up against the back of the door. I gasp from shock and he uses it to seal his mouth over mine in a long, lingering kiss.

"You smell like him," he says when we part.

"What?"

"You. Smell. Like. Him."

This won't be the first time we've fought about Murphy.

"He gave me a ride here."

He snorts. "And what else?"

I can't lie to people I care about. People I don't know? People who ask questions about my brother's motorcycle club? No problem. I can lie with ease to strangers.

I focus on a spot on the wall over Axel's shoulder. "Nothing."

"Please. He's been waiting for your birthday like a fat kid waiting for Girl Scout cookie season."

I snort at the absurd mental image Axel just painted for me. "That's stupid. His girlfriend's here."

He shakes his head as if he's disappointed he needs to spell it out for me. "She's not his girlfriend."

"You seem to know a lot about her."

Axel knows when I'm deflecting. "Don't." He takes his hands off the door and backs away from me. "I love you, but I'm not stupid. I've seen this coming since we got together."

His hands fist at his sides and he glances at the bed. "One, Heidi. That's all you get. I know he's an important part of your life. But I won't be played. I'll give you *one* fuck-up and that's it."

I don't bother asking him to explain this "one fuck-up" rule. It's pretty clear. Generous too. I don't think I'd be as forgiving if the situation were reversed. "There's nothing." The lie feels like slime on my tongue.

"I hope that's true."

I don't have it in me to fight with Axel on my birthday. Obviously he doesn't, either.

"I'm going to head home. You still want me to take you to Penny's tomorrow?"

"Of course I do."

Such sharp pain twists around in my chest. I hate that Axel's mad at me. Hate that I don't deserve his trust.

He gives me a kiss on the forehead and leaves, while I sit down on the floor and stare at the window, wondering if my brother's around to give me a ride home.

Some birthday.

I'm irrationally pissed with Murphy for putting me in this posi-tion.

You could have said no, slut.

Except, in a lifetime of loneliness and bad memories, some of the happiest moments of my life include him. Were *because* of him. There's too much history between us for *no* to be an option where Murphy's concerned.

Three

More than memories

Heidi

I realized I was in love with Murphy when I was eight. Maybe that sounds crazy, but I remember the moment perfectly. My eighth birthday. No card or phone call from my mother—no biggie. I'd stopped expecting anything from her by then. My grandmother gave me a dress—which sucked, because I didn't wear dresses. Reminding her of my preference for jeans got me a smack across the face and a lecture on graciousness.

Ten years earlier...

The rumble of my brother's bike pulling up in front of the house was the first thing to make me happy all day. But when I ran outside, it wasn't just Marcel who came to visit. Blake was there to show off his new bike. I'd seen him working on it with Rock for a long time and never thought much of it.

Ecstatic to get away from my grandmother, who seemed to hate everything I said and did, I flew into my big brother's arms and squealed as he spun me around.

"Happy Birthday, baby sis. You havin' a good day?"

"No. But I am now."

"Missed you, kid."

I choked down my tears, knowing they'd make my brother feel guilty. "I miss you, too."

He sighed and set me down, glancing at the house.

Like lots of kids, I collected Schleich figurines. Unlike most girls my age, I didn't want horses or unicorns with unrealistic rainbow-colored manes. Nope, I was obsessed with collecting the wildlife figurines. The more realistic the better. Even though I realize they were never that expensive, back then, to me, they cost a fortune. Marcel brought me one of the littler creatures almost every time I saw him, and I cherished each one, because to me it meant even though I didn't get to see him a lot anymore, he hadn't forgotten about me.

When my brother set me down, Blake motioned me over. At first I thought he wanted to show off his bike, but he crouched down, pulled something out of his saddlebag, and handed it to me.

"This is so cool!" I couldn't stop myself from jumping up and down at the roaring grizzly bear. "He looks so mad. What do you think he's growling at?"

"Maybe this?" He handed me a snowy owl figurine, and I thought I'd explode with happiness.

"Two?"

"Yup."

I plopped right down on the sidewalk to inspect my new treasures while the two of them talked about where to go next. I hated that they were already leaving.

"You bring her helmet, bro?"

My brother was slow to answer. "Yeah."

"Can I take her?"

That got my attention and I jumped up. "Can I, Marcel? Please, please, please?"

"Yeah, calm down." He glanced at the house, where my grandmother was either staring out the window trying to put a hex on Marcel, or not paying any attention at all. "Go put those inside and let

Gran know we're gonna take you down to Friendly's."

He didn't even get the last word out before I raced up the sidewalk and into the house. Grams was nowhere to be found, so I raced upstairs, tucked my new treasures away in my dresser drawer and flew back down. I yelled a quick, "Going to Friendly's!" before slamming the door shut.

"Ready!" I announced when I landed at the end of the sidewalk.

Blake handed me my helmet and chuckled at me.

Marcel put his big brother stare on Blake. "Go easy with her."

"Absolutely."

"Hang on tight," Marcel warned me.

Did I ever.

I wrapped my arms around Blake so tight, it was a miracle he could breathe. I'm pretty sure it ranks up there as one of the happiest days of my life.

I'd ridden with my brother lots of times and loved it. But riding behind Blake was different. Different but still familiar.

The boys chose Friendly's because they'd give me a birthday sundae for free and to check out one of the waitresses behind the counter.

It was the first time I'd ever thought about Blake having a girlfriend, and it bothered me.

It bothered me a *lot*.

Suddenly my sundae didn't interest me that much. I studied the girl they were both so obviously interested in. She had long blonde curls tied into a high ponytail that swished back and forth as she ran around the cramped restaurant. I glanced down at my own dark, whip-straight hair—windblown and messy from the ride here.

"What's wrong?" Blake asked when he noticed my ice cream had melted into a puddle.

"Nothing. Don't feel good."

Concern snapped Marcel's attention away from the pretty waitress and he pressed the back of his hand against my forehead. "You eat any real food today?"

"Yeah." I'd poured my own Cheerios this morning, but it wasn't the lack of food that'd turned my stomach.

Now that I had their full attention, I milked it for everything I could. After I rattled off a long list of ailments, Marcel squinted at me. "Sounds like we should take you to the hospital."

Whoops. I'd gone one too far.

"Can we go now?"

"Sure. I'll grab the check." He lifted an eyebrow and nodded at Blake. "Stay and watch her?"

As we walked out to the parking lot, Marcel gloated that he'd gotten the waitress's phone number and Blake shrugged.

"That means you're all mine," I said, throwing my arms around his waist. He stared down at me, patted my back.

"Always."

My heart fluttered and that one word meant more to me than Blake would ever know.

At the house, he promised to take me for a ride every year on my birthday.

I watched them take off and disappear down the street.

Then ran straight to my room and cried into my pillows until I fell asleep.

Four

Heidi

Thankfully, my brother doesn't have a lot of questions when I finally locate him and ask for a ride home. In fact, I think he's relieved to get me away from the clubhouse.

Not wanting to leave me alone on my birthday, he stops at Stewart's for my favorite ice cream and we make a plan to stay up late watching cheesy eighties horror movies.

After the last movie, he turns to me. "You're falling asleep. Time for bed."

"I'm eighteen now. You can't tell me when to go to bed," I tease.

He groans and runs his hands through his hair.

At my bedroom door, he pulls me in for a hug. "Love you, baby sis. I'm proud of you, too. I hope you know that."

Tears prick my eyes and I squeeze him tight. "I know. I love you, too."

"Did you have a good birthday at least?"

I mentally run over the day. Almost having sex with Murphy. Rejecting Murphy. Spending time with my club family. Fighting with Axel. Not the best birthday ever, but certainly not my worst.

"Yes."

"Good." He hesitates and runs his hand over his cheek before continuing. "I need to make a quick run out to Syracuse tomorrow, so I'll probably be gone when you get up."

"Okay." I don't bother asking what he's doing. It must be club business, otherwise he would have told me.

"I'll leave some money on the counter for you, so you can get breakfast. There's nothin' in the fridge."

On impulse, I reach up and give him another hug. "Thank you for always taking good care of me."

He seems surprised and shakes his head, but I rush to explain. "I mean it. I'm an adult now. I can get a job and help out around here."

"No. Your job is doing well in college."

"But—"

"No." He flashes a quick smile to cancel out the harshness. "I need you to get good grades so you can graduate and land a good job. Then you can take care of me in my old age."

I can't picture Marcel ever being old enough to allow me to take care of him. "Deal," I answer.

He places another kiss on my forehead before going into his own room.

I didn't have a drop of alcohol last night—you'd think the clubhouse would be the perfect place to sneak drinks, but you'd be oh-so wrong— and still, I wake up the next morning with a pounding headache.

Some of the pounding, I realize, is someone banging on the front door.

Annoyed at whoever decided to drop by this early, I turtle-walk my way into the living room. If it's one of Marcel's muffler bunnies, I'm getting out the shotgun.

It's Murphy.

For some reason, I didn't expect to see him for a while. A shiver of happiness throbs through me. I can't help it. It's how I always feel around him.

Then I remember seeing that girl clinging to his side and it pisses me off so much, I throw on a mask of indifference while he tries to talk to me about last night. I've got plenty of things to say about last night, but I'm too mad to have my words make any sense.

So instead, I act like the brat everyone thinks I am and piss him off. The slam of the front door jolts my heart, as if Murphy took a piece of it when he stormed out. Before I know what I'm doing, I'm up and running after him.

MURPHY

Last night did not go the way I'd planned. Not even a little bit. Nope. Heidi stayed glued to Axel's side all night, then I caught her sneaking him upstairs. I had no right to stop them. Her brother wasn't around for me to tattle on her. For a second, I thought Wrath would intervene. But he was no help either.

Confused by my inattention, Serena left the party early. Honestly, it was a relief. If I can't have the girl I want, then I'd rather be by myself at this point. Maybe it's too little too late as far as Heidi's concerned. I don't know.

I *do* know if I gave up every time life threw a challenge at me, I'd be dead in a ditch by now. So first thing the next morning, I ride over to Teller's apartment. Wrath casually mentioned how Axel left early last night and Marcel had taken Heidi home a while later. Words that gave me some hope. Maybe she ended things with him?

I know Teller's got club business to take care of, so he won't be home. I'm praying like fuck Axel's not using the opportunity to reconcile with Heidi or sneak in some alone time.

No other bikes in the parking lot's a good sign.

Heidi taking for-fucking-ever to open the door is not.

"Hey. What are you doing here so early?" she asks in a low morning-rough voice that has me thinking about what it would be like to wake up next to her every day.

I aim for cheerful, instead of the pervy bastard who threatens to make an appearance. "It's almost noon."

"In case you forgot, my birthday party was last night. I got in late."

At least I know the "got in late" applies to her brother giving her a ride home and not her boyfriend. I ignore her sarcasm. "We still need to talk."

She yawns and opens the door wider. "You could have at least brought me breakfast."

Jesus Christ. A braless Heidi in tiny flannel shorts, tank top, and not much else is not what I need in front of me right now.

"I'll take you out for breakfast later. First, we need to talk."

"About whaaat?" she whines as she walks back into her bedroom.

I'm trying not to drool over her long bare legs walking away from me or notice the swish of her ass in the tight flannel.

I expected her to shut her bedroom door, change, and come back out. But the door stays open. Cautiously, I stick my head inside and find her under the covers.

"Heidi?"

"What?"

"Can we talk?"

One of her hands flails out from underneath her comforter. "Speak."

Is she deliberately trying to tick me off?

After yesterday, I think it's best I stay away from her bed. But I'm irritated that she won't look at me.

"It would be easier if you'd look at me."

"Blake, I'm tired. Spit it out or let me go back to sleep."

"Never mind." I don't fuckin' need this shit. She made it clear last night, and she sure as fuck is making it clear right now, she doesn't give a fuck.

The slam of the front door behind me isn't as satisfying as I expected.

Five

MURPHY

I'm halfway to my bike when I hear the light *thud, thud, thud* of Heidi running down the stairs behind me. "Blake, wait!"

Everything in me stops moving. I turn around in time to catch her as she throws herself at me. "I'm sorry. Please don't be mad. I can't stand when you're mad at me."

Ah, shit.

I wrap my arms tight around her and squeeze. "I can't ever stay mad at you."

After a second, I realize she's still wearing the tank top, sorry excuse for a pair of shorts, and no shoes. "You shouldn't be out here like this."

By *this* I mean the barely-there clothes, but also the bare feet. "You're gonna get a splinter or something in your foot."

"I think I already did." Her mouth turns down. She picks her foot up and wraps her hand around it, inspecting for damage. The movement means she's hopping around on one foot. Braless.

Jesus. Eighteen or not, she's fucking clueless.

"Come on." I crouch down and she wraps herself around me for a piggyback ride, the same way she's done since she was little.

The pleasure of her body plastered against my back barely registers before the rumble of another bike enters the parking lot.

Fucking Axel.

"Shit," Heidi mumbles and tries to scramble off me. But I've got an iron grip on her legs.

"Blake, let me down."

"No."

"Blake, come on. He's gonna get pissed."

Something about her tone stops me. I don't know how to express the rage welling up in me, though. I find out Axel's ever laid a hand on her, I'll fucking murder him—slowly and painfully. I allow her to slide down, but wrap my hand around her arm. "What do you mean?"

"What do you think? We had a fight last night."

"About what?"

"What we always fight about. *You.*"

I'm too distressed that she spends a second being unhappy to take any pleasure in finding out they fight about me. "Did he hurt you?"

"No! Knock it off." She shakes out of my grasp about the same time Axel pulls into a spot next to my bike.

I have to give Axel credit. He's a brave little bastard, because he strolls right up to us and nods at me as if nothing's wrong. "Morning."

I fold my arms over my chest and acknowledge the greeting with a nod.

"You okay?" he asks Heidi.

"She's fine. We were in the middle of something."

Heidi smacks my arm, but it might as well be a tap from a butterfly.

Axel's done being polite. He ignores me and focuses on Heidi. "Are we going to Penny's or not?"

"Yeah, later. Just let me…"— her head swivels between the two of us—"take care of this. I'll call you."

Axel narrows his eyes at Heidi. "Fine," he says. I'm really not liking the disrespect in his tone. No one, don't give a fuck who, should talk to Heidi like that. But since I'm hoping soon it won't be an issue, I let it go.

He takes off without another word. You'd think a real man would stay and fight for his girl. "See, even he knows it's pointless to fight this."

"God, you're a caveman. What'd you want to do, fight to the death for me?"

Yeah, kinda. If that's what it takes.

By the look on her face, she knows what I'm thinking and it isn't appreciated.

She groans and turns to head back upstairs. I have to run to catch up with her. "Still want your piggy back ride?"

"No."

We don't say anything else until we're inside. I make the mistake of trying to kiss her and she wriggles away from me.

Confused, I reach for her again. "What's going on?"

"I explained last night. I can't do this."

"Heidi—"

"No. I made a mistake. I'm not *that* girl. I don't want to be. I don't cheat on my boyfriend."

"Then break up with him." There. Seems pretty simple to me.

She stares at me for a second—probably to see if I'm joking, which I'm not.

Her face screws into what at first seems like anger. "Does Serena know you're here?" By the soft tone she uses, I know she's hurt.

"She has nothing to do with us."

"So you invite her to family weddings and birthday parties, but she's not your girlfriend?"

"No," I answer evenly.

"Why the hell did you invite her to *my* birthday party? After you said... After we...?" She chokes on the last word and points at her open bedroom door. I'm furious at Axel for pulling that prank, but I don't offer him up as an excuse. Even though I'm one hundred per-cent positive he's the reason Serena ended up there last night, throw-ing the blame on him seems like a pussy thing to do.

I give her a simpler truth. "I didn't know she would be there. She's just a friend."

"Right. Your downstate girl."

Fuck. "Who told you that?"

This angry, frustrated groan works out of her throat. It reminds me of the noises she made yesterday when we were alone in her bedroom and I thought we could finally be together.

"You make me crazy and turn me into something I don't want to be," she snaps.

"What's that even mean?"

Frustrated, she waves her hands in the air. "You're not *good* for me."

"Heidi—"

"Don't 'Heidi' me. Did you tell your girlfriend about us?"

"Fuck no. She's *not* my girlfriend."

"Right. Just a girl you fuck from time to time. Well, sorry, I don't feel like being added into your rotation."

"My *what*? Why are you giving *me* a hard time, when you're with Axel?" I swear to fuck I'm tired of hearing that kid's name.

"Are you kidding me? First, that's none of your business. Second, my *one* boyfriend—who I happen to love, by the way—hardly compares to the volume of women who've been in and out of your bed."

"Volume of women? What the fuck are you even talking about?"

"Do you think I'm stupid? You think I'm dumb enough to think that horror show I walked in on a couple years ago was a one-time event?"

"That's—"

"No," she says, cutting me off. "You never even asked me why I showed up that day."

I'd been too fucking embarrassed to dwell on it. "Heidi, the whole thing was embarrassing for everyone. I wanted to forget it happened. I'm so sorry."

"I'm sure you are. Do you think I don't know you two were up to that shit for years? And kept it up even after—"

"You were thirteen! What was I supposed to do?"

She glances at the floor, then meets my eyes again. "Don't act like you've been pining away for me all this time. I've overheard plenty of stuff over the years."

"From who? Your brother?"

"No. I only have to be up at the clubhouse for five minutes to hear the kind of dirty shit you're into."

What the actual fuck? "What are you talking about?"

She doesn't hesitate with her comeback. "Please, everyone talks about how you have a different girl at every LOKI charter in the Northeast."

"Who? Axel? Of course he'd say that." That may have been true a couple years ago, but I've settled down a lot, so it pisses me off that she still thinks I'm like that.

"No. And leave him out of this. I've been hearing those stories since I was a kid. I never really believed it until—"

"You've got to let that stuff go. It has nothing to do with *us*." Even as I try to convince her, a bad feeling forms in the pit of my stomach.

"I don't *have* to do anything. How could I ever trust you?"

"I wasn't in a relationship with any of them!"

That was probably the worst possible thing I could have said.

She nods as if I proved her point, which I probably did. "I couldn't stand wondering who you were with all the time. It would break my heart," she whispers, glancing down at her intertwined hands.

All I want to do is comfort her. My fists ball up in frustration as I try to find the right words to explain she's all I've ever wanted. I'd rather lose a limb than ever hurt her. "You're all I want. When have I given you a reason not to trust me?" I hate how desperate my voice comes out.

She can't come up with anything. But she shakes off the question. "We won't work. I want to finish school—"

Now *that* pisses me off. "*I* want you to finish school. For fuck's sake, I offered to send you anywhere you wanted to go."

"I don't want your money. I'm not some whore."

"What?" Is every woman this frustrating? "Why do you even go there? You're my girl. I want to take care of you. What's wrong with that?"

"I'm not *your* girl."

"Forget the fucking money. You're right, I'm an asshole for wanting to make sure you go to college."

"I didn't say that. I can't take your money. It wouldn't be right. I'm with Axel."

She crosses her arms over her chest and glares at me. Shit, even that's fucking hot.

I ignore the *I'm-with-Axel* bit. "Heidi, I'm sorry if I've ever made you feel bad, but I've always cared about you. In one way or another, I've loved you since the day I met you."

"Then why'd you have to be so mean and push me away?" Her words are weighted with years of hurt that I unknowingly caused and it almost crushes me.

How do I explain it to her in a way that makes a lick of sense? "I didn't know how to deal with my feelings. I didn't want to end up doing something I'd regret later. I only ever wanted what was best for you."

Silent tears roll down her cheeks, and I have to stop myself from kissing them away. "Why couldn't you just say that?"

Her words punch me in the gut, because there were so many times I *did* want to tell her to wait and be patient. "How could I ever tell you that? You would have made things ten times harder on me."

"You—"

"It *hurt* waiting for you, Heidi. There were days when I'd see you and think I'd lose my fuckin' mind. That's why I had to stay away sometimes."

"But you kissed me—"

"I know, baby girl. And I shouldn't have."

"Please don't say that." Her voice, raspy from tears, slices right through me.

"I never regretted it for a second. That's not what I'm saying. I shouldn't have messed with your feelings. That's what I'm sorry about."

"But, why couldn't—" She breaks off, sobbing, and I have to gather her in my arms.

Leaning down to kiss the top of her head, I close my eyes and give her the truth she needs to hear. "I'm so sorry I ever hurt you. I love you so fuckin' much. You're the last person in the world I'd ever want to hurt."

She sniffles and wraps her hands in my T-shirt to get closer. "Blake?"

"Yes, Bug?"

As if that word's some magical, pissed-off switch for her, she flattens her palms against my chest and pushes me away. "Why do you have to ruin everything by calling me that?" She's not quite screaming, but a few more decibels and my eardrums might bleed.

"We all call you that."

"I hate when *you* call me that!"

"I don't—"

She's too mad to hear reason. "It makes me feel small and insignificant. It reminds me of every time you called me that to put me in my place. You say I'm your girl, but you never *listen* to me. I've told you a million times how much I hate it."

She's so wrong. When she was little, it was a sweet nickname that became a habit and later, I called her that to remind *myself* that she was off-limits. Never to hurt her. "Okay, okay. I'm sorry. I thought we were just joking around. I didn't know it bothered you so much."

"Well, now you know."

"So you're not going to give us a chance because I called you *Bug*?"

"There is no us."

"There will *always* be an us."

"I'm with Axel," she whispers.

"Heidi, do you love him or are you trying to get even with me?"

Her jaw drops. It's probably the most honest question I've ever asked her and I want a real answer.

"God, you're so full of yourself! Yes, every time we make *love*, I'm thinking 'This'll show Blake!' How'd you know?"

Fuck, fuck, fuck. That answer might have been a little *too* real. My vision swims red and the buzzing in my ears reaches an all-time high. Thinking about the two of them together has me about ready to lose my shit. I asked the question, though, so I deserve every bit of pain gathering in my chest.

"We can talk about this later." I try one last thing. "Hey, remember how I promised to take you apple picking for your birthday? Let's go—"

She shakes her head sadly. "I can't. Axel and I have plans."

I blow out a frustrated breath. "When can we get together and talk?"

"There's nothing to talk about."

"Bullshit," I growl.

I love her.

She can deny it all she wants, but Heidi's *mine*. Every stubborn, bratty little inch of her.

Six

The bond of true family isn't always one of blood

MURPHY

Fourteen years earlier...

The ride to the Lost Kings MC's clubhouse seemed longer on my own. Usually, I'd peddle as hard as I could to keep up with Marcel.

Rock was out behind Crystal Ball, the strip club located right next door to the MC's clubhouse. The guys could always be found there or in the garages behind the clubhouse. I'd gotten to stick my head in Crystal Ball once or twice. Never got to see any of the good stuff, though. Just poor lighting, ugly decorations, and throbbing music.

Rock lifted his head when he saw me coming.

"'Sup, kid? Where's your buddy?"

"Don't know."

He cocked his head and gave me a more serious appraisal. "Everything okay?"

I lifted my shoulders and prayed like fuck any tears were wiped clean on the ride down.

"Needed to get away for a bit?" Rock asked.

"Yeah."

He nodded and tossed his cigarette, grinding it out under his boot. "Come on. Let's teach you how to change some spark plugs."

Cool. I followed him next door to the garages. I tried not to act too eager, but inside I was bouncing with excitement. Usually Marcel was the one learning stuff, and I just got to watch.

Rock was patient and when I froze up because I was afraid I'd wreck his bike, he assured me I wouldn't. I was finishing up when screaming and shouting echoed across the parking lot. Ruger, the president of the Lost Kings, was tossing one of the Crystal Ball dancers out the back door. Rock's hand tightened around the wrench he was holding, but he didn't move.

Ruger slammed the back door shut and the girl focused on us. Rock called her over.

"What'd I tell you last time, Ashley?"

As usual, I was invisible to the girls that came out of the club. They either straight-up ignored me or wanted to mother me. Both sucked.

When Ashley turned, I caught the bruise forming along her cheek, her eyes wet, red and puffy from crying. Rock grasped her chin and turned her face.

"Christ, Ashley. You need to leave."

"I was gonna, but a flight home's like three hundred and thirty bucks. Then he called and was so sweet. I figured—"

"He ain't ever going to change, Ashley."

She stared down at the ground, misery all over her face. I should've probably looked away or gone away, but I didn't have anywhere to go.

Rock tipped her chin up again. "Where's home? Your family?"

"My momma's in Texas. I—"

"If I give you the money, will you go now? Don't stop by your apartment. Toss your fucking phone and get on the next plane."

"Shit, Rock. You don't—"

"Will you?"

"Yes, yes." It seemed to finally sink in that Rock was serious and a look of relief washed over her.

Rock yanked out his wallet, flipping it open and pulled out a handful of bills. "That's more than enough, Rock. I have some saved up. Thank you."

"You need a ride to the airport?"

"No."

They talked for a few more minutes, but I lost track of the conversation when I spotted Ruger watching them from just inside the back door.

"Rock?" My voice wasn't loud enough to catch his attention, so I waited until Ashley finally left.

Without turning my head, I gave Rock a low warning. "Ruger was watching."

"Yeah, I dare the fuck to say a word about it."

When I looked up again, Ruger was gone. Rock turned his stare on me. "I ever catch you hurting a woman, I'll break your hands."

"I wouldn't. But this ain't the first time he's knocked her around. Why she keep coming back?"

"'Cause he's a real good fucking liar."

I might not have been the brightest, but even I'd figured that out about Ruger.

"You're meant to take care of girls and protect 'em," Rock continues.

It wasn't exactly an issue since no girls would talk to me. I opened my mouth to say that and Rock's mouth curled into a smile, but he didn't laugh at me. "Don't worry. The ladies will be crawling over you in a few years."

Yeah, right.

"What if she just spends your money and comes back tomorrow?"

He shrugged. "Least I tried."

Rock's best friend, Wrath, stopped by. "Need to talk to you," he said in a low voice. He lifted his chin at me. "Hey, kid. You gettin' some work done?"

"Taught him how to do a few things," Rock says. "Picked it up right away."

"No doubt. Knew he'd be good with a wrench." I stood a little straighter. While Rock was always encouraging, Wrath's approval was harder to earn.

"What'd you need?" Rock asked.

They took a few steps away, and I inched closer so I wouldn't miss anything.

"Ruger set this fight up for me and I won't be ready for it. He's got me set up on a long run. Won't be back until right before the fight."

"Motherfucker," Rock grumbled. "You ain't lost one yet. We got some time?"

"Not much."

"We'll figure it out. Where's Z at?"

"Dunno. Riding with Lucky."

"Fuck me. Make sure he comes to see me when he gets back."

"Hey, guys," one of the girls next door called out.

"Christ," Rock muttered while Wrath chuckled.

"Hi, Meg." Wrath greeted Meg with a smug smile firmly in place.

"Why can't you keep your mouth shut?" Rock grumbled, which made Wrath grin even wider.

"What are you guys up to?"

"Nothing," Wrath said at the same time Rock answered, "Working."

Meg focused her attention on Rock. "That's too bad, I thought maybe—"

"You know I'm with Carla," Rock said in a bored tone. He motioned me to his side and handed his wrench over.

"Oh, hey, Blake."

"Hi, Meg." My voice sounded like a little girl's. So fucking embarrassing.

"You really gonna marry Carla?" I asked Rock after Meg left.

Wrath snorted at the question, earning a scowl from Rock. "Yeah, why?"

Because she never seemed too fond of Marcel and me hanging around. I figured once they were married we'd see a lot less of Rock.

Since this was the closest I had to a family, I'd miss it when it got taken away.

"Just wonderin'," I answered.

Marcel joined us, so I didn't get to say anything else. He was carrying his baby sister. Well, Heidi wasn't really a baby anymore. She was four and could talk your ear off. I couldn't be around her for more than five seconds without smiling.

"Where ya been, fucker? I stopped by your house. Your ma was throwing a fit, smashing dishes everywhere," he said when he stopped in front of us. Nothing would calm my crazy-ass mother down until she found some cash. Better I was out of her way, so she didn't aim the china at my head. Thanks to her, there was nothing of value in my room anymore. Didn't give a fuck if she tore it apart again. She wouldn't find shit.

In this garage, I felt safer than I did in my own house.

"Hey, Heidi-girl," Rock said and she beamed at him.

Heidi's arms reached out for me. "Blake. Blake. Blake," she chanted. Like I'd ever say no to her.

I grabbed ahold of her, and she wrapped her legs around me, little knobby knees digging into my sides. "Hi, Bug."

She pulled back, placing one of her tiny hands on each side of my face. "I am *not* a bug, Blake," she stated with the seriousness of a grown-up.

"Yeah, you are. You're *my* bug."

She huffed and wiggled in my arms. "Put me down," she demanded.

I set her down but kept hold of her hand. Couldn't have her taking off and gettin' run over by one of the dancers who blew in here like it was a raceway.

Rock lifted his chin at Marcel. "What's up?" I think what he meant was, *This isn't the best hangout for your little sister.*

Marcel shot a pleading look at Rock, and I figured things must be bad at home. Rock nodded in understanding and didn't force an answer out of him.

Besides, it wasn't Heidi's first time hanging out here. If you set her on the counter and handed her a few tools, she'd happily chatter about anything and everything all afternoon.

Marcel pushed me out of the way and took over working on the bike. Rock nodded at me, and I picked Heidi up, setting her on the counter and then hopped up next to her.

"Did you go to school today?" Heidi asked.

"Yeah." I hated school. Rock said if I ever wanted to join the club I had to finish, though.

"I can't wait to go next year! I already know a bunch of letters." Then she sung the entire alphabet to us, making Rock chuckle.

I stayed out of the way but still wished Marcel hadn't taken over. The roar of multiple bikes entering the parking lot reached us, and Rock and Wrath headed out to meet the guys. Heidi started squirming to get down so she could follow. I hopped down first and offered my back to carry her out into the parking lot. She wrapped her little arms around my neck and I concentrated on not choking.

"Ease up, Bug."

"Sorry."

I set her down long enough to say hello to Grinder, Lucky, and Z, then headed back to the garage. If I wanted to keep hanging out here, it was best to stay away when the guys had business to discuss.

Grinder was older than Rock, and from what I'd heard, he brought Rock into the club years ago. Lucky and Z were also tight with him, but we didn't see them as much as Wrath. None of them minded us hanging out here, but they were real careful about what they said around us, too.

Marcel lifted Heidi in the air, spinning her around until she yelped. Since he was busy with Heidi, I made it back to the bike first.

"You even know what you're doing?" Marcel asked, setting Heidi back down on the counter.

"Yeah. Rock showed me." *Before you got here and took over.*

Grinder's bike started up and a few minutes later Rock joined us. "Waitin' on me?" he asked.

"Yup."

I reclaimed my spot next to Heidi.

Even though I wasn't working on anything, I was just happy to be there. My father was in and out—mostly out—of my life. My mother was a mess who didn't even know what day it was most of the time. School was torture. From the outside, it might have looked like a scary place to hang out, but at least around the MC, I was accepted and included.

"You came dressed to work, Heidi-bug, why you sittin' up there?" Wrath nodded at her coveralls.

"My underwear have ruffles, wanna see?" she asked.

Everyone chuckled at her.

"No, Heidi. And don't let me hear you offer that around here again," Rock said. He was laughing, though, which made Heidi laugh, too.

Marcel nodded at his sister. "She wants to be a vet." He nodded in the direction of Crystal Ball. "Not a dancer."

"Careful, Marcel," Rock warned. "A lot of those girls are dancing to pay for college."

His face reddened. He hated sayin' something stupid around Rock and gettin' called out for it. "Yeah, well, not my sister," he grumbled and it surprised me he'd get mouthy with Rock. Whatever had gone down at his house earlier had him in a foul mood.

"I like to dance," Heidi blurted out. She jumped off the counter to show us her dance moves, making everyone laugh again. Abruptly, she stopped. "I'm hungry." She turned her glare on Marcel.

Rock pointed across the street. "We'll go over to the 76 Diner."

That was thrilling news for Heidi and a relief for Marcel and me. Neither of us had a single dollar, and it was doubtful either one of our mothers had bothered to buy groceries.

"I want a chocolate milkshake," Heidi announced.

"Heidi—" Marcel started, but Rock cut him off.

"Whatever you want, Heidi." He stopped to clean up and then patted his front pocket. "Fuck. Forgot Ashley cleaned me out."

Wrath rolled his eyes. "I got it."

"You don't have to," Marcel tried again. He had more pride than I did.

"No, you and Blake were a big help. Least I can do is buy you dinner." Rock's mouth turned up in a smirk. "Or have Wrath buy you dinner." He glanced down at Heidi. "And I can't say no to a pretty girl."

"That's me!" Heidi beamed. "Hold my hand," she demanded, sticking her hand out for Wrath to take.

"I think it's just easier if I pick you up." She squealed and chattered all the way across the road.

Marcel and I had no choice but to follow along.

The next few years were the most difficult I'd ever encountered. Rock married Carla, and as I feared, she wanted nothing to do with three wayward kids. Rock still made time for us, but he was constantly stressed. Not long after, Lucky died. Rock and Grinder ended up going to prison. Instead of the safe haven it had been for us, the club turned into a hostile place. But as much as we tried to distance ourselves, Ruger kept pulling us in.

Wrath and Z protected us from a lot of shit Ruger wanted us to do. But Marcel still spent six months in juvenile detention. I looked out for Heidi as best I could, and Wrath and Z looked out for us.

In return, Marcel and I did our part to help cut Ruger out of the club once Rock got released from prison.

I had no doubt Ruger was responsible for Rock and Grinder's imprisonment, as well as Lucky's death. So it didn't bother me a bit when one day Ruger just *disappeared*.

Things improved after that. Ruger's few supporters either retired or moved to other charters.

Rock moved the club in a more positive—although still highly illegal—direction. When I patched in, the club was more than family to me. It was a brotherhood in every sense of the word. I knew without a doubt I could trust every one of my brothers with my life. In return, I'd die to protect every one of them for the rest of my life.

Seven

MURPHY

After my fight with Heidi, I have to take a step back. Regroup. Rethink my approach. Here I'd assumed, well, I don't know what the fuck I assumed. Heidi's given me more than enough hints over the last year that she's over me.

Too bad I'm not over her.

Even if she won't admit it, she still feels something. Those kisses didn't lie.

My past. The things I've done. *Who* I've done. It never occurred to me that it might be an obstacle to Heidi and me being together when the time was right. That's just not how club life works. At least, that's not how I've seen it work. That she'd be mad at me for pushing her away instead of giving in to her? Sure, I expected to do a little groveling there. Was looking forward to it honestly.

But this?

I'm not sure what to do.

But I do know who can steer me in the right direction. And I find her sitting in front of the clubhouse when I return from my shift at Furious.

"Hey, First Lady. What're you doing out here?"

"Waiting for Rock." She stands and hugs me. "How are you?"

My shoulders lift. "Got a minute?"

"Sure. Pull up a slab of stone." She drops back down onto the stone bench and pats the space next to her.

Shit. Am I really doing this? I take so long to speak, Hope asks what's wrong.

"I, uh, had this fight with Heidi the other day and it's still bugging me."

"Okay," she answers slowly. She waits patiently while I decide how much to tell her.

"Well, the night of her birthday, I sort of explained how I felt about her and how I wanted things to be between us."

"Did you ask her what she wanted?"

Nope. Never even considered it because I assumed we wanted the same thing. "Not exactly. She was into it. What we were doing, but—"

Hope narrows her eyes, and I stop.

"Go on," she says, still looking pretty suspicious of me.

"You know how I call her Bug? I guess I didn't realize how much she hates it." As I'm saying the words, it all starts falling into place. I called her Bug after the phone call. That's when everything changed. Then she had time to think and remember all the reasons she doesn't want to be with me.

"Well, she's been pushing boundaries for a while. She wants to be seen as an adult, and it probably makes her feel childish."

"Yeah, I got that." Boy, did that come through shrill and clear.

"And?"

"Axel was all over her at the party, and Serena showed up, so we didn't get to talk again until the next day. When we finally did, she said some other stuff I don't know what to do with."

"You're going to have to be more specific, Murphy."

Christ, this is embarrassing.

"I think you understand how things work around here. With club girls? Heidi's heard stories, and—"

"Ahh." She nods knowingly, but doesn't laugh at me. "She's sensitive about that stuff." Hope pauses and seems to be considering what she wants to say. Whether it's so she doesn't hurt my feelings or she's searching for smaller words my brawny-man brain will understand,

I'm not sure. "More and more girls are rejecting the idea that it's okay for boys to have as much sex as they want, while girls are supposed to keep their legs closed and not complain."

What can I say to that? Definitely *not* the way things are in our world. "Maybe college wasn't the best idea."

Hope must think I'm kidding—which I sort of am. She giggle-snorts and nudges me with her arm. "Trust me. She had those ideas before she got to college."

I raise an eyebrow so she'll feed me a little more information.

"We've shared some girl talk," she says vaguely. "I can't be more specific with you."

"Oh." I really want to know if any of those conversations included my name, but she won't betray Heidi, and I respect that. "Okay."

"Anyway," she continues. "Yes. The girls…bother her a lot."

"But you know Rock—"

"Don't go there. It's not the same. I was married when we met. And I'm not a teenager."

"Sorry."

"It's okay." She pauses again, an uncertain expression clouding her face. "I think her grandmother also had some warped opinions on sexuality and made Heidi feel ashamed about anything related to sex."

That doesn't surprise me and helps me understand some of the things Heidi said the other day. "What should I do to fix it?"

Her bottom lip quivers, and she looks like she wants to hug me, so whatever she's about to say isn't going to be favorable.

"I don't know that you can. Maybe she needs time to grow up and sort of broaden her horizons and it won't matter as much."

I groan. More waiting. Great.

"Or maybe she just needs to have some sexual experiences of her own to feel—"

A frustrated growl bursts out of me, and instead of laughing, Hope pats my back. "I know."

I can't even deal with that idea right now. So I decide to ask her about the other thing that's been bothering me. "All right. Can I ask you something else?"

"Yes."

"Can you find out if Axel treats her okay? She made a comment about them fighting the other day…and I just got a bad feeling from it. But if I say anything"—I wave my hand at the clubhouse—"they're just gonna think I'm being a jealous little bitch."

She snorts again. "You're probably right." Her nose wrinkles but she seems to be thinking over my request. "I've only seen Axel be nice to her, and you know, couples do fight."

"I know. It was just…she was almost scared about how he might react, and that's not the Heidi I know. She's always been fearless."

She nods, seeming to take my request seriously, not just humoring a jealous, wanna-be boyfriend. "I'll see what I can find out."

"Thank you." I think for a second how fucking selfish I'm being. "Thanks for listening. I always unload all this Heidi crap on you, Hope. I never ask if you're okay or do anything for you."

She wraps her arms around me for a quick squeeze. "You're so sweet. And that's not true. I haven't gotten in my car once since I moved here and had less than a half tank of fuel. When it snows, my car's always cleaned off and ready for me. Rock says that's all you."

Pride turns my mouth up in a big grin. "Well, that's me making sure the prospects do it."

"I figured." She bumps me again with her shoulder. "Thank you."

"Everything okay?" Rock asks as he steps out the front door.

Hope doesn't jump or try to distance herself from me in any way, and Rock doesn't even raise an eyebrow. There are no games between these two. They trust each other absolutely. Well that and he knows damn well I'm no threat.

He walks over and she stares up at him as if everything she needs in the universe is right in front of her. A long time ago, Heidi looked at me in a similar way.

"You okay, Baby Doll?" he asks as he runs the back of his hand over her cheek. She leans into him and murmurs a yes. She doesn't offer up what we were talking about, and I appreciate that. I'm sure later she'll tell him all about it, but she has too much class to embarrass me in front of him.

"Need anything, prez?"

Rock sighs and shakes his head. "Sway called. He and a couple of his guys are coming up—not Bull."

That information makes me laugh. I'm sure Bull won't return anytime soon since I knocked him out cold after Rock and Hope's wedding. I'm not too fond of Sway showing up, though. Not after the way he treated Hope when Rock was in jail last summer.

"Ugh, just let me know when so I can steer clear of the clubhouse," Hope says and Rock glances down at her with a questioning face. I'm guessing no one filled Rock in on Sway's misbehavior.

Shaking my head, I catch Hope's attention. "He wouldn't dare be that rude in front of Rock."

"What the fuck are you two talking about?" Rock asks.

Hope makes an *oops* face. "With all the craziness going on and then our wedding, I forgot all about it."

Rock swings his icy glare to me. "What is she talking about?"

"Nothing. Sway was just a rude dick to her while he was here. We set him straight and he backed down."

His angry face softens as he turns back to Hope. "He touch you?"

"Not really. He was concerned that I should know my place."

"Interesting. Wrath never mentioned it," Rock grumbles.

"I think he had enough to worry about." Hope's quick to defend Wrath, and I find that funny since he treated Hope pretty harsh in the beginning. "The guys took care of me," she says, patting my leg.

Rock glares at me again. "Okay," he says in a way that means it's definitely *not* okay.

Church should be a big ball of fun this week.

Sway's visit should be entertaining too.

Teller rides up, and Rock walks over to meet him. Hope waves but doesn't leave my side.

"Anything else?" she asks in a low voice.

"Probably but I can't think of anything right now," I answer honestly.

The corners of her mouth tip up and she wraps her hand around mine for a brief squeeze. "Please stop being so hard on yourself."

Teller and Rock join us, and then Rock drags Hope home. "You see Wrath, tell him I need to talk to him," Rock says over his shoulder.

"What's that about?" Teller asks as he drops down next to me.

"Sway's comin' to visit."

He screws his face into pure disgust. "Gonna tell Axel to keep Heidi away while Sway's here."

My insides knot up at the mention of her name. "You still cool with that?"

His eyes narrow. "What? Axel dating my sister? No. I'd rather she not date anyone and just concentrate on school."

So would I. "That's not very realistic, bro."

"No shit." He eyes me again. "Why're you asking?"

My shoulders lift, but I'm not fooling him one bit. Fuck. Am I really gonna beg my best friend to talk his little sister into giving me a chance? "She's eighteen—"

"Don't." He throws his hand up. "She's not ready. She's not—"

"What?"

"She's not the girls you're used to."

Does he think I'm stupid? "I know that."

"So, what if she wants to take things slow? You gonna wait or...I won't have anyone disrespect my sister. Not even you."

Somehow he lost me. "I'd never do anything to hurt her."

"Dude. She ever caught you with someone else, it would kill her. She's already—"

"Wait a second. You think I'd cheat on her? Why?" Then it hits me. My brother's living in some deep denial. I won't be the one who bursts his carefully constructed bubble by telling him Heidi's not a virgin. Or at least that she told me she isn't.

"I'd do whatever she wanted at her pace," I finally mumble. "I'd never force her into something she didn't want or have someone on the side."

The weight of his stare drills into me and I lift my gaze. "If you're with my sister, you're *with* her. She's not ending up one of your many conquests."

Oh, man. He's begging for me to punch him in the fuckin' throat by suggesting I'd ever treat Heidi that way. "I know that," I growl. "That's not what I want."

"Since when are you *seriously* into Heidi?" he asks.

How do I put into words what Heidi means to me? "Since always."

His jaw drops and he continues glaring at me. "Why didn't you ever say so?"

"Because it wasn't right."

"Jesus Christ." He shakes his head, but finally drops the protective big brother shit and gives me a hint of a smile. "You tell her?"

"Tried."

"And?"

"We just argued."

"Figures," he mutters. "Give her some time to work stuff out. She's not going anywhere."

God, I hope not. Even if she's not mine, I don't know what I'd do without her in my life.

Eight

Heidi

It's easy to avoid Murphy when I want to. After our fight, I manage to avoid him for a couple of weeks. Things go back to normal for Axel and me. School's hard. My brother always thinks I'm so smart, but the truth is, school has always been hard work for me. What seems to take my classmates seconds to grasp requires a lot of studying for me.

I don't mind. It gave me an excuse to stay out of my grandmother's way when she was in one of her fits. My high grades were the only thing she ever liked about me. It gave her something to brag about. When my mother dropped Teller and me off at her mother's house and took off with her boyfriend, I wonder if she knew how bad things would get for me.

Everyone in my grandmother's small town knew my father split after I was born. My mother was a tramp who chose a random biker over her children. The Whelan kids provided a lot of gossip for narrow-minded neighbors. Angry at the world, Marcel fought with our grandmother a lot. *We* were that trashy family down the street who always had the cops at the door. She hated Marcel for embarrassing her.

Even after my brother moved out, he always made time for me. Murphy also remained a constant in my life. Those moments were precious and I never wanted to burden either of them with how miserable my life was. My grandmother always threatened to put me in foster care if I didn't behave. I feared if visiting me became too complicated, Blake and Marcel wouldn't do it anymore.

Axel's the first person I ever spilled my dark secrets to. Mostly because he walked in on one of the blowout fights my grandmother and I were always having. Not long after, he found the bruises on my back and demanded answers. When my brother fought her for custody, I prayed every damn night he'd win. They ended up compromising, but it didn't matter because she died a few months later.

I felt guilty about the relief that washed over me when she passed. She had taken me in when my mother tossed me out. Things were far from perfect, but I felt like the ungrateful brat she always accused me of being because I felt so free once she was gone.

The guilt I feel today is a bit different. I've been avoiding Murphy and I hate that. I just can't figure out a way to reach out to him after everything we said to each other.

As if he knew he'd been on my mind, I find him outside my last class leaning against a brick wall, arms crossed over his chest. His bored expression turns hard when he spots me with my friend, Lucas.

"I'll catch you later, Lucas."

The corner of his mouth quirks up. "You're not going to introduce me to your friend?"

I glance at Murphy's not-so-bored-now face. "Not today."

Lucas gives me a quick fist-bump and hurries away.

Murphy's face completely transforms as I approach him. "What are you doing here?" I ask.

"I needed to see you."

I cock my head and study him. "Is something wrong?"

"Yeah, I miss you."

Is he really here to see me? Axel said that girl Serena takes classes here, too. Maybe I only ran into Murphy by accident. I almost ask, but then bite my tongue. I don't want to argue again. I'm still ashamed of myself for being so mean to him.

We stare at each other for a few seconds before he holds his arms out. Not caring who sees, I drop my bag and fling myself against him.

"Missed you so much, Heidi," he says against my hair. His low voice vibrates through my chest, and I swear, I feel it all the way to my toes. My hands slide down the supple leather of his cut and over the familiar flannel softness of his shirt. I wrap my arms around him, holding on tight. Burying my face against his shoulder, I breathe him in. A hint of wind, leather, and all the scents I love most.

I barely choke back a sob. "I'm sorry."

His arms squeeze me a little tighter. "Me too."

I want to ask what he's sorry for when I was the one who acted so awful, but he pulls away. Under the weight of his gaze, I flinch and turn my head.

"Hey." His hand brushes over my cheek. "Want to go for a ride?"

"You have your bike?"

"You know it." He leans over and grabs my bag, and I follow him out to the parking lot.

"So, who was the guy?"

I'm trailing behind him, so he misses my eye-rolling headshake. "My friend Lucas. He's dating my friend Penny. Remember her?"

He snorts. "Yeah, I remember Penny."

I don't ask any follow-ups to *that*. He stops at my car. Naturally, he's parked right next to it.

"How did you know? And how'd you know where my class was?"

His mouth slides into a familiar half-smirk. "I know how to find you."

Some girls might consider that stalkerish. I like that I matter to him.

I unlock my car and he tosses my bag in the backseat. "Car running okay? You need anything?" he asks as he casually leans in and pops the hood.

"Did you really come here to check my oil?"

"No. But since I'm here, I might as well."

When he's certain my car is in perfect order, I lock it up. "You putting a lot of miles on it?"

I don't want to tell him that on nights when I know Marcel won't be home, I usually stay at Axel's, which has cut down on my mileage a lot.

"Not too bad."

"You got a jacket in there?"

"You know I do." He and my brother had lectured me endlessly about keeping spare stuff in my car "just in case." So, in addition to the usual tire-changing supplies, jumper cables, an empty gas can, and duct tape, my car is equipped with a spare jacket, gloves, extra sneakers, a blanket, and other assorted items.

Once I'm suited up, he hands over a helmet. A surge of guilt pulses over me as I wrap my arms around him. He's not my boyfriend. I shouldn't be on the back of his bike.

But it's *Blake*.

I didn't bother to ask where we're going, and it doesn't matter. I just enjoy the ride. Axel's working late so we didn't have plans tonight. Part of me wonders if Blake knew that, too.

Maybe twenty minutes into our ride, I pick my head up and actually take notice of where we're going. If I had to guess, Fletcher Park.

My ears pop as we climb higher into the mountains. He slows the bike as we enter the park, always aware of cops who wait right after the big Fletcher Park sign to pull over speeders.

"Thank you for parking on this side," I say as I shake out my hair and hand over my helmet.

"I remember, b—Heidi."

Warmth flickers in my chest. Blake's trying. Remembering at the last second not to call me Bug. Remembering how much the overlook side of the park freaks me out, ever since I saw one of my classmates in fourth grade fall over the side. I want to hug him again.

I think the hug takes him by surprise. He runs his hand over my head and down my hair. "You okay, Heidi?"

"Yeah."

"Wanna go for a hike or stay here?"

"Hike."

He chuckles when I don't let go right away. Finally, he takes my hand and leads me up the trail that will take us into the woods and to the bridge that stretches over the waterfalls.

"Did you have a good day in school?"

"It was okay."

"Learn anything useful?" he asks. "You still happy there?"

I know Blake had been hoping I'd go to another college. One Axel didn't attend, so I take my time answering.

"Yes. I met with my adviser to talk about an internship next summer."

"Already?"

"Well, yeah. It's a two-year program. I need the experience some time."

"That's scary. I don't know if I'd want you poking at me—"

"I'm not drawing blood, you goof."

He chuckles, not insulted. "I'm just messin' with you."

"How's everything in motorcycle and stripper land?"

He chokes on a laugh. "Okay." After a few seconds, he clarifies. "You know I spend more time helping Wrath over at Furious than I do at CB these days, right?"

"No. I didn't know that. How come?"

His shoulders lift, jerking my hand, reminding me that we're still holding hands.

"His other trainer's been out, so he needed the help."

"Oh. Is he paying you, or making you work for free?"

"We worked something out," he says with a smile.

"So, if I stop by are you going to teach me some cool self-defense moves?"

His smile fades. "Sure. You think you need 'em?"

"Doesn't every girl?"

Instead of laughing, my question seems to bother him. "I'd bury anyone who hurt you, Heidi. You know that, right?"

"Even you?"

He stops and turns to face me. "I'm sorry if I hurt you. I never meant to."

My chest squeezes. Once I'd calmed down, I'd thought over his words endlessly. His admission that he cared about me the same way I cared about him. It helped finally twist my way of thinking and understand his actions a little more. "I know."

He takes my other hand and rolls his lips as if he's not sure he should say what he wants to. "So, where's this internship going to be?"

I don't think that's what he planned to say. "Probably Empire Med."

"Wow."

"Don't get too excited. I'll probably just be watching and taking notes."

"Yeah. Still. It's—I'm proud of you. Knew you were smart from the time you were little."

"You did?"

"Hell yeah. You couldn't wait to go to school. You loved being there. You were the only kid I ever knew who was sad when she had to leave."

I chuckle, because he's right. "True. But that's because home sucked."

"I hated when you and Marcel moved out to your Grams's." His voice turns raw and he glances away. "Used to have a bitch of a time hitching a ride out there."

"What's wrong, Blake?"

He flashes a quick smile. "Nothin'. I—that money I told you I was saving for college for you. It's not...it wasn't 'cause I expected anything from you. You remember hanging around the old clubhouse when it was next to CB? Lots of those girls were dancing to pay for school, and your brother and I never wanted that for you. That's all."

My breath catches, throat tightening so I can't get out a response. Hot tears bubble up and I blink to clear them. "Blake," I whisper. "I'm so sorry I ever—" Shame slides over my skin and I pull my hands out of his grasp.

"Hey," he says, pulling me back in. "I didn't tell you to upset you. I just wanted you to understand."

"Why?"

"Why what?"

"Why me?"

"'Cause you're one of my favorite people in the whole world."

MURPHY

I mean it, too. Heidi and her brother are the most important people in my life. My first true family, before the club. She's a part of me, no different from the blood running through my veins.

"Hey." I take one of her hands again. "Let's keep walking."

We trudge up the rough trail in silence. The sound of water rushing on our left intensifies the farther we go.

"We're close to the falls," Heidi says in a low voice.

Trees break and the falls are in front of us.

"Oh, it's so beautiful." Heidi rushes forward, dragging me along.

"Careful, Heidi."

She tugs her hand out of my grasp. "I'm okay." She must have pulled harder than I realized, because she pitches forward, then tips right over the ledge.

"Jesus!" I'm flying through the air, landing on the ground hard, with her arm in my grasp.

"Blake!" The fear in her voice makes me forget the wind just got knocked out of me. I'm strong. No question. I spend plenty of time lifting weights, boxing, and strength training. None of it prepared me to hold a hundred and twenty pounds of scared teenage girl over the side of a ledge with one hand.

"Stop moving, Heidi," I shout as calmly as I can given the circumstances. "Can you get a foothold?"

"Yes." Her scared voice reverberates through me.

My wrist feels like it's about to snap. But her frantic movements stop enough for me to inch forward. Peering over the ledge, I find her balancing on the tiniest stone jutting out like some ballerina-mountain-goat hybrid. Shit.

I swing my other arm over. "Grab my other hand."

She's clutching a tuft of grass growing out of the side of the ledge. "I'm scared to let go."

"Honey, I'm stronger than that bunch of weeds you got there." As I say it, the patch tears loose. She lets out a short scream and grabs my outstretched hand.

"I gotcha. Hang on to me and climb up. I'll pull you back."

She whimpers but starts climbing while I inch back, scraping the shit out of my stomach and the undersides of my arms in the process. When her head and shoulders clear the ledge, I get a burst of energy and pull her up and over. She lands on me, wrapping her arms around my neck, crying against my shirt.

"Shh, you're okay. I got you."

She keeps shaking and crying.

"Hey, what's going on?"

Oh, sure. Now there's a park ranger.

I crane my neck, peering up at the park cop. "My girl almost went over the side. How is there no fence there?"

He ignores my question. "Need me to call an ambulance?"

Heidi's head snaps up. "No. We're fine."

He studies her for a minute before addressing me. "Come down to the guard shack and you can file an incident report."

Yeah, I'll get right on that.

I help Heidi stand and brush the dirt off her. When I glance up, Officer Useless is already half-way down the trail. "Big help," I grumble. "You okay?"

"Your arms. You're bleeding."

I don't feel the sting until I lift my arms and see what she's talking about. "Fuck." I'm scraped to shit and have all sorts of pebbles digging into my skin.

"We need to clean you up so you don't get an infection."

"I'm fine. Let's get out of here."

"You can't ride like that."

"I'm fine," I repeat, taking her hand.

At my bike, she throws her arms around me. "Thank you."

"For what? Almost gettin' you killed?" I'm so pissed with myself. I wanted to do something nice and instead she almost got hurt.

"No. For being strong enough to pull me up."

I chuckle. "I may not have speed, but I'm strong."

"You've got quick reflexes to catch me like that." She hugs me again and not wanting to get blood and dirt all over her, I just stand there with my arms out. "Are you mad at me?" she murmurs against my shirt.

"No, honey."

She pulls back and looks me over. Her hand reaches out and tugs my shirt up. "What are you doing?"

"You're bleeding." I glance down and find a few spots of blood that seeped through my shirt.

"I'm fine. Let's get out of here."

"Wait. There's a first aid station—"

"Are you hurt?"

"I don't think so."

"Then let's go. I'll get patched up at the clubhouse."

She opens her mouth to argue some more, but I thrust her helmet into her hands and strap mine on.

At the clubhouse, she follows me into the kitchen, where I grab the first aid kit.

"Let me do it?" she asks. "I'm a medical professional, remember?" she teases in a shaky voice. I get the feeling she needs to do this to calm herself down as much as she needs to patch me up.

"Thank you."

"Let's get this clean. We should have done it up there. You're going to get an infection." She fusses while she holds my arms over the deep kitchen sink and uses the sprayer to thoroughly spray down the scrapes. When she's finished, she inspects me closely, flipping the water back over me a few times when she finds stray bits of rock or dirt. I grit my teeth and bear it, even though it stings like a bitch.

Her hands are soft and gentle, and I'm impressed with her skill as she thoroughly fixes me up.

"Your ink should be fine. The scrapes aren't that deep."

I hadn't even thought of that.

She nods at my shirt. "Let me see your stomach."

"You trying to get me naked in the kitchen, Heidi?"

One corner of her mouth quirks up. "No."

The damage there isn't as bad as my arms. "You should really take a shower and clean it well. I can't do it down here unless you want to climb in the sink. Then I need to wrap your arms."

I toss my shirt over my shoulder. "Come up with me?"

She hesitates, but then gathers up the supplies and follows. I gesture for her to go first when we get to the staircase.

Mistake.

My arms and stomach may have been scraped raw, but the pain no longer registers. No, the only pain I'm feeling is the new one in my groin. I can't keep my eyes off her little round ass in my face. Doesn't matter that she's covered in dirt and dust.

She waits quietly while I open my door and leans up against the dresser. Her little jump when I close the door surprises me. "Are you okay?"

"Yeah. It's just weird being … in here. With you. Alone."

"Why? You've been in here before."

She shakes her head and glances down at the supplies in her hands. "Go take your shower. Make sure you clean out any stray bits of dirt."

"Want to come supervise?"

Finally, she picks her head up, but she's not smiling at my attempt at a joke. "That's not a good idea."

"Purely medical reasons."

She flashes a quick smile but stays put.

After I wash off, I get a better look at the scrapes on my stomach. They aren't that bad. I kinda feel like a pansy letting Heidi take care of me, but I also like it. It's a way to get her soft little hands all over me with no effort on my part.

As much as I'm looking forward to having her hands on me, I can't get the image of her falling over the ledge to stop repeating on a constant horrifying loop in my head.

Stepping out of the shower, I snag a towel to dry off and wrap it around my hips. When I open the bathroom door, I find Heidi in the same spot.

"You can sit."

She eyes my bed with something close to disgust on her face. "No, thanks."

I doubt it will make her feel better if I explain the only girl who's slept over recently is Serena—you know because that whole "volume of women" accusation has been rattling in my head since she hurled it at me.

I end up sitting on the edge and she kneels in front of me, which is awkward for a whole bunch of reasons.

No, actually one big reason.

I should have given more thought to parading around in a towel in front of Heidi. She seems to have the same thought and stands. "Hold your arm out."

Having her stand is almost worse. Now she's pressing her breasts into my face. More blood rushes south, making the towel situation critical.

I clear my throat and ask, "Are you almost done?"

"Do you see a bandage on your other arm?" she snaps.

"Great bedside manner, Bug."

She huffs and moves onto my other arm. When that's finished, she runs her fingers over my stomach, coming dangerously close to my very-happy-at-the-moment trail.

"I don't think I need to bandage this. Your shirt must have taken the brunt of it."

"Heidi?"

Slowly, she drags her gaze up my body and finally meets my eyes.

I press my palms on either side of her face. "I'm sorry."

"For what?"

"For almost gettin' you killed. Not lookin' out for you better. I couldn't live with myself if something happened to you."

She doesn't say anything.

"Are you hurt anywhere?" I ask.

"My shoulder. I wrenched it pretty good."

"Turn around."

"Can you put some pants on first?"

"Uh." Low laughter rumbles out of me. "Give me a second."

She moves so I can stand. Grabbing a pair of gym shorts out of my dresser, I duck into the bathroom and slip 'em on. I pluck a small jar of Tiger Balm off a shelf, too.

"Better?" I ask when I return.

She glances up and gives me a shy smile. "Yes."

I don't tease her about why she needed me to cover myself. I don't point out that she feels what's between us as much as I do. It feels as if we've called a truce, and I won't do anything to break it.

Heidi

"Where's it hurt?"

All over. But the worst pain has nothing to do with going over the cliff. It's the pain in my chest. From embarrassment that my clumsiness almost killed us. From the things Blake revealed to me before my epic *flail*.

From being so close to him.

I've never doubted my safety when I've been with Blake, and today he's proved again that he's as invincible as he is fearless.

As I settle on the floor at his feet, all my physical aches demand attention.

I shimmy the shoulder that's bothering me. He gently gathers my hair in his hands and drapes it over my other shoulder. "Thanks."

"Can I check to see if it's bruised?" His voice so rough and low, I shiver.

I freeze, barely breathing. Time seems to stop. Tension shimmers between us or maybe that's his heat, radiating against my back.

"Yes," I whisper, dropping my head so I'm staring at my hands, clasped in my lap.

But he doesn't lift my shirt like I expected. He tucks a finger in the collar and pulls it out. Warm breath tickles my neck and ear. This is almost worse than if he'd just asked me to remove it.

"I can take it off."

He goes stock-still and I wonder if that was a mistake. He pulls back and waits quietly while I pull my shirt up and over my head, leaving it covering my arms and front.

One finger, firm and rough, traces down my spine, skipping over my bra and stopping at my lower back. "You're good," he finally says.

Before I have a chance to slip my shirt back on, he starts kneading my shoulder. More heat spreads over my skin as his warm, slippery fingers keep working.

"What is that?"

"Tiger Balm. It'll help."

"Okay."

He keeps at it, using both hands, digging in. My head tips forward.

"Am I hurting you?"

"No, that feels good."

I untangle my right arm from my shirt and hold it out. "My arm hurts too."

He doesn't say a word, but works his hands down my arm.

"Other one?"

I slip my left arm out and hold it up.

"How'd you get so good at this?" As soon as I ask, I wish I hadn't. Now I can't stop picturing him with other girls.

"I like taking care of you, Heidi," he answers.

Not the answer I expected. But his soothing voice slides over me like honey.

This has to end.

My hands grapple with my shirt.

"You want one of my shirts to wear?" he asks.

"No, I've got clothes here. In my room. Down the hall."

Blake's hands falter. "Better?"

No, not at all. That's why I need to get out of here.

"I think so. Thank you."

His hands disappear and I hate the cold air that replaces the warmth of his touch. Finally, I find the armholes and slip my shirt back on.

I turn and find him watching me. "Do you want to go out to dinner?" he asks. "I was thinking we could go down to Hog Heaven?"

Not fair. He knows how much I love that place.

"They have Coffee Toffee Pie this week," he says with an enticing tone. The corner of his mouth quirks up because he knows I can't resist the special pie they only serve a few times a year.

"Yes."

Balancing on his leg, I pull myself off the floor. It was a stupid thing to do, because we end up face to face.

And he doesn't miss the opportunity to place his hands on my cheeks and pull me even closer for a kiss.

A kiss that goes on longer than it should.

I pull away but not because of the kiss. "Your hands are all sticky." I swipe at the smelly ointment that's now smeared on my face.

"Shit. I'm so sorry. I didn't mean to. I forgot."

He strides into the bathroom and the water starts running. I wander over and find him scrubbing his hands. "That stuff works great, but it's a bitch to get off," he mumbles. "Come here, let me clean your face."

"It's not that bad."

Still, he takes a washcloth and dabs at the spots on my cheeks.

"Better?"

"Yes."

He keeps staring at me, moving closer until I have no choice but to back up. I find myself against the wall looking up at him. Whisper quiet, he presses his palms against the wall on either side of my shoulders.

"Blake?" My voice comes out hushed.

"Are we ever going to talk about your birthday?"

"What about it?"

"Don't. You feel this as much as I do. We almost—"

"I *know* what we almost did. It would have been a mistake."

Pain flickers over his face and my chest tightens. I can't stand hurting him. "The love I have for you will never be a mistake, Heidi."

"I—"

He cuts me off with a kiss that I sink right into—for a moment. Abruptly, he pulls away. "Go change. I want to take you to dinner."

I'm too dizzy to respond, but that doesn't stop Blake from placing his hand on my lower back and guiding me to the door. "What are you doing?"

"Taking care of you."

He opens the door and we step into the hallway, smacking right into my brother.

His forehead wrinkles and his eyes light up. "Heidi? What're you doing here?" His angry glare shoots to Blake. "Why's she in your room, bro?"

"Knock it off, Marcel. I was patching up his arms."

A little of his anger disappears. For fuck's sake, is my brother ever going to back off and realize I'm eighteen years old?

Blake nudges me again. "Go change and meet me downstairs."

I eye my brother, trying to figure out if he'll behave himself, then reach up to give him a kiss on the cheek. "Chill, would ya?"

He gives me a quick hug then sniffs me. "You reek of menthol. What the hell?"

My mouth quirks up. "I'll let Murphy explain."

MURPHY

Teller waits until Heidi's door shuts before jabbing his finger in my chest, knocking me back into my room.

"Quit it, dick. We weren't doing anything."

He glances at my bandaged arms. "Tell me you didn't lay your bike down with my sister on the back."

"No." Fuck. I decide to give him the quickest version of what happened. "She fell at the park and I scraped myself up catching her. That's all."

"What the fuck were you two doing at the park?"

"Talking."

His eyes narrow. "You know I love you, brother. And I understand how you feel about my sister, but don't go putting her in an awkward place. You know she's with Axel."

I don't even know what to do with that so I just stare at him like an idiot.

"She can't say no to you. Don't push her into stuff that's gonna make her feel bad later."

"I…" Fuck. That's exactly what I've been doing. Is that why she spent the last couple weeks avoiding me? I figured she was pissed. I shake my head, but Teller knows me too well. We can practically read each other's minds after all these years. "Yeah, okay."

"I'll take her home," Teller says, making it clear it's not up for debate.

"I wanted to take her to dinner."

He cocks his head as if asking if I heard anything he said.

"Friends eat dinner, you know." It sounds lame, even to me, but we stare each other down for a few minutes before I back off. Now's not the time to get into it with my best friend.

"Fine."

I need a minute to replay the afternoon and think over the things he said.

Heidi

For reasons I don't want to think about, I'm anxious while I wait downstairs. Sparky's hanging out in the living room, so I end up talking to him while I wait.

It's my brother who finally comes downstairs. Not Blake.

Marcel ushers me out the door without speaking. Outside, in the parking lot, I shake out of his hold. "Wait a second. Where's Blake?"

"Upstairs. He's tired."

"What?"

He pushes me into his truck and shuts the door.

Tired of being manhandled, I hop right back out. "What do you mean he's tired? We were going to—"

"Get back in the truck."

"No."

"Heidi," he warns. "Leave him alone and get in the truck."

I don't answer, but I hoist myself back inside his big, jacked-up ride.

"What are you compensating for with this monster truck?" I ask when he slams his door.

"Very funny."

"You didn't hit Blake, did you?"

"No. Should I have?"

"No! Why are you being such a—"

"Careful, little sister."

I hate this. I hate when he pushes me into acting like a brat. I've been trying so hard lately, but sometimes he pushes all my bratty-little-sister buttons.

"He said you fell at the park. You okay?"

Unsure of just how much Blake told my brother, I say as little as possible. "I'm fine."

"Why were you up in his room?"

"Jeez. I already told you. I helped him bandage up his arms."

"Are you hurt?"

"No."

My shoulder still burns from the Tiger Balm, and I replay the few brief seconds wth my shirt off while Blake tended to me, our kiss, our second kiss after he tenderly wiped my face clean. I'm not sharing any of those moments with my brother, though.

"Heidi, you know you're the most important person in the world to me, right? Everything I've done. Everything I do. It's to make sure you end up okay. You know that, right?"

His words drive splinters of guilt through my chest. "Yes."

He sighs and reaches over to squeeze my hand. "How much do you remember about living with mom?"

"I don't know. Not much. I remember hanging out at the club with you guys more."

"She left us alone a lot."

"I know." I'm tempted to tell him to get to the point, but I'm also curious about where he's going with this.

"You remember any of the guys she used to bring home?"

If I think really hard, I do. Sort of. "I remember you sleeping in my room when she had guys over. You used to sleep in front of the door."

I'm watching him closely, so I notice the way his mouth twists down right away. "Yeah." His hands squeeze the steering wheel. "You were so *little*. And trusting. And sweet."

"Are you trying to say I'm a big, suspicious, bitter teenager now?"

He huffs out a laugh and glances over at me. "And so fucking smart."

"Smart *ass* you mean."

"Sometimes."

"Not that I don't enjoy strolling down crappy childhood memory lane, but do you have a point?"

"What did we always say when we were younger? Whatever Mom did—"

"We'd do the opposite when we were adults."

"You still happy with Axel?"

Confused and suspicious of the change in conversation, I take a second to answer. "Yes, why?" A shiver of excitement races over me. "Why? You think the club's going to vote him in soon?"

"Heidi, you know I can't talk to you about that stuff."

"Yeah, yeah," I grumble and cross my arms over my chest.

He chuckles then turns serious again. "If you're with Axel, be with him. But stop messing with Blake."

The familiar tingle of my blood boiling starts up. "What's that supposed to mean?"

"Exactly what I said. He's too old for you."

"I'm not *messing* with him." If anything, Blake keeps messing with my head. My heart. But I won't rat him out to my brother and cause problems between them. I love both of them too much.

He's silent for the next few miles and his words replay in my head. "Are you trying to say I'm like Mom?"

"No. Fuck no. You're nothing like her. I just don't want you making her mistakes."

"What would those be?"

"Heidi—"

"Axel's my only boyfriend."

"Good. I know you and Blake are friends, too. Just, be careful."

"Why? He wouldn't hurt me."

"You're not a two-guy type of girl, Heidi."

"How do you know?"

He takes his eyes off the road for a second to glare at me. "I know you."

"You're saying that because I'm your sister."

"How would you feel if you knew Axel had girls on the side?"

An uneasy prickle slides through my stomach at the thought. Axel spends a lot of hours at the club. Marcel knows my boyfriend in a whole different way than I do. "You haven't seen him…he doesn't mess around with other girls, does he?"

He chuckles because I fell for the bait. "Have I ever kicked his ass?"

I snort and shake my head.

"I won't tolerate anyone disrespecting my sister. Club or not."

A tight smile forms at the corners of my mouth, but I don't say anything right away.

"Marcel?"

"Yeah?"

"Have you ever considered those girls you mess with? Club girls. Maybe they're someone's little sister?"

"No."

"Maybe they've got big brothers warning them away from guys like you?"

His jaw tightens. "You're too smart for your own good."

My phone buzzes, interrupting our fun conversation. I pull it out and find a text from Axel.

Where you at?

With my brother.

"Who is it?"

"Axel."

"Tell him you're having family night."

I chuckle as I tap out the message.

"You need to drive me to school tomorrow. I left my car there."

"Okay."

I sit back and watch the highway rush by. Not for the first time, it occurs to me what a long drive this is for my brother. A huge inconvenience when I know he'd rather be hanging out at the clubhouse. Yet, he did it—rented an apartment near my grandmother's house—so he could share custody with her. So he could see me and not interrupt my last year of high school.

"Marcel, you can get rid of this apartment now. Grams is gone. I'm done with high school. There's no reason to still live out here."

"We can rent a place closer to Hudson Valley if you want."

Actually, Axel and I have been talking about getting our own apartment. But I'm not ready to tell my brother this yet.

"I can get my own place."

He glances over at me. "How you plannin' to afford that?"

"I don't know. I'll get a job."

"You worry about finishing school. Doing your internship. I'll worry about the rent."

"You're going to have to let me be an adult sometime."

"I will. When I'm ready."

I huff out a laugh.

My big brother will never be ready for me to grow up.

Nine

Heidi

As promised, Marcel drops me off at school the next morning. Axel's leaning up against my car with a bunch of flowers in one hand.

"Can't he go one night without seeing you?" Marcel snorts.

It takes a second to force any words past the lump of guilt in my throat. "Stop. Don't tease him."

"I'm not." My hand's on the door about to open it when Marcel stops me. "Just slow down a little. You're so young to be tied down."

"Aren't you the one who told me to pick a lane last night? Now, you're what? Telling me to take the back country roads?"

He laughs and stares out the windshield. "Something like that."

"You know I won't be a virgin forever, right?"

He claps his hands over his ears. "I'm gonna pretend I didn't hear that."

Leaning over, I place a quick kiss on his cheek. "Denial's an ugly place to live, big brother."

"Get out of here." He shoos me out the door. "Call me later."

Axel holds out the flowers as I approach. "What's this?"

He shrugs as I take the bouquet. "You sounded kind of down last night."

"Thanks," I murmur as I stick my nose in the middle of the blossoms. They don't have a lot of scent, but it's the best way to avoid looking Axel in the eye. I barely slept last night. My mind kept returning to Blake. The things he confessed to me at the park. The things he said in his bedroom. Our kiss. The sweet way he took care of me. My brother interrupting everything and then lecturing me on the way home. All of those things replayed on a constant loop. The thing I should have been the most worked up over—almost falling over the cliff, barely made an appearance in my recap of the day.

"Don't be mad, but I have to work again tonight."

"Oh. That's okay. I have some work I need to catch up on." I certainly didn't get anything done last night.

"We can meet up later. Maybe grab dinner?"

"Sounds good." Does it though? When I can't get my mind off of Blake?

Axel threads his fingers through my hair, holding me still while he leans down and presses a kiss against my lips. It's quick and sweet.

Then it's over.

He pulls away a slight frown darkening his face. "See you later?"

"Sure."

Leaving the clubhouse without saying goodbye to Blake last night still bothers me. After classes, I point my car toward Furious Fitness.

I'll just drive-by. If I happen to see his bike, maybe I'll stop in and say hello. Or so I tell myself.

The subtle shimmer of blackened green paint catches my attention. I'd spot Murphy's bike anywhere. It has a four-leaf clover with the club's skull and crown logo painted in a subtle way that's visible in certain light. He's had some version of that image on his bike for as long as I can remember. My mind strays to the up-close view of his chest where he has the symbol inked into his skin.

Bad Heidi.

As I reach out and wrap my hand around the door, I have second thoughts. Wrath will razz me to death if he catches me here visiting Murphy.

It's not enough to stop me, though.

Then I enter the gym and want to walk right back out.

Murphy's watching over a slim blonde girl on a treadmill, arms crossed over his chest. He says a few words to her and makes an adjustment on the machine. The flirty smile she gives him makes my stomach twist, but then he glances up. When his gaze lands on me, a big smile spreads over his face. He says a few words to the girl and walks toward me without his eyes ever leaving mine.

"Hey, what are you doin' here?" There's no hug or touch of any kind, which feels weird, even though it's probably for the best.

"I was driving by and saw your bike in the parking lot, so I thought I'd stop in and say hello. Is that okay?"

"Yeah. Absolutely." He jerks his thumb over his shoulder at the blonde who's now glaring at me. "Let me finish up."

"Yeah, sure. Sorry I interrupted. I can go."

"Don't you dare. I'll be right back."

I watch as he talks to the girl. Dejected, she takes off for the locker room. I'm not sure what to think about all the jealousy that seized my heart. I have no right. But I still can't help it. I just don't have to act on it. Right?

"So, what's up?" he asks as he approaches, swinging his arms to burn off the restless energy he's had for as long as I've known him.

"I…I felt bad about not saying goodbye yesterday. My brother said—"

"Yeah. I'm sorry, too."

I think he means about the way the night ended, but then he continues. "I shouldn't have…well, I get that you're with Axel." He almost sounds like he's choking on every word and I can guess why he felt the need to say all that—my meddling brother.

"What did Marcel threaten to do to you?"

Surprised, he stares at me with wide eyes. I'm too pissed to get lost in their emerald depths, though.

"Nothing."

"Well, he lectured me all the way home."

The corner of his mouth lifts into a smirk, but he still won't confirm my suspicion. An unusual awkwardness settles over us. He finally breaks it by throwing a few fake punches. "So, did you want me to show you some moves?"

That seems appropriate. "Do you remember when you told me what to do if a guy ever—"

"How could I forget? You punched me in the balls to make sure the advice was sound."

I cringe at the memory. Completely mortified at how obnoxious I was as a kid. "Sorry," I mutter without looking at him.

He laughs. "I think you cried more than I did."

"I felt bad I hurt you," I whisper.

Instead of responding, Blake's gaze strays to something behind me. "Hey, Twitch."

I turn and find a lanky kid hovering by the door. There's plenty of room to move past me, but I inch farther out of his way because he keeps staring at me. The movement pushes me into Murphy who wraps his arm around my shoulders.

"This your girlfriend?" Twitch asks.

It takes Blake a second to answer. "No. My friend Heidi. Teller's sister." I'm usually referred to as *Teller's little sister.* It may seem like nothing, but it means a lot to me that Blake introduces me as his friend first.

Twitch runs his gaze over me and Blake's hold drops to my waist, his hand resting on my hip.

"Yeah. I see the resemblance. You're way prettier than Teller, though."

"Thanks." With my brother's fair coloring and my dark hair, all my life people have questioned whether we're really related. So hearing that we look alike is honestly more flattering than the pretty comment.

"Move along. Wrath's waitin' for you," Murphy growls at the kid. Twitch hurries away and I step out of Murphy's hold.

"Really?" I can't stop the laughter popping out of my mouth.

He shrugs. "I don't know him that well yet." He turns and grabs my hand. "Come on, let's go out back." He ducks behind the counter and grabs two bottles of water out of the mini-fridge and takes my hand again.

"Sorry, I didn't come dressed to work out."

He glances at me over his shoulder as he pulls me through the gym. "That's okay. It's break time for me anyway."

"Murphy, where you going?"

I recognize Wrath's voice right away then spot him taking up the entire doorway to his office. He grins when he sees me. "What're you doing here, Heidi-girl?"

I've known Wrath my whole life, and he still scares me a little. I also respect him and his opinion means a lot to me. I don't want him thinking I stopped by his place of business to flirt with Murphy, although in the back of my head, I have to admit, that's exactly what I did.

"Hi, Uncle Wrath." Blake drops my hand and I walk over for a quick hug from Wrath. "Murphy said you crack the whip on him pretty hard, so I had to drop in and see if it was true."

He throws his head back and laughs, and I'm pleased with myself for coming up with something my gravely serious uncle finds amusing.

"Nah, Murphy's a hard worker. No whip-crackin' required."

Wrath has never handed out compliments to *anyone* freely, so I know it must be true. "That doesn't surprise me."

"Twitch come find you?" Murphy asks, changing the subject. I glance over, surprised he'd be embarrassed by the compliment.

"Yeah, he's cleaning out the break room."

"Okay. We'll be out back if you need me."

"Take your time. Kids won't be here for another half hour." He nods at me and then walks out onto the main floor to talk to customers.

"You guys seem to be popular with the ladies," I say, nodding at the crowd of females flocking to Wrath's side for "fitness advice."

Blake's mouth quirks up. "Yeah. There's one of those McMansion developments not far from here. I think he runs an ad in *Bored Housewife Weekly* or something."

"How does Trinity feel about that?"

His shoulders lift. "I think she finds it funny." He tips his head at the open office door. "She comes down and works in his office a few days a week. She knows what goes on. Besides, it's money. Helps pay for the after-school programs he likes to run."

"Oh." I mull that over while I follow him out the back door.

MURPHY

When I told Heidi I was working at Wrath's gym, I just wanted her to know I was doing something else with my time other than babysitting strippers. Especially after I realized how deeply my involvement with the club girls and dancers bothered her. I never expected her to show up for a visit.

I'm crazy-happy to see her though. Can barely keep the grin off my face. Twitch eyeing her like a safe he wanted to crack pissed me the fuck off. Need to keep an eye on that kid. I don't trust him as much as Wrath does.

One of Trinity's additions to the gym was a couple of picnic benches out back, so on days like today, we could spend time outside. We're the only ones out here and it's nice to be alone together—someplace safe where I don't have to worry about her falling over ledges and stuff.

"How are your arms today?" she asks.

I roll up my long sleeves. "Got taken care of by a professional. Bandages are still good."

The corners of her mouth quiver. She reaches out and runs her fingers over the gauze. "You should probably change these tonight."

"Wanna come supervise?"

"If you need me to."

She flicks her gaze up and catches me staring at her. Something's been bothering me since she stopped in. "You okay? You look tired. Hittin' the books hard?"

Her lips curve into a slight smirk. "Thanks a lot. Nothing better than hearing I look like shit."

"You're fucking gorgeous. I just worry about you."

Her face softens. "Yes. I've been studying late."

"I'm glad you stopped by."

"Really? I wasn't sure—"

"Yes, really."

"Your bike stands out. It caught my eye."

"Yeah?"

"Yup. Are you upset it's almost time to garage it for the winter?"

"Hell, yeah. But it's been pretty warm. You never know. Might be able to ride right up until Christmas."

"Always hopeful. That's good, Blake." She stares at where our fingers are sort of rubbing up against each other.

"I was thinking of going on a run. Haven't taken my bike for a long ride in way too long."

She peeks up at me. "By yourself?"

"Yeah. Unless you want to come with me. You used to beg me to take you all the time when you were little."

Her cheeks turn pink. "Yeah. Sorry."

"No. It was cute."

"You promised me a cross-country trip when I was old enough, remember?"

"I did, didn't I?"

"Yes." She looks away, sadness turning her mouth down.

"Hey, what's wrong?"

"Nothing. I just used to—never mind."

"You still want to be my co-pilot?"

Her surprised eyes meet mine. "Me?"

"Yeah you. Never had anyone go with me before. On the back

of my bike, I mean." I wait to see if what I'm trying to explain to her sinks in.

"Oh." She hesitates and I brace myself for the *I'm-with-Axel* speech. "I can't. I have classes…" she trails off.

Encouraged, I tap the back of her hand. "When's your break?"

"Not until Thanksgiving. But that's only like four days. Then winter break, but it's probably too cold… Spring break is a whole week. Can you wait until March?"

"For you, I'd wait forever, Heidi." Ain't that the fucking truth.

She flashes a weak smile. "Where?"

"Dunno. Not enough time to do cross-country, but I'll come up with something."

"Cool. You think my brother will bring Mariella?"

Fuck. Nope. She didn't get what I was asking at all.

"I don't know what's going on with them."

Nervous laughter spills out of her. "They're cute together, right?"

"Sure."

"But you weren't talking about a club run, were you?" she asks.

It must be spelled out all over my face that I was talking about a trip for two. "No."

She nods slowly. "I'll text you the dates when I get my spring schedule."

"Okay." Here's where I should say something like, "What about your boyfriend?" Except, I don't want to ruin whatever we just planned together. There'll be plenty of time to figure out the details later. Right now I want to enjoy making plans with Heidi. Something I've been waitin' to do a long damn time.

Noises from the front of the building reach us. The busload of kids from Empire High School getting dropped off.

"Should I let you get back to work?" Heidi asks.

I hate like fuck to have her leave, but I do need to get back inside and help Wrath. Trying to be a responsible adult sometimes sucks. Worse, I can't let a brother down when he's counting on me.

"Yeah. Wrath has me teaching the afternoon class."

She stands. "I can't picture you teaching."

"No?"

"That's not true. Actually, I bet you're pretty good at it."

"Thanks."

I take her hand and walk her around the building to her car. "Thanks for stopping to see me."

"Sure. Maybe next time I'll bring you lunch or dinner or something?"

"I'd like that." Warmth fills my chest as it sinks in that she's planning to come visit again. I can't help pulling her in for a hug. She feels so good pressed up against me. But I don't try sneaking a kiss or anything else. Something shifted, changed for us today, and I don't want to press my luck.

I watch her leave, feeling empty as her car disappears. Turning around, I find Wrath standing in the doorway.

"What're you doing, Murphy?"

"I don't know, brother." I can't wipe the grin off my face, though, and he shakes his head.

He doesn't step back as I approach but pats my shoulder. "I hope you don't end up gettin' burned."

"Me, too."

Ten

Heidi

What did I do?

Did I agree to go on a trip with Murphy? Did I make spring break plans with him?

Am I out of my mind?

It felt like the most natural thing in the world. The words just flew out of my mouth. Memories of plans we made when I was kid came back to me, and I realized I'm not a kid anymore. No one can stop me from taking a trip with Blake if I want to.

Except for the fact that I have a boyfriend.

What am I going to do?

Because I really, really want to go. That means I need to make a decision. Not today. But soon.

I can't deny how I feel about Blake any longer.

My mind keeps wandering to our talk. How happy he seemed to see me. I took a gamble stopping by and it turned out okay.

As if my body remembers what my head forgot, I end up driving back to school. I have a couple hours in the library ahead of me. After texting my brother to let him know where I am, I get to work.

Three hours into my studying, I'm falling asleep in my stack of books.

"Heidi?"

I pick my head up, blinking to clear my sleepy eyes. "Axel?"

Concern clouds his face and he settles his hand over my shoulder. "Are you all right?"

My mouth feels gross. I run my tongue over my teeth and sit up straighter. "A little tired. I thought you were working?"

"I wanted to see you." He runs his gaze over my face again. "You sure you're okay?"

Why does everyone keep asking me that? "Yes," I snap, then force a smile to take the sting out of my tone.

Axel doesn't seem flustered by my moodiness. He never is. "You want to grab dinner?"

"Sure."

"Taco Bell?"

My stomach twists and I groan. "Can we go somewhere else?"

He pats his pockets. "I only have a couple bucks."

"I have money."

He rolls his eyes and shakes his head. Any money I have comes from my brother and using it makes Axel uncomfortable.

"Never mind. Let's go there. It's close by." I blink a few times to clear my eyes and pack up my books.

Outside, Axel curls his hand around mine and leads me to the parking lot.

"Car or bike?" he asks.

"Car, but you can drive. I feel like crap."

He glances over, worry wrinkling his forehead. "You want me to take you home instead?"

"No. I'm probably just hungry. I haven't eaten since early this morning."

"How many times have I told you to stop doing that?" he scolds as he holds my door open.

My shoulders lift. "I forgot." I'd been too giddy from my visit with Blake to think about food, but I don't think that's an explanation Axel wants to hear.

The drive is short and the place is packed. Cheap food next to a community college? Taco Bell's parking lot is never empty.

Axel points at an empty table in the back corner. "Go grab a table,

I'll order."

While I wait, I watch the crowd. Some kids I recognize from school. Most I don't. It's not like I spend much time socializing. If I'm not studying, I'd rather be with Axel or at the clubhouse with the family. Even though I dislike a lot of the stuff that goes on up there, I'm happy I'm allowed to hang out at the clubhouse more often. In a way, it reminds me of when I was little and Marcel would bring me to the old clubhouse. Those were happy times. Before my mother dumped me at my grandmother's and ran off.

As I watch the people moving through the line, I wonder if I'd even recognize my mother if I saw her today.

Probably not. It's not like it matters any way.

"Need anything else?" Axel asks as he sets down two trays.

A flash of blonde hair catches my eye. A girl way too pretty to be hanging out here. Tall, skinny, she looks like a freakin' model and I realize I recognize her from my birthday party.

Murphy's girlfriend or *whatever* she is. She's with another girl, and they both study the menu vigorously before ordering.

I put my head down and play with my food.

"Do you want me to grab you something else?" Axel asks.

"No. I'm okay." I nibble on my Crunchwrap to make him happy. I have sour cream dripping off my chin when a girl's voice interrupts us.

"Hey, Heidi, right?" Serena asks.

Are you kidding?

I frantically swipe a napkin over my chin. "Yeah."

"Oh, hi, Axel," she says. Huh. They seem awfully familiar with each other.

I glance up at her again, waiting for her to introduce herself. For fuck's sake, she's even prettier up close. She looks like a frickin' Barbie doll come to life and here I am one of those Little Miss Matched dolls.

She holds out one perfectly manicured hand. "Serena. I'm a friend of your brother's. I saw you at your birthday party but didn't get to say hi."

"Sure. Yeah. Hi."

"Mind if we join you?"

Why the hell not?

I nod and she drops into the chair next to me.

Her friend slides into the booth next to Axel and he raises an eyebrow at me.

Serena eats like a dainty bird. It's annoying. She's all graceful and pretty and perfect. "So, do you know each other through the club?" she asks, nodding at Axel.

"No," I answer a little sharper than I meant to. "We've been dating since high school. I introduced him to my uncle Rock."

Her eyes widen and she sits back. "Oh." She flashes a perfect smile. "That's cool. So you know Murphy then, too?" she asks.

I'm really hating this chick right now.

"Yup. Known him my whole life."

"Oh," she says again. While she's pretty, she's not very articulate.

Just how Murphy and my brother probably like their muffler bunnies.

I glance at Axel and I swear he's trying not to laugh.

This blows.

She asks me about school and then subtly tries to shift the conversation back to the MC. This isn't the first time some club girl has tried to befriend me to get closer to my brother or Murphy.

"So how'd you meet my brother?" I ask.

"Oh, I used to hang out at the downstate charter. I actually know Murphy better."

"I'm sure you do."

She's not put off by my sarcasm. "Now that I'm up here, I hope I'll see him more."

My throat tightens and my eyes water. Haven't I cried over Murphy enough in my life? By sheer force of will, I push back any tears. I'm not embarrassing myself in front of this chick. Nor am I going to risk a fight with Axel if he sees me getting upset over Murphy.

Serena and her friend chatter about school, drawing Axel into their conversation. My stomach rolls.

"I'm ready to go," I say, pushing my tray at Axel.

I can't get up quick enough.

"Bye, Heidi. It was good to see you. Hopefully we can hang out sometime," Serena calls out.

Not fucking likely. "Sure," I say over my shoulder.

Axel's still laughing as we climb in my car.

"Fun times," he says with a smirk that's not endearing. At all.

"What? She seems nice. She's perfect for Murphy."

Axel chuckles and puts the car in reverse.

We don't have much to say as he drives back to campus.

After he parks the car, I push my door open without waiting for him to say anything.

"You comin' over?" he asks as I round the car.

"No. I don't think so."

His hands squeeze my shoulders. "Come on. Don't let those girls get to you."

"I'm not. I don't care. I'm just tired of muffler bunnies trying to use me to get close to my brother. I've put up with it since I was a kid."

He nods. "I can imagine."

"You seemed to know each other."

"I told you I met her downstate. Trust me, she's not my type."

I jab my finger into his side. "Oh yeah? What's your type?"

He leans over and kisses the tip of my nose. "You." He's so close. Even in the crisp autumn air, I feel his heat. Maybe it's silly, but all my irritation evaporates as I stare into his serious hazel eyes. Axel has always made me feel wanted and made it clear he only has eyes for me.

I slide my arms around him and lean against his chest. He holds me for a second before asking, "Come on. Follow me home. You don't have to stay if you don't want to."

"That's the problem. You know I want to."

His mouth curves into the boyish grin that drew me to him the first time we met. I lean in and he gives me another kiss. On my lips this time. A longer, lingering kiss. He angles his body until my back's pressed against my car. My hands settle at his side, drawing him closer. A soft moan leaves my throat and Axel lets out his own needy sound. His lips travel over my jaw, nuzzle my neck, kiss their way to my ear.

"Come home with me, baby."

"Okay," I whisper.

My mind's in turmoil the whole way to Axel's apartment. I intentionally get stuck at a red light, so I have a moment to think.

When I pull into his parking lot, he's already gone inside, so I take a second to check my phone.

And find a text from Murphy.

Get home okay?

Not yet.

My heart twists. I don't want to lie to him. Not after the nice afternoon we had. But I also don't want him to think I said I wanted to take a trip with him and then slept with my boyfriend a few hours later.

I glance up at Axel's apartment building. He's probably wondering what's taking me so long. Should I try to talk to him? Break things off?

The sick feeling that slithered through my stomach as I sat through dinner with Serena returns. I want to text Murphy about it, but all the words that come to mind make me sound like a jealous little brat.

I can't figure out how to cause the least amount of damage to the people I care about.

At Axel's. I finally add.

I wait a few seconds, but he doesn't send any more messages. I can't decide if I'm relieved or sad.

AXEL

Heidi takes so long, I wonder if she changed her mind. But then there's a soft knock at the door.

"You know you can just come in, right?" I ask when I open the door. "I want you to move in with me anyway."

Her eyes widen. Why, I don't know. We've talked about moving in together a bunch of times. "Won't Lucas get annoyed?" she finally asks.

My roommate has his girl Penny here so often, he has no business giving me shit about Heidi being here. "No," I answer. "Now, where were we?" I ask, pushing her up against the wall and leaning down for a kiss.

She smiles, but places her hands on my chest, gently pushing me away. "What's wrong?"

"Nothing. Just—give me a minute. I want to run to the bathroom."

Shaking my head, I step aside. She's still rattled from running into Serena, and it's starting to piss me off.

Heidi can't lie for shit and I saw the way she flinched when Serena mentioned Murphy's name. Sometimes I wonder why I keep trying to force this. I really do love Heidi. And I'm pretty sure she loves me.

I'm also pretty sure she's in love with Murphy. Whether she admits it or not.

Thinking about that sneaky ginger is the equivalent of a splash of cold water on my nuts, so I drop down on the couch and flip the television on.

Heidi emerges from the bathroom and yawns before snuggling up next to me on the couch.

"You okay?" I ask, running my hand over her hair.

"Yeah, just tired. I hope I'm not getting a cold or something. I've got a test Friday."

My phone pings and I pick it up to find a text from Hoot, one of the other prospects.

Church this weekend. Prospects invited.

It's not often we get invited to sit in on the club's business meetings. Or if we do, it's after they've already discussed the good stuff.

I know Hoot's probably flipping excited. Birch, too. They love being included.

I feel nothing.

"What is it?" Heidi asks.

"I guess Rock wants the prospects at church this weekend."

She shifts to face me. "Oh, that's awesome. Think they might be taking a vote on you?"

"Doubt it. I don't have enough time in. Has your brother said anything?"

"No. You know he won't."

"Yeah."

I flip through the channels, but before I know it, Heidi's snoring softly. I give her a poke. "Hey, wake up. I still wanted to talk to you."

She murmurs and twists her head back. "Sleepy."

I end up tucking her into my bed and going back out into the living room to watch television by myself.

It gives me time to think about this weekend. Do I want to be voted into the Lost Kings MC?

Unlike Hoot and Birch, I have family around. Stuck-up, country club types, about as opposite from a motorcycle club as it gets. They've been less than thrilled about me dating Heidi and hanging out at the MC. I've never let them see me with my prospect cut on. For one thing, they wouldn't understand what it meant, and if I explained it, they'd flip out. But they're still my family.

I thought hanging out at the MC was a fun diversion. Much to my parents' irritation, I've loved motorcycles and fixing them up since I was a kid. Since no one in my family cared about that stuff, hanging around other guys with the same interest was very appealing at first. And it got me closer to Heidi.

But now I realize it's not just a club. It's a commitment. A brotherhood. Those guys would die for one another. And I've never felt that way about anyone.

Heidi thinks her brother walks on water. The rest of the brothers, too. She idolizes all of them. Especially Murphy. I get that they were close growing up, but I figured she'd grow out of it.

Not so much.

I've always admired her intelligence. Even though she's had some lousy female role models, her need to be more than just someone's ol' lady or a club girl is what attracted me to her in the first place.

It's what makes me hopeful we'll stay together even if I don't patch into the club.

Eleven

Heidi

Yesterday I woke up sick to my stomach.

I'm not stupid. The first thing I thought of was pregnancy. I've been on the pill for a while now. I try to be meticulous about taking it, but obviously I fucked up.

If there is a '+' in the Result window when the line in the Control window appears, your result is "Pregnant."

Yup. That's a plus sign.

Same as yesterday.

I'm alone in my brother's apartment. I thought he'd never leave this morning, so I could take the test in peace.

He and Axel are at the clubhouse. I plan to go up there right after I finish freaking out.

I slide down to the floor and tip over, resting my cheek against the cold tile.

What the fuck am I going to do?

My brother will kill me.

No, first he'll kill Axel, then me.

Murphy. I can't even think of him right now.

Maybe my boyfriend—*the father of my baby*—is getting patched in to the club right now. That would make things a lot easier. My brother can't kill him if he's a member of the club.

My brother will be so disappointed in me.

He expects me to finish school. He's worked so hard to provide for me. How could I let him down like this?

You don't have to have the baby.

I don't have to tell anyone at all.

There's a clinic near school.

I always thought if this happened, that's exactly what I'd do. Was one hundred percent positive that's what I'd do.

Now, I don't know.

Tears roll down my cheeks, dripping onto the floor and soaking into my hair. My stomach lurches, and I can't catch my breath.

Shooting into a sitting position, I slap my hand over my chest and take several deep, wheezy breaths.

The tears fall harder.

My life's over. I've never had a job. I've just barely started college. If I even make it through this semester, I have three more left before I can get my associate's degree. How?

How am I going to do all of that with a baby?

Will Axel freak out or be happy when I tell him? Will he leave me to do this on my own?

I've been sitting on the floor for a long time now.

I'm so scared.

MURPHY

Church has a different vibe to it this week. After we sit down and go through regular club business, Rock points at Wrath.

"Tell me what went down with Sway and my wife while I was away."

Wrath frowns in confusion then glances my way. I give him a subtle shrug and his gaze skips to Z before answering. "Nothing. He was just a dick. Murphy was ready to kill him."

"We took care of it," Z explains. "He was bent because he wanted to know if, with you out of the picture, we were still against running guns."

Rock nods slowly. "Fucking prick."

"Pretty much," I agree.

"Oh, he was also surprised none of us were fucking her while you were away," Wrath adds, grinning and shifting away in anticipation of a kick from Rock.

"He say that to her?" Rock asks.

"No. Just us," Z says.

Rock nods, but I don't think the matter is completely closed yet. He runs his gaze over the rest of us. "Hoot and Birch, what are we doing about them?"

"Let's take a vote. They're both ready," Ravage says.

"We've waited long enough since Hoot's last vote," Stash agrees. Hoot hadn't been quite ready but he'd dedicated himself to the club since then and I agree with Stash that it's time.

Wrath glances at Rock. "Why don't we vote on Axel, too?"

"Fuck that," I snap. "He ain't been here long enough."

Dex elbows me. "He stepped up a lot over the summer, prez. Not a bad idea to see where we're at with him."

Rock smirks at me. "I think we already know."

I glance at Teller to see where he's at, but he's completely blank. Rock's still watching me and I nod at him. "I'm cool."

"Bring 'em in."

All three prospects stride in the door, all wearing uncertain faces. Hoot probably looks the most nervous since he's done this once before. Birch runs his hand over his bushy beard, then slips his game face on.

"Thanks for being here," Rock says to the prospects. "And thank you for everything you do around the club. I know we give you a ton of shit, but your hard work and loyalty is appreciated."

Hoot and Birch stand up a little straighter. I think they realize what's about to happen. Axel, on the other hand, seems confused. Or bored. It's hard to tell.

"I think it's time we take a vote and see if you three are fit to wear the Lost Kings' patch," Rock says.

Axel's eyebrows shoot up. Yeah, even he knows it's way too early to be voting on him. Not sure what Prez is thinking.

Hoot's up first and everyone votes yes. Z gets up and presents him with his full three-piece patch.

Birch is also thumbs up and gets a patch.

Then it's time for Axel.

AXEL

Murphy will be the reason I don't get voted into the club. I know it. I can feel his hatred from here.

Why I'm getting voted on so soon mystifies me. Hoot and Birch have been here way longer. In a way, it's a relief.

Doesn't mean I won't use it as an excuse to give Murphy a dose of reality.

For some reason, Rock starts the voting with Teller instead of Z this time.

"Yay," Teller says. I'm surprised. While I know Murphy will be a big fat *no*, I suspected Heidi's brother might also say no.

Rock points at Murphy next and I brace myself.

I'll give Murphy credit. He's not a coward. He looks me straight in the eye when he says, "No."

Even though I expected it, I'm pissed. I swallow, stare back at him, and sneer. "Let it go. Heidi isn't picking you. It's done."

Murphy jumps out of his chair and narrows his eyes at me. "Fuck you. You don't know shit."

"The fuck I don't," comes out of my mouth. Low, but loud enough that everyone at the table heard it.

At the head of the table, Rock slams his fist down. "Enough. Everyone out, except my officers and Axel."

They all file out fast. Hoot and Birch throw me a look like they don't envy me right now.

Can't say I blame them.

This needs to happen, though. And however it turns out, I'm fine with it. This trouble has been brewing since the day I signed up to be a prospect. Something I never would have done if it weren't for Heidi. I know in my heart, I'm not meant for this lifestyle. Murphy's doing me a favor, really.

Still pisses me off when I've busted my ass for the club for almost two years now. Even if I never patched in, I'd hoped to leave on good terms—for Heidi's sake. After this, I don't see how that's possible.

As soon as everyone leaves, I face Murphy. "If you think I don't know you tried to nail my girl before her birthday party, you're dumber than I thought."

The room absolutely explodes. Except for Murphy. He's got nothing. No comment. And no shame either, apparently. He crosses his arms over his chest and stares me down, a slight smirk tugging at the corner of his mouth.

Teller, on the other hand, has plenty to say. He brushes against my arm, bumping me out of the way to face his best friend. "Tell me that's not true, bro."

Before Murphy answers, I open my big, stupid mouth. "Oh, it's true. Asshole was trying to plant his flag first. Got a little pissed when he realized I'd already set up camp."

Was that an epically douchey thing to say?

Yup.

Do I care?

Nope.

Will it come back to bite me in the ass later?

Probably.

Teller jabs a finger at me. "You, shut the fuck up."

Yeah, I definitely shouldn't have said that in front of Heidi's brother.

Wrath and Z watch the scene unfold with the barest of interest.

Okay, they both look like they're trying hard not to laugh. Rock, on the other hand, seems ready to murder someone. I just don't think he's decided who needs to die yet.

"For fuck's sake, Murphy. We talked about this and you went behind my back anyway?"

This is news to me.

Murphy finally shows some remorse. "This was before our talk," he answers quietly.

"I've known you my whole life. How could you?" Teller's low voice really seems to shame Murphy, because he looks away.

Rock pushes out of his chair and grabs Teller's attention. "Simmer down. This is between the three of them."

Teller must be more enraged than anyone realizes, because he turns on Rock. Gets right up in his face. "Like fuck it is. Save that femi-nazi bullshit your ol' lady's been feeding you for someone else. This is between me and Blake—"

His tirade's cut off by Rock's hand around his throat, slamming him into the wall. Oh, Christ, I don't want to be the one responsible for getting Heidi's brother killed.

"Let's set aside the fact that I'm your president and speaking to me that way is grounds for me to beat the ever-loving fuck out of you. What I *will not* fucking tolerate is you talking about Hope—your *president's ol' lady*—with such disrespect when she's done nothing but try to help you and your sister out since the day she met your sorry ass. Are we clear?"

Teller's turning a bit blue in the face, but he manages to nod.

"Good." Rock releases Teller's neck. Teller staggers to the side, coughing and shaking his head.

Sitting back down, Rock pinches the bridge of his nose. "Jesus fuck, I don't even know where to start."

"It's Wrath's job to administer the beatdowns," Z throws out with a snarky grin. The reality that I might not survive a beating from Wrath settles into my skin, and I have to fight the urge to run from the room.

Wrath slowly turns his head and fixes Z with an *are-you-out-of-*

your-mind face before speaking. "I'm not sure where to start, either. Murphy for fucking around with another brother's girl—"

"He ain't a fucking brother," Murphy interrupts.

Wrath continues as if Murphy hadn't even spoken. "And disrespecting a fellow brother by fucking around with his sister. Or Teller for disrespecting the prez and his ol' lady." His scary-as-fuck eyes swing to me. "Or *you.*"

"Why me? I didn't do anything." Even to my own ears, I sound like a little bitch.

"I don't know. I just feel like kicking your ass all of a sudden. It was probably the *setting up camp* comment," he adds without a trace of amusement.

See, I knew that would bite me in the ass.

Even though Wrath terrifies the fuck out of me, I keep my feet firmly planted where they are. He seems to respect that and nods before turning back to Teller and Murphy.

"Given I might *accidentally* kill one of you, it's probably better that Z dole out the beatings you two assholes have coming."

It takes a second to comprehend Wrath's threat. I wonder if he's referring to his girlfriend's past relationship with those two jackasses. Personally, I've always thought that whole situation was pretty fucked.

Until I found myself in a similar situation.

Then I understood it a whole lot better.

MURPHY

I have to give Axel credit. I didn't see this coming.

Wrath kicking my ass? Sure, I've been waiting on that one for a while now.

Teller upset that I messed around with Heidi? I figured he might be uncomfortable. Maybe not thrilled. This level of pissed? No, I didn't expect that.

Axel having the balls to call me out in front of every one, though? I underestimated him.

That Heidi apparently confessed to her boyfriend and he forgave her and focused his rage on me? Nope. Never saw that coming.

When this clusterfuck dies down, I need to seriously consider having my head removed from my ass.

If I were a fraction smarter, I would've seen *all* of this coming.

Not that it would have mattered. Still wasn't voting Axel in. I know I'm a dick for letting a girl fuck with club business. And if it were any other girl in the world, I wouldn't. Which by the way, is probably the only reason Rock won't strip my patch for this epic fuck-upedness.

"Given I might *accidentally* kill one of you, it's probably better that Z dole out the beatings you two assholes have coming."

Wrath's deadly voice breaks into my thoughts. It should scare the piss out of me. The fact that I think he's referring to Trinity reminds me of what a piece of shit I am. I sort of welcome the ass kicking I've got coming.

"Did you touch her?" Teller demands.

No way am I talking about anything that's gone on between me and Heidi in front of all my brothers. I cross my arms over my chest and stare him down, letting him know this topic is off-limits.

Teller shakes his head. "Fucker." He turns on Axel. "And *you*. I catch you over at our apartment again, I'll murder you."

Axel backs up a few steps. "That's fine. We're planning to get our own apartment anyway."

Damn, the kid has balls. If this situation were slightly different, I'd have mad respect for him.

Teller isn't really seeing the grit in this kid. Nope. He lunges at him, tackling him to the ground.

"Enough!" Rock roars. "Get him off Axel." He points to Z, who hauls Teller away and throws him down on one of the couches in the back of the room. Wrath has his head down, but if his shaking shoulders are any indication—he's laughing.

I'd laugh too if I weren't so fucking miserable.

"Jesus Christ," Rock grumbles. "A simple fuckin' vote. You guys have to be shittin' me." He jabs a finger in the air at Teller. "Your sister's eighteen. She's an adult. I suggest you calm the fuck down before talking to her or you're gonna piss her the fuck off."

Rock swings his presidential glare my way next, but the corners of his mouth are ever-so-slightly turned up, telling me he's not horribly pissed at me.

Thank fuck.

Twelve

Heidi

As I arrive at the clubhouse, everyone except the officers storm out of the war room.

Axel doesn't come out, either.

That can't be good.

Maybe they voted him in?

I need to tell Axel about the baby. Maybe he'll think it's good news if he hears it on the same day he patched in to the club.

Ravage and Dex glance at me and Dex shakes his head. A strange, prickly sensation tickles my skin. I open my mouth to ask what's going on, but Birch's voice stops me.

"That shit with Murphy hatin' on Axel's just gonna get worse. No way is he ever gonna vote—" He stops when he notices me, and Dex punches him in the arm.

"Club business stays in there." He jerks his thumb toward the closed war room doors and walks out the front door with Ravage.

Hoot laughs and smacks Birch. "Christ, you're gonna lose your patch before you even get to wear it."

I know better than to say anything. Over the years, I've learned if I keep quiet and fade into the background, the guys will talk about all sorts of things in front of me.

Except, they both glare at me.

That's never happened before.

Since Axel's a prospect, I've hung out with Hoot and Birch plenty of times. They've always been cool to hang out with. Plus, my brother's the treasurer, so they'd be nuts to disrespect me.

But now they leave without speaking to me.

An uneasy feeling creeps through my stomach. More than the morning sickness that seems to attack me all day long. I run down to the bathroom to throw up and when I return, Trinity's walking in the front door.

She tips her head at the closed war room doors. "They still in church?" she asks.

"Yup. Everyone else left, except the officers and Axel."

Her forehead wrinkles and she crosses the room to stand in front of me. "That can't be good."

"Yeah, I thought so, too." I still feel awkward around Trinity. She's a girl, though. Maybe I should ask her what to do? I really need to talk to Hope, but she's not around this afternoon.

A few minutes later, Wrath and Z storm out. No sign of my brother, Murphy, Axel or Uncle Rock.

"What's going on?" Trinity asks.

Wrath's gaze slides to me and he shakes his head. "Nothing. Club business."

Club business is the guys' way of nicely saying, "None of *your* business." I've heard it for years.

The only good thing I can say is that they never use that excuse unless it really is about club business.

The bad thing is, I know it means Axel didn't get voted in.

AXEL

Rock's about to let us all go. Teller's calmed down. Sort of. Murphy doesn't have the stones to look at me at all.

"Can we talk, prez?" I ask, after the two of them leave.

"Yeah. Sit." He points to Z's chair and I feel a little uneasy taking it.

"Thank you for everything you've done for me. But I think...I think I'm done with the club."

He sighs and sits back in his chair, but his eyes never leave me. "I figured. I'm sorry. I know you've worked hard and you've been an asset to us. You know guys get voted down and still patch in later."

"We both know Murphy will never vote me in. I understand why it has to be unanimous. Honestly, I don't blame him. I don't one hundred percent trust him and I know that's a problem."

"You want me to put in a word with Sway for you? He wouldn't make you start over with a full two years of prospecting."

The thought of moving to the Lost Kings MC's downstate charter is incredibly unappealing. I spent some time there last year and they run things very different from the way Rock runs things.

"No. I—I like how things are run here. I don't think I could—"

He holds up a hand. "I get it."

Now, I understand in some clubs a prospect might not make it out alive. They've seen too much. Know too much. I have my guesses, but other than the strip club, I have no clue how the Lost Kings earn their money.

"This will make things difficult for Heidi," he says, completely surprising me that Heidi's his first concern here. This is why leaving the club is hard. Rock's a good guy and I respect him a lot. Respect the way he takes care of the members of his club. Yeah, Wrath and Z have ridden me pretty hard and thrown a lot of work on me, but they've also always treated me with respect.

"I won't stop Heidi from visiting."

"You're always welcome here for family functions. I want you to know that."

"Thank you. Appreciate it."

He stands and walks over to the locked cabinet where I've only seen him take stuff out of a handful of times.

"You done at the end of this semester?"

"Yes."

"Got anything lined up?"

"I have some leads. I can take care of Heidi."

The corners of his mouth lift. "Good. Glad to hear it. Even so, if you need a reference, use my name. I've got a contact at a diesel shop over in Ironworks I can put you in touch with."

"Thanks. That's…that would be a huge help." The school helps us with placements, but there's a ton of competition for coveted spots. Any extra edge I can get is great.

He returns to his chair and passes an envelope to me. "I want you to take this."

The envelope is thick, and when I peek inside, there's a lot of crisp hundred-dollar bills padding it. "Prez—"

"Just Rock now."

"Rock, I can't take your money."

"Yes, you can. And you will. You said you're planning to get an apartment near campus with Heidi?"

I nod, because yes, Heidi and I have talked about it a couple times.

"Find a nice place near campus for Heidi and use that for living expenses."

"I—"

"Need to concentrate on your schoolwork."

The intention behind his word is clear. This matter is closed as far as Rock's concerned. I slip the money into my pocket and stand. "Thank you."

He holds out his hand, but instead of a shake, he pulls me in for a quick hug and backslap. "You're a good kid. I'm sorry it didn't work out."

My throat tightens and I have a brief moment of regret. Am I making a mistake turning my back on this family who's, at times, treated me better than my own family?

I'm conflicted all the way out the door. But I don't think there's any way to take my words back.

Once you're out, you're out.

Thirteen

MURPHY

"What's going on, Blake?" Heidi's voice pulls me away from staring at the war room door. I did a shit thing in there, but I don't feel as bad about it as I should.

Marcel glares at me. Despite the assurances he just gave prez, I don't think we're cool yet.

He turns his glare on Heidi next, and I swear to fuck if he says something to her, or makes her feel bad, I will punch him in his goddamn throat.

"You here for Axel?" he asks his sister.

She squints at him, her gaze darting between Marcel and me. "Yes."

"He should be out in a minute," Marcel says.

"What's going on? Why is Axel still in there?"

"Not your concern, lil' sis. You know that," he snaps before walking out the door.

Heidi said she was here to talk to Axel. Not me. Fuck, that burns. We stare at each other for a few minutes without speaking. She's pale and shaky.

"Are you okay?" I ask.

Her lips tremble. "I'd be better if you would tell me what's happening."

"You know I can't."

She blows out an exasperated breath.

"I have some stuff to work on in the garage. Want to hang out there while you wait?"

She turns toward the war room door. Hesitates. Takes a step toward me. "I...I better wait here. I need to talk to him about something."

"Anything I can help with?"

She tucks her bottom lip in, biting down briefly before shaking her head. "I don't think so."

I hate leaving her, but I also don't want to get swept up into any more drama that involves Axel today. I've had about all I can take of that kid, and if he smirks at me one more time, I'll end up planting my fist in his face.

I'm in the garage maybe ten minutes before I hear her.

"Blake!"

Turning, I find her silhouetted in the doorway, tears on her cheeks. "It was you, wasn't it? You did this? Didn't vote him in? Why?"

"Not your business, Heidi."

Outside, the distinctive rumble of Axel's bike kicks up and Heidi's tears flow even faster. "You're ruining everything. Why? Why are you doing this to us?"

The way she says *us* sends anger through my veins, burning me alive from the inside. They shouldn't even *be* together. "Dammit, Heidi! You know club business isn't your business. Drop it."

Her fists ball up at her sides, and her face screws into that expression she makes right before she explodes. "I hate you! I hate you for doing this just to get even with me."

Yup. Sounds about right. "The world doesn't revolve around you, Heidi."

"Why can't you just let me be happy?"

Axel revs his engine, his cue to Heidi that it's time to go, I'm sure.

My head's throbbing. I'm so fucking pissed right now. "The club isn't here to make Heidi happy," I shout.

"Why are you trying to force me to choose?" A loud hiccupping-sob noise tears out of her throat.

Shaking my head, I take a few steps closer to her. "Choose what? Between him and the club? You're not a fucking member. You're the sister of a member, so why do you think anyone gives a shit what you want?"

Her lip trembles again and I hate myself for being so harsh with her. I haven't been able to stop thinking about all the shit Axel said at the table, though.

"Don't try to tell me this has nothing to do with me." A few tears tumble down her cheeks. Pain twists inside my chest. I can't stand when Heidi's upset. Can't stand being the one who upset her.

"It doesn't," I insist.

"Don't lie to me...on top of everything else, Blake."

I pin her with a stare. "Who's the liar here, Heidi? Because I seem to remember you planning a spring break trip with me not that long ago, but now I hear you two are moving in together? Are you fucking kidding me?"

Her mouth opens, she shakes her head. "You don't understand."

"Make me understand!" I yell loud enough that probably everyone in the clubhouse heard.

She flinches, then spins around and runs out of sight. A few minutes later, I hear Axel's bike leaving the property.

A string of curses bursts out of me, and I send every tool in front of me flying to the floor. Now that I know she's gone, I stalk back into the clubhouse.

Rock's still in the war room, shuffling through some papers when I poke my head in.

I take a few deep breaths to calm down before asking, "Can I talk to you, prez?"

He nods and motions for me to come in. "What's on your mind, brother?"

"Why'd you decide to vote on him today?"

He gives me a lazy shrug. "Why prolong the inevitable?"

"I—"

"Every one of your brothers has your back. Whether you're right or wrong."

I know that's how the club works. How the brotherhood works. Your brother's in trouble, you fight right next to him, protect him with your last breath, even if he's the one who got himself into trouble. That's why it's so important for it to be unanimous when we vote a member in.

Dragging my hand through my hair, I think about how to ask my next question. "How can I fix this?"

He tilts his head, considering my question. "I don't think there's anything to fix."

"You understand why I voted no."

"Doesn't matter why. It was never gonna work. Ultimately, you did the club a favor."

Now, I'm not so sure, and I guess the look on my face says that.

"He would never fully trust you, and you were never gonna fully trust him. Doubt like that can rip a club apart," Rock insists.

"Yeah, but everyone else was ready to patch him in. I'm the one who cocked it up."

"You don't know that for sure. Besides, I offered to get him into Sway's club."

"You did?"

Rock shoots me a glare, and yeah, I should know better than to interrupt him. "He said no. He made the choice to leave. His heart wasn't with the club." His face loses a little of its hard edge. "I understand how you feel about Heidi. Think what that would have been like for you." He glances at the open war room door. "I like to think we eventually learn from our mistakes."

I think he's referring to Wrath and Trinity, and it makes me feel even shittier.

Rock shakes his head. "It's not the same thing. I shouldn't have said that."

"Would you choose the club over Hope?"

I wish I would learn to think before shit comes tumbling out of my mouth sometimes.

Luckily, Rock's not offended by the question. "No. But she'd never ask me to do that."

"What do I do now?"

He sighs and stares out the window for a second. "Walk away. She made her choice, too, I guess. You keep pushing, you'll push her away permanently."

That's not exactly what I wanted to hear, even though I know he's right.

"How did you do it when Hope was married? How'd you walk away?"

This question does seem to piss him off, but I can't help asking.

"I wanted what was best for her. I thought she was happy. That's what mattered."

"How could you stand it?"

"I hated every second, but I didn't have a choice."

Ultimately, things worked out for them. A blessing for the club. I can't picture Rock without Hope anymore. Even if she's not a "member," she's just as vital as anyone else.

I don't think my story will have the same happy ending. "I need to get out of here for a while."

Regret and understanding play over Rock's face and he nods slowly. "Yeah, I get that. I know you don't want to spend time down at Sway's."

"Nah, not right now. Need more distance than that."

"Chaser's place is always open to us."

"I'd rather go some place warmer, maybe."

"Sparky's working out a deal with our friends near Phoenix."

"Yeah." Now *there's* a place that can help me get my mind off things. "Complete change of scenery might be best."

"Don't forget they're into harder shit than we are. Riskier."

"I don't even think I care right now."

Rock nails me with what Teller and I have always referred to as his *Dad Face*. "That's a good way to land in jail or dead, so you better get your head on straight on the ride down before you decide to stick around."

"I will. How much longer until Sparky needs me to go down there?"

"Should be any day."

"Good, I have some loose ends to tie up around here."

"I trust you not to leave us hanging." Rock's mouth curves into a slight smirk. "The only thing I ask, is that you make sure you see Hope before you leave."

"You know it."

Heidi

I end up driving behind Axel to his apartment. Eventually my tears dry. I'm still furious with Murphy. Hurt and embarrassed, too. A huge part of me is angry with Axel, to be honest. He acted so calm, like permanently leaving the club meant nothing to him.

My entire world's ripping apart. The reality that we're having a baby hasn't quite set in yet, and now I have to deal with a canyon-sized rift in my family. How will I ever spend time up there with Axel? I want my son or daughter to have the benefit of being around the club. Axel won't want to spend time up there after this. The club won't want him there, either.

I'm stuck.

I can't break up with the father of my child. That's something my mother would have done.

"You okay, babe?" Axel asks through my open car window.

"Just thinking."

He stares at the open road behind us. Is he having regrets about leaving the club? Or thinking of driving away and never coming back? "Come on. Let's go upstairs."

Butterflies flutter in my belly and my blood pounds through my ears. I'm not ready to do this.

But I have to.

When we're inside his apartment, he pulls me over to the couch. "I hope you're not mad at me," he says.

"About what?"

"That I'm not going to be a part of the MC."

"Was it Murphy? Did he vote you down?"

"You know I can't tell you that. It's for the best, though, Heidi. I know they're family and you love them, but that lifestyle isn't for me."

Lifestyle? What the— Forget it. I can't bother with that now.

He wraps his hand around mine. "Let's move in together. I found us a place near school, and Rock gave me some money for the security deposit."

"He did?"

"Yeah. He wanted to make sure I take good care of you. He's going to give me a reference for a job."

A small bit of relief washes over me. Maybe we *will* still be able to hang out with my family without it being awkward.

"Really?"

"Yeah. And he said I'm always welcome up there for family stuff. So, don't worry. This won't change things."

Sweet relief washes over me. *We're going to be okay.* "I need to talk to you."

My grave tone silences him and he cocks his head, inviting me to speak.

"I—I'm pregnant. I took two tests and they were both—"

"What the fuck?" He jumps up off the couch and paces in front of me. "Are you fucking serious, Heidi?"

His extreme reaction sets off sparks of fear in my stomach. "Calm down."

"What are we going to do? I don't want to be a father. I'm only twenty. How could you be so irresponsible? I thought you were on the pill?"

Oh, *hell* no. I practically fly off the couch and just barely restrain myself from choking him. "Do you think I got pregnant on my own?

This is as much your fault as mine, Mr. 'There's no sensation when I wear a condom.'"

He glares at me and shoves his hands through his hair again. "Did you make an appointment yet?"

My stomach churns, because I don't think he's asking if I made an appointment with my doctor.

"No," I whisper.

"Heidi. We're not ready. You're not ready for a baby. It's going to fuck everything up for both of us."

He's not saying anything I haven't thought of myself, but each word stings so bad. I wanted him to comfort me and wanted us to sit down and figure things out together. I never expected him to be so furious.

"Is it even mine?"

His question pierces my heart. "How can you ask me that? You're my only—"

"You and—"

"No!"

His eyes linger on mine, but I hold his stare. "Heidi, this isn't fair. You promised me if something like this happened, you'd get rid of it."

That's true. And at the time I absolutely meant it, but now? I can't. "I can't. I always thought…but this is different. It's real. And I can't."

I search his eyes, his face, seeking a trace of something I recognize. But all I find is anger.

"I'm out of here," he says, opening the door and slamming it behind him.

A nasty voice inside my head asks why I'm so surprised.

I've always been easy to leave.

Fourteen

Heidi

It's dark and I'm sprawled out on the couch. I should have left. Gone back to my brother's apartment, but I'm mad at him, too. If there's a chance of working this out with Axel, I need to do that before I tell my brother I'm pregnant.

My hand settles over my stomach. Even if Axel never comes back, this baby's mine. And at least I know when we made it, we loved each other.

I wonder if my mother ever thinks of me. Wonders if I'm okay? Stupid. I'm pretty sure I know the answer to those questions.

Much later that night, Axel returns to the apartment.

He closes the door quietly and stares at me for a minute. I scramble to sit up, pulling the blanket up to my chin. He sighs and drops down to the opposite end of the couch.

"What do you want to do?"

"Axel—"

"What do you want to do?" he asks a little harsher this time.

"It's our *child*."

He leans forward putting his head in his hands and curses under his breath. After a minute, he picks his head up and stares at me. "Explain it. How does this make sense for us, Heidi?"

I sit up, tucking my feet under me. "I know it doesn't…make sense. It's the wrong time, but"—my hand settles over my stomach—"I have this little person inside me who I want to know. I want to give her all the things I didn't have—"

One corner of his mouth lifts in a smile. "Her?"

"It's a feeling."

He cradles his head in his hands, staring at the floor for a few minutes before speaking. "We should get married then," he mumbles.

The shift in the direction of our conversation makes my head spin. "*What*?"

Finally, he picks his head up and looks at me "I don't want—we should get married."

"Earlier you wanted me to get an abortion. Now you want to get married?"

He lifts his shoulders. A quick, jerky movement. "At least maybe then your brother won't kill me."

His attempt at a joke sucks. When I don't say anything, he walks into his bedroom and returns with a red velvet box. "I was planning to give this to you after graduation anyway."

"What is it?" Stupid question. Obviously, it's a ring. He confirms it by opening the box and plucking out a delicate white gold ring that sparkles with tiny diamonds surrounding one larger diamond. There are scrolls and filigrees, giving it an antique look.

"It was my grandmother's," he explains after pushing it on my finger.

"It's beautiful. Your parents won't mind?"

His shoulders lift. "My grandmother left it to me, to give to my future wife."

"And you were planning to give it to me?"

"Yeah." His mouth turns up in a sad imitation of a smile. "When the time was right."

Fifteen

MURPHY

Things settle down at the club after Axel leaves. No one talks about it. Hoot and Birch don't ask any questions about where their buddy went. Axel's out. No further conversations need to happen.

Well, one conversation needs to happen, but Heidi won't speak to me. Won't answer my calls or texts. Nothing.

Teller finds me in the garage a couple afternoons later and stops to watch what I'm working on. Although I talk to him every day, we haven't talked about Heidi or the vote.

"You hear from her?" he asks while I'm sifting through my toolbox.

Asking which "her" he's referring to isn't necessary. "No."

"Fuck. Me, either."

I finally stop my search and motion him outside. "Where's she staying?"

"Must be with him. All her shit's gone from the apartment."

Guilt because of the rift I caused between Marcel and Heidi settles in my gut. "Stop by his place?"

"Not yet. I'm afraid I'll kill him."

"Did you talk to Hope? Bet you Heidi's spoken to her."

His mouth twists down. "No."

"What's your deal with Hope, anyway? You said some dickish things about her during that fiasco."

"I shouldn't have said what I did. I was just so pissed." My best friend shrugs and turns toward the woods. "I don't know. Been a lot of changes since she got here."

Maybe a joke will pull him out of his funk. "What's the matter? You mad 'cause Trinity caught monogamy from Hope?"

He glares at me. Guess it's too soon to rib him about Trinity.

"That was obviously never gonna happen," he says.

"No shit."

Teller keeps pining away over Trinity like this, Wrath's gonna straight up murder him one of these days, so I return to our first topic. "Rock's happier than he's ever been. Hope's good to everyone. What else you want?"

"Christ, keep it up, I'll think *you're* in love with her."

Now it's my turn to look away. "You know who I'm in love with."

"Don't go there, bro."

"She's been like a mother to Heidi."

At the word *mother* he turns and glares at me. "Yeah. And I don't want Heidi getting hurt when Hope decides she's had enough and takes off."

Whoa. We've been closer than brothers for years. Have seen and done everything together. There's nothing we don't know about each other. But it's not like we sit around discussin' our mommy abandonment issues. All that shit's in the past. At least for me it is. "Bro," I say gently so he doesn't take my head off. "She's *not* Heidi's mother. If she didn't leave when Rock was in jail, she's not going anywhere. Besides, even when she and Rock *were* apart, she didn't abandon Heidi. Took her shopping and all that other shit."

His fists open and close. "Yeah, I know."

I love him like a brother, but Teller can be a dick. He's also loyal to his core and protective of people he cares about. So I know he probably already feels like shit for disrespecting Rock, and figure I should drop it.

We're interrupted by Z riding in. He'd taken off right after the Axel clusterfuck and no one had seen him since. He parks his bike in the garage and joins us.

"Where you been, fucker?" Teller asks Z.

Z's mouth slides into a smirk. "Here and there."

We each get a brotherly hand-grab and hearty backslap.

"You need me to look at the ol' gray ghost?" I ask, nodding at the garage.

"Nah, I'll take care of it later. What're you two doing out here?"

I don't get to answer, because Hope jogs into the parking area from the woods. She's dressed to work out and smiles brightly when she sees us.

"What're you doing here, First Lady?" I call out. I'm dying to talk to her. But I want to do it alone. Not in front of Teller and certainly not in front of Z, who can't be serious for five seconds.

"Oh, geez. You're all here." She reaches up and gives Z a quick hug. "Where've you been?"

"Around."

Teller nods at her. "What's up?"

"We're going to use the yoga room for actual yoga," she teases. We turned the room—a room the hippie cult who owned our compound before us used for a yoga studio—into a champagne room, complete with shiny stripper poles and all. More often than not, it ends up being an orgy room. It's on the tip of my tongue to tell her to wipe down any surface she plans to touch first, but Z interrupts.

"Who's we?"

"Swan, Trinity, and me. Swan's finishing her hours to become a certified instructor, and Trinity and I volunteered for the free classes. Win-win."

None of us know what to say to that. I'm pretty sure all three of us know Swan—intimately. But I doubt one of us knows fuck-all about what she does when she leaves the MC.

Hope shakes her head, as if she's thinking the same thing I am and finds it pathetic. For the first time in my life, I kind of agree with her.

I keep that to myself.

"I'm still allowed to visit, right?" she asks.

"I think you just miss us," I tease, and she grins.

"Maybe a little. And I miss the gym."

"Surprised prez hasn't put a gym in your basement," Teller says.

For some reason, Hope's cheeks turn a little pinker, but she doesn't have a chance to respond.

"Nah, they put a sex room in the basement. No room for a gym." Z chuckles and takes two steps back from Hope, who blushes even redder.

"Who told you that?" she demands.

"Who do you think installed the keypad?"

She crosses her arms over her chest. "You don't have to blab about it."

"Ew, it's true? Fuck, I don't need to know what Mom and Dad are doing in their basement." I rumble with laughter and next to me, Teller does as well.

Hope turns her glare on me. "I am *not* old enough to be your mother."

"Thank fuck, otherwise his crush on you would be extra weird," Teller mutters loud enough for everyone to hear.

"Fuck you, asshole." My fist lands solidly in his bicep and he falls over, laughing. At least he's not being a moody prick anymore.

"All righty then. This has been…fun." Hope draws the word out, letting us know it's been anything but. "Now, I have a date with two hot chicks."

Z watches her walk away in a manner that would get his ass kicked if Rock were here to witness it. I lash my foot out, kicking him in the calf. "What the fuck's wrong with you?"

His head snaps back my way. "What?"

"Why you picking on her? Rock's gonna kill you."

His shoulders lift and he grins like an idiot. "Nah, she knows I'm only messin' with her."

Teller leans over and fake-whispers. "He's being a passive-aggressive fuckwad, because he's pissed Lilly won't return any of his calls."

"Ohhh." I exaggerate the word, nodding like a goof. "That makes more sense."

"Fuck both of you," Z grumbles.

"Dude, she was way too classy for you." I get a smack upside the head for that one, but it was totally worth it.

The front door bangs shut, and before Z knows what hit him, Wrath charges, lifting Z off the ground in a bear-hug style hold.

"Jesus Christ, you're gonna fucking kill me," Z wheezes when Wrath sets him down. "I think you cracked a rib."

"Stop being a little bitch. Where you been?"

"Hi, Z!" Trinity calls out. She joins us, giving Z a quick hug then tucks herself against Wrath's side.

"Where've you been?" she asks Z.

"What the fuck. Why's everyone tryin' to keep tabs on me?"

Wrath reaches over and punches Z's arm. "Quit your bitchin'. I'm pissed 'cause my girl had to take care of your dogs while you were off chasing wind."

"I don't mind," Trinity protests.

"*I* mind. She lets them sleep in the bed."

Z's face breaks into a grin. "Just set them on the floor if you want to…" He does a few hip thrusts, making Trinity laugh and Wrath look like he's gonna punch Z again. "*You know.*"

Next to me, Teller stiffens, and I notice he's taken an interest in his shoes all of a sudden. I give him a subtle elbow to the ribs, and he picks his head up. "Have Mariella watch the dogs."

"She did," Trinity says. "Really, it was fine, Z. They're the club's dogs. It's no big deal."

I lift my chin at the clubhouse. "Your yoga buddy's looking for you."

Trinity chuckles. "Yeah, I saw her. Came out to say hi to Z." She and Z wave and make goofy faces at each other for a few seconds before she wraps her arms around Wrath and lifts up on her tiptoes to give him a kiss. It's awkward for a minute, but then he lets her go and it's just the four of us. Wrath eyes each of us. "What?"

"Why you lettin' them fuck with our champagne room?" Z asks. He's laughing, though, so I doubt he gives a fuck.

Wrath shrugs. "Were you planning to use it this morning? No. So leave 'em alone."

Z throws his hands up. "Settle down, fucker. I'm just kidding."

Wrath lifts his chin at me. "Ready to head to Furious?"

"Yup." I slap Teller's back and get a punch from Z before we take off.

Heidi

I can't avoid my brother forever.

Especially not on his birthday. Every day since I left, I've regretted moving my stuff out without talking to him. Ignoring his phone calls. Punishing him for something that probably isn't even his fault. All of it.

Besides feeling bereft without my big brother around, I'm scared to tell him why I'm such a mess. Why I've reverted back to acting like a brat. Why I'm so damn terrified.

Yes, I'm hurt Axel left the club. And while at first I suspected my brother and Murphy had something to do with it, I realized the reason doesn't matter. Marcel and I have never gone this long without talking, and I feel like a part of me is missing.

The only thing that's been keeping me together is my schoolwork. There has to be at least one area of my life I don't fuck up.

I've aced all of my exams so far this year, so at least I have some good news to tell my brother. You know, right before I tell him Axel and I are getting married. He's going to question me. He'll assume I'm knocked up. I can't tell him that yet, though. Axel and I are the only ones who know.

I think Axel's still hoping I'll change my mind.

"Can we do something fun this weekend?" Axel asks when he

gets home.

"I wanted to go up to the clubhouse. It's my brother's birthday."

Axel stares at me for several seconds without speaking. "Yeah, okay."

I let out a relieved breath. I'd been prepared for another argument. "Thanks."

He nods.

"I'm just so stressed out and tired and I miss my brother."

"Maybe we'll get lucky and the stress will cause a miscarriage," Axel jokes. He might as well have punched me in the stomach with his words.

A couple seconds of intense silence pass. "How can you say that?"

"I'm just kidding."

"That's not funny."

He lifts his shoulders and walks into the kitchen.

"I want to tell him about our engagement."

"Okay," he yells back.

"But not the baby."

He pokes his head around the corner. "Good call."

"I was thinking of asking Trinity to help me put together the wedding. Maybe at the clubhouse since it's too cold now to do it outside."

"Whoa. I thought we'd have the wedding at my parents' country club."

"What exactly about me says 'country club wedding'?" I tease, but deep down I'm annoyed he even suggested it. "Besides, it's not open now."

"No. I thought we'd do it in June. After I graduate."

In my head, I'm counting to ten so I don't strangle him. "Axel, I'll be huge by then. No frickin' way."

"Oh, shit. Yeah. I didn't think of that."

Big surprise. He's still pretending the baby will magically disappear. And don't think I've forgotten that miscarriage comment.

I'm way too hurt to examine those words right now.

Sixteen

Every Mile a Memory

Five Years Earlier...

MURPHY

I barely stopped my bike in front of the house before Heidi came flying down the sidewalk. The sight of her left me struck dumb, mute, paralyzed. I was also pretty sure my jaw was hanging and drool dripped from my chin.

What the fuck?

The club had been keeping me busy for the last few months. A lot of long rides with Wrath, shoring up different business interests. Heidi and I kept in touch. Marcel got her a cellphone for her twelfth birthday and I either talked or exchanged texts with her every day. Even if it was just a word or two. I would send her postcards from each interesting place I'd visit, too.

Except for the occasional selfie she'd send my way, I hadn't seen her in months. She'd done a lot of growing up in those months.

Fuck me.

I didn't even have a chance to greet her properly. She grabbed my shoulder and threw herself on the bike.

"Happy Birthday, Bug."

"Thanks," she answered breathlessly.

"Helmet?"

"Got it."

Marcel was out on club business, so I offered to come see Heidi during the day. He'd stop by later that night. At least that way, we knew she wouldn't be alone on her birthday. It was doubtful her grandmother even acknowledged the day.

She wrapped her arms tight around me and squeezed me with her legs. "Please go."

The distress in her voice had me rethinking our ride. Maybe I needed to have a *chat* with her grandmother instead.

But she squeezed me tighter and I took off.

We ended up at Friendly's. Somehow we always came here first on her birthday. She hopped off and waited patiently for me. When I finally turned and faced her, she jumped into my arms, giving me a big hug. "I've missed you," she said against my neck.

"Missed you, too, baby girl. Everything okay?"

I swear she sniffled as she pulled back, but she nodded and let me lead her inside.

Once we'd placed our orders, I grabbed Heidi's hand. "What's wrong? You seem upset."

"Grams said she wasn't going to let me out of the house."

"Why?"

"I don't know. She's pissed at Marcel."

"Great. She gonna call the cops on me?"

Her mouth tipped down and her eyes widened, as if that thought had never occurred to her.

"Shit, Blake. I don't want you to get in trouble because of me."

"I ain't worried about it. Besides, if anyone's worth gettin' in trouble for, it's you."

That seemed to make her a little happier and a quick smile brightened her face.

I stared at her probably longer than necessary. Cataloging all the changes that had taken place. "Are you wearing makeup?"

Her startled eyes met mine and she ran her hand over her lips. "Yeah, why?"

"Nothing. Not used to it."

She pulled out a little mirror and checked her reflection, brushing a few stray strands of hair back into place. "Penny gave me an eyeshadow palette for my birthday."

It was fucking weird. Since when did Heidi care about any of that stuff?

"Are you planning to meet boys while we're out?" I teased.

Startled, she dropped the mirror on the table and it spun around a few times before she slapped her hand over it. "No. Why would you ask something like that?"

"I don't know. You seem different." Older, curvier, prettier. All sorts of things I shouldn't have been noticing about my best friend's thirteen-year-old sister.

"Maybe *you're* the one who's different."

There's my smart-mouthed little bug. "Maybe."

"Tell me about all the places you've been."

"Didn't you get my postcards?"

"Yeah, but it's not the same as hearing it."

So, for the next half hour, I gave her the clean versions of all my travel stories. She watched me, fascinated. Every now and then she stopped me to ask questions. Smart questions, like if the ride was better going east to west because the country "opens up" as you headed west and left the congestion and over-populated places behind. Things you wouldn't have expected a thirteen-year-old girl to know or think about. Other times she asked if I'd taken a picture of something or someplace I'd described. With Heidi, I felt free to share little details that I wouldn't have with anyone else. Like how pictures came out better at dawn or dusk, so I tried to be someplace interesting at those times to catch a good shot for her whenever possible.

She sighed. "I've always wanted to see the Bitterroot Mountain range."

"You will one day."

She glanced down at her plate and pushed her food around. "But it would be more fun with you."

"So, I'll take you when you're older."

"You mean it?"

"Of course."

One hand rested on her chin and she absently tapped her finger against her lips. Plush, pouty pink lips that made me wonder how they'd feel against mine.

"But, you've already gone so many places. I'd want to discover something new with you."

It took my brain a second to catch up to her words. "Okay."

More tapping. That finger against her lips drove me half-crazy. "Have you ever read about the Pan-American Highway?" she finally asked.

"Yeah, that's a hell of a long road trip. Lots of rough roads."

She flashed a grin at me. "Don't you always say the hardest roads take you to the most beautiful places?"

I couldn't help but smile back. I loved the way she remembered stuff like that. "It's true."

"We don't have to do the whole thing. But some of it would be cool."

"Okay. Is that what you want to do for your first trip?"

She drummed her fingers against the table while she thought about it. "What about the Blue Mountain Scenic Byway?"

"Oregon? You don't have something a little more local in mind? Shelburne Falls?"

Disappointment pushed her lips into a pout, but she nodded. "Sure. Anywhere's better than here."

"Heidi, is everything okay?"

I don't think she realized it, but she shook her head *no* at the same time she said, "yes."

"That doesn't sound very convincing."

"I just hate it here. I miss you guys. You're both gone all the time now, and Grams hates me—"

"She doesn't hate you."

Heidi just stared at me and I felt like I was missing a giant piece of the Heidi puzzle.

"It's just, you guys have the club and I have nothing. I'm all by myself and I hate it."

Every word made me feel worse, because I didn't know what I could do to fix things for her.

"You can always call me."

"I don't want to *bug* you."

"What about your friend, Penny?"

"Yeah. She and Skye and I are close. But Grams doesn't like either of them, so I can't have them over. We all mostly hang out at Penny's. Her mom's never around, so we have the house to ourselves."

That sounded like a situation I didn't want Heidi involved in.

My hand covered hers to stop the restless tapping. "I know you don't think so, but I do understand how you feel."

"How?"

A long sigh eased out of me. I wasn't comfortable bearing my soul in the middle of a crowded ice cream shop, but if it helped Heidi even a little, then I needed to suck it up. "You know before I met your brother I spent a lot of time on my own. My mom was off scoring drugs or whatever. You're one of the most important people in the world to me. So, if you need something, call me."

She lowered her gaze to our hands. "Okay."

The waitress dropped our check off, but I didn't take my eyes off Heidi. My mind was spinning, trying to figure out what else to say.

"What do you want to do next?" I asked.

Her eyes widened. "You're not dropping me off at home?"

"No. I'm yours for the whole day."

She bounced around in her seat and clapped her hands in front of her. "Oh, I wish it wasn't Sunday. I'd love to go to the drive-in. We haven't done that in years."

Marcel and I had been there recently—with girls—but I didn't tell Heidi that. I stuffed down a little of the guilt, too. It wouldn't have killed us to say no to girls who meant nothing to us, to do something nice for the girl who meant everything. "They're only open Fridays and Saturdays now, right?" I asked instead.

"I think so. Ooh…Penny's brother said next week they're show-ing *Final Destination Five* and *Red Riding Hood*."

First, I wanted to know how old Penny's brother was, and second, how much time Heidi spent around him, but I decided to sneak those questions in later. "Aren't you a little young for those?"

She shrugged. "I've seen the *Final Destination* films one through four, so does it really matter?"

"Guess not. I don't want to be responsible for giving you night-mares."

"Trust me. Plenty of other things give me nightmares."

"Heidi—"

"Hi, Murphy."

I didn't even have to look up to know the voice belonged to Jan-ice, a girl I hooked up with the last time I was out this way.

"Hi, Janice." I glanced up and found her studying Heidi. Heidi had a bored expression in place, but her jaw was so tight she might've been about to break a tooth.

"I didn't realize you were back in town."

"Just got back. I'm doing family stuff." My hand reached across the table and settled over Heidi's, so hopefully Janice would get the hint that she was intruding on family time and get lost.

"Oh." She glanced at Heidi. "Okay. Call me."

"Sure."

Heidi wouldn't even look at me and I felt like a complete jerk. "Let's get going, Bug."

She swiped her purse off the bench and slid out, marching to the front door and storming outside. Fucking great.

I stopped at the counter to pay the bill and headed outside to look for Heidi. She wasn't upset enough that she tried anything crazy, like walking home. No, she was waiting quietly by my bike.

"You okay?"

"Sure. Is that your girlfriend?"

"No."

"But you had to let her know I was family? So she didn't think I was competition?"

"Jesus, Heidi. Yeah, I didn't want her thinking I date little kids." Aw, fuck. That did *not* come out the way I meant. I waited for Heidi to start yelling at me about how she wasn't a little kid, but she didn't. And somehow her silence was worse.

"I'm sorry you're embarrassed to be seen with me," she said quietly.

"I'm not. That's not what I meant. I figured if she knew you were family, she'd go away quicker."

She peeked up at me and gave me a hint of a smile.

"Put your helmet on, brat."

That time I got a full grin out of her.

"Hey, Friday we'll go to the drive-in, okay?" Marcel and I needed to get our shit straight and visit Heidi more often.

"You mean it?"

"Yeah. I'll talk to Marcel about it later."

Her mouth turned down and I realized she expected it to be just the two of us. *Hellfuckingno.*

Instead of her house, I pointed us toward Rt. 30. There was a small hiking spot with some pretty views of the Catskill Mountains and that was where I ended up stopping. A short but steep hike led to some breathtaking views of the surrounding mountains and creek.

Heidi navigated the rocky climb easily, while I was out of breath by the time we got to the top. It was embarrassing.

When we stopped, she poked me in the gut. "Maybe more time on the treadmill and less time lifting weights."

Heidi had to be the only person, besides one of the brothers, who could get away with saying something like that. "No kidding. Too much time spent on my ass lately," I grumbled.

Her laughter was so sweet, I didn't even care that she was poking fun at me. Next thing I knew, she was wrapping her arms around my middle, resting her head on my chest. "I love you no matter what," she mumbled.

I was sort of off-balance from having her pressed up against me. She felt good. Too good. *Bad* good. My hands settled on her shoulders and I pushed her away a bit. She stared up at me and an uncomfortable skitter ran down my spine. Whatever was happening wasn't right, and I was the one who had to stop it.

Even if I didn't want to.

"So, who's Penny's brother? You've never mentioned him before."

"Bret?" Her shoulders lifted. "He's a junior."

"Junior what?"

She rolled her eyes. "A junior in high school."

"And he hangs out with a bunch of thirteen-year-old girls?"

Her face scrunched up. "Yeah, so what? Penny's his sister."

"Hmmm. He doesn't bother you, does he?"

"No. What's wrong? You hang out with me, and you're older than Bret."

Yeah, and I was starting to think that was a bad idea. "That's different."

"He did try to kiss me once."

"He did *what*?" Sounded like Marcel and I needed to have a face to fist chat with this kid. She stared at me as if she didn't understand my outrage.

"Nothing happened. I told him my first kiss was for someone else."

It took a second for her words to register in my overheated brain. "Who?"

"You," she whispered.

I was stupefied. Tongue-tied. I didn't know what the fuck to say or do. This was new and unfamiliar. Weird and awful, but her words also warmed me from the inside out. Because part of me really liked the idea of kissing her first. Part of me really, really wanted to be her first *everything*.

And I hated myself for it.

"That's a bad idea, Heidi-bug," I finally said.

Her mouth turned down and she took another step back. "Why?"

"Let's see. Because you're thirteen and I'm twenty-one." Christ, even saying it out loud made me feel like a dirty sleaze. "Your brother's my best friend and would probably kill me. And you're like my little sister."

"I'm not your sister."

Believe me, I was very aware of that fact right now. "I've known you since you were a baby."

She tilted her head to the side and studied me. "None of those reasons have anything to do with what *you* want."

I swear to Christ sometimes she was more like thirty than thirteen.

"Well, I don't want to kiss you, Heidi. You're a kid."

My lie did the trick. Hurt spread over her face. Her pain resonated in my chest. She was the sweetest person in my life, and I hated hurting her more than anyone. I was so fucked in the head, I didn't know what else to do to end this craziness.

"Come on, let's get you home before your brother hunts me down."

Although she was silent on the way, she wasn't finished torturing me.

At my bike, she paused and stared me straight in the eye. "You know I won't be thirteen forever, right?"

Present day...

For years, I couldn't wait for Heidi to be old enough that I didn't have to feel like a degenerate asshole for wanting her the way that I did.

Now she is and it doesn't matter because she's with someone else and she hates me.

Marcel's birthday party is this weekend, and I'm not even sure if she'll show up. I can't imagine her blowing her brother off on his birthday.

"Go find some pussy, would ya?" Z says, pulling me out of my thoughts. He shoves my shoulder, knocking me back a step. I take a half-hearted swing at him and miss because he weaves out of range.

I can't admit it to my brothers—hell, I can barely admit it to myself—but I'm tired of women who spread their legs for anyone who asks. I'm bored. Aching to settle down and *be* with someone. No, not just anyone—one particular girl, who isn't even speaking to me at the moment. "Believe it or not, pussy isn't the solution to every man's problems," I grumble as I drop my sorry ass into one of the dining room chairs.

"No, it's usually the cause of them," Wrath answers.

Z flashes a grin. "Careful, Trin hears you, she'll kick your ass."

Wrath rolls his eyes. "I'm touched by your concern."

"What's wrong, trouble in wedding-planning land?" Z taunts.

Wrath's smile would be terrifying if I didn't know him so well. "Nope. All good. Don't be jealous." He turns and focuses on me. "What's wrong, little brother?"

"You don't want to hear me bitch about the same thing."

He shrugs. "Problem of my brother's is a problem of mine. Spill."

"Ooo, can I join the girl talk?" Z asks as he pulls over a chair and props his head on his hand.

Wrath knocks his elbow out from under Z and his chin hits the table. "Ow, ya fuck."

"Don't be an ass," Wrath says with zero sympathy. He turns and lifts his chin at me. "You hear from Heidi yet?"

"No," I answer, not even giving a fuck at how pathetic I sound. "I don't think we've ever gone this long without at least a phone call."

"She was pretty pissed," Z says.

Wrath gives him the side eye. "State the obvious much?"

"I think I really screwed up."

Neither of them make any of the jokes I expect. "Nah," Wrath says. He glances at Z, who wipes the smirk off his face and sits forward.

"Look, I like the kid. He did good work around here. Never pulled attitude or bitched about anything—"

"Thanks, you're making me feel much better, Z."

A hint of a smirk tugs at the corner of his mouth. "But, something was off. He wasn't LOKI material. It's not your fault."

Wrath sort of nods along and I catch his eye. "Were you going to vote him in?"

He lifts his shoulders. "Guess we'll never know."

When I open my mouth, he cuts me off. "Because he bailed. Not because you voted him down."

"Oh, you heard about that?"

"I hear everything." The smug smile disappears and he's serious again. "Have you talked to Teller?"

"Yeah. She's not speaking to him, either."

"You know who she's—"

"Hope?"

"Yeah, or Mariella."

Z snickers. "You'll get better info from Hope. She likes playing matchmaker."

"Too bad I'm so unsuccessful at it," Hope says as she comes up behind Z and Wrath, settling a hand on each of their shoulders.

Wrath reaches up and pats her hand. "Where's my girl?"

"In your room. On the phone."

He stands and stretches. "I'll be right back." He not-so-subtly tips his head in Hope's direction before leaving.

"So, who needs matchmaking?" Hope asks.

My gaze slides to Z, hoping he'll take the hint and leave. By some miracle, he does.

After he clears the dining room, the corner of Hope's mouth turns up. "I assume you want to ask me about Heidi?"

"Is she okay? Have you heard from her?" I have to stop myself before a hundred other questions come tumbling out of my mouth.

"Yes. I talked to Teller about it. I'm surprised he didn't share."

I'm not.

"She's okay. Straight *As* in all her classes so far."

"Oh. Good." I'd hate if all this stuff interfered with her schoolwork.

"Besides asking about her brother, she wanted to know if *you* were okay. She feels bad about the things she said to you before she left."

"I deserved them."

"I doubt that." She cocks her head to the side. "You love her deeply, don't you?"

My answer's stuck in my throat, so I just nod.

"More than brotherly love," she persists.

My shoulders lift. Am I really going to admit this out loud? "My feelings changed from brotherly to something else at least five years ago."

She raises an eyebrow but doesn't seem shocked or disgusted.

Even so, I hurry to add, "I didn't *do* anything about it. Actually, that's not true. I found girls here and there to take my mind off her."

Hope scrunches her nose but doesn't say anything. It gives me a second to remember Heidi when she was younger. That beautiful girl used every single trick a teenage girl uses to make me notice her.

I didn't hold it against her—*much*.

"You wanted to reassure yourself it wasn't her age you were attracted to, it was her?"

"Shit. Yeah, probably." I never once thought of it that way. "It's still wrong." The way I say the words sounds more questioning than certain.

"Human beings are complex, Murphy. You didn't act on it, that's what matters."

I grunt because I still feel scummy about it.

"You forget all the family court cases I've worked on. Gosh, Murphy, you know for a while I did assigned counsel work. In half of my support cases, I represented teenage girls and almost half of those deadbeat dads were in their twenties or thirties. So there are plenty of men who wouldn't have said no to Heidi the way you did."

I'm not sure how I feel about her comparing me to pieces of shit who have to be forced to take care of their children and I think the look on my face says that. "I'm saying, you're *nothing* like that. These guys take advantage of a situation like that then blame it on the girl when they get caught. They don't distance themselves from the girl and do what's best for her the way you did."

"I guess."

"You *are* a good guy, Murphy. You're so hard on yourself. Even with Heidi throwing herself at you, you said no. Trust me, I know how persistent teenage girls can be."

I consider her words carefully. Hope has a way of flipping everything I *think* I know upside down.

"Thanks, Hope."

"Can I ask you something?"

"Shoot."

"You don't have to answer, but I know Heidi and Teller's mom ran off." She hesitates before asking her question. "You mentioned your mother once, but is she around?"

Pain that's dulled over the years spreads through my chest. "No. She OD'd right after I graduated from high school and patched-in."

Her jaw drops slightly. "I'm sorry. I shouldn't—"

"It's fine, Hope. Long time ago. She probably doesn't remember, but Trinity helped me through it."

Hope reaches out and pats my leg.

"Don't feel bad for me, Hope. I'm fine. Even when she wasn't high, she was a shit mother."

"I'm sorry."

My shoulders lift. "Teller and Heidi's mother was just never around. When mine was, I wished she wasn't."

"Is that how the three of you got so close?"

"Yeah, I guess. I couldn't have *stuff*, you know? My mom would sell anything in our house for drugs. Or destroy it when she had a fit of rage or whatever."

"But Heidi was yours?"

For the first time in days, I smile. "Yeah. Teller needed help since his mom was gone all the time, and I needed a place where I didn't have to sleep on the floor."

"She'd just leave them?"

"Pretty much from day one."

"She left an infant with a ten year old?"

"Yup. Child Services showed up once or twice. She'd stop running around for a bit and then be right back at it."

"Jeez."

"Why do you think we turned out the way we did?"

"I think you turned out pretty well."

I lift an eyebrow inviting her to explain how she arrived at that conclusion.

"Well, I don't see you drinking or abusing drugs. That was your role model, right? You could have gone that route. Plenty of people do. Instead, you're part of this family and help take care of everyone in it."

It's not until right this second that I think about how odd it is that Rock sort of adopted us the way he did. How as a kid, I felt safer around a group of hardened bikers than with my own mother. I've always been thankful and considered myself lucky to have the club but never thought about *how* I ended up here. "That's all Rock's doing."

A slight smile flickers at the corner of her mouth. "Yes, but I think he had good raw material to work with."

"You were appropriately named, you know that?"

She laughs and bumps my shoulder.

"Come on, you've seen the way we treat the girls around here."

"I've never seen you guys abuse one of them or be…disrespectful."

"Rock wouldn't allow it."

"But, neither would you," she says absolutely confident of every word. "Besides that" she hesitates and seems to think over what she wants to say. "These *are* grown women making their own choices, you know? If you're honest with them and they get their hearts broken, that's not your fault."

"I guess."

"It cuts both ways, no? How many of the girls really try to get to know you? Besides the patch, the badass bike, the muscles, and tattoos?"

"Now you're making me blush, Hope." But as I think it over, except for Serena, none of them cared enough to know me outside of the club. "I get what you're saying, though."

"Good because I feel like a traitor to my gender now."

Hard laughter rumbles out of me.

"You still buggin' Hope?" Wrath says from behind us. I turn and find him grinning. Dying to razz my ass.

"None of you bug me," Hope insists.

"He grill you about Heidi?" Wrath asks as he sits down.

Hope rolls her eyes and doesn't answer the question.

"Why you gotta be a dick?" I ask.

Teller's laughter stops our bickering.

"Glad things are normal here," he says as he sits next to me. He glances around the table, finally setting his gaze on Hope. "Talk to Heidi again?"

Poor Hope. She's like our Heidi hotline.

Wrath catches the scowl on my face and laughs. "Hope doesn't mind. She's our Wendy."

"Our what?" For a scary-ass motherfucker, Wrath says the strangest shit sometimes.

"It's been a few years since I saw Peter Pan, so I'm not sure if I should be flattered or insulted," Hope says without a trace of humor.

"I think we're the ones who should be insulted, Hope," Teller says dryly. "Wendy's the one who mothers all the Lost Boys living in Neverland."

Seventeen

Heidi

After my last class, I meet Hope at her office for lunch. We've been meeting up for lunch or shopping at least once a week since my senior year of high school, and I've missed her.

"Hi, honey. I've missed you," she shrieks, wrapping me up in a big hug.

I'm too choked up to say anything, so I just hug her back.

"Your brother's worried sick," she says when we part.

Even though she doesn't say it in a scolding way, shame warms my cheeks. "I know."

"Please, at least call him."

"I will. I'm planning to come up for his birthday party."

"Oh good! M—everyone will be happy to see you."

I think she was going to say *Murphy* will be happy to see me. And it makes me wonder if Murphy asked Hope about me.

Focus.

I'm not here for info on Murphy. I need Hope to help me break the engagement news to my brother. I glance around her office. "Can we talk?"

"Sure." She leads me down the hall into her office. It's a cramped space that's hardly bigger than a closet.

"What's wrong, Heidi?"

"If I tell you, will you promise not to tell anyone yet? Not even Uncle Rock? And especially not my brother."

"Why don't you tell me first? Then I'll decide if I want to keep secrets from my husband."

"What if I'm asking for legal advice?"

She wags a finger at me. "Don't try that."

My mouth tips into a grin. When I asked Hope to take me to Planned Parenthood, I spilled some stuff to her and made her swear on her lawyer-client oath not to tell anyone. Obviously, she hasn't forgotten.

I let out a heavy sigh and hold up my left hand.

"Oh, how pretty!" She grabs my hand and studies the ring. After her inspection, her big green eyes meet mine. "Is it what I think it is?"

I nod. "Axel and I are getting married, and I could use your help breaking the news to my brother."

She sways a little then rounds her desk and drops into her chair. "When?"

"Ah, as soon as possible."

"Heidi—"

"I'm pregnant, Hope." Tears flow down my cheeks. I can't believe this is my life.

"Oh, honey." Hope's up and pulling me into her arms so fast, I don't have a chance to get any more words out. Wave after wave of shame threatens to drown me. I'm so damn angry with myself for being so careless.

"Are you sure?" she asks.

"I have an appointment with my doctor, but yeah. I've taken like five tests." Axel insisted I take one every morning for a couple of days, hoping the outcome would be different, but I keep that to myself. I need Hope backing me on this if I'm going to sell it to my brother, and if she suspects Axel's been anything less than one hundred percent supportive, I can kiss that goodbye.

"Shit," she mutters under her breath and it makes me chuckle. "What do you want to do, honey?"

The tears roll faster down my cheeks, and I let out a few sobs. "Keep it."

She hugs me tight again. "Okay." She hesitates then pulls back. "Heidi, you don't have to get married just because—"

"No. I do. We want to. It's the right thing to do."

"Heidi—"

"I know I'm too young and am probably ruining my life, but I just can't—" I bury my face against her shoulder. When she doesn't say anything, humiliation forces me to ask, "Are you disappointed in me?" I mumble the words into her sweater.

"What? No, Heidi. I won't lie. It's not ideal. You're both *so* young. But we'll get through it. We'll figure everything out."

We. She says *we* and for the first time, I don't feel so alone.

For the first time since that evil little plus sign popped up, I have hope.

AXEL

"I don't think it's a good idea for me to be there, Heidi." This is maybe the fourth or fifth time I've expressed my opinion on joining her at the clubhouse for her brother's birthday party.

"Well, I need you there."

"He's going to figure it out and kill me," I warn her.

"Then stick to our story. We need to get married in order to qualify for student housing."

Teller may be a lot of things, but he's not stupid. "He's never going to go for that."

Where did everything go so wrong?

I always figured I'd marry Heidi. Not like this, though. I feel like a schmuck about the whole situation. I'll never say it out loud but I'm also fucking pissed with her for—

"What's wrong?" Heidi asks.

"Nothing. Just hoping you don't end up widowed before we even get married."

"Stop. You're making it worse than it is."

Must be nice to be an optimist. Not only did I steal his baby sister away and move her into my apartment, but the way Teller probably sees it, I've been keeping his sister from speaking to him, too.

All these extra complications are not what I signed up for. I'm trying hard to finish up school and land a decent job. Wanted to enjoy some time to myself now that I'm not the Lost Kings' bitch.

Instead, I'm planning a shotgun wedding and trying to wrap my head around being a father.

Guess it's time to prepare myself for the beatdown her brother's going to give me when he finds out we're getting married.

Heidi

We take my car to the clubhouse. I had no clue what to buy my brother for his birthday, and I hate coming to his party empty-handed.

"He'll just be happy to see you," Axel reassures me after I mention my lack of a gift for the tenth time.

The closer we get to the clubhouse, the more anxious he seems. "Maybe I should drop you off instead."

"Where? In the woods, so I can hike up to the clubhouse by myself?"

He grumbles some more but doesn't offer up any more stupid suggestions.

We have to call up to the clubhouse before the gates open. That's new. It hurts that the club thinks they can't trust me anymore. But, I suppose I deserve it.

I send Hope a text letting her know we're almost there. She promised to meet us out front. Axel parks down the hill—not too far from where Murphy parked the night of my birthday party so we could talk.

Things have changed so much since that night.

As promised, Hope's waiting out front. I'm surprised Uncle Rock isn't with her, but also grateful.

"Hi, honey." She rushes over and gives me a warm hug. I cling to her probably longer than necessary, but I can't help it. The fear beating inside of me won't go away.

When she releases me, she hesitates before saying hello to Axel.

"Let's go in. The party hasn't quite started yet, and your brother's really anxious to see you."

He meets us at the front door. We don't say anything at first. The fierce, protective hug he sweeps me up into speaks more than any words could.

"Are you okay?" he asks against my hair.

My throat's so tight, I can't answer. Instead, I nod vigorously until he sets me down. I'm worried we're making a scene in front of the club, but the four of us are the only ones in the living room.

"Where is everyone?"

"Dining room. Finishing up dinner," Hope answers.

"Sorry."

My brother shakes his head. "I'm just glad you're here." He looks past me at Axel and nods, but I still detect a bit of murder in his eyes.

Reaching behind me, I take Axel's hand and follow my brother to the dining room.

Everyone, except Murphy, stands up and says hello. The guys neither ignore nor fuss over Axel, which is fine. Eventually, Marcel asks us to sit next to him.

"No singing," Marcel insists when Trinity gets up to help Mariella bring in dessert.

"You're gonna love this thing she came up with," Wrath says to Teller.

I see why a few minutes later after everyone blatantly disregards my brother's "no singing" rule.

"Rocky road cheesecake," Mariella says with a wide grin. Her gaze shifts to my brother to gauge his reaction.

"Appropriate," Z says and receives a smack from Wrath in return. It makes me laugh, because it's true, and Z grins at me.

"That looks good. What is everyone else having?" Marcel jokes. I glance at Mariella again, who's beaming at my brother. *Interesting.*

Trinity sets a tray of cupcakes down in front of my brother. "Whiskey-maple-bacon cupcakes."

"Christ. You two trying to fatten me up?"

Once everyone's on a sugar high, I peek at Hope, who raises her shoulders slightly. Now's as good a time as any.

Under the table, I grab Axel's hand and he squeezes me back.

"I have news."

All eyes are on me, so I go for it. Holding up my left hand, I show off the ring and announce, "We're getting married."

Stunned silence falls over the table.

Murphy's fork clatters onto his plate and everyone stops talking. When he doesn't say or do anything except stare at me, Hope awkwardly jumps in.

"Congratulations," she says.

Rock glances at my brother, probably giving him some subtle signal about where to bury Axel's body.

Everyone else is slow to follow Hope's lead and offer their congratulations.

I risk glancing up into Murphy's eyes and almost cry from the disbelief reflecting back at me.

I'm so sorry, I want to tell him.

"Do you have a date in mind yet?" Trinity asks.

Slowly, I tear my gaze away from Murphy to answer her question. "We were thinking after the holidays, but before spring semester starts."

"Are you serious?" my brother asks in his low, scary, big brother tone.

Murphy's chair scrapes against the floor and he leaves the table without another word or glance in my direction.

Axel squeezes my hand, then clears his throat and leans forward so he can see my brother. "There's, uh, married student housing we'd like to get into. Nice apartments, right on campus, and cheap, but you have to be married to apply."

"How romantic," Marcel snarks. He turns his glare on me. "Outside, little sister. We need to talk."

Axel moves to stand, and Marcel stops him with a look. "You stay put."

I follow my brother through the kitchen and out the back door. "Are you fucking out of your mind? You're barely eighteen!" he shouts at me.

"Don't yell at me. Yes, I'm serious. I love him and he loves me."

"Great, then wait until you're finished with school."

"I don't want to."

"Don't give me this married student apartment bullshit, Heidi. Did he knock you up? Tell me now so I can put a bullet in him tonight."

"No! And you can't go threatening my fiancé every time I do something you disagree with." The lie burns my tongue. I briefly consider coming clean, but he's so furious, I'm afraid he really might shoot Axel.

"Like fuck I can't," he fumes.

"Everything okay?" Rock calls out.

"We're fine, prez," my brother answers without taking his eyes off me.

"Heidi?"

"I'm okay, Uncle Rock. Thank you."

"What's the fucking hurry?" Marcel asks after Rock goes back inside.

"We told you."

"Fuck that. I'll give you money for an apartment."

"Axel won't take your money. We want to do this. We want to get married now. I don't need your permission. But I'd like you to be happy for me."

"Well, I'm not," he says, using his matter-of-fact big brother voice and planting his hands on his hips.

"You told me yourself, you think Axel's a good kid."

"Yeah, a *kid*. Just like you're a *kid*. Too young to know what the fuck you're doing."

Tears well up and I'm pissed because I swore I wouldn't cry. "This is happening, Marcel. You can either be there, or I'll send you pictures later."

"Heidi—"

"I mean it."

He plows his fingers through his hair, and I almost feel sorry for him. "Christ, Heidi. I want what's best for you. I want you to finish school and be able to support yourself. What about all the traveling you wanted to do?"

"Axel and I will do it together." Although, that seems unlikely now.

"I don't want you dependent on some guy," he insists.

"Axel's not *some guy*." He's the father of my baby. "This won't change anything. I'm not dropping out of school. Axel wants me to finish, too." Actually, Axel and I hadn't talked about our plans once the baby comes.

One thing at a time.

All the fight seems to go out of him and he holds his arms open. "Come here."

I throw myself against him. "Please be happy for me. Please?"

"I want what's best for you, Heidi, and I don't think this is it."

"It is. I promise."

I wish…I wish so badly I could convince myself that were true.

AXEL

After Heidi and Marcel leave the table, things get even more uncomfortable. Rock leaves to check on them, and when he returns, he pins me with a hard stare. "Let's have a word," he says, pointing in the opposite direction Heidi and her brother went.

Shit. I fully expected Marcel, maybe even Murphy, to kick my ass. Not Rock.

He leads me into the war room. Never thought I'd see the inside of this room again.

We don't sit. But he does close the door.

"Is this really what you both want?" he asks.

"Yes, sir. We were planning to get married after I graduate, but then the apartment—"

"Cut the bullshit, son. Her brother might swallow that asinine story, but I'm not."

Fuck. Me.

I could strangle Heidi right about now. I warned her this was never going to work.

Our eyes meet and I lift my shoulders. "What do you want me to say, Rock?"

His gaze slides to the closed door. "Nothing. Fuck. You better make sure she finishes school."

"I will."

"And you better find a damn good job."

"I'm trying."

His harsh stare is so terrifying, I'm afraid to move wrong. "I know someone looking for a good mechanic. I'll set you up with an interview."

"Thank you. I appreciate it."

"She plannin' to tell her brother the truth?"

"Not tonight."

"Fuckin' great," he mutters and shakes his head.

"Uh, we really are moving into an apartment on campus. You know, so it's easier for her to get to her classes and stuff."

"Good." He stares at me a few seconds longer. "You're trying to do the right thing. So that's a start."

I wait because I don't think he's finished yet.

"Warn me before she tells him, so I can at least try to keep him from killing you."

"Yes, sir."

"You need anything, let me know. Or if Heidi needs something, she knows she can always call Hope, if she doesn't want to tell me."

"Uh, I think she's already done that."

His mouth slides into a half-smirk. "Oh, really?"

Fuck. Like I want to cause problems between Rock and his wife. I should have kept my mouth shut.

"And don't let her go so long without calling her brother. He's been a wreck."

"I told her. But you know Heidi can be—"

"Headstrong. Yeah, I'm familiar with the type." He grins and I'm able to relax because I don't think I'm getting murdered.

Not tonight anyway.

Eighteen

MURPHY

We're getting married.

Swallowing ground glass would have hurt less than hearing those words come out of Heidi's mouth. He's not good enough for her. No one will ever be good enough for her.

The cold night air slaps me in the face when I storm out of the clubhouse. I don't know where to go or what to do.

My heart feels like it's being torn out. I look down, surprised there's no blood gushing from my chest.

She's really gonna *marry* him? She's eighteen for fuck's sake. I knew she was mad about Axel leaving the club, but marriage seems like overkill just to get even.

Marcel won't let her go through with it. I know he won't. He can't.

I don't know what to do. Am I going to go back in there and beg her not to do this? Try to make her love me instead of him?

No.

Soft crunching gravel draws my gaze toward the corner of the clubhouse as two girls appear under the spotlight shining over that area. Serena and her friend Amanda. "Hey, Murphy," Serena calls out as she tries to move faster in her ridiculously high sandals. "What're you doing outside?" she asks when she reaches me. She wobbles and I steady her with one hand.

"Waitin' for you." I flash a fake-as-fuck smile to go with the lie.

Heidi's marrying *him*, so I guess it doesn't really fucking matter anymore *what* I do or *who* I do it with.

I raise an eyebrow and paste on a cocky smirk. "What are you ladies up to tonight?"

Heidi

I survived.

My brother's far from happy. But at least he isn't threatening to shoot Axel anymore. Rock and Axel are nowhere to be found when we return to the dining room. Marcel keeps glaring at my fiancé's empty chair in a way that suggests murder might still be on his mind.

My stomach rolls. Shit. The last thing I need is to get sick here. Then they'll all know, for sure.

Murphy still hasn't returned. My feet twitch, wanting to check on him. Talk to him. Except, I can't. What would I say to him? I'm sorry? I'm a careless idiot? I got myself in trouble and I'm trying to be mature and do the right thing even though I don't have a clue what that is?

"I'll be right back," I say, pushing my chair back and running down the hall to the bathroom. Everything I ate comes up along with a rush of tears.

It takes a few minutes to get myself under control, wash my face, and swig some mouthwash before I leave the bathroom.

Voices in the living room draw me in that direction.

Murphy.

Correction. Murphy, with Serena and her friend. The girls are giggling and hanging all over him. He turns his head my way. His severe face seems older than it was a few minutes ago. I barely recognize the angry man staring back at me.

My heart thumps wildly. "Can I talk to you?"

He takes a step forward, leaving the girls behind. "About what?" he asks in a dismissive tone he's never used with me before.

"Uh, um." Dammit. If those stupid girls weren't here, I almost think I'd break down and tell him the truth.

"What, *Bug*? You want me to say congratulations? Ask you where you're registered?" I flinch from the ice in his voice.

The door to the war room opens and Rock steps out, Axel right behind him. Rock catches my eye and smiles. Not the loving or patient smile I'm used to. More of a tired, slightly disappointed smile.

Murphy raises an eyebrow at me, daring me to say what I wanted to say in front of Axel. But I'm frozen in place. After a few seconds of silence, he nods slightly.

Serena takes his hand, whispers something in his ear. Without looking at me again, he leads the two girls over to the couch to talk to Sparky.

Axel slips his arm around my waist, and we walk back into the dining room. Trinity and Mariella are busy clearing the table. I grab a few plates and follow Trinity out to the kitchen where she packs up a bunch of cupcakes and a hunk of cheesecake for me to take home.

"Have you thought about where to have the wedding?" she asks.

"Huh?" I mumble stupidly. I'm still chilled from the ice in Murphy's voice. Even when we've fought in the past, he's never been so cold to me. Along with everything else I've screwed up in my life, I've also lost his friendship. The thought leaves me hollow and hurting.

Trinity touches my shoulder. "Wedding?" she asks gently.

"Oh." Focus. Wedding. Future. "I'd love to have it here, honestly."

Her eyes light up, but her smile falters. "I can help. You know, if you want me to, I mean."

"God, yes. Please? Hope's wedding was so beautiful. And she said it was all your doing." I force myself to forget what just happened and concentrate on the future. I brush my hand over my stomach, *our future*. "I don't need anything as elaborate, though. Something simple."

She raises an eyebrow but doesn't question me. "Well, you need a dress, flowers, food, someone to do the ceremony." She ticks off each item on her hands then turns to grab a notebook and pen from one of the kitchen drawers.

"Don't go crazy. For me. You don't have to."

"Sure I do. This is a big deal."

"But, you're planning your own wedding."

She dismisses my concern with the wave of her hand. "We can't get the place where we want to have the wedding for a while. Wyatt's more focused on starting construction on our house. Don't sweat it."

This is all news to me. And *Wyatt*? I can't remember anyone referring to Uncle Wrath as anything but *Wrath*.

"Thank you."

We talk a little longer and make plans to meet next week.

My chest aches a fraction less as I return to the dining room. Axel's standing by the table, talking bike modifications with my brother and Z. He wraps an arm around me and pulls me to his side.

Noise from the front of the clubhouse reaches us. Party guests arriving.

Rock glances at Hope and tips his head toward their house. They won't be sticking around to watch the guys get down and dirty. Honestly, after what I've already witnessed tonight, I'm ready to go home. Watching girls vying for a night of my brother's affection is very low on my priority list.

After my second yawn, the guys chuckle and we start working our way toward the front door.

The living room's more crowded now. Full of smoke, too. Sparky runs over and embraces both of us, smushing us together. "Congrats, guys," he shouts and runs off. Rock shakes his head.

"You kids headed home?" he asks us.

Axel answers. "Yes, sir."

I snuggle closer to Axel and he gives me a squeeze. "Ready to go, babe?"

Before we leave, Serena's friend comes clomping downstairs, throwing herself on the couch next to Dex and Swan.

I wonder what happened.

No, I don't.

It doesn't concern me.

MURPHY

What's the best way to get over a girl? Get on top of another one.

Or two.

Couple years ago, I'd have been all over this scenario.

Now, I don't even care.

What was Heidi about to say to me downstairs?

It doesn't matter.

Married, married, married. How can she be getting married? Where did everything go wrong? I ask myself as I lead two girls I don't feel a thing for upstairs.

At my bedroom door, Serena hesitates and glances at her friend.

"What's wrong?" I ask.

"Um…" Serena shakes her head. "Well, I—"

"You don't want her here?"

Her lashes flutter and she shakes her head.

Fine by me.

I lift my chin at Amanda. "Go wait downstairs. Sparky'll take care of ya."

She rolls her eyes and fake-punches Serena in the shoulder.

"Sorry," Serena says after Amanda leaves.

Pushing open my door, I usher her inside. "It's fine."

"She'll probably ditch my ass. She drove."

"It's fine," I repeat. "I'll take you home tomorrow."

She smiles and looks so damn hopeful about me wanting her to stay. It makes me feel shitty because it has less to do with Serena and more to do with me not wanting to be alone tonight.

But really, isn't that what *this* has always been about anyway?

Serena closes the door and leans against it, tucking her hands behind her back. "Are you okay, Murphy? You seem really down."

"Long day." Nothing major. Just had my heart ripped out and shredded to pieces.

"Can I make it better?"

I lean in, placing a kiss on her lips then pulling away. "Yeah, I think you can."

"Do you want to talk about it?"

The question throws me for a second. I run my fingers over her cheek. Serena's a beautiful girl, no denying it. But I can't stop thinking about the most beautiful girl I know.

Who's downstairs with her fiancé.

How can she *marry* him?

I wish I felt something *more* for Serena. I *like* her. I even enjoy spending time with her outside of the bedroom. But, I'm an empty shell of nothing right now.

I lean in to kiss her again, hoping to chase the emptiness away. Fill it with something—anything—else. Even if for only a few moments.

Serena places her hands on my chest, under my cut, curling her fingers into my shirt. She presses closer, pushing me backward.

We stumble to my bed without breaking our kiss. She drops down on the bed, staring up at me. It's a practiced look. Seductive but sweet. She's good at it.

"What do you want?" I ask.

"Well," she says, reaching up and hooking her fingers in my belt. "First, I want to suck your dick."

A huff of laughter eases out of me. I cup her face with one hand and gather her hair in the other.

"Well then, you better get to it, darlin."

Nineteen

MURPHY

I'm a real piece of shit, because I wake up disappointed Serena's still in my bed. She's busy playing on her phone when I finally open my eyes.

"Amanda didn't leave, so you don't have to take me home," she says without looking over.

"Good."

She turns at the sound of my voice and sets her phone down.

"Are you mad I'm still here?" she whispers.

Fuck. Fuck. Fuck. "No." But I took so long to answer, hurt's already shining in her eyes.

"I'll get going," she says, throwing back the covers and slipping into her shirt.

"You don't have to."

"It's okay. I have stuff to do."

"I'm sorry."

She turns and raises an eyebrow at me. "Why? I'm just a club girl. You don't owe me anything."

"I like you."

Her eyes widen.

"But, I'm in love with someone else. So it isn't really fair to keep doing this to you."

I'm officially the biggest douche in the world.

She slips into her jeans. "I wasn't…I don't *expect* anything from you. I never have."

"I know you moved up here—"

She snorts. "I moved up here for school, Murphy. Not you."

"Okay."

"If you don't want me to come to the clubhouse any more, just say so."

When I don't answer, she snatches her shoes up off the floor and walks out, slamming the door behind her.

I grab one of my pillows and press it into my face. Maybe I can smother myself. But it smells like Serena, so I toss it across the room.

One shower and thirty minutes later, I text Teller.

Is Serena gone?

How the fuck would I know?

Where are you?

He doesn't answer, so I finish getting dressed and head to his room. I knock, but no one answers. Someone's definitely inside, though. As I'm about to pound a little harder, Mariella opens the door.

"Morning." Her cheeks turn red and she scurries down the hall to her own room.

Teller glares at me.

"Bro, did you hear nothing Rock said?"

He shakes his head and steps into the hall with me. "It's not...she can't...it's not like that. Just let it go." He hesitates. "You can keep your mouth shut, right?"

Realizing how serious he is, I drop all the jokes I'd been gathering. "Yeah. Of course, brother."

"Thanks. So, what's wrong with Serena?"

"Nothing. I just pissed her off and I don't feel like seeing her again."

Teller stares at me as if he knows what I did last night and why. "Pussy," he finally says.

"You have no idea."

He snorts and punches my shoulder.

I have to ask about the only thing on my mind. "So, you let Axel leave in one piece last night? Or you got a body you need help burying?"

"If only."

"You're not really gonna let her go through with that shit, are you?" I'm counting on Marcel to throw his big brother status around and put an end to this wedding bullshit.

"What the fuck do you suggest? Pissing her off so she doesn't talk to me for another month?"

I open my mouth but none of my suggestions are helpful so I shut it.

He opens and closes his fists a few times before speaking. "She's eighteen. Short of chaining her to the wall in the basement—which believe me, crossed my mind—I don't know what else to fucking do."

"Maybe Hope can talk her out of it."

"Would you stop treating her like our unofficial fairy godmother."

"Fuck off. She listens to Hope, you tool."

Neither of us say anything as we pound down the stairs. Never know who you'll find in the living room.

This morning, it's Hope and Trinity sitting on one of the couches, flipping through magazines together.

Wedding magazines.

Fuck me. Really?

Trinity sets them aside when she notices us. "Morning."

"Yes, it is," Teller quips.

Hope shakes her head. "Cute. How are you this morning, big brother?"

He opens his mouth—probably to snark at her—but then shakes his head. "I don't fuckin' know."

Trinity gathers her things and stands. "I'll be right back, Hope. Will you be here for a minute?"

"Sure."

As soon as Trinity clears the room, Hope focuses on us. "Okay. You two look ready to burst. What's up?"

Teller lets out a humorless laugh. "Not me. Him."

I flip him off and he returns the gesture.

"I gotta run." He slaps my shoulder. "We'll talk later."

Hope watches him leave before turning to me. "You okay? I didn't see you again last night, after the *announcement*."

"The announcement. That's one way to put it," I say as I drop down next to her.

She lowers her gaze. "Serena tore out of here a little while ago. She seemed upset."

"That's my fault. I told you, every time I try to do the right thing, I just fuck it up."

Her mouth turns down. "I'm sorry. I know it was probably a shock."

"You weren't shocked, though, were you?"

She reels back and blinks a few times before shaking her head. "Heidi tries so hard to be the opposite of her mother, I worry it'll push her into making even bigger mistakes."

It's an interesting theory and I wonder if there's more to Hope's words. "Heidi's always been stubborn. When she was little, you could tell her 'don't touch that or you'll get hurt' and she'd have to test it out anyway. Got burned a bunch of times that way." I shrug. "You can only give her so much advice."

Her mouth lifts in a tired smile. "Tell me about it. You know I care about her, but I also worry about overstepping. I'm not her mother."

"You think her marrying Axel is a mistake, don't you?"

She takes a deep breath before finally nodding. Her big, green eyes bore into me. "Yes. I do."

"Did you tell her that?"

"I tried. Gently."

Something else is bothering Hope, but no matter how hard I try, I can't get her to spill it.

Twenty

Heidi

Life moves quickly after our announcement. We really did apply for married student housing. That wasn't a lie. But the school's pretty flexible about the *married* part these days.

Our best friends, Lucas and Penny, for example, are also *engaged* and live right across the hall from us.

Even though no one in our foursome is twenty-one yet, Penny brings a bottle of wine over to our apartment the first night we're there.

"I can't." My cheeks must be bright red. We haven't officially told anyone yet.

Lucas, predictably, but good naturedly high-fives Axel. "Congrats, guys."

"Holy shit. What did your brother say?" Penny asks. She's been interested in my brother for years, so it always creeps me out when she asks about him.

"We haven't told anyone yet. Well, except for you guys."

Lucas shoots a dirty grin at Axel. "You lucky fucker. Do you have any idea how horny pregnant chicks are?" Lucas waggles his eyebrows, while Axel fake-shivers with disgust.

Gee, thanks.

"Gross. Dude, that's my kid in there." He runs his hand over my barely-there baby bump. "And my wife-to-be you're talking about." He flashes a sweet smile that almost makes me forget the yuck face he just made at the very idea of pregnancy sex.

Penny slaps her boyfriend's arm. "How would you know, perv?"

"I read it somewhere." He glances at me and winks so fast, I almost think I imagined it. "Don't be a dick, man. You knocked her up, it's your duty to satisfy all her needs."

Aw, thanks, Lucas.

"Can you all worry about your own sex lives? I'm not even past the wanting-to-puke-every-five-minutes stage."

Lucas shows more sympathy than Penny, which is not unusual. "Sorry, Heidi. If Axel won't man up, let me know so I can kick his ass."

Axel doesn't laugh. But I do. So hard I can't catch my breath. "That's okay. I'm sure my brother will kick his ass as soon as he finds out."

"Christ. Not to mention the rest of the club," Axel moans. He glances at me. "Rock already figured it out, you know."

Now that disappointed face Rock gave me makes more sense, and I'm hot with shame. Talk about someone I hate letting down.

"He's going to set up an interview for me at a friend's garage."

"Oh. That's good news."

Lucas leans over and slaps Axel's leg. "You should come to Alaska with us after graduation. I can totally hook you up with a job on my uncle's oil rig."

I snort, because obviously that's a joke, right? Lucas shifts his gaze to me. "I'm serious. Even the entry-level jobs pay really well." He turns and thumps Axel's arm "But, you've got a special skill set with the welding and mechanics—my uncle would kill to get you on his crew."

"You're seriously moving to Alaska?" I raise an eyebrow at Penny and she nods.

"Yeah, it'll be fun."

"Well, all our family is here. I don't think taking a newborn to Alaska makes a lot of sense."

Axel's still quiet, so I elbow him in the ribs.

"What? Oh, yeah."

"Sorry, Heidi. I wasn't thinking about the baby," Lucas says.

"It's going to be a big adjustment." What an understatement.

Penny cocks her head. "Are you going to finish school?"

"Duh. Of course."

Axel turns and raises an eyebrow. That's right, we haven't talked about our plans for after the baby comes.

"We'll have to find daycare or a sitter or something," I mumble.

"You guys have plenty of time to figure it all out."

Somehow, it doesn't seem like it.

MURPHY

By the next time we sit down for church, no one's worried about Heidi's wedding. Except me. And maybe Teller. I don't know, because he hasn't mentioned it again.

I can't dwell on it, though, or it'll drive me nuts.

The need to be on the road consumes me. Rock knows it and promised me he was working on something. I appreciate it, because at least then I'll be doing something for my club instead of just going off on a pity joyride.

We go through the agenda the same way we do every time. Rock grills each of the officers. Everyone does their part for the club and does it well.

"Need more bodies at Furious?" Rock asks Wrath once we've gone over everything else.

"Nah. Murphy's been a big help while Jake's been out. I'm gettin' busier, so if you don't need him anywhere else, I'd like to keep him on permanently."

Rock glances at me with a raised eyebrow.

Fuck. Originally, I wanted to get out of working at Crystal Ball because I realized how much it bothered Heidi. Since *that* doesn't matter anymore, I could go back. Truth is I'd rather keep working at the gym with Wrath. I like helping him out. The work is more challenging. And I'm in the best shape I've ever been in.

At the moment, though, I need some time away from everything. Distance. Wrath should understand that better than anyone.

Rock seems to read the dilemma I'm working through in my head. "Long-term, yeah. We'll find someone else for CB."

Ravage raises his hand, waving it in the air to get Rock's attention. "Right here, prez."

Rock chuckles. "Yeah, yeah. Simmer the fuck down." He turns back to Wrath. "Can you spare Murphy for the next couple weeks? The club needs him for something."

Wrath raises an eyebrow. "Okay." Rock may have phrased it as a request, but we all know it wasn't.

Sparky practically bounces in his seat trying to get Rock's attention. "You sending Murphy to Arizona for me?"

Our president doesn't hesitate. "Yes." He points to Dex. "You up for a trip?"

While I'd been hoping for some solitude, I get why Rock doesn't want me riding solo.

"Fuck, yeah."

Sparky narrows his eyes at Dex. "You're there on business. Not to fuck around."

A shocked hush falls over the table. All eyes are on Dex while we wait to see his comeback. Finally, his mouth slides into a sneer. "Yes, sir."

Sparky settles back in his chair. "Sorry. It's just that this is important."

Rock sighs and sits back. "Sparky, why don't you explain."

Our mad-scientist, weed-growing brother sits up, hands flailing in the air. "Okay. Okay. So, you know our friends in Arizona started up a grow-op, right? The dude who's overseeing it is an old buddy of mine. He's got this crazy amazing strain from Nigeria. Real rare stuff. Seven times the THC for a quick high…"

I try not to let my eyes glaze over. When Sparky gets talking about plants, he can get pretty in-depth.

"Sparky," Rock warns, redirecting our favorite stoner.

"Yeah, yeah. Sorry. So he's got this mega-awesome strain. I've got our Deepest Gray that I've bred. We're going to swap clones."

"You're gonna let someone have one of your masterpieces?" Z asks with only a hint of sarcasm.

Sparky's face screws up into a scowl. "This shit is worth it. They're far enough away that it's not going to impact our business."

Rock tosses his hands up in a *what-the-fuck-ever* gesture. "You wanna vote on the swap?" he asks Z. "It's club property."

Z's shaking his head before Rock even finishes the question. "No. I trust Sparky's judgment *on this*. I'm surprised, that's all."

I feel like I missed something. "So, what does this have to do with me?"

Brother has nerve, because Sparky rolls his eyes. "I need you to transport the clones."

"You can't just mail some seeds back and forth?" Bricks asks.

Sparky slants a look in Brick's direction. "No. Seeds won't cut it. No. No mail. Federal. Easy peasy."

I look to Rock to interpret that answer and he shrugs. Across the table, Wrath's leaning back in his chair with his hand on his chin, fingers covering the laughter on his lips.

"So, here's where I'll explain the risks involved, since Sparky seems to be forgetting that part," Rock says. Sparky waves his hands in the air and grumbles about the Feds. "How many plants?" Rock asks.

"Twelve." Sparky points at Dex, then me. "Six each."

Rock nods. "Okay, so one to forty-nine plants, the penalty is the same. Five years and up to a million dollar fine."

Ouch.

I've gone on plenty of drops where the amounts could land me in prison a lot longer than five years, but those are low risk since they're local and quick. This is a cross-country trip through areas where we have no influence.

Still, I think the risk is pretty low.

"Does the club need these plants, Sparky?" I ask.

He sits up and nods, taking the questions seriously. "It'll help us meet the higher GSC demand and give us a new strain to offer that can't be found anywhere else in the northeast."

"We already have the best stuff in the northeast," Wrath says dryly. "This shit make that big a difference?"

I think Sparky's feelings are hurt by the question. "Yes," he answers. "This is a high-producing plant, so we might be able to get ahead and reopen our western NY deal, too."

Yeah, backing out of that deal made us look like amateurish assholes. But Loco's Green Street Crew has us by the throat, demanding everything we produce. If we can get some breathing room that would be good for the whole club.

"I'm in."

"Me, too," Dex says.

"You do realize it's almost winter, right?" Z asks.

Dex blows off the weather concern. "Fuck, it's still like sixty-five degrees."

Now, this is *my* area of expertise. "Weather's clear for the next week. That gets us to Arizona. If there's some freak storm, we can always rent a truck and trailer the bikes back."

"Three days," Sparky says.

"What?"

"Three days. The clones can*not* be on the road longer than that."

"Jesus Christ, it's a day and a half ride at least. And that's without any stops, you prick."

"Oh no, you need to stop to check the plants, water them, breathe on them…" Sparky keeps listing tasks, while Dex and I roll our eyes.

"You can *stay* down there long as you want. But the drive back? Three days."

"Sparky, be reasonable," Rock says.

"Maybe four if you promise to talk to them."

"I'll sing them a motherfuckin' ballad if it makes you happy, brother," I tell him.

Everyone cracks up. Even Sparky.

We wrap up our meeting and after everyone leaves, Rock motions for Dex and me to stay.

"You sure you're all right with this?" he asks me.

"I'm a big boy. I'll be fine."

A slow smirk turns the corner of his mouth up. He sits back and regards both of us carefully.

"Dex, you good?"

"I'm in, prez."

Once we're cleared by Rock to leave, we head to the basement where we are treated to a lengthy botany lesson. "Sparky, I'm never gonna remember all this. Can't you write it down?"

He throws a glare at me. "Nothing in writing. I'll Skype with him."

"*That's* safer?"

Another fuck-off stare.

"Whatever. Just show us what you need us to do."

After what feels like a hundred hours later, Sparky finally releases us.

"Morning?" Dex asks as we head upstairs.

"Yeah."

"Looking forward to a change of scenery?"

"Fuck yeah."

Twenty-One

Heidi

"**A**re you sure I look okay?" I ask for the third time.

Axel runs his gaze over my green sweater, jeans, and boots. "Do you have a dress?

Although I've outgrown my *tomboy-who-refuses-to-wear-dresses* phase, the question still annoys me. I'm not a fan of being told what to wear.

"No. It's cold out."

"You look fine. Come on, my mother will be more annoyed if we're late."

Goody. Can't wait.

I met Axel's parents once. When he graduated from high school. They weren't impressed with me then, and I don't think they're thrilled we're still together. Definitely not happy about us living together.

Wait until we tell them we're getting married.

I spent a couple afternoons studying at Axel's house before we officially started dating. While the old Victorian I lived in with my grandmother was probably as big, it had more character—stuff that needed fixing. Axel's parents live in one of those generic, expensive, perfect McMansion types of houses. He walks us up the sidewalk, with a hand on my back, as if he's worried I might try to run away if he lets go.

Maybe I would.

"Hi, honey," Mrs. Ryan fusses, kissing Axel's cheek like she hasn't seen him in a million years. She turns her chilly gaze my way and nods. "Heidi."

What, no kiss for me, Lorraine?

I've never been a picky eater—couldn't afford to be if I wanted to survive. My brother hunts, so I'm not squeamish. I've eaten lots of Bambis and Thumpers over the years. But the bloody red roast his mother serves turns my stomach.

"I can't eat that," I whisper in Axel's ear. Never mind how unappetizing it looks. It can't be good for the baby.

A wave of unpleasantness rolls through my belly. Nope. Definitely not eating that.

"Heidi?" Mr. Ryan points to the roast.

"Uh, can I have my piece cooked a little longer?"

His mother's face twists into a scowl, as if I spit on the table instead of wanting to avoid a case of E. coli. She huffs as she reaches over and snatches my plate away. "I can do it, Mrs. Ryan. Don't go to any trouble," I say, following her into the kitchen.

"It's fine," she says without looking at me.

My stomach lurches again and I hurry to the bathroom, making it just in time to throw up in private.

When I return, everyone's waiting for me. I suppose it will be obvious that I'm knocked up now, but no one says anything.

The beef still doesn't look good, but I pick at it, cut it into tiny pieces and push it around my plate.

His mother's voice cuts into my thoughts. "Why is she wearing my mother's ring?"

Axel takes my hand and gives it a squeeze. "Well, that's what we came here to tell you. We're getting married in January."

She pins Axel with a flinty glare. "You gave her my mother's ring?"

Interesting she has no comment on the wedding.

"Yeah," Axel snaps. "Gram gave it to me to give to my future wife." He points at me. "Heidi."

"Congratulations," his father finally says.

"Thank you."

No one asks why we're getting married. Or where. His mother doesn't ask about my plans.

After dinner, I try to be a good guest and help her clear the table. In the kitchen, she whirls around and glares at me. "How did you talk my son into marrying you?"

Stunned from the accusation, I can't come up with anything more intelligent than, "What?"

"For reasons I can't comprehend, my son is obsessed with you."

"He loves me. I love him," I answer weakly.

She shakes her head as if that can't possibly be true. "You've done nothing but drag him down since he met you, but this is beyond comprehension."

"Axel wants… He proposed to me."

"Only because you convinced him. He'd never marry you if you hadn't talked him into it."

Her words strike hard. Will Axel end up hating me? Hating our baby?

"You haven't heard a thing I've said, have you?" she screams at me.

"Mom!" Axel shouts, storming into the kitchen. "Enough." He slips an arm around my shoulders and I lean into him for support. "We're getting married whether you like it or not. We want you and Dad to be there—"

"Like hell," she snaps.

"That's too bad. I guess you'll see pictures of the wedding."

She turns her ice-cold glare on me. "You're pregnant, aren't you?"

My stomach drops.

"Why can't you get rid of it? Why do you have to ruin my son's life?" she yells.

Axel's arm tightens around me. "That's it. We're leaving. If that's your attitude, we don't want you around our child."

I'm so relieved when we're finally in the car driving away, I burst into tears.

"I'm sorry," Axel says quietly, placing his hand on my leg.

"Am I ruining your life?" I ask.

He takes a long time to answer, and I'm not exactly reassured when he finally does.

"No. It's just going in a different direction than I planned."

Twenty-Two

MURPHY

Dex doesn't question me when I explain the two-hour detour I want to take into Arkansas to steer clear of the Kansas border.

"This is your show, brother."

I'm pinging with the need to get on the road, but Wrath insists we have breakfast before leaving.

"This is all getting a little too happy family," I grumble as Wrath's big hand settles on my neck and steers me toward the dining room.

"Bullshit. You love it."

After breakfast, Sparky oversees the loading of the clones into our hard bags. I hate the look of the stretched bags, but they fit our needs. I designed a tray to fit over the plants. It won't stand up to a serious search, but it provides some cover.

Sparky, naturally objects.

"Sweet pannies, Murphy," Z jokes, bumping my arm.

"Trying to blend in as much as possible."

"Christ, you're gonna make us look like a bunch of pussies when you roll into Romeo's compound with those dressers."

I punch him back. "You want to join us? Butch us up a little, ya prick."

He glances at the house. Then back at us. "Fuck it. Yeah. I'll ride ahead, like the lone outlaw while you two look like a couple of RUBs touring the countryside."

"Fuck you." I'm laughing as I insult my brother, so he's not put off one bit.

While Z jogs into the house to grab some stuff, Rock strolls over. "Something's up his ass lately. Can't sit still for more than a day."

"Yeah, I noticed."

"Keep an eye on him."

I don't have an answer for that. Never thought I'd see the day when Rock was asking me to look after Z.

Hope rushes in as we're about to go and gives me a fierce hug. "Have fun. Be careful," she whispers in my ear. I think she says it to Dex and Z, too, so I'm not insulted. Sparky takes her hand, squeezing it tight as we roll out. He must be nearing a meltdown watching us whisk his babies away.

Heidi

Trinity doesn't fuck around when it comes to wedding planning. Although the theme of the wedding seems to be *broke bride on a budget*, she manages to make everything beautiful instead of pitiful.

"Thank you so much, Trinity."

"You're welcome, honey."

I've known Trinity for years. Hated her for years, too. But the more time I spend at the clubhouse, the more I see what a vital role she plays here. Maybe not as *vital* as she used to, but important.

"Has, uh, Murphy said anything?" I can't look her in the eye while I ask. It's all too weird, but I need to know how he is. We haven't spoken in so long. He probably hates me.

She glances down at her hands. "No. He's on a run."

"Oh. Where?"

"Southwest."

"Oh."

I take a few deep breaths before asking my next question. "Was he upset?"

She finally meets my eyes. "Probably."

"Trinity, I never—"

"There's my girl," Wrath's low voice startles me, and I find him creeping up behind Trinity. She squeals and jumps out of her chair. I glance away while they greet each other with so much affection it makes me blush. If Wrath can get over the past, then I have no business being mad at Trinity. Especially when she's always tried so hard to be nice to me. Not because she wanted something from me—she was already plenty close with my brother—but because I was part of the family.

They approach the table with their arms around each other, and it's weird to see Uncle Wrath so…content. Weird, but nice.

"Hey, Heidi-girl." He pats me on the head and musses my hair. "Whose wedding are you working on?"

Trinity's mouth curls into a smirk. "Heidi's."

"Fucking bullshit, Heidi. Aren't you like eight?"

"Eigh*teen*, Uncle Wrath."

"Too young. Where's Axel? I want to kick his ass for making me feel old."

My hand flies up, covering my mouth while I laugh. Wrath never seems to age. At least not to me.

Trinity slips right back into wedding planning mode "I just remembered. We still have a lot of mason jars left over from Hope's wedding. Although, it's winter, we should do something like hot cocoa in pretty mugs or something."

"Good idea, since the bride isn't even old enough to drink," Wrath says, throwing a smirk my way.

I roll my eyes.

Wrath listens to Trinity rattle off a bunch of wedding details with a smile on his face. Like every word out of her mouth matters, no matter how trivial. It's a side of him I've never seen. When she finishes, he glances at me. "How many guests, Heidi?"

I know his job is security for the club, so he's not asking because he wants to pull up a chair and write out wedding invitations with us.

"Uh, just the club. You know, whoever wants to come. They don't have to, obviously. And four of our friends."

His puzzled expression reminds me of how crappy this whole situation is. "What about Axel's family?"

"They're, uh, not coming."

Puzzled morphs into pissed pretty quick. "What do you mean *not coming*?"

"They think it's a mistake for us to get married. They're uh, well, they're not fond of me, so—"

"Fuck them. None of us are thrilled about it either, but we'll sure as fuck be there."

I'm not really sure what to do with that.

"You're mad at me, too?" I ask, sounding unbelievably pitiful.

"No. Heidi-girl. Just worried about you. I don't want to have to kill Axel if he does anything to upset you."

"Ah, there's the Wrath I know and love," I tease to lighten things up.

"Murder's always on his mind," Trinity says and he laughs with her.

I love this crazy family. I'd rather spend a hundred years right here in this clubhouse than ten seconds with Axel's stuck-up parents.

All of this has me so emotional, I tear up. Crap. Everything makes me want to cry lately. If I keep it up, someone's going to figure out I'm pregnant.

"You okay, Heidi?" Trinity asks after Wrath leaves.

"I'm good."

"Good, because we have a long night at the craft store ahead of us."

I laugh so hard, I tip sideways in my chair, making Trinity laugh with me.

"Can't wait."

Twenty-Three

MURPHY

Turns out, 2,500 miles isn't enough to get Heidi out of my head. Fuck, instead of taking off to the other end of the country, should I have stayed and tried to talk her out of marrying him?

Normally, being on the road calms me and I can find some sort of inner peace. The road noise lulls me into a quiet state. But not this time.

She's eight-fucking-teen. What the fuck is she thinking marrying that asshole?

Not even the low seventies weather cheers me up. The whole time I was home, I couldn't wait to get away. Now, I'm in Arizona, visiting a club we're on good terms with. Their clubhouse is loaded with hot, half-naked chicks, and I just want to go home. Girls aside, things are pretty calm tonight. Either I'm getting older or the Bulls have settled down. This clubhouse isn't nearly as wild as I remember.

Just as I have that thought, the club's president, Romeo, joins us. He waves a hand at the open room. "See anything you like?"

I couldn't care less, but I don't want to insult the guy in his own clubhouse, either. "Too many."

He chuckles then gets down to the real reason he stopped by our table. "I gotta give you guys props. This grow-op shit ain't easy. Or cheap."

"Nope." Sparky makes it look easy, but he also lives in the basement taking care of our plants twenty-four-seven. The bits of the process that I *do* help out with may not be as complicated as the growing part, but they're still pretty detailed.

"Rebel's been draining us dry setting up our grow house."

"Lot of upfront costs. It should even out."

"You guys must think it's worth it though?"

My shoulders lift. "We do all right."

He signals one of the girls, Sadie I think, over with a bottle of Jameson and a few glasses. Dex smirks at me when I take the bottle but send Sadie away.

Romeo claps me on the back. "I'll catch you tomorrow." He nods at Dex before taking off for the night.

Dex shrugs. "Luck says Romeo's all wifed up now."

Christ, even degenerate pricks like Romeo are settling down? I lower my head and bang it on the table a few times, making Dex laugh. I just want to go home.

That need intensifies when Teller sends me a text with the wedding date.

This is really happening?

Dex and I kill one bottle, and another one lands on our table. "You gotta tell her," Dex says. We're both pretty wasted, so I hope to hell he forgets this conversation tomorrow. Thank God Z's nowhere to be found. Drunk or not, he'd remember every word and torture me later.

As if he knew my attention wandered, Dex slaps his hand down on the table. "Go home and tell her. Don't let her marry that douche without telling her how you feel."

"I have told her. She thinks I'm a filthy manwhore who can't keep his dick in his pants."

"Well, if the rubber fits—"

"Fuck you. Wait, you don't like him? I mean I know why I don't like him. What's your issue?"

Dex shrugs and finishes his beer. "I dunno. Kid always had a bit of attitude. Seemed to think he was better than all us filthy bikers."

"*You* think you're better than all us filthy bikers."

"No. I think you're all whores flirting with dick rot, but I don't think I'm any better than you."

"Uh, it kind of sounds like you do, brother."

He thinks that's hysterical and sets his head down on the table, shaking with laughter. After a few minutes, he picks his head up. "It's not just that. He had attitude down at CB, too."

"Really? Maybe that had more to do with Heidi giving him shit about hanging out there." Fuck, am I really defending the asshole marrying my girl? I must be drunk.

"Nah. Maybe. I don't know. He'd stand around like he had a stick up his ass. Take Wrath, he hates hanging out there more than any of us, but he still walks the girls to their cars and makes sure no one bothers them."

"Axel's a kid."

"I dunno. Manners are manners. If you don't know by his age that you should walk a lady to her car at two in the morning, you're already a failure in my book."

Dex's words burn a hole in my brain the whole four days it takes us to ride home. It makes me wonder if Axel treats Heidi right. I've had my suspicions but I'm not exactly a reliable judge of the kid's character.

Twenty-Four

Heidi

Axel joined us once for wedding planning stuff, then opted out of any future meetings. That's fine. Trinity doesn't need any assistance.

Not even mine.

If I had a mother, I suppose we'd go dress shopping together. I don't have a chance to feel sorry for myself over it, though. Hope takes me back to the dress shop where she bought her wedding dress and our bridesmaid dresses.

"Do you think I'm allowed to wear white?" I ask, pointing at my stomach.

She giggle-snorts. Not in a mean way, in a fun aunt way. "Heidi, that's such an old, outdated tradition. Wear whatever color you want."

"Well, I know you didn't wear white. But you'd been married before."

"And I hated the white dress my mother forced me to get the first time. But really, honey, if you want white, get white. If you don't, don't. This white dress thing is a recent thing. You know in Eastern cultures, dresses are red. I think blue is popular in Ireland. But it depends what you want."

"Ooh, red would be pretty."

"Come on. Let's find a dress."

I stop her on the way into the shop. "Thank you for doing this… for everything, Hope."

She pulls me in for a quick hug. "No problem."

"I…I mean it. You realize this is the third time you've taken me dress shopping?"

Laughter spills out of her. "I must love you."

She's teasing, but my throat tightens. "Well," I say, forcing the words past the lump in my throat. "I just want you to know it means a lot to me."

I think I embarrassed her because she flashes a nervous smile and tugs me into the dress shop. But I'm glad I got the words out.

For all my bravery of doing something different, I end up picking out a white dress. In the interest of being unique, the dress I choose has a skirt made up of layers of fluffy tulle and the bottom is embroidered with red and orange flowers.

"Orange is Axel's favorite color. I think he'll love the dress," I gush to Hope on our way home. Because of the way the dress and skirt fall, even if I'm showing by the time of the wedding, you won't be able to tell.

That was an important detail to me.

I end up leaving the dress in Rock and Hope's old room. "We can have you get ready up here, and then you can walk down the stairs. Oh, that will be perfect," Trinity says after she checks out the dress. She whips out her notebook and takes some more notes. "We need more ribbon," she says. Whether it's to me or Hope, I'm not sure. Hope shrugs and we all head back downstairs. My gaze strays to Murphy's door, wondering if he's home yet. My brother's useless as far as getting information. And I'm too embarrassed to ask Hope.

No matter how much I smile and pretend to be excited about the wedding, I can't stop thinking about the pain and anger in Murphy's eyes the night of our announcement. We've never gone this long without speaking. This should be a happy time, but there's a huge hole in my world and I don't know how to patch it up.

Downstairs, Sparky's hanging out in the living room with Wrath and my brother. Sparky gives me a big hug. "Are you excited?"

"Sure."

"Don't feel bad about Murphy. After your bomb, he needed to get out of here, but he's doing something good for the club, so it's okay."

"What?"

"Sparky," my brother warns.

"What?"

Wrath doesn't do subtle warnings. "Shut it, Sparky."

He huffs and heads back downstairs.

"Seriously, what was he talking about?"

"What do you think, Heidi?" Wrath asks. "You know how he feels about you."

"Wyatt—" Trinity says.

"Oh, was it a secret?" he asks with wide eyes.

"Stop picking on me, Uncle Wrath."

He stands and kisses the top of my head. "I'm not. I swear. Murphy's a big boy. He'll be fine."

"I'm sure he found someone to ease his suffering," my brother mutters.

Hope sort of gasps. I'm not sure if it's because she's upset with my brother or shocked about Murphy.

Wrath gives him the side-eye. "Really, bro?"

"What? Heidi's an adult now, or so I hear. Getting married. Why shield her from the truth?"

Tears prick my eyes. "Shut up, Marcel."

But he doesn't. He sits up and drills me with a big brother look that borders on nasty. "You're *marrying* Axel. Why do you care if Blake nails every skank from here to Arizona?"

"Teller, that's enough," Hope says.

He turns his glare at Hope and opens his mouth.

"Think it through, bro," Wrath warns in a low voice.

Hope stares right back at my brother and raises an eyebrow.

"What's going on?" Rock calls from the front door. He runs his gaze over the scene in front of him and narrows his eyes.

"My brother's being a jerk, that's all."

Wrath snorts.

"Tell me something new, Heidi-girl," Rock says with a smile. He gives me a quick hug then slaps my brother on the back. "What's up, knucklehead?"

"Nothing."

Rock looks to Hope who shakes her head and puts her arm around my shoulder. "Come on, I'll walk you out, honey."

"Thank you."

As soon as the door shuts behind us, the guys' voices can be heard raising in volume.

"What's gotten into my brother?" I ask.

"I don't think he's handling the wedding well, Heidi. You're young. He loves you and wants what's best for you."

"Great, wait until I tell him about the baby," I mutter.

"Maybe we'll just call him from the hospital," she teases.

She gives me a warm hug before I slide into my car. Why couldn't I have gotten someone like her for my mother? All this wedding stuff has me wondering about my mother a lot lately. Even if I wanted to invite her, I can't because I have no idea where she lives.

Or even if she's alive or dead.

MURPHY

We're treated to a regular clubhouse welcome when we return. Sparky dances around the parking lot, thrilled with his new baby plants. He and Stash inspect all twelve plants and carry them downstairs.

"Won't see them for another month," Rock jokes. He slaps me on the back. "Glad you're home safe, brother. Feelin' any better?" he asks low enough that only I hear him.

"Not really. Is it still happening?" I don't have to be more specific. He knows what *it* I'm referring to.

"'Fraid so."

"Fuck," I grumble.

He nods at the house. "Trin's turned our living room into half a wedding chapel, so…"

"Fuck me, really?"

"You can come stay at our place—"

I crack a smile. "I'll be fine, prez. I'm not that big a pussy."

He slaps my back again. "Never said you were."

After so much time on my ass, I need a shower and a long workout. I make a quick stop at my room to drop off my stuff and change, then head downstairs to the gym. It's empty, thank fuck, because I'm not in the mood to talk to anyone.

My luck runs out about halfway into my workout. Trinity's door across the hall opens. She smiles and waves when she sees me.

"Hey, I heard you were back. How'd it go?"

"I'm alive. Out of shape, but alive."

She ducks her head and laughs.

"Whatcha up to, Trin?"

The smile fades from her face, and she clutches the folder in her arms tight to her chest. "Nothing."

I roll my eyes. "You can tell me if it's wedding stuff, I won't fall apart."

"I know you won't."

"How's it going? The wedding stuff, I mean."

"Fine. Hope took her to get a dress earlier."

"That's nice." I mean it. I imagine planning a wedding has Heidi missing her mother something awful. I'm glad Hope's there for her. I'd be happier if Hope were helping Heidi plan *our* wedding. But whatever.

Trinity glances over her shoulder and then back at me. "Her brother said some mean shit to her earlier."

"She was here? Today?"

"Yeah, she just left a little while ago."

"Oh," I answer, trying to sound uninterested and failing. "What's Teller's issue?"

"Sparky implied you took off because you were upset about the wedding."

"Thanks a lot, Sparky," I mutter. "And?"

"Teller made a comment about you finding plenty of comfort in your travels." The way Trinity phrases it is a lot nicer than what Marcel actually said, I'm sure. "What'd he say, I was nailing chicks across the country?"

"Pretty much."

"Nice."

"I don't think he's handling the wedding well."

"Yeah, well he doesn't need to throw me under the bus."

Actually, the more I think about it, the angrier I get.

I shut down the treadmill and pat Trin's shoulder. "He upstairs?"

"I think so."

I take off to confront my best friend but get stopped by Rock before I hit the stairs. "Hey, Sway and a few of his guys are headed up here tonight. Will you be around?"

For Rock, I'll set my plans to kick Teller's ass aside. "Yeah, sure. Why, what's up?"

"Nothin', just want as many of my guys here as possible."

"You worried he's gonna bother Hope?"

"Or say something stupid to Trinity that gets him shot."

I chuckle at that, and Rock's stony glare intensifies. I drop the smile. "I'll be here, prez. Whatever you need. He say why he's coming up?"

He rolls his eyes. "A business deal to discuss. Fuck only knows what."

"Guns probably." That's the only "business" our downstate charter's involved with that I know of.

"I'm gettin' tired of answering the same question." A growly sound of irritation punctuates his frustration.

"I hear you."

"I need to have a word with him, so send me a text as soon as you see him?"

"You got it." I have a feeling the word he wants to have with Sway involves his fist and Sway's jaw for disrespecting Hope over the summer.

Later that night, as I predicted, Sway has a fresh bruise forming on the left side of his face. Whatever happened between them is done. Brothers don't hold grudges. We beat the snot out of each other and move on.

It's a good system.

I'm sitting next to Rock. Hope's curled up in his lap and Sway's next to me.

It's not guns Sway wants to discuss. It's porn.

I'm facing Sway when he brings it up, so I can't see Rock's face. I don't have to see him to know he's rolling his eyes, though.

"*Why* are you getting involved in that?" Rock asks.

"Why else? Money. Trying to move the club in a more legit direction like you did."

I don't buy that for a second and I doubt Rock does either. "I thought all the good porn studios were in Florida or California?" I ask, sitting back and trying to keep the disbelief off my face.

Sway waves his hand in the air. "You're thinking of that fake, cum-splatter porn. This is arty, classy, lady porn."

Huh?

"We're investing in this chick's company," Sway continues, ignoring our *what the fuck?* faces. "I want to protect our investment. She meets regular, ordinary dudes, fucks 'em in hotels or wherever, and films it."

"Sounds classy," Rock says in a flat voice.

Rock's sarcasm goes right over Sway's head. "She has a big following. Stella Starr."

Rock and I shake our heads.

"Oh, she's beautiful!" Hope says, making all three of us stare at her.

Rock squeezes her a little tighter. "Why have you heard of her and I haven't?"

She lets out a soft laugh and puts her hand on his face. "She writes a column for a feminist blog I follow."

Sway snorts. "Just admit you watch her movies, Hope."

The muscles in Rock's jaw clench, but Hope laughs. "Oh, I have. She's quite talented. Her film company's making a lot of money from what I've read. Sounds like an excellent investment, Sway," she says, sounding completely sincere.

He nods and puffs out his chest before getting up to find a drink. Once he's out of range, Hope jokingly raises her hand. "Question— *why* was he okay with me sitting in on *this* business discussion, but he had such a hissy the last time he was here and I was at the breakfast table?"

Rock shakes with laughter and pulls her against his chest, so I answer the question. "If I had to guess, he was trying to make you uncomfortable, hoping you'd flip out and do something crazy, like forbid Rock to go anywhere near the girl. That's what Tawny would do."

"Exactly," Rock says, pointing at me.

"Oops, sorry. Should I pretend to be outraged when he comes back?"

Again, Rock laughs, then pulls her closer and whispers in her ear something that sounds an awful lot like, "Do you need to be fucked?"

"For fuck's sake, prez," I grumble. "Take that to your house, would ya?"

He grins and slaps my arm, while a red-faced Hope laughs.

"Do I even want to know?" Wrath asks, walking up and tapping the side of the couch with his boot to get Rock's attention.

"Probably not," I answer.

Hope flashes a wicked grin before asking, "Feel like playing security guard to porn stars?"

Wrath's gaze darts to Rock. "Uh, *no*. The only thing worse than babysitting strippers is babysitting porn stars." His forehead wrinkles. "Why?"

"Sway's investing in porn," I explain.

He turns around and leaves the room without another word.

"Well, I guess Wrath won't be signing up for that job," Hope jokes.

"You're full of it tonight, aren't you?" Rock asks.

"I may have had some wine with Trin earlier," she confesses.

I'm wracking my brain, trying to come up with a subtle way to ask about her going shopping with Heidi, but finally give up and just blurt it out. "Have you seen Heidi?"

All humor disappears from her face. "Actually, yes. I took her shopping today."

"How is she?" I ask, trying to hide my eagerness and failing miserably.

Her green eyes blink under worried brows and she glances at Rock, as if asking whether she should answer the question. "We found a dress," she says softly.

I can't stand her feeling sorry for me, so I swallow down the pain in my throat and force a smile. "That's good. I'm sure she looked beautiful."

She doesn't say anything else, so I attempt to shift the conversation. "I heard Teller was a dick to her."

"I think he's having a hard time with his little sister getting married."

"Aren't we all?" I mutter.

Twenty-Five

MURPHY

Today's the day.

I wake up sick to my stomach. Not from alcohol, which I haven't touched since Arizona. Not from having a strange girl in my bed—I'm alone. No, I'm ill from the sounds in the hallway. Happy, girlish voices.

Heidi and her friends. Hope and Trinity. They're using Hope and Rock's old room right down the hall to get Heidi ready for the wedding.

This is it. My last chance to convince Heidi not to do this.

Dex catches me outside my bedroom door. My intentions must be clear, because he holds out his fist. "You got this, bro." I bump his knuckles.

I run into Hope next. "Can you buy me a few minutes to talk to Heidi?" I ask.

She stares at me for a minute. "You're not going to upset her, are you?"

"I don't want to. I just need to talk to her for a minute."

"Okay. She's almost ready. I'll grab Penny and have her help me downstairs."

"Thank you."

Once I have the all-clear, I slip into the room. Heidi glances up. She seems startled to find me instead of Hope or one of her girlfriends.

"Murphy? W-what's—what are you doing here?"

"I need to talk to you."

Her bottom lip wobbles. "About what?"

I take a few steps closer, drinking in all the beautiful details about her. Hating that everything is for another man. The right words won't come to me, but if I don't say something, I'll regret it for the rest of my life.

"Please don't do this." There. It's out. I can't believe I fucking said it.

The tears threatening to fall when she meets my eyes make me feel like shit. But I said it, so I better fucking finish before I lose her for good.

"I love you. I've always loved you. We can work things out between us." My voice is rough from fear and the unfamiliar sound of begging.

"Blake, I love you, too."

Thank God.

"As a friend."

Fuck me.

My mouth opens to plead my case again, but she cuts me off. Her cheeks are red but the shine is gone from her eyes. "I can*not* believe you have the arrogance to come here on my wedding day and do this to me."

What the what?

"How many more ways should I explain it? I love Axel. We're getting married. If you're really my friend, you'll sit in the front, with the rest of the family, and be happy for me."

"Heidi—"

Her fists ball up and she stomps her foot. It reminds me of all the times she did it in the past, and I'd laugh because it was so fucking cute.

It's not cute now. It feels like life or death. "Just stop!" Shit. She yells any louder, everyone's gonna come running up here. "Can you do it or not?" she asks in a quieter voice.

"What?"

"Be happy for me."

"No."

She reels back as if I slapped her and sucks in a deep breath. "Then you should leave."

"How can you expect me to be happy about watching the woman I love marry another man?"

"You don't love me in that way."

There are lots of things I'm on the fence about. Heidi has never been one of them. "I love you in every single way."

"You don't know anything about me," she insists. But her voice sounds forced, as if she's trying to convince herself.

I take a step closer. "You're wrong. I know *everything* about you."

She shakes her head while her mouth curves into a sad smile. "You know the pain-in-the- ass kid sister, the girl who annoyed you with her crush on you—"

"You never annoyed me."

She snorts. "I'll never be the kind of girl you want."

"You're already the girl I want. Just the way you are. I love the woman you've become. I love how strong you are. How fearless." I reach out to brush a loose strand of hair off her cheek and she flinches. "I love your beautiful face."

"You just want to cross me off your list and move on—"

"Jesus. How can you say that? You're the one who doesn't know me."

"Yeah, I do. You're the big manwhore who should probably be dipped in a vat of Lysol along with my brother."

I should be insulted, but I can't help chuckling. Heidi laughs, too, but there's no joy in it. "Heidi, can you be reasonable for one second? I'm eight years older than you. What did you want me to do? Half the time I was just trying to forget about you."

She makes this groaning sound of disgust. Apparently, she didn't find my admission flattering.

"What about our ride? Our spring break trip?"

"I can't. At the time, I thought maybe we could—but now. I can't."

Her gaze slides to the door and her teeth nibble at her bottom lip. For a brief second, I'm almost sure she's about to say fuck it and leave the clubhouse with me. Forget all about the wedding. Bye-bye, so long, Axel.

Then, she opens her mouth and rests her hand over her stomach. The pain in my chest threatens to crush me, whatever she's about to say will shred every last bit of hope I'm clinging to. "I'm pregnant. We're having a baby. Axel and I are having a baby," she whispers.

A thousand emotions and memories slam into me at once. Heidi begging me to play dolls with her when she was little. How scared she must be right now. How much I want to murder Axel.

Why this wedding happened so suddenly.

It takes a few seconds to process the news that Heidi's going to be a mother, but my response is automatic. "It doesn't matter to me. You don't have to marry him because of—I—"

She cuts me off before I explain that I have enough love for her and ten children. "He proposed before we found out. I said yes *before* we found out," she says more forcefully.

I struggle to come up with another argument. Anything to stop her from making a huge mistake out of fear. "Does Marcel know?"

Her cheeks redden and she lowers her gaze. "No. And if you're really my friend, if you really care about me, you'll let me tell him on my own when I'm ready."

Fuck that are the words on the tip of my tongue. But I stop myself. If I break her trust and tell her brother, it will make every shitty thing she thinks about me true. Even if she's marrying someone else, I love her too much to have her hate me.

"I won't say anything. I promise."

She meets my eyes briefly. "Thank you."

Someone knocks on the door and my throat closes tight.

Time's up.

My chest's ripping apart. Despair like I've never known burns through my veins. I've used every last argument, and I'm still losing the person I love more than anything. I'm all out of words.

Heidi takes a few deep breaths and swipes under her eyes before calling out, "Come in."

"Are you almost ready, honey?" It's Hope. I can't turn around and face her. Can't let her see how I laid out my heart to Heidi.

And it didn't change a thing. She's still marrying him.

There's nothing left for me to say.

Heidi

My heart pounds so hard, I'm positive Murphy can hear it. Our eyes meet and hold. It takes every ounce of self-control not to curl my hands into his flannel shirt and ask him to take me away.

No matter what he said earlier, saddling him with a kid that's not his is a horrible thing to do. To him and to my baby. My mother tried it several times, and I always suffered because of it.

And I love Axel. I do.

I'm barely even aware of Hope in the room as Blake shakes his head, turns and walks out the door. I can't take any air into my lungs, knowing I hurt him.

Lied to him.

"Heidi?"

I gasp, struggling to draw in a breath, and tears well up.

"Honey, please don't cry. We don't have time to re-do your make-up." Hope pulls me into a hug, and I try not to smudge my makeup off on her pretty dress.

"I—I hurt Murphy. I didn't want to hurt him."

"I know you didn't. He'll be…fine." There's a catch in Hope's voice, as if she doesn't believe her own words, and it cuts me even deeper.

My pathetic sniffles fill the room, but I manage to somehow keep any tears from rolling down my perfectly blushed and glowing cheeks.

"I told him about the baby," I whisper.

"Oh boy," Hope mutters.

"He promised not to tell my brother."

She nods. "Then he won't."

"It doesn't matter if he does. I hate that I hurt him."

"I know."

"I don't even think he cared, Hope. When…when I told Axel, he was *so* angry with me. But—"

"Heidi?"

Too late, I realize what I just admitted.

"Never mind. I better get out there."

She bites her bottom lip and then opens her mouth, but someone knocks on the door before she says anything.

"Hi, beautiful bride!" Hope's friend Mara says as she walks in. Her husband's a judge and will be performing the ceremony. I spent a lot of time with Mara when we were getting ready for Hope's wedding and like her a lot. She's really sweet and never talks to me like I'm a dumb kid.

She embraces me and kisses my cheek. "You're beautiful. Are you ready?"

"I think so."

Hope's still wearing her worried expression. "Heidi, let's take a minute—"

"No. Hope, it's fine. Will you tell Uncle Rock I'm ready?"

I have to endure a few more seconds of her intense stare before she leaves to find Rock. Mara steps out of the room and I'm all alone. My only friend from high school who I'm still close to, Penny, is up front with Lucas and Axel.

Honestly, for a hastily thrown together affair, everything is beautiful. I can't believe how much Trinity accomplished on such short notice. I try to focus on wedding details, because being alone gives me way too much time to let my mind wander where it shouldn't.

How many hours of my life did I squander daydreaming how perfect life would be if Blake and I could be together? Marrying Axel splashes gasoline all over that bridge and drops the match. I can never go back. This is it.

I said a lot of horrible things I didn't mean to Blake in order to push him away. Otherwise, I would have given in and left the clubhouse with him.

Marrying Axel is the *right* thing to do. It only feels wrong because I'm scared. It's the *only* thing I can do. Axel hasn't been enthusiastic about the baby yet, but he will be in time.

"Hey, Heidi-girl. Are you ready?" Rock asks from the doorway.

Clutching the skirt of my dress, I cross the room. "I'm ready."

One of his big hands settles under my chin, lifting my face so he can look in my eyes. I'm scared of whatever words he's considering. "Heidi, are you sure this is what you want?"

"Yes. Very much, Uncle Rock."

Lie.

He blows out a frustrated breath but nods and holds his arm out for me.

My brother decided this morning he was too furious to give me away, so Rock stepped in. He's been the closest I've ever had to a father, so it seems appropriate.

My breath catches when we walk down the stairs. Every member of the club is here. Bricks is here with his girlfriend and their kids. Even Sparky made his way out of the basement. A few guys I recognize from the downstate club even came. They all turn to watch us descend.

We stop at the bottom landing to meet Marcel. He wraps me in a tight embrace. "I love you so much, baby sis," he rasps out. When I pull away, I swear I see tears glittering in his eyes. I've never seen Marcel cry once in my life, and the thought of him fighting tears because of me has me ready to bawl.

I barely manage to keep it together as he and Rock nod at each other. Then, my brother holds his arm out to walk me down the aisle, something he swore he wouldn't do.

Warmth replaces some of the uncertainty in my heart, and my hand flutters over my stomach. My child will grow up with a big, loving family around and never, ever be lonely, the way I was. She'll know who her father is and grow up feeling loved and wanted. I'll be the best mother ever. Once the baby's here, Axel will be the father I know he can be.

My whole life, hope and heartbreak have been pretty much the same thing.

As we walk down the aisle, I'm not sure which emotion is stronger.

MURPHY

After leaving Heidi, I trudge down the stairs like a zombie. Trinity has turned the clubhouse into something beautiful for the wedding. She spots me and strides over, setting her hand on my arm.

"Are you okay?" she whispers.

I can't lie to Trinity and there's no point. I'm sure my misery's written all over my face. Her concern makes me feel worse. She's someone else I've treated like shit over the years. I don't deserve her concern.

I can see the hesitation on her face. She wants to hug me. But she won't. Not because Wrath's watching us from a few feet away, but because she doesn't want to do anything to embarrass me in front of everyone. I love her even more for it.

"I'll be okay."

"We all thought it would be you."

"I know."

She doesn't apologize, but I see remorse in the way her eyes shine. "Don't go there, Trin. I fucked this up on my own. It's on me."

She shakes her head but doesn't say anything.

"You look beautiful," I say, nodding at her dress.

"Thanks."

"You did an incredible job here." The words hurt like nails in my throat, but I know how much effort Trinity put into this, even though

Heidi hasn't always been nice to her—also my fault. "Everything looks perfect for her."

Her smile is forced.

"Get back to your man before he kicks my ass," I say, giving her a small shove.

Her mouth quirks up and she pats my shoulder.

Wrath slips his arm around her waist and whispers in her ear when she returns. I watch them together for a minute and all I want to do is leave. Eat concrete for as many miles as it takes to forget all the mistakes I've made. Everywhere my gaze lands, I see shit I've fucked up.

Trinity. I've been half in love with her since I was sixteen years old. Never treated her right.

Axel, who I chased out of the club.

Wrath. I unknowingly fucked him over for almost as long as I've looked up to him.

My best friend, Marcel, who I disrespected.

A gentle touch on my shoulder can only be Hope. I turn and the way she smiles up at me chases the chill out of my chest. Even though she has to know by now what a jerk I am, she clings to this stupid notion that I'm a good guy, and I never want to disappoint her.

Behind Hope, at the top of the stairs, I catch a glimpse of Heidi's white dress. Rock's up there with her.

Waiting to walk her down the aisle.

"We're about to start. Walk me to my chair?"

I hold out my arm and she takes it. *Man the fuck up.* I can do this. I have to do this. There's no other choice.

"Are you okay?" Hope asks before she sits.

"Not really."

Axel glances over and nods at me. The absence of a smug smile is what stops me from putting a bullet between his eyes. That and the way he can't stand still. I imagine the thought of being a father at his age is terrifying.

And that's about all the empathy I can come up with for the kid.

I lean over. "Did you know?" I ask Hope softly. By my raised eyebrow, she knows exactly what I'm asking.

"Yes. She told me a while ago."

"That's good." Hope looks surprised. I don't feel like it's a betrayal if that's what she's thinking. "I'm glad she has you to be there for her."

It's killing me because I want to pinpoint where I went wrong and go back in time and fix it, so it's *me* standing in front of the room waiting for Heidi. But that's pointless because it's not *one* thing. It's a culmination of little things. Things I did without thinking that hurt Heidi. The last person in the world I'd ever want to hurt.

Numb, I watch Marcel walk Heidi to the front. Reluctantly, he steps aside and nods at Axel. Rock slips into the chair next to Hope and takes her other hand.

All I see is Heidi smiling up at Axel. When they repeat their vows, it's nothing more than muffled pain. Each word a shard of glass in my heart.

As blood thunders through my ears and I struggle to pull in a lungful of air, I finally think I understand how Heidi felt all those years. Except, she's in love with Axel.

Somehow that makes the pain in my chest worse. But it's the one thing that stops me from hating her and maybe that's the difference.

Twenty-Six

MURPHY

I did what I guess some would say was the right thing and sat quietly through the wedding and watched Heidi marry Axel.

Now, I need to get the fuck away from this place.

The party's casual and upbeat. Just the way she probably wanted it, but I can't stay here another second.

I'm done. Out.

Need one hell of a long ass ride to clear my head. To get it through my thick skull that it's truly over. In the back of my mind, I kept figuring we'd work it out eventually.

Fuck, a couple months ago we were *so close*. We were planning a trip together for fuck's sake. How did it go so wildly wrong?

What a monumental jackass I am.

"Murphy?" Hope calls out. I wait by the front door for her to reach me. "Where are you going?"

My eyes meet hers and she looks so damn worried, I fake a smile. "I need to go for a ride."

"Please don't." She lowers her voice. "Not when you're upset or—"

"I haven't been drinking, Hope. It's okay. Really, I'll be fine."

"Well, maybe Teller will go with—"

"I need to be alone."

Her eyes shine with unshed tears. For me. Shit, I can do better. Reassure her better than this. Before I have a chance to make up something convincing, Rock joins us, slipping an arm around her waist and pulling her to him. "Let him go, babe. He's fine."

His steady gray eyes drill into me, silently asking if his statement's true and I nod.

"How long will you be gone?" Hope persists.

"Don't know. Couple days maybe?" Until the clubhouse is clear of all reminders.

"Will you send me a text later and at least let me know you're okay? No matter how late it is."

Fuck me if she isn't the only woman in my life who has ever worried about me. This time my mouth stretches into a more genuine smile. "Yeah. I can do that, First Lady."

She pulls out of Rock's embrace and gives me tight hug. Over Hope's shoulder, my gaze strays to Heidi. "Make sure she's okay?" I croak out.

Hope nods but doesn't say anything else.

No one else stops me.

Not until I'm on my bike and the cold air hits my face am I finally able to breathe again.

I don't make it nearly as far as I need. Exhaustion pulls me into stopping at our downstate charter.

Sway's more than happy to see me, and I get a warm welcome from the club. Tawny sets me up in a room. I send Hope a text so she doesn't worry about me ending up as road pizza all night.

Numb, but hurting, I end up staring at the wall until sleep takes the pain away.

Twenty-Seven

A Thousand Miles From Nowhere

MURPHY

Now I remember why I don't spend a lot of time downstate. We're all brotherly/friendly, on good terms now, but there's a reason Sway's president of the downstate charter, even though he started out in our charter. Most of the guys in his crew are dicks.

Bull, Sway's Sergeant-at-Arms, has to be the worst, though.

He definitely hasn't forgotten how I knocked his ass out for talking shit about Trinity and Serena after Hope's wedding. I've been spending a lot of time down here, and he's baited me in one way or another every chance he gets.

"Why don't we just take this outside, bro? Have a nice sparring match?" I suggest with a cold grin stretched across my face. Lots of Lost Kings at this party to witness me legitimately kick Bull's ass. Tonight's a good opportunity to end this once and for all

"Nah, I don't want to embarrass you in front of the girls." He nods to CeCe, a club girl who's been giving me subtle hints about visiting my room all night long. She seems nice enough. Pretty girl, too, but at the moment I'm more interested in pounding my fists into Bull's face than pounding pussy.

"Come on, Bull. I got twenty on Murphy to whoop your ass," Sway shouts.

Aw, isn't that sweet?

Finally, we amble outside. Someone constructs a makeshift ring. Or rather cleans up the one that's already there.

"Ain't gonna sucker punch me tonight, fucker," Bull grumbles while he tapes up his hands.

My mouth twists into a grin. I haven't given that punch a whole lot of thought since it happened, but obviously Bull's been nursing his wounded pride. "Learn to watch your mouth and show respect, and I wouldn't have to knock you out."

He spits at my feet. "Fuck you, choosing ass over brothers."

"You disrespected *my brother's* girl."

He shakes head as if he doesn't get the concept.

With outsiders, it's fuck with one, you take us all on. Between brothers? No one's gonna stop this fight. Not unless one of us is half-dead or taps out.

Nothing but imminent death will force me to tap out.

I used to think Wrath's whole fighting, getting the shit kicked out of him thing to unleash his anger, was fuckin' nuts. But I find myself eager to pound the piss out of Bull and not really caring if I take a beating in return. If Wrath were here, he'd probably recommend I tire Bull's out-of-shape ass and then go with an uppercut to the jaw or temple. So, that's my plan.

"What's wrong, Murphy? Still sulking over your buddy's slutty little sister?"

Unrestrained anger pulses through me at the low taunt. But I'm not completely stupid. He's using shit like that to provoke me. I grin at him instead, which seems to confuse him.

Shadow, one of Sway's guys, gives us the go ahead.

Bull's not only dumb as an ox, he lumbers like one, too. Around and around the dirty square, throwing fake punches to, I don't know what, scare me? He's drunker than fuck. I'll go easy on him. Maybe I won't bother tiring him out, and I'll just put him down for the night with a swift punch. Fuck knows I've done it before.

A few rounds later, I'm rethinking my strategy. What was supposed to be a simple sparring match and puttin' on a show for the rest of the club has turned into a nasty brawl.

"Bring it, old man," I taunt, but I don't think he hears me.

Sweat, maybe blood, drips into my eyes. I shake it off and bounce up and down a few times on the balls of my feet. My next right hook connects with Bull's jaw and snaps his head to the side. Fucker's still on his feet, though. I must be gettin' weak.

Pain explodes on my side and I back off. We circle each other again. Honestly, I'm pissed with myself for not ending this sooner.

After absorbing a left hook to my right pec, I have to rethink Bull's impairment. His aim seems fine. He's definitely aiming to knock the wind out of me. Thankfully, he doesn't have a tremendous amount of power behind the blows. Otherwise, I'd be fucked.

The next time he moves in close for a body punch, I tighten my stomach and shift slightly so the blow lands on my side. Not gonna lie, it hurts, but my obliques take the brunt of it and I'm able to land a few solid hits of my own.

He backs off.

This time, I duck and jab my way in for a few body shots. It's my hard right straight above his floating rib area that finally does him in. There's a sickening squishing-crunch on impact. Bull drops to the ground and starts spewing.

Sway seems pissed that his guy lost, even though he claimed to bet on me, but he calls it, raising my hand and congratulating me.

A group of girls swarm around us. Each one vying to give me the congratulatory blowjob, I'm sure. At the back, I spot Serena and she raises an eyebrow. I finally make my way to her and she kisses my cheek.

"What're you doing here?" I ask.

"Don't be mad, I'm visiting my friend Lisa and heard you were here, so we came over. Thought I'd say hi."

"I ain't mad at all, darlin'. Good to see you."

Her eyes shine with interest, and I'm uneasy about leading her on again. Any one of the bunnies at my back would be fine for the night.

But I know Serena. She's not a psycho bitch who will try to jack my wallet. She doesn't feel the need to hang all over me in front of everyone. I can actually talk to her. I hold my bloodied hands out to her. "Come help me clean up?"

She gives me a flirty smile. "Sure, I'll take care of you."

Instead of any form of excitement or elation from the win, I'm *tired*. I sling an arm over her shoulders and lead her down the hall to my room

On our way, someone stops me, places a bottle of Jameson in my hand, and gives Serena an ice bag and first aid kit.

Glancing down at my throbbing hand, my middle knuckle's swollen. Wrath would give me shit for my sloppy form.

When I shut the door to my room, Serena leans in to kiss me.

"Fix my hand first?" I ask, pulling away.

She blinks. "I can do that."

Taking my hand, she tugs it toward her to inspect the damage. Gently, she prods each knuckle. I let out a pained hiss when she gets to the swollen one. "Does it hurt?"

"Nah."

"You can tell me," she teases.

"It stings," I concede and she nods.

"Can you wiggle it for me?"

She focuses on my hand as I stretch and flex each finger.

"How's school?" I ask.

She seems surprised and it bothers me. I've asked her about stuff like that before, haven't I?

When she seems satisfied nothing's broken, she grabs some antiseptic wipes, cleans and bandages my hand. "Good. I ended the semester with a three-point-seven."

"That's great." I hope I don't sound too shocked. It's not that I think Serena's dumb. We usually end up talking about me, the club, or not talking at all. I realize I don't know a whole lot about her. "What's your major again?" I ask as she takes my other hand, turning to inspect all four knuckles that got scraped by Bull's teeth when I punched him in the mouth.

This whole situation is starting to remind me a little too much of when Heidi did something similar for me, and I have to sit down.

Concern creases Serena's brow and she puts the back of her hand on my cheek. "Are you okay? He got a few good shots in."

"Yeah. I'll live. Tell me. What's your major?"

"Exercise Science."

I must look confused—that's a thing?—because she rushes to explain. "When I'm done, I'll transfer to a four-year school for sports medicine or occupational therapy. Something like that." She grabs my hand again. "Ouch," she whispers.

"I barely feel it."

"You'll feel it tomorrow."

"Maybe." I squeeze her hand. "You like it? School, I mean."

"Oh, yeah." She finishes taking care of my hand and dabs at my forehead. "We don't have to talk about me, though. I want to take care of *you*."

She sets all the supplies aside, and I slide one of my hands into her hair, pulling her in for a kiss. "Thank you."

Her lips quiver into a nervous smile. "Sure."

"I'm glad you're here."

One of her eyebrows shoots up and a voice in my head warns me not to reel her in again. It's not right.

"Really?" she asks.

But I'm an asshole and do it anyway. "Yes, really."

Serena and I spend the weekend together and don't venture out into the club much. She's the perfect way to distract myself from why I came down here in the first place.

Sunday morning, Tawny bangs on my door. She scowls when she sees Serena in my bed. "What?" I ask.

Her gaze roams over my bare chest, and I wish I'd taken the extra two seconds to put on a shirt. "Give me a second, Tawny."

I duck inside to get dressed and Serena scurries into the bathroom.

"Okay, what's up?" I ask.

"The cops are here," she whispers.

Out of habit, I mentally go over anything I'm carrying that might be incriminating. "Why?"

She rolls her bottom lip. "They found Bull dead, out on route twenty."

"Holy shit. Are you serious?"

She nods solemnly and twists her hands together. It's unnerving because I've never seen Tawny in anything but one hundred percent biker bitch mode.

"They asked for you right away, Murphy. Someone told them about the fight Friday night."

"So? I haven't left here since Friday."

She shrugs and motions for me to follow her.

Two plainclothes detectives are waiting for me outside. Naturally, Sway wouldn't allow them inside without a warrant. I go with them willingly to get them away from Sway's compound.

The questions they throw at me at the precinct make no sense.

"Wait a minute. I haven't seen him since Friday night. We had a friendly boxing match outside and that was it."

Friendly might be exaggerating a bit.

The one questioning me raises an eyebrow at my bandaged hands. "Yeah, but we heard you two have history."

"History of what? We're in the same club."

One of the detectives rolls his eyes. "Yeah, 'cause all you brothers are so close."

Every brother in *my* club, yeah. Down here, not as much. But of course I won't say that.

"We also heard you had an altercation a few months ago at your prez's wedding over a different girl."

Whoa. Who the fuck would have told them that? Inside, I'm rattled, but I keep it together.

"We weren't fighting over a girl Friday. We were just messing around. And the girl I knocked him out over is the same one I spent the entire weekend with. In fact, I was in bed with her when you guys showed up at the clubhouse."

They don't seem to like that, because it ruins their neat little theory.

"Who?"

I give them her name and they tell me to wait.

I'm waiting for a few *hours* before they come back. Someone comes in and allows me to make a phone call. Rock's the logical one to call. He's my president. Gotta let him know first. It's possible Sway already called him, but that's still who I dial first.

"I'll get in touch with Glassman. Keep me updated," he says.

Finally, the two assholes who brought me here come in. "All right. We verified your alibi. You managed to find the only articulate, classy piece of ass in that shithole clubhouse."

"Watch it," I growl.

He chuckles, happy he got a reaction out of me.

"One final thing, Mr. O'Callaghan. You wouldn't happen to know anything about a barn that was burned to the ground last year, would you?"

"Barn? No," I answer, genuinely confused.

Then, I remember. It was pitch black the night Sway drove us out to the middle of nowhere to collect a stolen shipment of guns. Sway and his guys had burned the place to the ground when we were done. But, we'd also left quite a few bodies behind that night.

The cops don't mention the bodies, only the arson.

"You're free to go back to the clubhouse or home to Empire. But I wouldn't leave New York any time soon."

"Not plannin' to."

I don't expect Rock to be the one who shows up to collect me from the jail. He pulls me in for a quick hug. "You good?"

"Yeah. They got nothin'."

Once we're inside the car, he's silent. We leave the police station, but a few miles down the road, Rock pulls over.

He turns and fixes his *give-it-to-me-straight* stare on me, and I know what's coming.

"I'm only going to ask you this one time. You know I've got your back and the club has your back no matter what. Did you do it?"

I understand why he's asking and I'm not insulted. "No. Fuck no. We boxed at Sway's Friday. I worked him over pretty good. Sway called the match. I didn't see Bull again after I left the ring. But he was breathing."

"Well, they think he died sometime early Saturday morning."

"I was with Serena until Sunday late morning. Like twenty-four-seven."

He rolls his eyes. "You start that back up?"

My shoulders lift. "Might as well stick with what I know."

"Yeah, well, she give a statement backing you up?"

"From what I heard, yeah."

"Christ, you better not piss her off."

"Nah, she ain't like that. Even if we…she's a good girl. She wouldn't lie just to get even with me."

"All right. Call her anyway. Keep her happy until this blows over."

"Yeah, okay. She's probably back at Sway's. I'll have her ride home with me."

"Good. Let's go see Sway. I need to have a chat with him anyway."

I don't ask. If Rock wants me to know, he'll tell me.

"Prez, there's another problem. No one outside of LOKI should've known about our sparring match. Not that quick anyway. But the cops asked me about it almost right away."

"That ain't good."

"No, but this is worse. They knew Bull and I fought at *your* wedding. How the fuck would they know about that?"

"Don't know. It's not good, though."

"They also asked some pointed question about the arson that went down when we visited Sway last year."

"Fuck me."
"Yeah."

It's a full house back at Sway's place. Every member's in the building. I head to my room, looking for Serena. I run into Tawny first.

"You seen Serena?" I ask.

She waves her hand down the hallway. "Took off with Shadow a few minutes ago," she says with a fake *I'm sorry* face.

Anger, sickness, irritation, one of those emotions settles in the pit of my stomach. Serena and I sure as fuck aren't exclusive, but we did just spend an entire weekend together. Did she really go fuck someone else while I was busy getting questioned at the police station?

Yup.

I didn't realize Rock followed me down the hall, so we're both standing there when Serena stumbles out of one of the rooms, wiping her mouth and fixing her hair. She freezes when she sees us.

Rock's hand clamps down on my shoulder. "Talk to her," he warns me in a low voice, reminding me there are bigger things at stake than my ego. "I'll be out front."

"Murphy? I didn't realize you were coming back."

"I'm back."

"Everything okay?"

"Not really." I nod at the door. "Who were you with?"

She glances at the floor. "No one."

"Bullshit. Don't lie, Serena. We ain't a couple."

"Shadow grabbed me out in the living room when the police dropped me off."

"He force you?"

"No. Not really."

I'm burning with a number of emotions. Anger, because while I doubt Shadow *forced* himself on her, I'm sure she felt like she didn't have any other option and just went along. That blurry gray area of consent goes on in Sway's clubhouse all the time. That shit doesn't happen in ours. A girl says no or clearly isn't into it, we move on.

"I'm sorry," I say.

Her eyes widen. "Why are *you* sorry?"

"I just am. Come on, I need to talk to you."

She follows me to my room and leans against the door once we're inside.

"What'd the police ask you?" I ask while I change.

"If we were together. I told them we were side-by-side all weekend and only left the room to grab food."

"Thanks."

She shrugs. "It's the truth."

"I'm headin' home in a bit. Do you need a ride?"

"You'll still—you're not mad at me?"

"I'm not thrilled, but it's not like I ever gave you a reason to think we were together or something either."

Tears fill her eyes. Why the fuck do I always seem to make girls cry?

"Thanks. Yes, I'd appreciate a ride home."

"Give me a few minutes to collect my shit, and then I need to meet up with Rock."

"Okay." She turns to open the door.

"No. Wait here." I'm not risking her taking off with someone else. In fact, I want to get her away from here, before someone talks her into changing her story and I lose my alibi.

Call it a gut feeling.

We meet up with Rock in front of the clubhouse.

"I'll follow you up the Thruway," I say, "but I'm gettin' off at twenty-three to take her home."

He nods at me. "I'll stick with you."

Obviously, Rock's anxious about letting me ride alone. I always trust his instincts. Not that I would question my president anyway.

The ride goes by quick. I pull into Serena's apartment complex, and she hesitates after she gets off. "Do you want to come in and talk?"

"I would, hon. But I need to get up to the clubhouse." I tilt my head at Rock's SUV patiently waiting by the exit.

"Oh, sorry. Yeah. Call me."

Yeah, not happening.

Although, in her head it might not seem clear where we stand, in mine it's crystal clear.

We're done.

Twenty-Eight

The ride itself is home.

MURPHY

"You okay, bro?" Teller asks outside Heidi's hospital room door.

"Yeah."

Haven't seen Heidi in over six months. Not since her wedding day when I laid out my heart to her and she went ahead and married Axel. Teller called to let me know I was an uncle this morning, and I drove straight to the hospital without thinking.

Now, I stop to consider if I can really do this.

She's not mine.

Not my baby she just had.

I still want to see her so bad, I feel it in my bones.

Teller's waiting with his hand braced on my shoulder. Waiting to make sure I won't do anything to upset his baby sister.

"I'm good, brother. I swear it."

"Okay."

He pushes the door open and suddenly I'm not okay. Not at all. Axel nods at us. Heidi glances at me and a pained smile turns the corners of her mouth up.

"Hey, Heidi-bug. How you doin'?"

Her smile turns a little more genuine. "Hey, Blake."

Teller throws himself into a chair across from Heidi, leaving room for me to move closer.

"Congrats, man." I shake Axel's hand and try not to choke on the words.

"Thanks for coming." He seems sincere. That's the problem. Can't even hate the guy.

"Hey, hon, I want to run down to the cafeteria. You want anything?" Axel asks Heidi.

She raises an eyebrow in a sweet, hopeful expression I remember her using to get her way when she was little. "Ice cream sandwich?"

"You got it."

He glances at Teller and me. "Need anything?"

"Nah, but I'll run down with you." Teller pulls himself out of the chair and slaps my shoulder on the way out.

"So, where is she?" I ask after they leave.

Heidi gestures to the little rolling crib on the other side of the bed. Been so focused on her I didn't even notice. Walking around the edge of the bed, I stop and stare down.

"Oh, shit, she's pretty."

Heidi chuckles.

I guess having me looming over her wakes the baby, and she waves her plump little fists in the air. Heidi reaches over and scoops her up.

"Can I hold her?"

She gives me a cautious look. "You ever held a baby?"

"Yeah, *you*. When you were little. I was only eight and didn't drop you, so I think I can manage now."

The memory I offered up doesn't make her laugh like I intended. She sighs instead. Then leans down and presses a kiss to the baby's cheek. "You want to meet your uncle Blake, little one?"

Swallowing over the lump in my throat is impossible.

"Meet Alexa Jade," she says as she hands the baby over.

"Hi, Alexa." I find myself babbling like an idiot to this teeny-tiny little person Heidi just handed over. "She's so tiny."

Heidi's silent, so I glance up and find her red-faced, staring at the baby. "She was a little early."

By the tone of her voice, it sounds like there's more to it than that, but I don't know the right questions for this situation. "She's beautiful, Heidi."

"Thank you."

Alexa settles into my arms, letting me rock her back and forth. "How do you feel?" I ask Heidi without taking my eyes off the baby.

"Tired. Sore. But we're going to be fine."

This is fucking weird. I want to hug Heidi and the baby and do everything I can to make sure they're safe and protected.

But I can't. Heidi's married to someone who isn't me and has a baby who isn't mine. It's like she went from a child to an adult in the snap of two fingers, and I can't catch up.

This isn't the way I pictured our lives turning out.

"What have you been up to, Blake?"

"Not much. I was helping out downstate," I say with a shrug.

"Marcel told me. Rock's okay with that?"

"Yeah, he understood." Shit, I wish I hadn't said that.

"Are you coming back?"

Looking down at little Alexa's sweet, chubby face, I know I won't be able to stay away any longer. Even if being around her mom and dad kills me. "Yeah, I think so."

"That's good."

"So, how'd you get a room to yourself?" I finally manage to meet Heidi's eyes. A smile pulls the corner of her mouth up.

"I work at this hospital."

"Really? Since when?"

"Well, I interned here over the summer. But they offered me a job after I graduate."

It takes a second to find my voice again. "That's great. Did you like it?"

"I loved it."

"Think you'll take the job or stay home with Alexa?"

For a second her eyes narrow, and I wait for her to snap at me.

"They understand. I'm taking this semester off, so I'll have some time to figure it out. The hospital has a really nice day care for employees. But Axel's doing well at his job, so…I don't know."

"Are you happy?" I blurt out.

Her gaze strays to Alexa. "Yes."

Alexa chooses that moment to scream her little head off.

"Holy shit. Some lungs on her."

"She's had people poking and prodding her all morning. She's probably hungry now." Heidi holds out her arms and I hand the baby to her.

"I'll uh." I drop into the chair in the corner and stare at the ceiling.

"Blake, I'm covered."

"I'm fine."

We're interrupted by Hope opening the door. Her gaze goes right to Heidi. "Hi!" She rushes over and coos at the baby before noticing me.

"Murphy! Oh my gosh. When did you get here?"

"Little while ago. Teller called me this morning."

"That's great. Are you coming up to the property?"

"It's my next stop."

"Good. Rock will be so happy to see you."

"You came here first?" Heidi asks.

"Of course."

The corners of her mouth turn up and she holds her hand out for me to grasp. "Thank you," she says. "I'm really happy…it was good to see you. I missed you."

Hope takes a step away from the bed, giving us some privacy.

"Missed you, too, kid. I'm glad you're okay…you're happy." I squeeze Heidi's hand and take another look at Alexa. "If you need anything, let me know."

"Thank you," she whispers.

Regret? Relief? I'm not sure what settles over me as I leave the hospital. I point my bike southwest of Empire on the road to take me home. Half-way there, I take a detour to Fletcher Park, stopping at the overlook to stare at the view of Empire and the surrounding areas below. The last time I was here...*fuck it*. Everything reminds me of Heidi. Doesn't matter where I am.

My mind's blank as I leave the park and take the familiar back roads to the clubhouse. It's the only place that's ever truly felt like my home. How often will Heidi and the baby come up to visit? Fuck, that's gonna hurt every single time I see her.

I'll have to get over it.

Heidi

Seeing Murphy again hurt. I feel like I've lost one of my best friends. I can never give him what he wants, so pushing him away is for the best.

"Is everything okay?" Hope asks after he leaves.

"Yes. It was nice of him to come visit."

The hospital social worker speed walks into my room. I spoke to her yesterday. Apparently, my age makes me a high-risk mother or something. On top of that, Alexa came earlier than expected, so they're concerned about making sure I have enough people to support me when I leave.

"Hi, Heidi. How are you feeling?"

"Better."

She leans over the bed, checking on Alexa. "She looks great. Very healthy baby girl."

"I did everything the doctor told me to." I've gotten a little defensive about everyone acting like I'm a moron because I'm only eighteen.

"Are you grandma?" she asks Hope, who scowls at the question.

"No, this is my aunt. Hope."

"Well, you're getting discharged tomorrow. What's your plan?"

Fear spreads through my chest. I don't know if I can do this. My lower lip trembles. "I'm scared to be alone with her. What if I screw something up?"

Nervous laughter bubbles out of Hope. "You're not going to screw up, Heidi."

The social worker doesn't seem to agree. "It would be better if she had some family to either stay with her or that she could stay with, until she feels more comfortable."

"My *husband* and I can handle it," I protest.

Hope taps her fingers against the bedside table. "Rock and I talked about it earlier. Maybe you, Axel, and the baby should come up and stay at the clubhouse for a couple of weeks. That way there will be people to help you out in the beginning."

"Really? The guys would let me do that?"

"Well, Rock will bring it up today and see how they feel. You can stay in our old room, so it will be more private. I'll go up today and clear some of my junk out of your way."

Tears start rolling down my cheeks. "I don't know what to say, Hope. I can't… I'd feel much better."

"Good." She whips out her cell phone and taps out a text. "I'm letting Rock know."

The social worker seems confused but relieved that I won't be going home alone.

"Sounds good." She makes some notes on her folder and nods at me. "I'll check back with you tomorrow before you leave." She hurries out as Axel steps back into the room.

"Your brother had to go back to the clubhouse," Axel says to me.

"They're having a meeting," Hope says. She raises an eyebrow. "You can explain it to Axel." She leans over and kisses my cheek. "I'm heading home."

"Thank you for everything, Hope."

After she leaves, Axel pins me with a hard stare. "Explain what to me?"

"Hope offered us their old room at the clubhouse for a few weeks after I get out of the hospital."

His face twists in anger. "Fuck that. You did that behind my back?"

Axel's shifts from happy-about-the-baby to stressed-out got a lot worse toward the end of my pregnancy. So his outburst barely registers. "No," I answer calmly. "The social worker was in here pestering me again about not going home alone. So, Hope offered."

"Fuck her. That social worker doesn't have any say over what we do."

"Can you try to be reasonable, Axel? I'm already exhausted. You're at work for eleven or twelve hours a day—"

"I'm working to pay for the baby you just had."

Ignoring that, I continue with my reasoning. "If I'm up at the property, people will be around to help me with the baby."

With a heavy sigh, he says, "Christ, Heidi. Babies sleep all day. How much help do you need?"

I take a deep breath and count to ten so I don't scream at him.

"This is all new to me and I'm scared, okay?"

"You're doing fine. And it's not as if Hope or Trinity know what to do with a baby, either."

He's not getting it. "But at least I won't be alone."

Axel pinches the bridge of his nose. "It more than doubles my drive to work."

"I don't want to move up there permanently. Just for a few weeks until I get used to things."

"Why don't you ask Hope to come stay with us?"

"That's not fair to her. And our apartment is barely big enough for us and the baby. Where's she supposed to sleep?"

"Okay. But just for a week or two. I'm not comfortable up there."

"I know."

"Promise me this isn't just so you can be around Murphy."

Is he kidding? Except for today, I haven't spoken to Murphy in months. I cut an important person out of my life to keep the peace with my husband, and he still won't let it go. "That's so stupid, I'm not even going to answer it."

Axel stares at me and exhales. "I'm sorry. I'm exhausted."

Like giving birth was a tropical vacation. "No kidding."

"You know why it's weird for me to be up there, right?"

"I understand. But they're still my family."

"*I'm* your family now."

"Yes." I answer with more patience than I'm feeling. "But they're my family, too."

Why does he always seem to forget that fact?

MURPHY

When I walk into the clubhouse, Rock has all the members currently living there—except Z because no one has been able to find him—assembled downstairs. Trinity, Mariella, and Hope are also there. If there were a party or church going on, it wouldn't be unusual. Middle of the afternoon on a weekday, it's a little odd.

"Everything okay, prez?"

"Yeah, take a seat."

"What's going on?"

Rock glances at Teller and gives him a go ahead signal.

"I'm worried about Heidi going home alone with the baby. Axel's working long hours, and—"

"You want to have them stay here for a bit?" Sparky asks. By the way he's bouncing around, he's clearly excited about the idea.

"Rock and I discussed it this morning, and if it's okay with you guys, we were going to offer them our old room," Hope says.

What the actual fuck? "You're *what*?" I snap.

Hope bites her lower lip, and Rock glares at me. No doubt for the sharp tone I just used with his wife.

"Sorry, Hope. This is just weird."

"It's temporary," Rock says.

"A baby in the house will bring good energy for the plants," Sparky assures us. Rock gives him the side eye.

"You're gonna have to confine your smoking to the basement while the baby's here," he warns Sparky and Stash.

Sparky nods as if he doesn't mind one bit and all this makes perfect sense. "I get it, prez."

Teller paces and runs his hand over his chest. "I'm sorry. I know it's gonna disrupt the whole clubhouse, but I'd really appreciate it. The hospital social worker's been on her ass, too, so this will make them back off."

Wrath sits up. Finally. No way our enforcer will let this happen. "Fuck it. I'm gettin' sick of the place gettin' trashed every weekend and havin' to throw people out Sunday nights, anyway. She's family. Of course we'll help her out."

Has the entire club lost their minds? "Do we get to vote on this?" I ask.

Rock narrows his eyes and turns my way. "Seriously? I thought *you* of all people would want to help her out?"

Shame burns through my anger. This isn't about me or my wounded whatever. "You're right. Sorry. I'm cool."

Hope finally flashes a smile. "Thank you. I talked to her this morning, and she seemed so relieved when I asked her. She really needs all the support she can get right now."

My face still burns even though Hope doesn't seem to be judging me. "I know."

"Thank you." Teller squeezes Hope's hand.

"You can thank me by helping me spruce up the room for them."

Teller shakes with laughter and turns to Mariella. "I'll help you, Hope," she says.

"Well, one of you muscle-y wonders is needed to help me move some heavy boxes."

"Hey," Rock protests, making all of us laugh.

Hope pats his arm. "Your muscles are needed elsewhere, Mr. President."

Wrath sits up and waves his hand in the air. "Before you two start going at it, when's she gettin' discharged?"

Hope's mouth quirks, but it's Teller who answers. "Tomorrow morning."

"Oh, shit." Wrath gestures at Teller and me. "You guys better hurry up."

"Why'd I get roped into this again?" I ask.

Teller slaps my arm. "Don't be a dick."

We follow Hope upstairs. All she needed was for us to move a couple of boxes of books into her closet. Mariella stays and helps her make the bed.

"Feel good to be back home?" Teller asks on our way downstairs.

In spite of everything, it does feel good to be home. I'm not so sure I'll have the same opinion tomorrow when Heidi and her *husband* move in a few doors down the hall from me. "Yup. It's good to be back."

My best friend doesn't call me out on my fake smile or strained voice. He slaps my shoulder. "It's good to have you back. Missed you."

Twenty-Nine

Heidi

My whole life's become surreal. How did I end up with a baby before my nineteenth birthday?

Axel, the baby, and I arrive at the clubhouse after I'm discharged from the hospital and are given Rock and Hope's old room.

After a few days, I've settled into a bit of a routine. Even so, exhaustion pulls at me. The kind that leaves my head fuzzy and achy. Curling into a ball on the floor sounds good right about now.

Alexa's a good baby. From what I've read, she could be way fussier than she is. Even so, I'm tired. After Axel leaves for work, I put Alexa down for her nap and crawl into bed.

A soft knock on the door has me groaning. Sleep. Just a few more precious minutes before she wakes up again. Why is that too much to ask?

Z's on the other side, so I'm happy I dragged my butt out of bed. "Uncle Z!" He gives me a big hug, lifting me off the ground a bit.

"I'm so sorry I didn't come see you in the hospital, Heidi-girl. I just got home."

"That's okay. It was too hectic anyway."

"Can I see her?"

"Sure. She's sleeping."

"I'll be quiet."

By appearance alone, Z is probably pretty terrifying. He's a big guy and covered from neck to fingertips in tattoos. When he smiles, though, he flashes dimples worthy of a college quarterback. As soon as he sees Alexa, he grins. "Aw, shit, Heidi. She's so tiny. She looks just like you when you—" He stops and glances over at me. "Fuck, this is weird. In my head, you're still four years old."

"I know. I think my brother's having the same problem."

"No doubt. Where's that husband of yours? I feel like kicking his ass."

"Don't you dare. He feels awkward enough about all this." I wave a hand in the air to explain I mean staying here.

"Nothing to feel awkward about. There're no hard feelings. He's family, too, now."

Z doesn't realize it, but that gives me a piece of information I've been missing. Axel refused to tell me the circumstances of why he left the club. I assumed it was Murphy voting him down, but now I'm not so sure.

"Well, he's at work anyway."

He slips his arm over my shoulders and pulls me to his side. "You need anything? You okay?"

"Yeah. Just tired."

"I bet. That's why you're here though, right? So we can help you out?"

The face I pull makes him laugh.

"Okay, so Hope, Trinity, and Mariella can help you out."

"Hope's already done enough for me." My cheeks heat up. "I haven't always been nice to Trinity, so—"

"Trin ain't like that, Heidi. She loves you. You're family."

"I know. Mariella's been a big help. I guess she had a lot of nieces and nephews."

"Cool."

Alexa kicks and blinks up at us. My dream of a nap floats away as I pick her up. Z holds his arms out. It's strange for me to explain to my uncle Z how to hold her and support her head. I have a bit of anxiety when anyone besides me touches her, but he's so gentle, I ease up quickly.

"Oh my God. That pouty-pissy face she's making. You made the same one when you were little."

"I did not."

"Yeah, you did. You're doing it right now." Z chuckles. "See?"

"Shut up."

He laughs harder, jostling Alexa. She grunts and waves her fists, smacking Z's chin. "Ouch. She's got a good right hook."

"I think she needs her diaper changed."

"That's all you, Mom," he says as he hands her back to me.

"Thanks."

"Hey. What's goin' on?" Murphy calls from the doorway.

"Hey, brother. I just got in and wanted to meet the newest member of the family," Z explains.

"Yeah. Welcome back." He hesitates, his gaze darting between Z and me.

"You can come in." Why not? Rock and Hope's old room feels like party central since we got here.

Both of them watch me as I change her, talking about Z's trip.

"I gotta go check in with Rock. I'll see you girls later?" Z asks me.

"We'll be here."

He gives Alexa a kiss on the forehead and ruffles my hair.

After Z leaves, Murphy leans up against the wall by the door.

"What's up?" I ask.

"Nothing. Wanted to say hello. See if you need anything," he says, hovering in the doorway.

"I'm okay."

"You have breakfast?"

"Yeah."

"Got any plans?"

"Honestly? I think I'm going to feed her and pray she takes a nap, so I can take one."

Murphy ducks his head and chuckles. "Okay. I'm headed into Furious." He runs his hand over his beard, then down his chest. "If you need something, call me."

My throat tightens from the simple offer. "Thank you," I whisper.

"Hey, what's wrong?"

"Nothing. I told you. I'm tired."

He approaches slowly and asks to hold Alexa. "You can always ask one of us to watch her for a while if you need some rest."

"I can't yet."

He cocks his head, inviting me to explain.

"I…I don't know. I can't really let her out of my sight yet."

Some of the tension eases out of his face and he glances down at her. "Yeah. I can understand that."

"Besides, she's my responsibility. I can't dump her on other people because I need a nap."

"Uh, yes, you can. That's why you're here. So your family can help you out."

I can't because it's too much like something my mother would do, but I don't feel like bringing that up now. Murphy was there. He knows my history.

"Everything okay? Being here?" he asks.

"I guess. Are the guys mad we're in the president's room?" I meant it as a joke, but I'm so tired, my question sounds more serious than I meant.

"No, Heidi. We all just want to help you out the best we can."

"Yeah, right. My brother's probably plotting my husband's murder." That time it does sound like the joke I meant.

Murphy chuckles, jostling Alexa, who makes little squee noises. "I think she likes that," I say.

"She's really good."

"I know. Our next one will probably be a holy terror."

Murphy reacts as if I punched him in the gut. "Christ, you're not already planning—"

"No. God, no. We didn't plan *this* one."

I swear he rolls his eyes, but he doesn't say anything, so I let it go.

He tilts his head, and his dark green eyes study me for a few moments. "I guess I won't be taking you for your birthday ride this year."

I barely choke back a sob. "I think those days are over," I whisper.

"Yeah. Guess so."

Neither of us seem to know what to say.

Finally, he hands Alexa back to me. He almost seems conflicted, as if he doesn't want to let go. "I'd stay and help you out, but Wrath's out today—"

"It's okay."

"Hey, lil' sis," Marcel calls out, not bothering to wait for me to invite him in. "What up, Murphy?"

"Heading into work. Just stopped by to say hi to Alexa."

"Not me?" I tease.

His mouth curls up into a teasing, brotherly smile. "Yeah, you too."

My brother sets a box down on the dresser and holds his arms out for the baby. "How come everyone wants to hold her until she needs her diaper changed?" I grumble.

Both of them crack up.

Murphy hesitates then gives me a clipped wave. "Catch you later." I watch him go, feeling like we had so much more to say to each other.

"What's in the box?" I ask after Murphy leaves.

Marcel grins and hands me the box. It's small. Plain cardboard. Inside I find a bunch of photos thrown in. "Found those today. Think I grabbed them when we were cleaning out Grams's place. Meant to give them to you to put in an album or something."

"Oh, wow." I drop down on the edge of the bed and flip through the photos. "I don't think I've ever seen these."

Marcel sits next to me, still holding Alexa, and looks at the photos with me. I stop on one of a younger Marcel, holding a tiny pink bundle. "That's *you*. The day mom brought you home from the hospital."

"Really?" I glance at the photo and then Alexa.

"She looks exactly like you," Marcel says, reading my mind.

"That's crazy."

"Keep going."

Pictures of the same baby taken over a series of days. "I took a photo of you every day."

"Why?"

"So I could flip through them and see you change."

"Really? You thought of that? You were ten."

"I know. You were like my own personal science experiment."

I bump him with my shoulder. "Jerk."

The smile slides off his face, and the fierce big brother look I know well takes its place. "I think I saw one of those news shows about how you should always have a recent photo of your kid in case of kidnapping. Mom was so erratic, I was always worried something would happen to you."

Tears fill my eyes. My brother's always been good to me. But this is a side of him he rarely allows to be seen.

There's another photo of Murphy, sitting on the twenty-year-old avocado-green couch my mother refused to get rid of, holding me. A goofy expression on his face has me either laughing or screaming, it's hard to tell.

"He was so much more ginger back then," I joke.

Marcel snorts. "Yeah. Don't know what I would have done without him sometimes, you know? He used to help me steal formula when Mom forgot to leave money."

"Seriously?"

"Hell yeah. We were destined to be outlaws."

"Stealing baby formula?"

"That shit's expensive. Pretty badass for a ten-year-old."

"Figures she didn't even breastfeed me."

He pulls a disgusted face. "Trust me, it's a good thing. You would have been high as fuck if she did."

While we're joking about some pretty fucked-up stuff, it also hits me how young my brother and Murphy were. They've always been older, obviously. Big brothers I looked up to. But in reality, they were both children. "Why did you take care of me?"

"What do you mean?"

I shrug, not sure how to put it into words. "You were ten. You didn't have to do that stuff."

His face turns hard. "No one else was gonna do it."

"I know. Well, I get *you*, I was your sister. But why'd Murphy do it? I was nothing to him."

He stares at me as if he doesn't understand the words hanging in the air between us. "We did everything together. I told him I had to take care of you." Marcel's shoulders lift. "He wanted to help." He stares at the pictures in my hands. "He loved you, too."

I don't know what to say, so I keep going through photos. Strangely, I actually recognize my mother. "Is that Helga?"

"Yup."

I study the photo, finding hints of my brother and me in her. My mother was actually a pretty woman and I say that to my brother.

"Yeah, too bad that's all she had going for her."

"What? Her looks?"

"Yeah. She didn't bother to finish high school. Made it hard to find a decent job. She moved from guy to guy."

"Grams always called her a slut and a whore. She used to say I'd end up just like her." Tears fill my eyes and I can't say anything else.

Marcel gently grips my chin and turns me to look at him. "Hey, you're *nothing* like her. And Grams was a bitch, but she was partially right. Mom hooked up with any guy she could for money or stuff they could give her. That's why she was never around."

"Where do you think she is now?"

"Hell?"

I roll my eyes. "I meant Mom."

"Who the fuck knows. She doesn't deserve to know either of us anyway."

I glance down at the photo again. "She was too pretty for such an ugly name."

He snorts at my observation. "Yeah, and you always complained about Heidi. It would have been so much worse if Grams had her way."

"Why?"

"She wanted Mom to name you after her."

"Sue Ann?"

"No, her real name. Olga."

"Ew. Yuck. *She* hated it. Why'd she want to stick me with it?"

He shakes with laughter. "Tradition?"

"God, we come from a fucked-up family."

We spend most of the afternoon talking, reminiscing. I learn a lot of things I never knew about my mom *and* my big brother. I guess having a baby makes me an adult in his eyes, and he feels free to share all sorts of stories I've never heard before. I soak it up, loving every second.

"Hey," Axel says as he comes in. He lifts his chin at my brother. "How you doing?"

"Good. How was work?"

"Long." He glances at Alexa. "I hope she sleeps tonight."

"She slept last night."

"You were up every four hours with her."

"Yeah, she's a baby. The doctor said she needs to eat every four hours."

Marcel drills my husband with a stern stare that Axel either ignores or doesn't notice. Instead of saying something, my brother stands and kisses my forehead. "I have to go. Call if you need anything."

"Come here," I say to Axel. "I want to show you these."

I flip through the photos, skipping the ones of my mother and any picture with Murphy. "Oh shit. Is that you?" His gaze darts between the photo and our baby. "Shit, she looks just like you."

"I know. Freaky, right?"

He chuckles for the first time in days, and some of the tension seems to ease from him. "If she ends up being half as pretty as you, we're totally fucked."

"I know, right? I'll kill her if she gets knocked up at eighteen."

He leans over and presses a soft kiss on my cheek. "Amen to that."

Thirty

AXEL

It's been almost two weeks at the clubhouse, and Heidi shows no signs of moving back to our apartment. She's loving the attention of having everyone visiting our room constantly. The guys all want to see the baby. Hope and Trinity fuss over Heidi and Alexa, which is nice, but it's also getting old.

We have zero privacy.

I hate knowing Murphy's only a few doors away from us. Even though he's been civil to me, I'm on edge from being in such close proximity to the guy who basically kicked me out of the very clubhouse I'm now living in.

Awkward doesn't even begin to describe it.

"Babe, we're going on week two. Don't you think it's time we think about going home?"

Heidi pushes her bottom lip out, and even though I used to think it was cute, tonight it annoys me.

"This was only supposed to be temporary," I remind her.

"Okay. Give it another week and then, yeah, it will be good to be close to campus again. I need to talk to my adviser about getting back in next semester."

"How are you planning to do that?"

She gives me a blank look.

"Who's going to watch the baby?"

"We'll have to figure something out. I'm finishing my degree."

"Okay. Whatever you think is best."

I'm stretched out on the bed and Alexa's napping on my chest. She's so tiny, I barely feel the weight of her, but every now and then, she twitches or kicks and I rub my hand over her back.

"What do you think she's dreaming about?" I ask Heidi.

Her lips curve into a soft smile. "I don't know. My psychology professor once told us that considering babies' limited experiences, they probably don't dream for the first few years of life."

I make an interested *hmm* noise. This is what made me fall for Heidi in the first place. The interesting pieces of information she keeps stored in her head. The way she's so inquisitive. I don't know much outside of machines and how to fix them. Heidi knows something about everything.

"Come here," I ask, holding out my hand.

She approaches slowly and entwines her fingers with mine. After a few seconds, she drops down next to me on the bed. "How are you?" I ask.

She seems surprised and I feel like a real shit. I've been so wrapped up in working as much overtime as I can and adjusting to this life I didn't plan for that I've been short with her a lot lately.

"I'm tired, Axel. All the time."

I run the back of my hand over her cheek. "Lie down with me."

She curls up next to me, resting her head on my shoulder so she can see the baby. "I'm sorry I've been working so much," I say. I've been meaning to tell her that for a while now.

"I understand. I do appreciate it, you know."

"I know you do. You know I love you, right?" The way she hesitates hurts. I hate that I've made her question how I feel about her.

"Yeah."

I squeeze her a little closer, resting my hand on her hip. "Get some rest, baby."

"I love you, too," she whispers before she falls asleep.

Heidi

At her two-week check-up, the doctor seems surprised Alexa's doing so well. I'm not insulted, I'm surprised myself, since I feel like I'm screwing up all the damn time.

It's a beautiful day and it feels good to be out of the house. Axel's at work, so after the doctor, I decide to stop in and visit him.

"Hey, what're you doing here?" he asks as he jogs over to my car. "Did everything go okay at the doctor?"

He pulls me in for a quick hug as I step out of the car. "Yup. She gained a whole pound."

"Is that good or bad?"

I chuckle and stop myself from pointing out that he didn't read any of the baby stuff I asked him to. "It's good."

"So, what's up?"

"I missed you."

He gives me another quick squeeze and leans over to whisper in my ear. "How are you feeling?"

"Not that good. Four more weeks, bud."

He throws his head back and laughs. "Am I that obvious?"

"Yes."

"Lucas and Penny wanted us to come over tonight. They want to see the baby. You up for it?"

"Sure. I'll stop by the apartment now actually. Check on things. See if they want us to bring something."

"Thanks." He glances up and nods at someone. "I have to go back."

"I know. Sorry."

I watch him jog back into the garage, and some of the heaviness in my chest eases away.

"We're leaving for Alaska Monday," Lucas announces after dinner.

Penny and I ended up making hamburgers that the guys grilled outside on the patio.

"What?" I ask, although I seem to be the only one surprised by
this information. "Since when?"

"Since my uncle got me a job. There's one waiting for Axel, too,
if he wants it."

By the look on my husband's face, this isn't new information to
him. He slides his gaze away from me. "I was going to talk to you
about it."

"What's to talk about? There's no way we can do that."

"They have babies in Alaska, Heidi," Axel says almost under his
breath.

I ignore it and we have a fun night hanging out with our friends.

Too tired to drive to the clubhouse, we crash in our apartment.

Axel's wide awake and waiting for me in the morning.

"How can you shut me down on Alaska without even discussing
it?" he asks as I stumble into the kitchen.

"What?"

"The job. In Alaska. You didn't even consider it. Didn't bother
asking me about the salary. Just *no*. Since when do *you* make the decisions for both of us?"

"Uh…" It takes me a second to shake myself awake and into this
conversation. "One of us needs to act like a responsible parent. You
have a good job here. Our families are here."

"My parents don't give a shit about us. They haven't had any interest in meeting Alexa or being part of her life."

"Yeah, but mine does. I don't know what I would have done without them the last two weeks, and now you want to yank us away from
all of that?"

"It's only for a year."

"What if they offer you another year? Or a promotion? What
then?"

The corners of his mouth turn up slightly. "I'm glad you think
so highly of my skills. I haven't even taken the job and you're talking

promotions."

"You know I think you're good at what you do."

"Come here."

I cross my arms over my chest and stay planted right where I am.

He stands and takes a few steps in my direction. "What if we love it up there? What if it turns out to be really good for *our* family?"

"I want to finish my degree. I don't have—"

"UAA has a Radiologic Technology program."

"How do you know?"

"Because I looked it up," he says in a matter-of-fact way that makes me suspicious.

"Wait a minute. How long have you known about this job offer?"

"Couple weeks."

"A couple *weeks*?"

"Will you at least consider it?"

I uncross my arms and allow him to pull me into his embrace. "Fine. Convince me," I mumble against his sweater.

Thirty-One

AXEL

"Like fuck are you moving my sister and my baby niece to Alaska. Are you out of your fucking mind?"

I knew Heidi's brother wouldn't take this well. Bringing this up first thing this morning was probably a mistake. We've been back at the clubhouse for the last couple days and this is the first time it's been empty. Heidi's over at Hope and Rock's with the baby. So, I decided to seize the opportunity to get this out in the open.

"I'm telling you, it's a possibility. Not asking for your permission, Marcel."

"Good, 'cause you ain't gettin' it. I'm the only family—"

"They are *my* family. I'm doing what's best for *my* family."

"You think it's best to take Heidi away from anyone and everyone in her life? Who's gonna help her with the baby when you're off for weeks at a time?"

"Our friends are up there, too."

"Who? Penny? That skank won't lift a finger to help Heidi if she needs it."

"You're more than welcome to join us."

"Fuck you. You know I can't leave—"

"The club. Yeah, I know all about it. Maybe if you'd bothered to choose your sister over the club just once in your life, I'd have more sympathy."

"What the fuck are you talking about?"

"You're a selfish asshole." I'm too furious to slow down now. "You were too busy whoring around and playing outlaw to see what was happening to Heidi."

He takes another step into my space. "Watch your mouth, and remember where you're standing." The threat in his voice sends a shiver of fear through me, but I don't back away. "The club helped me take care of Heidi. How the fuck else was a sixteen-year-old kid supposed to earn enough money? Please enlighten me, Mr. Silver Spoon."

"She would have been better off in foster care than with that witch."

"What's going on?" Murphy calls out from the staircase. Of course he has to be here to stick his nose where it doesn't belong. My blood boils as he lazily walks up behind Marcel.

"None of your fucking business, Murphy. This concerns *my wife* and me."

Murphy raises an eyebrow and slides his gaze to Teller, but otherwise shows no reaction. I hate how intertwined the two of them are. No matter what, they always have each other's backs, even when one of them acts like an asshole. I can't wait to cut them out of our lives.

"I'm about two seconds from beating your arrogant ass, Axel. Explain," Marcel threatens.

I'm committed now. "Go ahead. Kick my ass. I'm sure that will make Heidi want to stay."

Murphy drills his stare into me, and I'm reminded that while he seems jovial and good-natured, he's also a violent prick when he thinks he has a reason to be. "Where's she going?"

"None of your fucking business," I spit out. Murphy reacts by widening his stance and hooking his thumbs in his pocket. Silently letting me know he's not going anywhere. *Asshole.*

"Axel here thinks he's moving my sister and niece to Alaska so he can take some job on an oil rig where Heidi will be left alone for weeks at a time."

Okay, when he puts it like that, it sounds bad.

"Is that what she wants?" Murphy asks quietly.

Murphy questioning my plans pisses me off so much I can't see or think straight. It's the only excuse I have for what I say next.

Ignoring Murphy, I jab my finger into Teller's chest, but he doesn't step back. "Where was all this big *brotherly* concern when your grandmother was taking a belt to Heidi's ass and all the other fucked-up shit she did to her?"

Both of them explode and I have a small measure of satisfaction at their surprise.

"What the fuck are you talking about?" Teller shouts. "Heidi—"

"Heidi was busy getting smacked around by your grandmother for every damn little thing she did wrong." I'm yelling so loud now, Heidi can probably hear me betraying her secrets all the way over at Hope and Rock's house.

Teller's jaw drops. "No. She would have said something."

"She was a kid. She had nowhere else to go."

"But—"

"You abandoned her to—"

"I didn't fucking abandon her! I saw her every week. She never said a thing."

"Axel! What's going on?" Great. She couldn't stay out a little longer? I turn to find Heidi holding Alexa with Hope and Rock right behind her. Fantastic.

Rock lifts his chin at us. "Everything okay?"

Teller glares at Rock, which surprises me. "No. Everything is *not* okay." He points to Heidi. "We need to have a talk, little sister."

"You told him?" Heidi gasps, staring at me with hurt eyes. Alexa bursts into tears.

Hope holds out her arms. "I'll take her, honey. Why don't you guys discuss this quietly somewhere else." She nods at the hallway that leads to the dining room.

"No. Please stay, Hope." Heidi asks without taking her eyes off me.

Murphy moves away from us. "I'll take her, Hope." As I watch him carry my daughter down the hall, the only thing I feel is relief that he's finally out of my business.

Heidi

My entire body shakes with fury. But, I don't want anyone to know how pissed I am at my husband. I don't want to hear any shit from my brother, or even worse, Murphy about how I got married too young. I'll die if I see one pitying look from Rock or Hope.

I made my bed and I'll lie in it if it fuckin' *kills* me. It's what's best for Alexa. Taking care of her, both parents loving and providing for her, are all that matter right now.

Even though at the moment, I want to smack my husband upside his head.

United front.

Flashing a tight smile, I curl my fingers around his and let Uncle Rock lead us into the war room. I'm shocked he's letting us use the sacred MC table for family business, but he ushers us inside and shuts the door. Rock and Marcel take what I assume are their regular seats.

Axel and I sit across from my brother. Hope hovers behind Rock's chair, unsure or unwilling to take a side. I kind of wanted her to be my moral support, since at the moment, I'd rather junk-punch my husband than lean on him.

Rock points at my brother. "What's going on?"

Marcel glares at Rock—his president—in a way I've never seen him do before. "You don't need to involve yourself in this, Rock."

Rock's eyes narrow. "I'm *not* getting involved. I'm here to make sure things stay civil." He nods at me. "For her sake. What I saw out there wasn't helping anyone."

Marcel relaxes a notch. His gaze skips right over Axel, landing on me. "Your husband informed me this morning that you're moving to Alaska."

Godfuckingdammit. I wasn't aware the decision had been made by *us*. And Axel went ahead and told my brother without talking to me? Under the table, I give his leg a sharp pinch, but he doesn't react at all.

"Then while we were discussing *that*"—he stops and clasps his hands together, swallowing hard—"he said something about how I abandoned you at Grams's and that she hurt you." He almost chokes on that part, and I want to run around the table and wrap my arms around him. I never, ever blamed my brother for what my grandmother did. My mother? Absolutely. She knew what would happen when she left me there.

Why Axel felt he had the right to talk about this with my brother is beyond me. I'm so angry, so frustrated, heat sears my skin and tears fill my eyes. "It's not your fault," I choke out.

"So it's true?" Marcel asks.

Warm arms gently wrap around my shoulders. Hope. She doesn't try to fill the silence with useless sympathetic words, just hugs me. When I don't think I'm in danger of crying any more, I tip my head back and thank her. She pulls out the chair next to me and sits.

"What did she do to you?" Marcel asks.

I shoot a glare at my husband before answering. "It doesn't matter. She's gone. I'm fine and have bigger things to worry about now."

"Why Alaska?" Rock asks.

Axel squirms in his seat. "I got offered a good job on an oil rig—"

"In *Alaska*," Marcel growls.

"Simmer down," Rock says without looking at my brother. "Cain told me he was keeping you on permanently."

Yes, my idiot husband already has a damn good job. A job that Rock went out of his way to help Axel land. So what my husband's doing feels a lot like spitting in my family's face.

"He did offer. But this job will pay almost double what I make there and the benefits are really good. We can use the extra money with the baby and all. It's only for a year."

"Yeah, and who's going to help my sister with the baby when

you're out at sea for weeks at a time?" my brother asks. "How is she supposed to finish school in *Alaska*?"

Axel shrugs and the urge to smack him returns. "She can take online classes."

"Bullshit," my brother snarls. "She can't take her clinicals from fucking Alaska. She can't finish her program in Alaska and get certified by New York State."

"She can transfer her credits up there."

This is partially true. At least for the basics that I've completed so far: English, Psychology, Anatomy and Physiology, and History. But most likely, my Radiographic Positioning, Radiographic Physics, and the two clinicals I've already taken won't transfer.

Axel knows this because we discussed it at length after I spoke to my adviser. This is the main reason I thought we had *not* made a decision on Alaska yet.

Marcel looks at me with a *please-be-reasonable* expression, and it almost makes me want to cave. My brother's right. I'm furious with my husband right now, but I don't know what to do.

"I'll figure it out. Or I'll just finish up my last year when we get back from Alaska. We're only going for a year."

"This is what you really want, Heidi?"

"It's what's best for my family."

He throws his hands up in the air. Defeated. I hate myself for lying to my brother, yet again, but I don't know what else to do.

My brother storms out of the war room and a few seconds later the front door slams shut. I choke down my anger, paste on a smile, and thank Rock for playing mediator.

Axel leans over and gives me a kiss. "See you upstairs?" The smile he's wearing borders on smug, and I want to smack it off his face.

After he leaves, Hope takes my hand. "Are you sure you're all right? You don't have to leave right away. You could maybe let Axel go up first, scout out an apartment. You can stay here."

"We have a guest room, Heidi, if you and the baby would be more comfortable at our house," Rock offers.

"No. I—uh, I'll be fine. Alexa should be where her dad is."

Hope's face screws into a scowl, but before she can say anything else, I slip my hand from hers. "Thank you both, for calming my brother down."

I leave before they say anything else and run into Murphy in the living room. Alexa shrieks when she sees me and he holds her out. "She's been looking for you, Mom," he says as he hands her over.

"Thank you for watching her."

"No problem." His words are light, but when I look in his moss-green eyes, they're empty and sad. "Are you really moving to Alaska?" he asks quietly.

"I don't know for sure."

"You husband seems pretty sure."

I don't have an answer, so I stare down at Alexa. Murphy stands and brushes his hand over Alexa's head. "I'll miss you if you go."

I'm not sure if he's speaking to me or the baby. But it's all he says before he walks away.

Sighing, I trudge upstairs.

For the first time, I agree with my husband about the lack of privacy at the clubhouse, because I want to go into our room, close the door, and yell at him.

Instead, after setting Alexa in her crib, I drop down on the bed and stare at him. "How could you?"

Axel's mouth twists into something a little too close to a smirk for my liking. "He had a right to know the truth."

"Bullshit. You just wanted to hurt him and make him feel like shit."

"He *should* feel like shit over what happened to you," he says, not bothering to deny my accusation.

"It wasn't his fault." If I'd known Axel would react this way, I never would have told him all my secrets. "Besides, that's not even what I'm upset about. We hadn't decided on Alaska yet. Why are you acting like we did?"

"They upped the offer this morning." He walks over and sits next to me, taking my hands in his. "They want me bad, Heidi. They're willing to help us with some of the relocation expenses. This is a really big opportunity for me."

"But—"

"You're not ready to go back to school. You told me yourself, you hate leaving Alexa with anyone. Who's going to watch her when you're in class? Take the year off and re-enroll when we get back."

"You still should have talked to me first."

"I'm sorry. I was going to. I swear it, but it came up—"

I snort out a humorless sound, feeling like I've already lost this battle. "How exactly did Alaska come up in conversation with my brother?"

He waves the question away. "Come on. It'll be fun. For as long as I've known you, you've wanted to travel and see different places."

"Yeah, I wanted to *visit* Alaska. Not live there permanently."

"So think of it as a year's vacation."

Not that I feel like I have much choice, but I drop my resistance. Axel makes the move easy for me. He or his new employer arranges everything.

All I have to do is decide which stuff to bring with me and which stuff to leave behind.

"Hope, can I leave some boxes here?" I ask one afternoon as I'm going through my things.

"Of course you can, honey. Leave them on the shelf there, or if it's clothes, store them in the closet."

"Yeah, I doubt I'll need shorts or sundresses up there," I mumble, glancing down at my favorite pair of lavender shorts. "Not that I can fit back into these, anyway."

Hope chuckles. "Heidi, you're beautiful."

I stop and glance down. "I'm okay with the bigger boobs. The bigger hips, not so much."

Hope chuckles and from the doorway, someone clears their throat.

"Hey, Murphy," Hope calls out. She waves him in and he stands inside the doorway looking uncertain.

"Need any help?"

"No. I think—well, maybe." I point to a stack of boxes in the middle of the floor. "That stuff I want to ship up there."

Hope checks her phone and stands. "I need to run back to my house for something." Her gaze darts between Murphy and me as if she's asking me if we'll be okay.

"Thanks for your help."

Murphy watches her go then turns to me. "So you're really doing this?"

"Looks like it."

He glances at Alexa. "Can she even fly at this age?"

"Doctor said it was okay. Axel found a new doctor up there, so at least I'm all set with that."

"That's good." By the sound of his voice, none of this is good as far as he's concerned. After a bit of silence, he tips his head up and focuses on me. "I hate that you're going so far away."

"Me too. But it's just a year."

"Is this really what you want, Heidi?"

"No." Might as well be honest. I'm sick of lying to the people I care about all the time. "I'm trying to make the best of it. Who knows, maybe I'll finally get to check out the Pan-American Highway."

His head snaps back as if I'd sucker-punched him.

"It's okay, Murphy. I'm excited, too. You know I've always wanted to see new places."

"I—Yeah, okay." He stares at me for a few more seconds, then taps one of the boxes with the side of his boot. "Where you want to ship these from? FedEx?"

It's good that he moved to a more practical topic of conversation, because inside, I'm slowly unraveling. "I don't know. Axel said there's a freight service company in Seattle we can ship them to, and they'll send it up from there? But I don't think it's enough stuff to do that."

"I'll figure it out for you."

"Thanks. I'm going to have to buy so much crap when we get there."

"Sounds like it."

"Hey," Axel says as he comes in the room. He sends a sharp look Murphy's way before wrapping an arm around my waist. "What's going on?"

"Nothing. Murphy was going to help me ship those boxes—"

Axel shoots a glare at Murphy. "I got it covered."

Murphy's eyes narrow and I catch his hand flexing into a fist, then opening again. "Sounds good. I'll catch you two later."

"Why was he in here?" Axel asks as soon as the door shuts behind Murphy.

"I told you why. Hope was here, too, but she had to go."

"Oh, she was here?"

"Yes."

That seems to calm him down. "Come on, let's go down for dinner."

Reluctantly, he follows behind me.

Since we announced our move, every meal we've shared in the dining room has been awkward. My brother's anger seems to be simmering below the surface. Part of me misses being sheltered by my big brother and wants him to make this all go away. The rest of me says, *You're an adult, suck it the fuck up and do what's right for your family.*

I can't stop wondering, *is* taking my daughter away from my bigger, extended family the right thing to do?

The club has welcomed Alexa with open hearts, and I hate taking her away from family.

"What are you planning to do with your car?" Murphy asks, jerking me out of my thoughts.

"I—uh, haven't thought about it."

"Sell it," Axel says.

I barely manage not to glare at him. "I don't *want* to sell it."

"You can garage it here. I'll make sure it gets taken care of," Murphy assures me with a confident smile. "It'll be all ready for you when you get back."

My heart thumps at his offer. After, well...everything, he's still my friend.

"You found new prospects?" Axel asks without lifting his gaze from his plate. It's the first time anyone has remotely come close to mentioning Axel's time as a prospect.

Murphy's jaw ticks. He glances at me and back at my husband. "Nah, I got this. What are you doing with your Indian?"

That catches Axel's attention and he lifts his head. "I put an ad in the Digest for it."

"You can't sell your bike," I say and Axel shrugs.

"I'll buy it," Murphy offers.

Axel glares back. "We don't need your charity."

"It's not charity," Murphy answers calmly. "I like the bike. You don't see many of them around. You did good work on it. You want to buy it back when you guys return, I promise not to gouge you too hard."

My brother laughs and slaps Murphy's arm. "Get in line. If he's selling it, I want a crack at it."

The guys go on like that until they work something out. I think Axel's actually relieved he found a home that he trusts for his bike. Or maybe that's my wishful thinking.

After dinner, Marcel steers me into the kitchen and out the back door.

"You're not planning to yell at me are you?" I ask.

He shakes his head and I hate how defeated he seems. "Marcel, everything's going to be fine. This year will go by fast."

"Yeah, exactly my problem. Alexa will probably be walking by then."

Please, please, please, don't do this to me, Marcel. Inside I'm crying because I've thought the same thing over and over. "I'll come home and visit."

"Yeah, listen." He pulls an envelope out of his pocket and hands it over. "This is for *you*. I don't want you trapped up there. Or dependent on *him* for everything. There's more than enough money here to get you and the baby home." I open it and find a debit card and a statement showing it's linked to an account with a hefty amount of money already in it."

"It's in both our names, so it's easier for me to make deposits," he explains.

"Marcel—"

"I'm serious, Heidi. I hate you being so far away. Something ever happened, it'd take me for-fucking-ever to get to you."

"Thank you." I fold the envelope up and shove it in my pocket.

"If you need anything at all—I don't give a shit what it is—you tell me. It's not just you anymore. You have a baby now, and I don't want you afraid to ask for something because you're embarrassed or anything."

"I won't, I promise," I whisper.

"You can also call me if I need to come up there and kick his ass."

I snort, knowing he'd love any excuse to kick Axel's ass. "Thank you so much for everything. You're—" I can't finish because I'm sobbing so hard. I want to tell him how sorry I am for making a mess of my life when he tried so hard to give me everything I needed to succeed.

"Please don't cry, sis." His raw voice makes me cry even harder. "I won't be able to let you go if you cry," he says, gathering me in his arms.

I squeeze him back and almost beg him *not* to let me go. I can't imagine being away from my brother for a year. "You've always been the best brother a girl could have."

Thirty-Two

Stop Signs and Red Lights

Heidi

"You can't whip your boob out for the whole flight," Axel says low enough that no one should overhear him. It's still annoying, though.

"She's a baby. The sucking will help with the pressure changes."

"Oh."

"And my boob isn't out."

"I'm just jealous."

"I think you're *nervous*," I tease.

"Probably. I've never been on this long a flight."

"Well, I've never flown at all, so I'm freaking terrified."

He chuckles and slides his hand over my leg. After a few minutes, he leans over. "Is she okay?"

"So far so good."

Lucas and Penny meet us at the airport and we follow them to our new apartment building. They'd done some of the legwork finding a place for us that happens to be right next door to them.

"Just like home," Lucas jokes.

It's actually a nice place. Bigger than our apartment back home. I'm trying to keep an open mind about everything.

About a week later, we're barely settled into the new place when Axel has to leave for his first shift.

"Drive me out to the office, so you can have the truck while I'm gone." We'd spent a fortune shipping Axel's truck up here so we at least had one vehicle.

We meet Lucas and Penny in the hallway. Lucas is pumped up for the trip. "You're going to love it, Axel. Long hours but, well, you'll see."

We end up following Lucas's truck. "Are you nervous?" I ask.

"A little."

"Promise you'll be careful?"

"Promise." He leans over and kisses my cheek. He turns and pinches Alexa's toes, making her kick and let out a bunch of happy baby sounds.

"Shit. This is harder than I thought."

I'm not sure what to say to that. It never occurred to him he might miss his family?

After the guys take off, Penny runs over, jumping up and down. "We're going to have so much fun while the boys are away."

I let out a humorless snort. "Doing what?"

"There's this awesome club that—"

"Penny, I have a baby. I can't go clubbing."

She glances inside the truck at Alexa. "Oh, yeah. Well, we'll find you a sitter or something."

Yeah, no thanks.

Later that night, I discover what Penny means by having "fun."

Our living room wall is on the other side of their bedroom wall. And since Lucas is away with my husband on an oil rig, I don't know who's helping her bang the headboard into the wall, but it goes on for so long, I have to go to bed to get away from the noise.

The next morning, she doesn't say anything. I'm not sure what to say either, so I don't.

During this time of year here, there's maybe six hours of daylight.

It's freezing. People keep telling me it's not that much colder than up-state New York is in the winter. But those twenty-five to fifty degree differences are a lot.

The worst though? The short days. Alexa and I barely leave the apartment. Since one of the reasons Axel dragged us up here is the high-paying job, it's unfortunate he didn't take into account the high-er cost of living. Or the probationary period where he's earning a lot less than we budgeted for. I run through our money pretty fast each month just paying our rent, buying groceries, and diapers.

And that's our routine for the next few months. Axel's out on the oil rig for two weeks and home for one. Without Alexa, I doubt I'd bother to crawl out of bed most days.

By month three, I'm ready to snap. Underneath it all, I'm angry with myself for letting Axel talk me into moving here.

My life feels like the hardest road I've ever traveled, and there doesn't seem to be a beautiful destination in sight.

MURPHY

I'm not sure why I'm in Rock and Hope's old room or what I'm look-ing for. I just know that since Hope casually mentioned Heidi stored a bunch of stuff in there before she left for Alaska, I've been curious.

Four large cardboard boxes take up two of the bookshelves in the corner. One with a tiny heart with a *B* in the middle catches my attention, so that's where I start. There's no other writing indicating what's in it.

Inside, I find two smaller boxes. One's plain. The other is cov-ered in drawings and doodled words. I recognize Heidi's handwriting right away and a soft chuckle eases out of me. That laughter turns to surprise when I pull the lid off and find the box stuffed with things I'd given Heidi over the years. Her animal figurines are all neatly wrapped in bits of cloth. But that's not what yanks the air out of my lungs. It's all the *other* little things. Postcards I'd sent her, stubs from movies I'd taken her to, seashells I brought back for her after my first run to Florida. The little notes I used to stick in her lunch bags, birthday cards, all these small personal things she's kept forever. There are also nuts, bolts, and screws I assume she swiped from the garage for reasons only Heidi knows.

At the bottom are a bunch of photographs. I can't even look at them right now or I'll lose it.

I should stop. These are her personal things. She'd be furious if she knew I was poking through them. As I'm about to put everything back, a small notebook catches my attention.

Childish handwriting. Then more mature, neat, cursive writing spells out dozens of different variations of "Mrs. Blake O'Callaghan," "Heidi O'Callaghan," and "Heidi Whelan-O'Callaghan" all over the outside cover. More signatures are scrawled over the inside cover. "Mrs. Murphy O'Callaghan" surrounded by a bunch of doodled shamrocks is probably my favorite.

It's the sweetest, most painful thing I've ever seen, because now she's Mrs. Ryan.

I consider going up to Alaska and dragging her home. But I'm not sure what that will accomplish.

I know she *thinks* she's doing the right thing for her daughter.

I still miss her as much as the day she left. Although having her here with *him* hurt, at least I was able to see her every day.

The clubhouse feels empty without Alexa's four a.m. squeals. And there's no glimpse of Heidi's shiny brown ponytail when I hit the dining room in the morning.

I've been such a moody prick, everyone pretty much steers clear of me.

Everyone except Marcel, who can't seem to let me suffer in peace.

On my way out of Hope's room, he stops me. "What're you doing?"

"Nothing. Checking on some stuff."

He levels one of his challenging looks at me. "Come on, Blake. I know—I understand how you feel about—"

"I don't want to talk about it," I snap, cutting him off and then completely contradicting myself when I ask, "Have you heard from her?"

"Yeah, she texts me every day."

"Is she okay?"

"I guess. Hard to tell, you know?"

I grunt and try to sidestep him, but he blocks my path.

"Come out for a ride with us."

"No, thanks. It's forty-five fucking degrees out."

"Yeah, but the roads are clear. Come on. I'm taking Mariella out on the bike."

"Really? She wants to go?"

"She asked."

That cheers me up a bit. Mariella's sweet and she's been a big help around the clubhouse, but she's also terrified to ever leave the property. Marcel's been trying to coax her into a ride for a while now.

"You guys have fun. Be careful with her."

"You know it." He gives me a slap on the shoulder and heads downstairs.

A few hours later, I regret not going with them.

Thirty-Three

Some roads can't be found without getting lost.

Heidi

My phone vibrating across the nightstand wakes me up. "Who the fuck is calling at six in the morning?" I grumble as I roll over and grab my phone.

Hope.

"Hi, Hope."

"Heidi?" Her anxious voice pushes the last bits of sleepiness from my system, and I bolt upright.

"What's wrong?"

"Honey, there was an accident—"

"Who? Is Marcel okay—"

"He's in the hospital." She's sobbing so much I can't make out her words.

"Hope?"

"Mariella didn't…it's bad, Heidi. He woke up a little while ago and asked for you."

"Hope, what happened?"

"He was on his bike."

Please tell me Murphy's okay. "Was he alone?"

"No. Mariella was with him."

"Is she okay?"

"No, Heidi. She's not."

"Oh my God," I whisper. "Marcel?"

"They're administering steroids now and then they're sending him for a CT."

Spinal injury. "What about an MRI?"

"I don't know," she answers through sniffles. "He may have to go in for surgery."

"Give me a couple hours. I'll see if Axel can get off the ship. I'll call you when I have my flight information, okay?"

"I'll see you soon."

Sick, I race into the bathroom and wretch until tears stream down my cheeks. Mariella. My brother. What if he's paralyzed? Oh my God, what if—

Freak-outs and what-ifs will have to wait until I'm on the ten-hour flight home. I pull myself off the floor and dial Axel's cell phone. He's not supposed to have it on him when he's on shift, so I'm not surprised he doesn't answer.

It takes me a few minutes to find the number for the ship phone. Even then, I can't reach him.

"I'll give him the message, miss, and have him call you back."

"Please, it's a family emergency."

I'm a wreck waiting for him to call me back. I want to book my flight, but I'm not sure how long it will take Axel to come home. Maybe I should book mine and Alexa's first?

Finally, he calls me back.

"Heidi? What's wrong? Is Alexa okay?"

"Yes, she's fine. My brother was in an accident. It's bad."

"Oh, shit. I'm so sorry, baby. Was he by himself?"

I choke on a sob and have to repeat myself a couple times before I force the words out. "No. Mariella. Mariella was with him."

"She okay?"

"I don't think so. Hope wasn't very clear. I'll find out more when I get there."

"You're going home?"

"Yes! I have to." How is it even a question?

"Why? He's got his club. He's got plenty of women willing to take care of him. He doesn't need you."

"Are you serious right now? Do you actually hear the words coming out of your mouth?" I practically scream into the phone. "He's my *brother*. He's in critical condition. If something happens and I don't get to see him—" The thought of it makes me choke on a sob.

"Calm down. Wait until I get back and I'll go with you. I don't want you and the baby traveling alone."

Why not? We're alone all the time anyway. "Can you come home now?" I ask, trying to compose myself.

"No. I'll be home at the end of the week."

Fuck. That. "Axel, I can't wait. I won't. When you're done with your shift, fly down and meet us."

His groan travels through loud and clear. "We don't have the money for all these flights back and forth to New York, Heidi."

No, *we* don't. "I have money from my brother. I'll use that for our tickets and I'll move some into our joint account so you can buy your ticket."

Axel doesn't respond. The silence goes on for so long, I'm afraid he hung up on me.

"Yeah, okay," he finally answers.

I make the travel arrangements and actually manage to find a flight out tonight. My next call is to Hope, who promises to pick me up at the airport.

"How is he?"

"No change."

"Is he breathing on his own?"

"Yes."

"Okay. That's good." My mind's spinning with the possibilities. My limited medical knowledge isn't helping. Not surprising since I'm flying through the apartment packing random things. I can't think straight.

"I'll text you when I get to the airport."

"Okay, I can't wait to see the three of you."

"Uh, it's just me, Hope. Axel can't get away for another week."

She falters. "Oh, sure. Will you be all right traveling alone with the baby?"

"I'll have to be." It's pretty much me and Alexa on our own. Even when Axel's home, he doesn't seem to know what to do with her. I don't say any of that to Hope.

Next, I stop at Penny's. She's more than happy to give us a ride to the airport and sends me off with a big hug.

I'm a wreck the whole flight, praying I get there in time.

"Murphy? Where's Hope?"

First his eyes widen, then his forehead wrinkles as he takes me in. I didn't exactly dress up for the ten-hour flight, so I'm sure I look like hell. Great.

Alexa thankfully slept for most of the flight, but she's been cranky since she woke up. She lets loose with a howl as soon as I stop the stroller.

Murphy immediately picks her up, rocking and talking to her. "Oh, shit. She's gotten so big, Heidi."

He's so sweet with her, so excited to see her, that I feel awful. My daughter should be growing up around family, not up in Alaska where we have no ties to anyone.

After a few minutes, she seems to remember him and pulls on his beard. "Good grip, kid." He laughs and makes a silly face, which encourages her to smack him a few times.

"How's Marcel?" I ask.

His eyes meet mine, but they're unreadable. "Stable. I'll tell you more on the way. It's hard to explain."

I don't know what to make of that. But he's stable, so I'm able to relax a notch.

"Come here, kid," he says, giving me a brief, one-armed hug.

"How are you?"

"Anxious."

"Let's go." Murphy holds my baby with one arm and pushes the stroller ahead with the other, all while talking all sorts of baby nonsense to her. I enjoy having my arms free for the first time in what feels like forever.

At the luggage carousel, we stop and Murphy tucks Alexa back into the stroller.

There's no luggage yet and I'm not sure what to say to him.

Murphy's fingers skim over the ends of my hair. "Your hair's gotten so long."

I shrug, a little self-conscious about how sloppy I probably look. "I haven't had time to get it cut or anything." No time. No money. No will. No one cares about their appearance in Alaska. Hell, it's dark most of the time.

"It's nice," he says before looking away.

I don't have to point my bag out to him. He spots the hulking red suitcase and effortlessly snags it off the carousel.

"I can push her," I offer, reaching for the stroller.

"Okay. Give me this, though," he says, slipping my carry-on, bursting with baby gear, off my shoulder.

I'm too tired to argue, so Alexa and I follow him out to his truck.

MURPHY

"So, why are you here instead of Hope?" Heidi asks when we're settled in the truck.

"She had to go down to the hospital."

Heidi's terrified face almost makes me feel bad for lying to her. "Is Marcel okay?"

"Yeah. He'll be happy to see you two. Every time he's woken up, he's asked about you."

The truth is, when Hope let it slip she was picking Heidi and Alexa up at the airport, I begged her to let me do it instead.

Beg is probably exaggerating. Hope didn't need a whole lot of convincing.

I didn't ask why Axel let her and the baby fly alone. Honestly, I'm not all that surprised.

No, I won't be an asshole and do something inappropriate. I get that she's married now, even if I think her husband is a piece of shit for letting her travel by herself at a time like this. But after what happened, after my best friend almost *died*, after Mariella did die, I *need* to see Heidi. I need to be near her for a few fucking seconds. Reassure myself she's okay.

Even though there were times in our lives where I tried to keep some distance between us, these last three months, having her so far away, have hurt in ways I never imagined.

"So, he's awake?"

"In and out."

"What's going on? Hope said they were giving him steroids?"

"I don't understand all the medical jargon, but he's lost feeling from his lower back down. There's fluid or something?"

"Spinal shock?"

"I think so. They gave him steroids for the first twenty-four hours."

"Jesus, that can have some nasty side-effects."

"I know. They explained."

"What happened?"

I grip the steering wheel so hard, I'm afraid I'll snap it off. "He took Mariella out. He asked me to go with them. I should have gone."

Her hand settles on my leg, trying to reassure me. "It's not your fault." Somehow her words only make me feel worse.

I choose my words carefully. "It looks like someone might have run him off the road."

"Do you know who?"

"No." My jaw tightens from the lie. Marcel was adamant that it was Killa, the enforcer for the Vipers MC, a rival club we have a long and bloody history with. But that's club business I can't share with Heidi. Nor should I.

"Don't lie to me, Murphy. Is it another MC? Did something happen?"

Of course, Heidi's not stupid. "Heidi—"

"Don't give me *club business* bullshit today, Murphy! Did someone try to kill my brother?"

"Maybe."

"Mariella?"

Christ. Poor Mariella. That sweet girl lived through fucking hell only to be rescued by us and then killed a few months later anyway. "She didn't make it. We haven't told him yet."

A frightened silence fills the inside of the truck. "Jesus Christ, Murphy. I'm fucking scared to be here now."

I slow down and catch the next red light, so I can face Heidi. "Look at me. You're safe. I won't let anyone hurt you or Alexa. I promise."

"Yeah, I'm sure my brother told Mariella the same thing."

I flinch at her words, because they're true.

"He's not in trouble, is he?"

"No. From what I understand it was pretty clear he was run off the road."

"Did they catch the person?"

"Not yet." Wrath and Z are hunting down Killa and Ransom, the Vipers' president, so they won't be on the loose for long. But again, not something I can share with Heidi.

"Mariella doesn't have any family," Heidi says.

"I know. We're taking care of everything."

"Is everyone else okay?"

"Yeah. They're all taking turns at the hospital. Hope's been there since we first found out. I actually need her to go home, so if you can help me with that later, I'd appreciate it."

She huffs out a laugh. "Sure. No one's probably told her it was club-related either, I bet."

"I don't know what Rock shares with her. Not my business. Right now, she's just worried about your brother."

"The light's green," she says softly.

The hospital waiting room is full of Lost Kings who are here both for support for their injured brother and for protection. Hope and Trinity are both here, and there's no way they're going anywhere without escorts.

Hope rushes over when she sees us. She grabs Heidi, pulling her into a hug. "He's okay. The doctor's reviewing his CT now."

"Can we see him?"

"I'll ask."

Thirty-Four

No road can take us back to the way we were.

Heidi

Don't cry. Don't cry.

Oh, but it's a struggle to see my big brother so…banged up and not burst into tears.

Murphy's standing behind me quietly, offering support by holding Alexa for me while I speak to my brother.

"Marcel?"

They have him immobilized in a rigid brace, but the fact that he's breathing on his own gives me a small sliver of relief.

"Hey," he says, his voice a shadow of what I'm used to. He lifts his hand to motion me closer.

"Don't move," I warn him and he huffs out a brief laugh.

"When'd you get here?"

"Just now."

His eyes close and he seems to slip back into sleep. Murphy's hand rests on my shoulder. "He's been in and out."

"Is there a doctor around?"

Murphy takes me into the hallway where one of the doctors treating my brother stops to talk to me.

"We won't know the severity of the damage for a few days. Methylprednisolone was administered within a few hours of the trauma, but there's still some inflammation at the base of the spine. As far as we can tell, he landed on something hard that caused some trauma. We stabilized the spine to prevent any additional damage, but the swelling hasn't gone down as much as we'd like."

"Will he be able to walk?"

"I can't say this early. Right now, we need to keep him calm and as immobile as possible. We may schedule surgery to go in and remove any debris that could be causing the swelling."

The doctor walks in to check on Marcel, and I turn to Murphy. "What are we going to do? What's he going to do? Oh my God."

His free arm wraps around my shoulder and he pulls me up against him. "Shh. Your brother's a tough son of a bitch. He's gonna be fine."

"I know," I mumble, but I can't stop myself from clinging to his shirt and weeping all over him.

My crying makes Alexa cry so I gather her in my arms, rocking her back and forth until we both calm down.

"Hey, Heidi-girl," Rock calls out, entering the room with Hope. He gives me a kiss on the cheek. "You must be tired."

"I'm not leaving."

The corner of Rock's mouth quirks up, and he slides his gaze to Murphy. "Heidi, it's late. They're not going to let you stay in his room overnight."

Hope settles her arm around my shoulder. "He's stable now. I've got a room at our house all set up for you and the baby."

"You do?" I end up crying again.

Somehow, they talk me into leaving with them. Murphy stays behind at the hospital and some of the guilt for leaving my brother lessens.

I'm so exhausted, I barely notice the room Hope set up for us. After taking care of Alexa, I fall into a sleep full of dreams where I'm falling and burning at the same time.

The next morning, I wake completely disoriented. My phone rings at the same time Alexa starts screaming.

"Heidi?" Axel's voice sounds so distant.

"I'm here. Alexa just woke up and I'm trying to calm her down."

"How'd she do on the flight?"

"Okay."

"How's your brother?"

"Bad. It's really bad, Axel."

"Shit. I'm so sorry, baby."

"Thanks. I'm headed back there in a bit."

"Where'd you stay?"

"Rock and Hope set up a room for us at their place."

"Oh. That was nice of them." I can hear the relief in his voice that I didn't sleep under the same roof as Murphy.

We talk a little longer. He doesn't mention coming down on his week off, and I don't bring it up.

I'm too tired to fight about it or to have my feelings hurt when he says he's not coming.

Hope and Rock are in the kitchen talking softly at the counter when Alexa and I join them.

"Sleep okay, hon?" Rock asks.

"Like the dead." I cringe at my choice of words but neither of them say anything.

I don't have much of an appetite, but Rock goes to the trouble of making breakfast, so I choke down some eggs and toast. As we're finishing up, someone knocks on the door. Rock shouts for them to come in.

"You don't have to knock, Murphy," Rock says.

"Yes, you do," Hope corrects.

Murphy chuckles and ambles over, dropping into an empty chair across from me. Exhaustion is etched in every line on his face.

"How's Marcel?" I ask.

"No change really. The doctor wants to do an MRI today."

"Why haven't they done it already?" I ask and he shrugs.

Murphy's gaze slides to Rock, and he jerks his head at the back porch. They get up and leave the table while Hope shakes her head. "Your brother's tough, honey. He'll get through this."

"It was hard seeing him like that."

"I know. I still don't know how we're going to tell him about Mariella. I'm not sure what their…relationship was, but they spent a lot of time together."

"He'll take it hard. He was driving, he'll blame himself. It won't matter that someone ran him off the road."

Hope gives me a curious look, and I wonder if no one told her the part about Marcel being run off the road.

"I need to make some arrangements for Mariella today. Do you want me to drop you off at the hospital?" she asks.

"I got her, Hope," Murphy says as he and Rock step back inside.

"I'm with *you*, Baby Doll," Rock says, settling his hands on her shoulders. She tips her head back and he presses a kiss to her forehead. Their easy affection makes me feel lonely almost. I don't know how to describe it. Maybe I'm just tired.

Hope pins me with a motherly stare. "Are you sure you'll be okay?"

"Yes."

"I'll be at the hospital after I'm done."

Murphy taps my arm. "Let me know when you two are ready." By the sound of his voice and look on his face, he's planning to leave.

"I'm ready. Just let me grab some stuff for her."

He takes Alexa while I run down to my room and hastily throw together a bag.

There's an Alaska-sized lump in my throat when I return to the kitchen. Murphy's entertaining Alexa by playing drums on the table with his hands and a utensil or two. He's got her propped up in his lap showing her how to make different sounds with her fingers and hands. She can't quite grasp the fork he's using and ends up slapping it away. The fork spins across the table and she laughs.

Her first laugh.

Alexa's been cooing, gurgling, sighing, and making a variety of noises for weeks. This is her first laugh, well more of a sweet baby-chortle.

"Oh my God."

Murphy's head snaps up. "What? We're just playing drums." He seems worried that I think he did something wrong.

"That's her first laugh."

"Oh yeah?" He leans over and kisses her cheek. "You like drums, baby?"

She makes another giggling sound—she really seems to like hearing her own voice and seeing his reactions.

It makes me feel like a failure. I realize how miserable I am in Alaska. I haven't done a lot of fun, silly playing with her, something the doctor and the social worker in the hospital stressed was important for babies.

"Ready to go?" he asks, picking her up and grabbing my bag out of my hands.

I follow along over to the clubhouse. He's still got her car seat in the back of his truck. "You can move that over to my car if you don't want it in here," I offer. His brow wrinkles, but he doesn't say anything as he stands back to let me strap her in.

When I'm finished, I turn and face him. "You can't go driving around with a car seat, you'll scare the ladies away."

His face darkens. "Get in the truck," he says, his harsh tone leaves my mouth hanging open. I think I hurt his feelings. He jumps in the truck and slams the door.

"I was just kidding around," I mumble as I climb in and click my seatbelt.

We're quiet as we bounce down the driveway. Well, *we're* quiet. Alexa fusses a lot. I dig through my never-ending bag of baby stuff looking for her favorite squeaky polar bear.

"Shit."

"What's wrong?"

"Nothing. I have this special polar bear I let her play with when we're in the car. It seems to soothe her usually. But I think I left it home."

"I can turn around."

"No. Alaska home."

"Oh." He fiddles with the radio, finally finding something Alexa seems to like.

"Classic country? Really?" I tease.

His shoulders lift. "What? *You* liked it when you were a baby."

"I did not."

He lets out a gruff sound—somewhere between a grunt and a laugh. "Yeah. You did. The twangier, the better."

"Bullshit."

He laughs at me some more. "So, how do you like Alaska?"

It's on the tip of my tongue to blurt it all out. How much I hate it there. I can't, though. It feels too much like talking about my husband behind his back—like criticizing the place Axel chose for us to live—to Murphy. I choke the words down. "It's okay. It's mostly cold and dark right now, but the locals assure me summer is pretty. Plus, it will be light almost twenty-four freaking hours a day."

"Fun," he says dryly.

"One of our neighbors says she grows these freakishly large cantaloupes and cabbages because of all the summer sun."

"Yum. You gonna be a farmer now?"

"No. I think she's just hoping I'll help her out. And she likes seeing Alexa."

"So you're making friends?"

"If you count the eighty-year-old lady across the hall, sure."

"I thought Penny was up there, too?"

"She is." I don't mention how Penny's free time consists of meeting guys on hook-up sites and bringing them back to her apartment when Lucas is out of town. I don't want Murphy thinking I'd ever do anything like that or that I condone her behavior.

We don't have a lot to say after that. Or maybe there's too much to say. Murphy and I have never run out of things to talk about before. But I can't come up with anything that isn't a conversational minefield.

Luckily, we arrive at the hospital.

Marcel doesn't look any better. Not that I expected him to in twelve hours. Murphy picks up a magazine and drops into a chair in the corner. I have the feeling he knows that chair intimately. "You stay here last night?" I ask.

"Yeah, as long as I kept out of their way, the nurses said they wouldn't kick me out."

"Gave them a dose of ginger charm, did ya?"

His face screws into a scowl. "Despite what you seem to think, my life doesn't revolve around nailing every woman I meet."

"Since when?"

He stands and tosses the magazine down on the chair. "I'm going down to the waiting room to talk to Bricks. Stay here with him?" Once again I said the wrong thing, because I don't know how to act around Murphy anymore. Our friendship seems easy one minute. Forced and strained the next.

"Blake," I whisper, reaching out to grab him as he walks past me. "I'm sorry. I was only kidding. I'm so tired, I guess it came out mean."

He nods, but I don't think he's completely forgiven me. We've never been this awkward around each other, but I don't know who we are to each other anymore.

Alexa and I take over Murphy's chair, but I pull it closer to my brother, taking his hand and talking to him.

"Alexa laughed for the first time today. Blake made her do it. Figures, right?"

Nothing.

"Alaska sucks, by the way. You were right. I hate it up there."

Still nothing.

Sighing, I sit back in the chair. Alexa settles against my chest and we snooze together.

I'm woken up a few hours later by the doctor checking on Marcel. "Good morning, Mrs. Ryan."

I sit up and frantically swipe my messy hair out of my face. Alexa helps by yanking on it. "How is he?"

"The imaging looks encouraging. Nothing broken. There is a significant amount of swelling. I'm sending a neurologist up to do an examination. He'll be able to better diagnose the severity and predict your brother's road to recovery."

"Will he be able to walk?"

"It's still too soon to tell. But he's a healthy young man in good shape. That will make rehabilitation easier."

"Okay."

I'm left already trying to figure out how much longer I'll be able to stay and help my brother.

Thirty-Five

Lost on the wrong road

Heidi

It's been three long weeks. Visiting my brother. Spending time with the club. Despite the horrible circumstances that brought me home, I'm happier here than I've been in months.

"Are you all packed, honey?" Hope asks from outside my door.

I let out a deep sigh and sweep my gaze over the room one last time.

I don't want to leave.

Axel has already called several times to make sure I'm coming home for his week off.

"I think so. I hate leaving my brother."

The misery in my voice must be painfully obvious, because Hope rushes forward and wraps me up in a hug. "Teller's doing so much better. You'll be back to visit soon, sweetie."

That's when I lose it. Hard sobs burst out of me and I cling even tighter to Hope. "I don't want to go." I cry even harder. "I hate it up there. I hate it so much."

"Oh, honey."

Distressed from my wailing, Alexa adds her baby screams to the mix.

"Everything okay?" Rock's low, gentle voice asks. "Hey, what's the matter, Heidi-girl?" A strong, comforting hand slides over my back—Rock—and I cry even harder.

Hope must give him some signal, because his hand disappears and I hear him cooing at Alexa. Her cries fade, and I realize he carried her out to the living room. "I'm sorry." I pull back and sniffle.

Hope reaches over and grabs a bunch of tissues, pressing them into my hands. "Sit down. Let's talk for a minute."

"We need to go. I have to see Marcel before we go to the airport."

"We have time. Talk to me. Why do you hate it?"

"If I tell you, you can't tell my brother. Or Murphy. Please? Not now. It will just make my brother worry when he needs to focus on getting better. And I can't stand hearing an *I-told-you-so* from Murphy."

"I won't. I promise."

Am I finally going to share my private misery with someone? The whole time I've been here, I've managed to keep it together. To smile and nod when the guys asked me how I liked Alaska. To lie to my brother about what an awesome adventure I'm having.

"It's awful. It's cold and dark. I'm trapped in our apartment with the baby by myself all the time. Even when Axel's home, he doesn't help me out. We end up fighting a lot." I choke back the rest of my words. It feels wrong to say anything bad about my husband. Even if my confession is to Hope and even if every word is the truth.

"Heidi—"

"I love Axel. I do. But I'm so mad at him for making us move up there. Money's tight because everything is so damn expensive. Besides Penny, there's no one my age around. All she wants to do is go out and party. I can't do that. Not that I want to, anyway."

All the words, every bit of the misery I've been stuffing down for months, comes bursting out of my mouth.

Hope sighs and seems to struggle for words.

"What should I do, Hope?"

"Are you asking me as a friend or as a lawyer?"

Lawyer, shit. I hadn't even thought of that.

"Both."

"Well, as your *friend*, I'd tell you that you're still young newly-weds, with a baby, and that alone is hard to handle. A move to an unfamiliar place makes it even harder. Especially if he's gone all the time."

"Okay. That's the Cliffs Notes version of my miserable life. Where's the advice part?"

She doesn't laugh. "The advice part is you're married now. You took vows to work through things in good times or bad."

"I—"

"I'm not finished. You need to work on your marriage. But it takes *two* people to do that. Axel needs to be more involved. Whether he has to change his schedule so you're able to spend more time together, or he needs to take a parenting class, or you two find a counselor up there."

Huh. None of those things had occurred to me.

"Okay. Now, what's your legal advice?"

She lets out a long sigh. "Did you get your driver's license up there?"

"No. I didn't see the point if we're only staying for a year."

"Good. Okay. So, your residence could still be considered here. New York has no-fault divorce now." I flinch. Never did I imagine contemplating divorce at nineteen. "We'd have to show the marriage has been irretrievably broken for at least six months," she explains, slipping into lawyer mode. "We could file for custody here. You'd have a strong case for full-custody since he's away all the time, and she's so little that no judge will make you send her to Alaska. He'd have to come here for visitation. You'd have to sort out custody, support, and all that other stuff before you'd be granted the divorce."

"That all seems so ugly."

"It *is*. That's why you need to try to work things out first. Un-less"—she reaches out and grabs my hand, prompting me to look her in the eye—"he hurts you or the baby."

Just with his words and indifference. "No. Never."

"Okay. I didn't think so. I always liked Axel. He seemed polite and respectful. But like I said, you've got a lot of stress heaped on both of you and that can change anyone."

"I think he's still upset about having Alexa. I know he loves her, but sometimes he acts like she doesn't exist. And I never realized how strongly he dislikes my brother. Murphy, I understand, but not Marcel."

Her brow wrinkles at the mention of Murphy's name, but she doesn't ask me to explain. "Is he upset about the club?"

"I don't know. He's never explained why or how he left."

She gives me a tired smile and pats my leg. "I know how much you wanted that to work out."

"I *did*. But I shouldn't have tried to force it. I thought everything would be perfect if he were part of the club. I never considered what it would mean for him. Axel's always been very much a *make it on your own* kind of guy—"

"And here everyone's in your business all the time?"

I snort. "Yeah, something like that. *You* didn't grow up around a club. Did you think it was weird?"

She glances at the open door again. "It's different, that's for sure. But it's a family by choice and I think that's amazing. Plus, now that I understand how much everyone cares and supports one another, it makes complete sense. I wouldn't trade it for anything."

Her words weren't intended to hurt, but they do. Because I feel like I traded away the few good things in my life for the one thing I thought I needed, and I don't know how to untangle my life from the mess it's become.

"Everything all right?" Rock asks when we come out of the bedroom. He hands Alexa to me and grabs my suitcases, leading us to the front door.

At the door he stops and raises an eyebrow. "Heidi?"

I realize I never answered his question. After everything he's done for me these last few weeks, I owe him the truth. "I don't know."

"You don't have to go back today." He sets my bags down and

levels a stern look at me. "Take a few more days, stay here, and think things through."

It's a tempting offer. The thought of going home and having a serious talk with Axel turns my stomach upside down. Worse, I hate leaving my brother while he's still in the hospital. I'm only able to do it because I know Rock, Murphy, and the rest of the club will take care of him.

Hope gently touches my shoulder. "Honey, do you want me to change your flight?"

"No, Hope. You're right. I need to go home and talk to Axel."

Rock nods. He reaches out, rubbing the back of his hand over my cheek. "I'm proud of you, Heidi."

Alexa wiggles in my arms and I tip my head at her. "Really?"

He doesn't crack a smile. "Yes. You took a hard road, but you're handling it well."

His words mean the world to me. They give me the extra nudge I need to face my problems.

MURPHY

"Hi, big brother!" Heidi shouts as she comes in the room.

Teller picks his head up and actually smiles for the first time today. The smile disappears when he remembers why she's here. To say goodbye.

I don't feel like smiling much, either.

Even though I've kept a respectful distance from Heidi, I loved having her near again. Knowing I could take a quick stroll through the woods and find her at Rock's house. Giving her rides to the hospital. Playing with Alexa. Getting to know Heidi as an adult. When she's not stressed out or mad at me, she's pretty funny. She's an amazing mother, too. Not that I ever thought otherwise, but I love spending time with the two of them.

And now she's leaving. Again.

To go home to her husband.

The prick who never bothered to fly down here. I doubt Teller gives a fuck one way or another, and I sure as shit didn't need to see the little fuck. But the fact that he didn't care enough to come support his wife when she's going through hell visiting her brother in the hospital every day? Going to a funeral for a friend who never should have died? Worrying night and day if her brother will ever walk again? The fact that he couldn't be bothered tells me all I need to know about him. I kept my mouth shut and didn't make Heidi feel worse about the situation, but if Axel were in front of me right now, there's a good chance, I'd beat the arrogance right out of him.

I've been so lost in my violent daydreaming, I missed most of their conversation.

"When are you coming back?" I ask.

Everyone turns and stares at me. What? Why shouldn't I ask?

Heidi ducks her head. "I'm not sure. I'll see what Axel's schedule looks like."

No one's been able to give me a reason that makes an ounce of sense for why she needs to fly all the way home, when her husband will only be there for a week before he takes off again. She's not working. Not going to school. She should just stay here.

I keep all of that to myself.

Teller grabs her hand and pulls her attention away from me. "I'm getting sent to a rehab facility this week. So hopefully, when you come back, I'll be walking."

"Oh, thank God! Why didn't you say that first, you goof?" She playfully smacks his shoulder and bursts out laughing.

"Give me my niece. I want to hold her for a few minutes before you take her away again."

Heidi's mouth turns down, but she hands Alexa over. That baby girl is the only thing that kept Teller from losing his mind when he found out about Mariella. She's the only person he's happy to see every day.

And now Heidi's taking her home. Teller's putting on his big brother face today, but I wonder how this will affect him tomorrow and the next day.

"I can't get over how big she's gotten, Heidi," he says as he lifts her up and down. Alexa kicks and giggles the whole time, loving it.

"Are you bench-pressing my daughter?" Heidi teases.

"My legs are fucked, but my arms are fine. Besides, she can't weigh more than what, fifteen pounds?"

Heidi's smile fades. "Around that, yeah. I don't know. She has her check-up this week. I'll let you know."

"You better call me right after. Murphy finally dropped off my new phone this morning. You better send lots of pictures."

"Okay." Heidi looks like she's about to cry, and Teller pulls her down for a one-armed hug.

"You okay?"

"Yeah, I—everything. I'm going to miss you and worry about you, that's all."

He studies her face for a few seconds, then nods and releases her. Alexa gets a few more kisses and silly faces before he reluctantly hands her back.

Rock stops in the doorway. "Ready, Heidi-girl?"

"Yeah."

I glance at Teller. "I'm going to walk down with them. You cool?"

He nods. I still stop in the waiting room and ask Trinity to go sit with him while I'm downstairs.

"Rock, hold up," I call out, jogging down the hall to catch up with them.

They stop and wait by the elevator.

"I can carry her if you want," I offer. Heidi gives me a brief smile and lets me take Alexa. As if she knows how much trouble I'm having letting both of them go.

Hope and Rock make superficial small talk with Heidi. About her flight and what her plans are for the week. Crap that makes me want to yell, "Why are we all pretending like this is okay?"

The pressure in my chest only gets worse as I walk them out to the parking garage. "Hey, I have something for you. Let me go grab it?" I ask Heidi.

Rock takes Alexa from me, and I jog over to my truck. I dig out the bag and when I turn, Heidi's standing behind me.

"Oh, you didn't have to follow me over."

"No. It's okay. You'll…I know you'll take care of him, right?"

I almost want to tell her I'm scared shitless he's going to have nothing to look forward to now. But, the last thing I want to do is heap a bunch of guilt on Heidi's shoulders. Especially since I don't think it will make her stay. "Of course I will. If you need anything, you know you can always call me, right?"

"I do. Thank you." She nods at the bag. "What's that?"

"Uh, here. Spur of the moment purchase." Okay, that's a total lie. I'd never been to a baby shop in my entire life before yesterday. "For Alexa. For the plane. You know to keep her busy."

Her eyes widen as she takes the bag and pulls out the plushy lion. "It has a mirror and all these different textures on his paws." I shrug, feeling a bit silly. "You know, stuff to keep her entertained," I explain. Reaching over, I pull the other item out of the bag.

Heidi's smile makes all this awkwardness worth it. "Keys?"

"Motorcycle and keys," I correct, pointing at the loop full of colorful plastic keys.

"She'll love them." Her arms wrap around me and I hesitate before hugging her back. "Thank you, that was really sweet."

Somehow saying good-bye feels worse than when I had to sit through her wedding, and I can't pinpoint why.

Thirty-Six

MURPHY

After saying goodbye, I trudge back upstairs.

"You all right, bro?" Teller asks when I sit down next to his bed.

I don't know what to say. We haven't spoken about Heidi's situation much, but Teller and I don't lie to each other. "I hate that she had to go back."

He doesn't give me shit. "Me too."

We don't talk about much else until Hope comes in about an hour later. She looks as twisted up as I feel.

"What's wrong, Hope?" Teller asks.

"Nothing." She flashes a fake-as-fuck smile. Hope would be a terrible poker player. She can't bluff worth a fuck.

"Rock dropped me off and ran up to the clubhouse."

"Is he coming back, or do you need a ride?" I ask and she shrugs.

I stand and offer her the chair next to Teller's bed. After taking it, she leans over and taps his hand. "How are you feeling?"

He rolls his eyes and pulls a half smile. "Come on, Hope. You ask me that like ten times a day. Tell me about my sister. She make it to the airport okay?"

"Yes. We waited until her plane took off. She promised to text me when she lands."

I cock my head and stare her down until she fidgets. "Come on, something's bothering you."

She blows out an exasperated breath, and I fight the urge to shake the information out of her. Her gaze darts between me and Teller.

"Listen, she specifically asked me *not* to tell you two. You can't say anything to her."

Teller sits up, clearly agitated. "What's going on, Hope?"

I drop into the chair on his other side and wait.

"She…" Hope hesitates, and I know it's probably killing her to break a promise to Heidi. Hope's usually locked up tight like a vault. "This morning she admitted how unhappy she is in Alaska."

"Aw, fuck," Teller mutters. "I knew it. Knew she wasn't right."

"Axel's away working and she's alone with the baby all the time…" Hope's voice trails off. Teller and I share a look. My chest aches for Heidi. I know how much she hates being alone and cut off from family. She already spent so much time alone as a kid. Everyone abandoned her. Now, her husband's doing the same damn thing. It pisses me off so much, I'd pound the shit out of Axel if I got ahold of him.

"That motherfucker. He *promised* me. Promised he'd take care of her," Teller grinds out.

"He's trying to take care of them the best way he knows how. Working and earning money," Hope says. Although, by the look on her face, I don't think defending Axel agrees with her.

"Fuck that. He didn't need to drag her up to Alaska," Teller snaps. "What about Penny? She any help?"

"Not really. Heidi made it sound like when the guys are away, Penny likes to go out and party. Heidi can't do that with a baby at home."

Teller curses. "She's got people to help her here. Why didn't you make her stay?"

Hope glares at him. "I can't *force* her to do anything. She's married now. I told her she needs to work on her marriage, maybe find a counselor."

Teller's making a *fuck-that* face similar to mine. The only "counseling" Axel needs is an ass kicking.

"I suggested she talk to Axel about changing his schedule." Her mouth snaps shut after that.

"What else," Teller demands.

"I can't…she asked for my *legal* advice, so I can't violate her trust more than I already have."

Teller curses and I think about the implications of what Hope's saying. They must have discussed Heidi's options for divorce. It's the only thing that makes any sense.

Holy shit.

Maybe deep down, there's a part of me hoping Heidi chooses option B. Mostly though, I'm overwhelmed with how much I hate knowing Heidi's alone and unhappy.

"I gave her my advice and told her I'm here if she needs me. What else could I do?"

Teller keeps glaring at her, so I'm the one who answers. "Nothing, Hope. You're right." I flick Teller's side. "She's a wife and mother now, bro. You can't boss her around. She has to figure it out on her own."

"Fuck that." He slams his fist into his leg, making Hope jump. "I feel so fucking useless. I can't do anything for her. I *hate* this."

"That's why she didn't want me to say anything. She wants you to worry about getting better."

Teller mutters a few more curses and Hope rolls her eyes. "She's a smart girl. She's capable. A good mother. But, they're both so young. Newlyweds. A new baby. New job. A big move. Any one of those things would stress a couple out. All of them together?" She shakes her head. "That's rough."

"He treat her okay when he's home at least?" Marcel asks.

"Yes," Hope answers, a little too fast for my liking. "I specifically asked about that. I *wouldn't* have let her go back if I thought he hurt either of them." Marcel accepts her answer with a nod.

We don't talk about much else after that. Dex and Swan show up with dinner.

"They let you in with that?" I ask, nodding at the bag Dex has.

"Sure."

"You should have seen him sweet-talk the nurse into looking the other way," Swan says, making Teller pull a half-smile.

"Come on, Hope. I'll give you a ride home," I say, holding my hand out for her. She leans over to give Teller a hug. Before she leaves, he grabs her hand and pulls her to him.

"Hey, I'm sorry I was being a dick. Thank you for lookin' out for her and being someone she can talk to."

Her eyes well up, but she nods. "Of course."

We're silent as we walk down the hall, but once the elevator doors close, I turn and face Hope. "Tell me the truth. I saw your face when Teller asked if Axel's treating her right."

Her face pinches in anger and she puts her back against the elevator wall. "Listen, Murphy, I already feel horrible for the way I broke her trust back there. Don't make me feel worse."

"Hope, you *had* to tell us something like that."

She shakes her head. "You don't understand, Murphy. She broke down in *tears* this morning." Hope's eyes glisten and I reach out to wrap my arm around her. I'm gutted finding out Heidi's so unhappy. "I feel so guilty for not doing more to stop their wedding," she says miserably.

"What? Why?"

"You *can't* tell Heidi I told you any of this. She'll never trust me. And if she has no one to confide in, it will make things worse for her. You get that, right?"

"Yeah, Hope. I get it."

"She let it slip before the wedding that Axel wasn't happy about the baby. And now it sounds like they probably argue a lot and he's no help with Alexa when he's home." Her fists ball up at her sides. "I should have said more and stopped her before the wedding—or convinced her not to go to Alaska. Rock and I tried to offer our guest room, but—"

The elevator dings and the doors open at the parking garage level. She shakes her head and pushes off the wall. "I hated sending her back. But I didn't know what else to do."

"Nothing you could do. She made her choice." I feel like a bastard for saying that, but it's the truth. Heidi made her choice when she married Axel. If she reaches out to me or needs my help, I'll be there in a heartbeat.

Otherwise, as much as I hate it, she has to figure it out on her own.

Heidi

Heavy doesn't describe my heart as I board the plane to return to Alaska. The smile I forced at Hope probably didn't fool her one bit. Especially after I unloaded all my misery on her back at the house.

As if she senses my unhappiness, Alexa fusses and cries while we're waiting for the plane to take off. The woman in the seat across from us throws a lot of dirty looks my way.

Remembering Murphy's sweet gifts, I dig them out of my bag. Alexa's immediately fascinated by the plushy lion and ends up playing with it until we take off.

I'm tired but too anxious to sleep for most of the trip. Alexa's good until the last half hour when she screams pretty much the entire time.

"I know, baby. You've already traveled an awful lot in your short life," I coo to her, ignoring all the dirty looks and comments from the nearby passengers. They can fuck right off, it's not like I want my baby to be miserable.

Right before we land, she falls asleep with her fingers wrapped tightly around my index finger.

As much as I hate Alaska, it's a relief to be done traveling.

Except, no one meets us at the gate.

I text Axel. He has all our flight information. Where the hell is he?

We're at the airport.

Nothing.

What the fuck?

Tired of waiting, I call Penny. "Is Axel home?"

"I don't know. Where are you?"

"At the airport waiting for him."

There are some muffled thumps in the background and more shuffling. Sounds like she's banging on our apartment door.

"He's not answering the door."

"Shit."

"Do you want me to come get you?"

"Do you mind?"

"No. I'm leaving right now."

"Thanks, Penny."

We hang up and I drop down onto one of the benches. I don't know whether to be pissed or worried.

Are you okay?

Nothing.

Penny's coming to get us.

A half hour later, Alexa's had her fill of airports, traveling, and life in general. She lets a scream rip and nothing I say or do calms her down this time.

"I feel you, baby."

I'm trying to comfort my daughter, but inside I'm seven years old again. Waiting for someone to pick me up from school. Hoping someone remembers I even exist.

I jump up the second I spot Penny's car, so damn happy to leave the airport I almost cry.

"I called Lucas. They're on opposite weeks now, but he said Axel left for home yesterday."

"That's what I thought."

Penny helps me drag all my stuff upstairs and waits while I go inside to set Alexa in her crib.

The sound of the shower draws me to the bathroom. "Axel?"

Pushing open the door, I find him under the spray. "Uh, we're home."

"Hey, babe. I'll be right out."

I'm so angry, I turn and walk out of the bathroom without responding.

"He's here," I say to Penny. She gives me a curious look but waves and shuts the door behind her.

Work on your marriage. Strangling your husband does not count as working on your marriage.

Axel strolls into the living room dressed in shorts, damp hair dripping everywhere.

"Where were you?" I ask as calmly as I can.

"I'm sorry. I got home and crashed. By the time I saw your texts, you said Penny was coming to get you, so I thought I should stay put."

Is he serious?

"A *nap* was more important than picking up your wife and baby from the airport?"

"Hey, I didn't want you going by yourself in the first place."

"Well, instead of taking an extra shift, you could have flown down."

"You didn't need me in the way. And we could use the extra money."

He hasn't even asked about my brother. Or his daughter. I'm so frustrated and plain *sad*.

Am I the one being unreasonable?

"I'm exhausted."

"It's two in the afternoon."

"Yeah, but I've been up since sunrise, New York time."

I push past him and check on the baby. She's out, thankfully, which means I should get some rest while I can. Obviously, I can't trust Axel to be of any help.

The TV comes on in the living room and I shake my head.

Welcome home, Heidi.

MURPHY

Even though I feel Heidi needs to work stuff out on her own, it doesn't mean she's not on my mind.

The next morning as I'm on my way to work, a flash of silver on the passenger side catches my eye. When I pull into the parking lot behind the gym, I reach over and grab what turns out to be Heidi's hairbrush.

A fucking *hairbrush* has stolen my breath. I can't stop picturing her sitting next to me, brushing her hair and throwing it in a ponytail every morning on the way to the hospital. At the time, I'd teased her about leaving all her girly crap in my truck. Now, I reach over, flick the glove compartment open and smile when I find her lip gloss, a pile of hair ties, and one of Alexa's rattles.

The pain of missing *both* of them hits me. Hard.

I'm sitting there staring out the windshield but not seeing anything in front of me. Slowly, the picnic bench where she and I sat a little over a year ago and planned a spring break road trip, comes into focus.

The hollow, lonely ache in my chest expands. The pain that has only ever gone away when I'm with Heidi.

I grab my cell phone.

My thumb hovers over Heidi's number.

I should check to make sure she got home all right.

At least that's what I tell myself.

"Blake?" she answers on the third ring.

"Hey, kid. Get home safe?"

She hesitates, and I hate how far away she is. Hate that I can't see her face. Hate that I can't do a damn thing to make things easier for her.

"Yeah."

"How'd Alexa do on the plane?"

Something like a sob or a sniffle comes over the line. "Heidi? Are you okay?"

"I'm fine. Alexa? She was pretty cranky at first. She loved the lion, though. It kept her busy for a while."

"No one gave you shit, did they?"

"Just the usual dirty looks a teen mom gets."

"Heidi—"

"How's my brother?"

"Misses you." As soon as I say the words, I wish I could take them back. I didn't call to make her feel guilty.

She sighs, such a sad sound, it makes the pain in my chest even worse. "I wish—I should have—never mind."

"What?"

"I'm sorry. I'm still tired."

"I didn't wake you did I?"

She snorts softly into the phone. "No."

I feel guilty knowing stuff about her that she told Hope in confidence. It makes this call so much harder. I want to tell her to come home. Not for selfish reasons. For *her*. So she's not alone all the damn time. "Axel pick you up at the airport?"

"No. Penny did."

"Oh." *Not your business. Leave it alone.*

"I should go—"

"Yeah, yeah. Sorry. Just happy you made it home safe."

"Thank you."

I hope my call made her feel a little better, because as we hang up, I feel a thousand times worse.

Thirty-Seven

Heidi

At my request, Axel changes his shifts so we can have two weeks together. He's not interested in counseling, but after I mention it, he makes more of an effort. He takes me to some of the parks I've wanted to visit but was afraid to navigate alone with the baby. He spends more time with Alexa and seems less confused by her.

He doesn't ask me about my visit home, and it bothers me. I lost a friend. My brother's paralyzed and might not walk again. But, my husband doesn't seem to care about that part of our lives any more. I'm tired of arguing, so I don't say anything. But his indifference stings.

After he goes back to work, I think I might try counseling on my own. Someone who can help me figure out what the fuck to do. Is this normal? Does this happen to couples so soon after getting married?

Gradually things improve. Marcel lets me know when he moves into the rehab facility. He hates it, of course. Axel finally asks about my trip and holds me when I burst into tears over Mariella's funeral.

After a long day at the zoo, we're in our little kitchen cooking together. Today has been the most fun we've had since we moved here. I finally saw polar bears up close. Alexa seemed to love everything.

Overall, it was a perfect day. I feel closer to Axel than I have in a long time.

Since she was exhausted from all the new experiences, I put Alexa in bed as soon as we got home.

Axel wraps his arms around my waist and rests his chin on my shoulder watching as I toss a mixture of diced salmon, garlic, panko, and green onions together.

"Where's my egg white mixture?" I ask, teasing him with my bossy kitchen tone.

He places a kiss on my cheek. "Right here, chef."

After I form the burgers, he takes over transferring them to the sizzling hot pan and cooking them, while I assemble the rest of the dinner.

Things feel so easy and calm for a change, I blurt out what I've been thinking about for a few days now. "I'm thinking of flying home after you go back to work."

He stares at me for a few seconds. "Again?"

"My brother's still pretty messed up. Do you want me to wait until you're home so you can go with us?"

He doesn't even pretend to think about it. "No. Go while I'm on shift."

"Fine."

"I thought he was in a rehab facility now?"

"He is. Hope says he's had a few setbacks. Maybe seeing Alexa will help."

"It can't be good for Alexa to do so much flying."

As if you give a shit.

That's not something a good wife—a wife who's working on her marriage—says, so I choke the words back down my throat. My shoulders lift. "She did fine. I think it was good for her to be around the family. She loved playing with my brother." I leave out the part about Murphy getting her to laugh.

He rolls his eyes and I resist the urge to smack him. Barely.

"I don't like you traveling alone with her."

"Axel, I'm basically a single parent while you're away. What does it matter if I do it here or somewhere else?"

"That's not fair, Heidi. I'm doing all this for us."

I really don't want to fight with him. But it's so hard not to call bullshit. Instead, I point at the frying pan. "I think they're done."

AXEL

I fucked up when Heidi returned home. Such a stupid, simple thing. Forgetting to pick her up at the airport. I felt like a piece of shit, but sorry was all I came up with.

So, when Heidi asked me to switch shifts so I could spend two weeks with her instead of one, I jumped at it.

Having her back in New York for so long scared me. I feared she might not come back. And I couldn't bear the thought of life without Heidi.

When she mentioned counseling, I realized how bad things had gotten and promised myself I'd work harder.

Now she's telling me she wants to go home again. What if she doesn't come back this time?

She points at the salmon burgers. "I think they're done."

But all I hear her saying is *I think we're done.*

I grab the spatula to flip the burgers out of the pan and onto our plates. "When can we make these for Alexa?"

She chuckles as she carries the plates to the table and sets them down. "If you read any of the baby stuff I gave you, you'd know."

"I'm a real slacker, huh?"

A quick smile brightens her face and she pokes me in the side. "Yeah, you are."

I catch her hand and bring it to my mouth. "Don't go home by yourself. I'll go with you." The words fly out before I have a chance to think them over. But the relief on her face, the way her eyes shine, the wide smile, all let me know it's the right decision. As much as I don't want anything to do with the club any more, I really should do this.

Besides, it will be easier to break my news to her.

"You haven't told me a lot about what you do on the rig," she says as we dig into our dinner.

I haven't talked about it much, because I feel her unhappiness about the job and things in general and don't want to rub in how happy I am. "I love it, really."

She raises an eyebrow for me to continue and seems genuinely interested. "Yeah, it's exciting. I'm not stuck under a truck every day or hoping enough vehicles come in for me to keep my job. It's long hours and hard work, but it's challenging and each day is a little bit different. It's intense."

"It seems so isolated."

The solitude is one of my favorite things about the job, but I'm afraid that will hurt Heidi's feelings so I don't say it. "It is. But we have a good crew. Everyone gets along. There aren't any slackers or whiners. The work's dangerous, and Lucas says throwing one bad apple into the mix can fuck up the whole crew."

Heidi's mouth turns down at the dangerous part. It's been one of her biggest complaints about the job. The hefty life insurance policy the company provides didn't make her feel any better about it. I haven't even told her about the new job I'm training for. It's mostly underwater repair work. Dangerous, but the pay is crazy. Lucas was insanely jealous when I told him about the offer. I felt a little guilty since he's the one who brought me into the company.

Heidi taps the back of my hand with her fork to get my attention. "Do they have any rigs in New York?"

"You really want to go home bad, huh?"

"I'm trying, Axel." She sets her fork down and sits back, staring me right in the eye. "But I hate it here. Maybe it will be different in the summer, but honestly, I'm miserable."

I clear my throat then bite back my words. Now's not the time to tell her my news. "Well, it's only another eight months."

Heidi

"Do you *have* to go?" I whisper when Axel's alarm goes off.

He turns and pulls me into his arms. "Yeah, baby. You know I do."

"But now you have to work three weeks?" I already know the answer, but the three weeks looming ahead of me feel so bleak.

"It was worth it to spend extra time with you."

I love the way he says that. We snuggle together a little longer before Alexa starts wailing, and I groan. "I'll get her," he says, kissing the tip of my nose.

He carries her in and gives her to me so I can feed her. "Think she'll be able to eat solid food when I get back?" he asks while watching me.

I try to do the math in my head. "Maybe. I can always pump if you want to feed her."

"No. It's good bonding for you two. She's used to it."

The three of us are quiet for a few minutes. Quiet and together. It's nice. Then it's time to get ready to drop Axel at his office, where he'll get flown by helicopter to his rig.

He doesn't have a lot to say on the drive there. In my head, I imagine it's because he's going to miss us, or maybe he's worried about what work is waiting for him on the rig.

I park the truck and he taps my hand. "They want to promote me," he blurts out.

"That's great! Why didn't you say so sooner?" The words tumble from my mouth before I realize what he's saying. More time in Alaska.

"The project's in Indonesia. It doesn't start until I'm done here, but I need to give them an answer soon."

I'm stunned. Every bit of air has been sucked from my lungs so I can't even give him the answer spinning through my head, which is *fuck no* or *fuck that*, I'm not sure, but fuck is definitely part of it. Because by the look on his face, I can tell he wants to take the job.

"Axel," I say a whole lot calmer than I feel. "I can't think of any place I want to live *less*. Aren't there any oil rigs in say, Texas? Or Louisiana? Maybe Florida? At least some place that if I can't be home in New York, where you *promised* me we'd be next year, it'd be someplace I'd want to be?" I'm pretty close to yelling now, so I stop and take a few deep breaths. Behind me, Alexa squeals, agitated by my raised voice. I reach back and tickle her toes to calm her, and myself.

"There's another project I can sign on for here, but it would be the same position."

"Did you hear anything I just said?"

"I heard you."

"What about school? I'm supposed to finish next year when we're home."

"So, enroll here and finish."

"Axel, I hate it here. I don't know if I can finish out *this* year, and you're asking me to stay for another one? When you promised me it was only for one year?" I feel it's important to keep mentioning that last part.

"Heidi. I'm good at this job. I like it."

"Well, good for you. At least one of us gets to be happy."

"You don't understand, the pay is—"

"I don't care about the money!" I shout, finally losing it. "Money won't give us more time together. Money won't give Alexa back all the time she's missing with her father. It won't give me back the time I'm missing with my family. Don't you get it?"

He drops his head and covers his face with his hands. "Fuck. This is why I waited to talk to you about it. I knew you'd be pissed."

"Ya think?"

"Look, it sucks now because it's winter. Wait until it warms up. Summer is supposed to be beautiful here. Maybe you'll like it. Maybe I can arrange my schedule next year so we can take off during the worst part of it, or you can go home then or something. We'll figure it out."

"How could you do this?"

He has the nerve to ask, "What?"

"Make a decision without consulting me. Again."

"I didn't. I haven't—"

"Bullshit! You're doing it again. You're telling me instead of discussing it with me. I'm your wife, not some stuffed animal you drag around on all your adventures."

He reaches out and brushes his hand over my cheek. "I'm sorry."

"So am I."

Penny and Lucas pull up next to us and wave.

It's time for my husband to go.

What is it about me that makes it so easy for people to leave me?

"He's back on your rotation?" I ask.

"Yup." He flashes a smile, clearly thrilled to get back to his job. "Thank God. It's really boring without him there." He leans over and kisses my cheek. "I love you. We'll figure all this out."

I can't answer or I'll start sobbing.

There's no figuring it out. We want opposite things and can't seem to meet in the middle no matter what.

As I watch him and Lucas walk away, laughing and joking with each other, I struggle to shut down the little voice in my head that says *this is the end.*

Thirty-Eight

MURPHY

"You planning to give him the good news today?" Wrath asks as I get up from the war room table.

"Fuck yeah, I am."

The good news is that Killa has been found and dealt with. Wrath found him, and I ended him.

Justice for Mariella—an innocent. And justice for my best friend who still can't fucking walk.

I didn't lose any sleep over it.

Maybe that makes me a bad person. I don't waste a lot of time worrying about it.

In our world, payback is swift and brutal and often *final*.

That leaves one remaining Viper on the loose. Ransom. In time, we'll find him and take him out, too.

Rock nods at me. "Go ahead. Hope and I will be down later."

"Trinity and I will be down, too," Wrath adds

Having us all visiting Teller is less about security now and more about keeping his spirits up. Rehab hasn't been going well for him.

He's looking gloomier than ever when I walk in.

We've known each other so long, he knows something's up.

"It's done."

"Killa?"

"Last night," I confirm.

"Should have been me."

"I know, brother. But we couldn't risk—"

He grabs my arm, stopping me. "I understand. Thank you."

That's the last we talk about it.

He's grumpy about everything else. Physical therapy, his therapist not working him hard enough, but then ten seconds later he bitches that he's seeing her too often and he's tired.

I'm a little relieved when Hope and Rock show up. Although, watching them hold hands and be so affectionate with each other is a bit nauseating in my current mood.

Wrath and Trinity show up next. Wrath jerks his head toward the hallway, and Rock and I follow him out.

"He's bitchier than usual, so good luck," I say to Wrath.

"Great."

Inside the room, I hear Hope and Trinity fussing over Teller. An effort to distract him from the fact that the three of us are in the hall talking about him like he's a two year old.

Wrath pins Rock with one of his scary faces—one that has no effect on Rock whatsoever—and explains what he thinks is bothering Teller. "He said something about how if he never regains the use of his legs, he's out of the club."

"For fuck's sake," Rock groans. "He got injured over a club beef, and he thinks we're gonna toss him out. Asshole," Rock mutters.

"Yeah, well, try to work it into the conversation that he's not going anywhere," Wrath suggests before taking off down the hall.

"Did you give him the news?" Rock asks as I'm about to step inside.

"Yeah. It made him happy for about a second."

"Wanted it to be him, right?"

"Yes," I answer. He slaps me on the back and places his hand at the back of my neck, walking me into the room.

Teller lifts his chin at me. "Hey, Fucker."

"Can't you be nice to each other?" Hope teases.

"Morning, Blake, are you finished ratting me out to dad?" Teller says with a big smirk on his face. Well, I guess being a cocky dick is better than the usual attitude we've been getting from him lately.

Rock groans and Hope playfully slaps Teller's shoulder. "That's *not* what I meant."

Wrath returns with lunch for everyone, and we're our regular rowdy selves. So much so, that one of the nurses stops in to ask us to keep it down.

"I'm pretty sure I'm the youngest person here," Teller says after she leaves.

I'm trying to come up with a casual way of asking if Teller's heard from Heidi when he leans over and grabs his phone. "Got this from my sister the other day." He passes it to Hope, and I restrain myself from snatching the phone out of her hand.

"Aw, cute. She told me he took some time off, and they were doing a lot of family stuff."

Hope passes it to me, and it's a picture of Heidi and Alexa at what looks like a zoo. "Cute," I say, handing it back to Teller.

I'm happy for her. I really am. Glad the little punk is finally treating her right.

"She say when she's coming back?" Rock asks.

Hope jumps and pulls her phone out of her back pocket. "It's like she knew we were talking about her," she jokes. "Hi, Heidi, we were just—"

Hope's eyes widen, her jaw drops. "Heidi, calm down." She paces to the other side of the room, while every one of us focuses on her side of the conversation. "What did they tell you?"

"Hope, what's wrong?" Marcel demands.

She shakes her head and holds her hand up. Teller turns his glare on Rock, silently asking him to get a hold of his wife, I guess.

Wrath gets up and closes the door, while Rock joins Hope by the window. He gently pries the phone out of her hands and hits the speaker button.

Heidi's anxious voice fills the room. "I don't know what to do, they're not telling me anything, but the explosion was bad. It's all over the news. The other families are meeting at the company's local office to wait for information, but I don't want to bring Alexa down there—"

"Heidi, it's Rock. Calm down."

She bursts into tears.

Teller and I exchange a look.

"Honey, I'm visiting with your brother," Hope says calmly.

"Oh. Oh, okay."

Hope crosses the room and sits next to Teller.

"Heidi, what's going on?" he asks.

"I don't know." She sobs. "They just called and said there was an explosion. Half the crew is missing, the rest are either injured or—"

Trinity gasps and even though Heidi can't say the word, we all know.

An avalanche of guilt lands on my shoulders. *Shit.* I may not have liked the kid. Didn't think he was right for Heidi. Might have wanted to kick his ass a few times. But I'd *never* wish this on him. Or her.

Hope shoots a pleading look at Rock and he nods. "Heidi, is Penny around?"

"Yes. She's on the phone with Lucas's family."

"Okay. Have you called Axel's parents?"

"No. Not yet."

"Do that," she directs, utterly calm and unruffled. "Let them know what's going on. Then stick with Penny. I'm going to find a flight up there. I'll be there as soon as I can."

"You'll do that? Come all the way up here?"

"Yes. Give me a little time to figure it out. I'll call you back."

"Thank you."

Hope's trembling as she ends the call and sets her phone down. She held it together the whole time she was on the phone, but now she leans against Rock and cries softly. I know she spent some time with Axel when he was prospecting for us and liked him.

Teller looks like he wants to strangle something. "I *hate* this," he growls. "Fucking *hate* that I'm stuck here."

I know where I'm headed. I'm just waiting for prez to give me the go ahead. He stares at me with a raised eyebrow and squeezes Hope tighter. "I can't have her going up there alone. I need to be here for that meet."

"I got her, prez."

"Thank you," Teller says.

Rock nods at me. "Okay." The *I'm trusting you with my wife* in his expression isn't lost on me.

Hope wipes her face and straightens up. "Shit. If he's… If he's really…we'll have to help her pack up their apartment and whatever else she needs. We might be gone for a while, Rock."

"Whatever you need to do. If you need me after Saturday, I'll be there."

She doesn't even question him. Just nods.

Teller picks up his phone and starts checking for flights.

"I can do it," Hope says.

"Please. Let me do something. I feel fucking useless."

Teller can't get us on a flight until later that night. And it leaves from Boston. So we basically have enough time to run up to the property, throw some clothes in a bag, and have Rock drive us to the airport.

Heidi

Penny hasn't stopped crying since she hung up the phone. We've been sitting on my living room floor watching the news for hours. I have Alexa propped up on her Boppy pillow in front of me playing with her toys. She's quieter than usual, as if she knows something's wrong.

Me, I don't know what I am. Numb? Guilty? Angry?

At the moment, I land on angry. Axel's company has confirmed five workers were killed, six injured, and seventeen still missing. They've also started subtly shifting the blame to two other companies involved in the project. The news keeps talking about a ruptured pipeline and gallons of crude oil that were spilled. Experts talk about risk management and how there hasn't been an accident of this magnitude in five years.

No one mentions the families who are sitting on the floors of their darkened apartments waiting to hear news. Some news. Any news.

Hope called me from Los Angeles where she said there was an hour layover. She gave me a time but asked me to stay at the apartment. She said she'd rent a car when they get here.

I don't ask who came with her. I assume it's Rock. I can't think beyond that.

After dropping the news of his "promotion" in my lap before leaving, I've been furious with Axel. I hate that we left on such bad terms. We spoke briefly yesterday, and I'd sent him a picture of Alexa and me before I tucked her into bed last night, but it doesn't feel like enough.

Penny sniffles and looks up. "God, Heidi, what if they're disfigured or disabled or something horrible?"

"Then we deal with it and thank God they're still with us."

She snaps her mouth shut at my sharp tone and focuses on the television again. A few minutes later, there's a commotion out in the hallway.

"I better check in case that's his parents," she says.

"Go ahead. You know where I'll be."

Alexa gets a quick kiss before Penny runs out.

I end up dozing for a few minutes before my phone wakes me. I'm almost afraid to answer it, fearing what might lie on the other end.

Thirty-Nine

MURPHY

I need a lot of coffee when we finally make it off the plane. Keeping Hope upright helps me focus. She's even more exhausted than I am.

The guy at the rental car counter gives me lip when I point out we reserved a large SUV and he tries to hand me the keys to some shitty little subcompact. "Hope, can you go look up that receipt for me?" I ask nodding to a quiet corner. She gives me a curious look but does as I ask.

As soon as she's out of hearing range, I lean over the desk. "Listen, asshole. You know that explosion that's all over the news?" I nod at the television that's been covering nothing but the oil spill since we walked in here. "My friend's husband was on that rig, and I'm here to help her out. I just traveled thirteen fucking hours to get here. Don't fuck with me." I figure it's better to go with a generic threat before I give him the details about what I'm going to do to him if he doesn't straighten this out.

His bored expression turns into a pale-faced stare quick. "Give me a minute."

Christ.

"Sir, all I have left is an Infiniti QX80, from our Prestige Collection."

"Perfect." I slap down my credit card and he raises an eyebrow. I guess my scruffy appearance has him doubting whether I can afford the prissy SUV. I flick my license across the counter. "I don't have all night, dude. Move it along."

"Yes, sir."

"Jesus Christ."

"Did you threaten him sufficiently?" Hope teases, sneaking up behind me.

"Not even close."

"If you're tired, I can drive," she offers.

The face I make clearly says that's not happening. "I got ya, First Lady."

After lots more waiting, our vehicle's finally ready. Hope reads me the directions, and we find our way to Heidi's. "Here, Spruce Loop."

I pull into a modest apartment community. At least, from what I can tell, it's in a nice area. Looks safe, anyway. That had been my biggest concern with Heidi on her own so much up here.

Hope makes a comment that echoes my thoughts, and I give her a tired smile.

"Here, this one," she points to a spot in front of building seventy-six.

We trudge up the stairs and knock on the door. Heidi answers teary-faced and hiccupping.

Hope rushes in and gives her a big hug while Heidi clings to her and cries even harder. I stand there feeling useless and unsure what I should do.

"Blake, you came?"

"Yeah," I answer lamely.

"Thank you." She lets go of Hope and gives me a hug. She's so small and warm in my arms, I want to pick her up, cuddle her, and make all the bad stuff in her life disappear.

"I just got a call. Still nothing."

Hope moves to the couch to pick up Alexa while Heidi and I say hello. "Hi, baby," she coos and makes silly voices at her until Alexa laughs.

I glance down at Heidi, still not ready to let go of her. "Are you okay?" I ask.

"No. Not at all."

I don't know what to say. We've both lived through enough bad stuff that saying stupid shit like "it's okay" or "don't worry, they'll find him" is pointless.

Heidi sways to the side and I put my arm out to steady her. "Whoa, you all right?"

"Just tired."

Hope glances up at me. The whole trip, we never discussed where we were staying.

"Hope, you can sleep in my room. I have a daybed in Alexa's room I can use. Murphy—"

"I'm fine on the couch."

"Good, because I'm out of beds."

I crack a smile because that sounds more like my Heidi.

"I don't want to kick you out of your room, Heidi. I can—"

"Don't worry about it, Hope. I've slept in there plenty of times."

There's a lot of information in that sentence that my tired, caveman brain can't pick apart right now. Another time.

After Hope goes to bed, I try to settle into the couch. I keep the television on in case the news story changes. I'm half-asleep when Alexa's screams yank me awake.

Should I check on them?

I'm up and moving through the apartment before my brain really answers the question.

Alexa settles down as I reach her door. "Shhh, baby. It's okay," Heidi says in a sleepy-hushed voiced.

Pushing open her door, I find her feeding Alexa and look away. "You two need anything?" I ask the ceiling.

She chuckles at my discomfort. "We're fine. Thanks, though. Are you comfortable out there?"

"I'm fine."

"You can shut the television off. I have my phone on in case they call."

"All right. You're sure you're good?"

"Yes. But, thank you."

I leave them be and finally manage to fall asleep.

A few hours later, someone's banging on the door. Completely disoriented, it takes me a few minutes to remember where I am.

Door. Answer it.

An older couple scowls at me on the other side. "Who are you?"

The uppity tone reminds me of Axel, so I'm guessing this is his dad.

"Friend of Heidi's from home."

The mother sniffs and looks me over. From my wild slept-on-the-couch hair, scruffy beard, to my bare feet. "Mr. and Mrs. Ryan?"

They seem surprised I know who they are. "I'm a friend of Axel's, too." A bit of a lie, but there's no one around to call me on it, now is there?

They pull the sticks out of their asses and decide it's safe to come in.

"Oh, hi, Mrs. Ryan. Mr. Ryan," Heidi greets them as she joins us, carrying Alexa. It's not lost on me that she's not on a first-name basis with her in-laws. Not a surprise, since Axel's mom has to be the coldest woman I've met in a damn long time. She barely blinks in Alexa's direction. Don't grandmothers usually get all mushy over their grandbabies?

"Hi," Hope says.

Heidi introduces her as her "Aunt Hope," which is cute.

Axel's mother finally snaps. "Enough with the introductions. I don't care who these people are. Where's our son, Heidi?"

Well, now.

I understand why the woman's upset, but she has no business taking it out on her daughter-in-law. Before I cause a scene, I wait to see how Heidi handles it.

Heidi hoists the baby higher and rubs her hand over the back of Alexa's head. Then she straightens up, lifts her chin and answers calmly, "I don't know yet. I'm still waiting for news from his company."

"What do you mean you don't know?" she yells.

I hold up a hand. "Hey—"

"It's fine, Blake," Heidi says without looking at me. Hope moves in and slips her arm around Heidi's shoulders, giving her support and leaving me free to beat the crap out of Axel's parents if they snap at Heidi again.

"What have they told you so far?" the father asks.

Heidi recounts every detail, which isn't a whole lot. They only seem more agitated when she can't answer their questions.

"Do you want to sit down?" Hope asks.

"No," Mrs. Ryan snaps.

"Thank you," Mr. Ryan says, clamping his hand over his wife's arm and dragging her to the couch.

Heidi flips the television on. "I was watching for updates, but it's just the same stuff over and over."

Alexa squeals and flails her hands around. Heidi leans in and kisses her cheek. "I know, baby," she murmurs against her face, just loud enough for me to hear because I'm standing directly behind her. Both grandparents continue to ignore all the other cute, gurgly baby noises Alexa makes.

This couldn't be more awkward.

"It's amazing, she looks nothing like Axel," the mother says to her husband, jerking her chin in Alexa's direction.

I guess it *could* get more awkward.

"No. She looks exactly like Heidi did at that age," I answer.

All three of them turn and stare at me. "Didn't your brother give you those photos?" I ask Heidi.

"Uh, yeah." She points to a shelf next to the television, and I spot what she's asking for right away. Side-by-side baby photos of Heidi and Alexa. Someone had them framed and labeled "baby Heidi" and "baby Alexa." I hand it to Heidi, who leans over to show it to the Ice

Queen.

"Axel had this made for me for Christmas."

Can a nod be snotty? Because this woman's quick head bob is full of uppitiness. "That's nice, dear."

Who actually talks like that?

I'm really not liking the way this bitch seems to be implying Alexa isn't Axel's kid.

During a break in the news, they throw more questions about the accident at Heidi. Questions she doesn't have answers for.

When one of the hotline numbers scrolls across the bottom of the screen, the mother snaps at Heidi, "Why aren't you at the headquarters with all the other family members?"

Heidi explains to them, the same way she did to us last night, "I didn't think it was a good place for Alexa to be. The representative I spoke to said she'd call as soon as she had news."

The mother sniffs and glares at her husband who pats her hand. "She's right. There's nothing we can do there that can't be done here."

Oh, great. I guess that means they're sticking around.

"Can I make you breakfast? Or do you want something to drink?" Hope offers on her way to the kitchen.

They both shake their heads and things go back to awkward.

Someone knocks—well *bangs*—on the door. I open it and Penny jumps back. "Shit, Murphy, right? What are you doing here?"

I don't bother answering, just let her in.

"Oh, Heidi!"

"What?" Heidi jumps up and rushes over to meet her friend. "Did you hear something?"

"Lucas. They found him. He's at the hospital. I'm supposed meet his mom and dad there."

"Oh, thank God. He's okay?"

"No. I guess it's really bad." Penny's lip trembles and she squeezes Heidi's arm. "Lucas worked on the platform, so he got thrown into the water with the blast…" Penny trails off and Heidi bursts into tears.

I don't understand what the significance of that is, and now isn't the time to ask. The two girls sob together. Hope comes out of the kitchen to see what's going on and takes Alexa. She talks quietly to the two of them for a few minutes before Penny leaves.

"This is ridiculous. Sitting around waiting here. We're going down to headquarters," Axel's mother announces. His father shrugs and gives us a weak wave.

"We'll call you if we find something out, Heidi," he says before shutting the door.

"Friendly in-laws, Bug."

"They don't care for me." She shrugs and grabs Alexa from Hope. "Whatever. Axel hates them."

That explains why it was no big deal for him to move all the way to Alaska.

"I always wondered why his sister moved all the way out to California. But now I know."

"Yeah, I remember him telling me about her," I say. "She's got kids, too, right?"

"Yup."

"Are they that cold to her kids?"

"Don't know." She lifts Alexa up. "We don't really care, do we?" she asks in a playful, silly voice. Alexa laughs and kicks her little legs in the air, clearly not giving a fuck what her grandparents think of her.

"Well, breakfast is ready," Hope says. She takes Heidi's elbow, pulling her into the kitchen. "You need to eat something."

A few hours later, we get the official call. Given the nature of the explosion, and the extreme water temperatures, the probability of finding any other workers alive after all this time is considered highly improbable.

Forty

Sometimes the road we fear the most,

is the one that takes us home.

Heidi

I can't leave Alaska without saying goodbye to Lucas. Hope says she'll stay at the apartment with Alexa, and Murphy drives me to the hospital.

The last few days have been horrible. No, horrible isn't enough. No words cover what I'm feeling.

The worst has been dealing with Axel's parents. Subtly blaming *me* for him taking this job. I finally got fed up and explained in lengthy detail how much I hated it here and how Axel dragged me up here, not the other way around.

I'm pretty sure Murphy has been plotting their deaths and drew a map of where he plans to dump their bodies before we leave for home.

He's quiet the entire ride, and I don't have it in me to come up with any small talk.

"I'll wait in the car," he says when we finally find a parking spot.

My hand's on the door, about to push it open, but I fall back in my seat. "Oh."

"Shit. I'm sorry. Do you *want* me to come in with you?"

"If you don't mind."

He opens his door and hurries to my side, offering me a hand.

I'm limp and drained. So damn tired, I end up leaning on him. "You okay?" he asks.

"No."

His jaw clenches, but he's quiet as we cross the parking lot. At the sliding glass doors, I stop and pull Murphy to the side. "Are you mad at me?"

"What? No. Why would you think that?"

"You're so quiet."

He takes one of my hands and doesn't speak again until I meet his gaze. "Heidi, I want to make everything better for you and I don't know how. That's all."

"Oh." Tears wet my lashes and I try to blink them away. "Having you here, helping me with packing up the apartment, and all the other small details. It makes it easier. I don't know what I would have done if you and Hope hadn't come."

He nods, but his serious expression never changes. His hand settles on my lower back and he guides me inside the hospital. "Come on, let's see your friend."

"Are you coming in with me?"

"I should probably wait outside the room. I've never really met the kid."

Clearing the air between us helped. A little.

We find our way to Lucas's unit. Barely more than a sheet separates his bed from the patients on either side of him. "Lucas?" I call out before entering.

I've worked in a hospital and unfortunately spent a lot of time in hospitals visiting injured family members. None of that prepared me for seeing Lucas, and I try not to gasp when I take him in.

"It's not as bad as it looks, Heidi," he rasps in a voice I barely recognize.

I take a deep breath and force a smile. "Is this your new method of picking up chicks?"

He snorts and rolls his head toward the window. "Might as well. Penny left me."

"What?"

"It's fine. Good to know she wasn't down for the sickness and health part before we got married, right?"

Even in his condition, he's trying to joke with me, so I laugh even though it's the last thing I feel like doing.

"What are you going to do?"

"My parents are staying."

"I…I'm headed home. I can't stay here by myself."

"Christ, Heidi. I'm so fucking sorry. This is my fault. If I hadn't dragged you guys up here, Axel would, well, he'd—"

Pain's etched all over his face, and I settle my hand on his shoulder to calm him. "It's *not* your fault. He wanted to visit Alaska way before you ever took the job here."

The small lie seems to comfort him, so I don't waste energy feeling guilty about it.

"He loved you, Heidi. I know you two were having problems." I raise an eyebrow, surprised Axel expressed our issues to anyone. Lucas squeezes my hand. "He didn't know how to deal with being a dad. But he loved you both. Every time you texted him a picture, he'd run around and show everyone 'his girls.'"

So much for not crying and snotting all over myself. "Thank you," I whisper when I can finally force some words out.

"When are you leaving?"

"Tonight."

"Good. My parents are going to try to get me transferred to a hospital at home, when I can travel."

"Let me know as soon as you're back so I can come see you."

His eyelids drop and his voice is much weaker than it was a few minutes ago. "Bring Alexa with you?"

"I will."

I give his hand another quick squeeze before leaving.

"How'd it go?" Murphy asks while we're waiting for the elevator.

I choke down a sob. "Not great."

He wraps his arm around my shoulders, offering support. After a few minutes, I'm able to spit out part of why I'm so mad. "Penny ditched him. He's better off. She cheated on him all the time. But still."

The doors open, and he ushers me inside. "I'm sorry."

"He's such a good guy. He didn't deserve that."

The rest of the afternoon goes by swiftly, yet in slow motion. I'm a robot as I take a last walk through the apartment. Too many emotions overwhelm me as we leave. I don't know which one beats stronger in my chest. Anger with Axel for taking this stupid job? Guilt because I'm so damn happy to go home?

The one thing I'm sure of? I'm terrified of what happens next.

Forty-One

Heidi

I'm a wreck the day of Axel's funeral. I haven't slept much since we returned to New York. To be honest, I haven't slept since that first phone call.

After a week of waiting and getting the runaround from Axel's company, I was told due to the special gear required by Axel's below-deck job, they found "remains." No one explained what specifically that meant, but the gruesome images my head came up with haunt me all day, every day.

While we were packing up the apartment, I was asked to turn over some of Axel's things for DNA testing and the remains were determined to be his.

Axel's parents have fought me on everything since the official word about their son's death was made public. Axel and I never exactly discussed things like funeral arrangements. Who thinks about that stuff when you're nineteen and twenty-one years old? His parents already have burial plots picked out for themselves, and that's where they want to put their only son.

Given how little there is to bury, I don't think it makes a lot of sense, but it seems like a horrible thing to quibble over, so I don't object.

Besides, it's not as if I have something better in mind.

When we returned to New York, I realized Alexa and I had nowhere to go. Axel and I had given up our apartment when we moved.

My brother had moved out of his apartment and was still in his rehab facility re-learning how to walk. It wasn't even a question for Hope, though. She and Rock took me back into their house and set me up in the guest room I stayed in last time. Hope and Rock stepped in a few times when Axel's parents got too demanding. I don't know what I'd do without them.

I haven't seen Murphy since we got back from Alaska. But then again, I haven't wanted to see anyone.

I'm angry. Boiling mad. About everything. Confused as hell about what I should do next with my life. The only thing that gets me out of bed every morning is Alexa. Every day, I wake up, take a deep breath, and listen for sounds of what she's up to. I see Axel every time I look at my baby girl, it hurts, but I fall in love with her all over again. Nothing matters except doing the right thing for her.

If only I knew what that was.

Today, I dress her in a black velvet jumper with footies. Probably meant for taking happy holiday photos—not for attending funerals. I found it on clearance. It came with a matching black velvet hat, which is good because it's a cold day.

On the way to the funeral, I sit with Alexa in the back of Rock's SUV and try to convince her to keep the hat on.

News of Axel's death must have spread. The parking lot of the funeral home is full of motorcycles. Lost Kings here to show their support.

I burst into tears when I see them.

When we step inside the funeral home, Trinity takes Alexa from me and pulls the diaper bag out of my hands. Hope never leaves my side.

Axel's parents barely speak to me. His mother glares at each biker who approaches and offers condolences.

It's a bitterly cold day at the gravesite. Too cold for the long service his parents planned. Alexa starts screaming. I think she's had enough of the cold, too.

"Heidi, why don't I take her back to the clubhouse, so you don't have to worry?" Trinity asks.

"That's probably better. Thank you."

"No problem." She embraces me and I kiss Alexa's cheek. "There are bottles and stuff in her bag," I remind Trinity before she leaves. I haven't been able to nurse my daughter since before we left Alaska. Another thing that makes me feel like a failure. The doctors and counselors had stressed over and over the importance of breast-feeding, and now I can't even do that.

"Where is that girl taking Alexa?" Axel's mother snaps at me.

Now you care about your granddaughter?

"That's my friend and she's taking Alexa home." My hands twist nervously in front of me to keep warm. I forgot gloves. "It's too cold for her to be out here."

His mother's eyes zero in on my hand. "You should give that back."

"What?"

She points at my left hand. "My mother's ring."

"My engagement ring?" I ask stupidly, unable to follow this woman's logic.

"Yes. It belongs in the family."

I'm so utterly confused by her words. "It is."

"*My* family. It should go to Annabelle's daughter when she's older. Not you."

I don't have a response. I'm too stunned and hurt.

Luckily, Hope's full of words. She wraps her arm around my shoulders and squeezes. "Mrs. Ryan. That ring legally belongs to Heidi. Axel gave it to her in contemplation of marriage. They married. You don't have any claim on it. It will go to their daughter when she's older."

Mentioning Alexa reminds me of how Axel gave me the ring. As an afterthought when I told him I was pregnant. What kind of story is that to tell my daughter? *Hey, when your dad couldn't talk me into an abortion, he proposed.*

"No." I twist the ring off my finger. "Here. Take it."

Hope tries to stop me. "Heidi, she has no right—"

"No. I don't want to think about *you* every time I look at it," I snap, throwing the ring at Mrs. Ryan. "Just so you know, he was planning to give it to me after graduation. Whether I'd been pregnant or not, we still would have gotten married." I don't know if that last part is true exactly. Axel said he wanted to give me the ring after he graduated, but if I hadn't gotten pregnant would we have even been together by then?

I'm so angry. I want to lash out at someone. I want to scream at her. She might think I'm biker trash who lured her son to the dark side, but at least my "trashy" family loves me and came here to support me, when her precious daughter couldn't be bothered to fly home for the funeral of her only sibling.

Mr. Ryan stoops down to pick up the ring. "How dare—"

Rock steps up next to me. "Enough. I know you're hurting, but you have no business taking it out on her," he says calmly. "I knew your son pretty well. He loved Heidi. He wouldn't want her treated this way."

Mrs. Ryan glares at him. "She ruined his life. He's dead because—"

Rock holds his hand up, stopping her. "Stop right there. I'm telling you politely to have some dignity for the sake of your son." He lowers his voice and leans in. "But if either of you say another word to upset Heidi, I'll personally escort you out." He puts enough menace behind the words that Axel's parents snap their mouths closed and move away from us.

"I'm sorry, Heidi-girl," he says, turning me to face him. "Are you okay?"

"Yes. Thank you. I didn't know what to do." I glance out to the parking lot and catch my brother's truck pulling in. Seeing it feels like a baseball bat to the stomach. I've been so miserable since returning home, I haven't visited my brother nearly enough.

There's only one other person Marcel would allow to drive his truck.

Murphy.

I'm flooded with emotions. Each one dark and painful.

"I'll be right back," I say over my shoulder.

Hope calls out to me, but I'm already running toward where Murphy's helping my brother out of the truck and into a *wheelchair*. It hurts so much seeing my brother like this. I know it must be killing him to depend on others for something so basic. Tears cloud my vision. Mrs. Ryan's accusation echoes in my head. My anger with Axel for moving us to Alaska and lying to me—something I haven't been able to admit to anyone yet—stirs inside of me.

All these agonizing emotions strangle me, stealing my breath. I feel so helpless. So frustrated and so damn angry.

A burning ball of anguish fills my chest as I watch Murphy pushing my brother's wheelchair over the rough ground.

My brother shouldn't be in a wheelchair.

Axel should be alive.

My feet slap painfully against the hard ground as I run to meet them.

"Why are you even here, Murphy?" I shout.

His head snaps up. "What?"

Marcel reaches up and grabs my hand. "Hey, baby sis. Calm down."

"Calm down?" I throw my glare at Murphy. "You hated Axel. You drummed him out of the club. We never would have been up there in the first place—"

"Heidi!" my brother snaps, jerking my arm to get my attention. "That's enough."

Painful sobs tear my throat apart. My heart's throbbing with so much anger and hurt, I don't know where to put it or how to make it stop. Shame slithers over my skin. I hate myself for every awful word I flung at Murphy.

"Heidi," Hope says, wrapping her arm around my shoulders and steering me back to the funeral. I'm so ashamed of my behavior, I bury my face against her coat and cry. She walks us to the front row and sits us down. Rock's on my other side. He settles his arm over the back of my chair, embracing both of us. For comfort and probably to keep me in place so I don't cause another scene.

"I'm sorry," I whisper.

Hope tips her head down and smiles through her tears. "I know you are, sweetheart. It's okay."

But, it's not okay. Nothing is okay.

MURPHY

Heidi's words sting.

Because I wonder if there's any truth to them.

Mostly her words burn because I know she's hurting. She's way too young to be dealing with any of this. She was dealt a shitty set of parents and had a rough childhood because of it. Things should be easier for her now. But they're not.

She'd been such a robot those last days in Alaska, she scared me. I'm glad she's finally showing some emotion. Even if it is by screaming at me in the parking lot.

"I'm sorry, bro," Teller says, reaching up to grab my hand.

"It's fine. She's upset."

"She didn't mean it."

I'm dealing with my own shit today. Picking my best friend up from his rehabilitation facility and wheeling him around is fucking with me. Inside, I'm shredded raw. Outside, I'm trying to stay upbeat and positive for him. I'm terrified his condition may be permanent, but I don't dare voice my fears to anyone. Afraid then it will become real.

Worse, I know how much he hates being seen out in public like this. *Weak.* If it wasn't for Heidi, he would have stayed in bed and told me to go fuck myself when I came to pick him up.

"You feeling all right?" I ask. A dangerous question. Even with me, he's touchy about his condition.

"I'm fine, dick."

I smack him in the back of the head for that comment. I mean, he won't get better if I baby him, right?

"Ow. It's not nice to beat up the disabled, you know."

"You're not disabled, you fuck. You're temporarily out of commission."

He lets out a dark chuckle and points to the back row. "Park us back here."

Dex and Swan join us and fuss over Teller, which I know makes him even more uncomfortable. My mind wanders to Heidi. Up front. With her head on Hope's shoulder. Rock has an arm around both of them. That's good. They've taken such good care of her since we got home. Rock gives me an update on Heidi almost every day because I felt it was better to keep my distance.

Across the aisle, Axel's stone-hard parents sit, glaring at everyone.

While Swan's still catering to Teller, Dex leans over. "I take back everything I ever said about Axel being uptight. Those parents of his are two of the coldest fish I've ever met."

"Yeah. Dealt with them up in Alaska."

"Did you hear the shit they said to Heidi? I'm surprised Rock didn't kill that mother. What a piece of work."

"No. What happened?"

He gives me a brief rundown that makes my blood bubble and my fists flex. I've never hit a woman. Axel's mother may be my first.

The service is long. As soon as there's a break, Teller asks to go.

"You don't want to stay and talk to your sister?"

He glares at me.

"Okay. Okay. Let's go."

In the truck, he explains he's not feeling well, and I know it killed him to admit it, so I just nod and drive him back.

When I finally make it to the clubhouse, it's virtually empty. Wrath's truck's in the yard, so he's here somewhere. I don't go looking for him, though.

Usually, I can't stand being alone.

But right now, I can't stand the thought of being around anyone.

Forty-Two

Heidi

I need to do this before I lose my nerve. Or fall asleep.

I'm wrung out and exhausted, ready to crawl into bed and not come out for a month.

After checking on Alexa, I hike up the clubhouse stairs. This trip has never seemed so long before.

Outside Murphy's door, I hesitate. What if he's with someone? *Stop making excuses and apologize.*

He answers after the third knock, looking as worn out as I feel.

"Hey, Bug." His gaze roams over me, concern etched on his face. He's still worried about me, even though I acted so horribly before.

I open my mouth, but instead of an apology a harsh sob bursts out.

He pulls me into his arms, against his chest, holds me tight and lets me cry. "I'm so sorry," I cry the words into his shirt.

"What're you sorry for?" With my face mashed up against his chest, I hear and feel his softly spoken question.

Is he serious? I wriggle away enough to stare up at his face. "For yelling at you at the funeral. I'm sorry. After his parents—and my brother and…I'm sorry. I never should have taken everything out on you. You're my—I—you helped me out so much. I don't know what I would have done without you. I'm so sorry," I babble all the words out and cry some more.

His chest rises as he pulls in a long breath. There's no hint of the smile I'm used to when he opens his mouth. "Heidi, I'm always here for you, no matter what. You take whatever you want out on me."

My jaw drops and I squeak out, "Blake."

He pulls me against him again. "It's okay," he reassures me while rubbing his hand over my hair and down my back.

"I didn't mean any of it."

"I know you didn't." He holds me tighter and I'm still so chilled from the funeral, I cling to him, soaking in his warmth. We stay like that, him holding me while I cry, rocking us from side to side, until I settle down.

"Where's my brother?" I finally ask.

"I brought him back early. He wasn't doing too good."

"Oh, shit. I should go see him."

"Let him rest today. I'll take you to see him tomorrow if you want. Maybe give him a call later and let him know how you're doing."

"I will."

"Where's Alexa?" he asks before I fumble out any more words.

"Downstairs with Wrath and Trinity," I whisper.

One corner of his mouth lifts into a smirk. "Come on. I want to say hi to her. Can't have Wrath being her favorite uncle."

He's trying to make me laugh, but I'm still too torn up. Instead, I let him guide me down the stairs.

Alexa's happy baby giggles ease some of the pain in my heart. Although when I see *why* she's making all the noise, I'm a little less enthused.

Wrath stops his game of airplane and settles Alexa against his chest, which makes her squeal and kick in frustration. "Don't worry, Mom, I was hanging on to her tight."

"I know. I saw you." Wrath's big and scary to everyone else, but I trust him completely with my daughter.

"Training for your own?" Murphy jokes.

Trinity wrinkles her nose. "Bite your tongue." Yeah, Trinity's much more interested in playing auntie than mommy.

"Thank you for watching her today."

"No problem," Trinity says as she passes Alexa to me. "Things looked intense with your mother-in-law."

I roll my eyes and drop down onto the other couch, keeping Alexa on my lap. She leans and wiggles trying to get Murphy to pick her up, and eventually I hand her over to him. My bare ring finger catches my attention.

"I can't believe I let her take my ring."

The three of them stare at me. "She did *what*?" Wrath asks.

My shoulders lift. I don't feel any sense of loss over the ring. More disbelief that I let that awful woman bully me into giving it to her. "It was his grandmother's, so I guess his mom felt like she was entitled to it."

"That's bullshit," Trinity says. "You should have Hope talk to her. That ring should go to Alexa."

"Hope said something to her." I laugh, a sad, pathetic sound. "It's not a super romantic story about how he gave it to me, anyway. I don't care."

"You might care later," Trinity says gently and I shrug.

We talk a little longer, then I stand and gather Alexa's things.

"You need me to walk you over to Hope and Rock's?" Murphy asks.

"No. We'll be okay."

I shouldn't have bothered. Of course Murphy won't let me walk home alone. He doesn't say anything as he walks beside me, carrying Alexa. When we get to the house, Hope's on the front porch.

"I was looking for you." Her gaze slides to Murphy. "Everything all right?"

"We're okay," I answer.

She holds her arms out for Alexa. "I'll put her down for her nap."

"Thank you."

Why didn't I go inside with Hope? Wrath and Trinity had been a good distraction back at the clubhouse. But now I'm alone with Blake, and I still can't look him in the eye. I'm embarrassed over the easy way he forgave me for my awful behavior.

"Heidi?"

I take a chance and meet his eyes. "Is there anything I can do for you?" he asks.

"I don't think so."

I hate all this…stuff. All this weirdness between us that I caused.

"If you need anything, call me. Okay?" he says quietly.

"I will."

"Doesn't matter what time it is. And if you ever need to talk, I'm a short walk that way." He points toward the clubhouse.

"I'll call first." My attempt at a joke comes out sad, and I think he misunderstands.

"That's not—I'm not—there's no one. Don't worry about that."

"Murphy—"

"No." He leans over and kisses my forehead. "Call me if you want to visit your brother tomorrow." Then, he takes off before I can say anything else.

My legs feel too heavy to carry me up the stairs. Inside, I find Hope and Rock talking quietly in the kitchen.

"You okay, hon?" Rock calls.

"Yeah," I answer, joining them.

"Hungry?" Hope asks.

"No. Is Alexa all right?"

"Yup. Went right down. She doesn't know…" Hope trails off.

"I know she doesn't." It makes me sad she'll never have any memories of her father. Kind of like me. "I think…I need a nap."

Rock pulls me in for a hug and kisses the top of my head. "You need to take care of yourself and the baby. We'll take care of everything else, okay?"

"Thank you."

MURPHY

Walking away from Heidi kills me. I want to be the one to help her through this. To be there for her. It hurt to find her outside my door in tears, so torn up because she thought she needed to apologize to me.

"She get back okay?" Wrath asks when I walk back inside.

"Yeah."

"Heard she let loose on you at the funeral."

"Yup." After hearing what her in-laws did to her, I understand her outburst a lot better. Not that I was mad at her in the first place, but at least I know where all that rage came from.

Wrath motions for me to join him. He has the whip for the house vaporizer, a grinder, and a glass jar of bud laid out on the coffee table. "Brother, I don't think there's enough weed in this house to make me feel better," I say, dropping down on the couch.

"You know how I like a challenge."

A half hour later, I don't necessarily feel *better*. In fact, I don't feel anything.

"How was Teller?" Wrath asks.

"Wrecked. I don't know what to do for him. He's not over losing Mariella."

"Probably why he keeps having setbacks with rehab."

"Yeah," I agree. "He's upset that he can't help Heidi, too, you know."

"Of course he is. She's been his whole life as long as I've known him."

The simple, heartfelt way Wrath says it leaves me speechless. Plenty of people probably think he's a meathead biker who only cares about lifting weights and motorcycles. That couldn't be more wrong. When it comes to his brothers, he's as perceptive as he is protective and loyal.

Saying any of that mushy shit will earn me an ass-kicking I'm not in the mood for. "Where'd Trin go?" I ask instead as I fall over and rest my head on the couch cushions.

He jerks his chin toward the back of the house. "Working or with the pups, I'm not sure. She's either been takin' care of babies or dogs all day."

"Aw, you want her to take care of you?"

"Fuckin' A." He grins at me, not at all offended by the question.

Z joins us and snaps the whip out of Wrath's hand. "Watch it," Wrath grumbles.

"You sound like a pit bull." I laugh like it's the funniest thing I've ever said.

"Cut him off," Trinity says, perching on the arm of the couch and patting my head.

"Where you been, Trin?"

"Working."

Z's dogs followed her in and immediately run over to him. "Down." He blows a cloud of vapor away from them. "You two don't need to lose any more brain cells." Wrath and I both crack up at that and Trinity shakes her head.

"Trin, you workin' on your beefcake covers?" Ever since Wrath let it slip that Trinity has a side business designing book covers, Z loves teasing her about it.

"Yeah, when you gonna model for me?" she asks.

Z must already be high, because he yanks his shirt up. "I'll do it right now, get your camera, Trin."

"Put your shirt on, dick," Wrath growls.

"I have a male-male cover coming up. Maybe you two can pose for that for me," she suggests with a big grin on her face.

"What's that?" Z turns to Wrath who shakes his head.

"Just say no," he advises.

"I love you guys," I blurt out.

Wrath leans over and slaps my leg. "We love you too, little brother. You need one of us to carry you to bed?"

"Nope. I'm good right here." Surrounded by family.

Forty-Three

Welcome to the daylight

Heidi

Murphy shows up to drive Alexa and me to visit my brother almost every day. I think he's truly forgiven my rotten behavior on the day of the funeral. He's never mentioned it and when I tried to apologize again, he blew it off.

"I can drive myself. You must have other things to do besides play chauffer for me every day."

His shoulders lift. "I'm visiting him anyway. It's nice to have company."

It's true. All the guys have arranged their schedules so someone is with my brother pretty much round the clock.

Marcel isn't stupid. He knows what they're up to and bitches about the guys babying him.

His complaints don't stop one of the brothers from being at his side every day, though.

After his physical therapy appointment, his physical therapist Violet takes me aside, while Blake takes my brother and Alexa back to his room. "Your brother's shown a lot of improvement since you've been home."

"Really?" It's the first thing I've had to smile about in a long time.

"Yes. He really loves your daughter. I think having her around motivates him a lot."

Her words leave me a little shaken, so I don't respond. I'm so torn about everything. Returning to Alaska meant leaving my brother, but if I hadn't gone home, I never would have seen Axel again before he… and at least I have good memories of our—

"He's a lucky guy," she continues, breaking up my gloomy thoughts. She nods at the hallway where we can still see Blake and Marcel. "To have such big family support. A lot of my patients don't have that."

"Are you saying he might be ready to go home soon?"

She checks over his chart and seems to contemplate her answer. "Yes. Things are definitely improving." She looks up at me again. "Are you sticking around?"

"Uh, well, yeah. My husband just passed away…"

Pink sweeps over her cheeks and her eyes widen. "Oh, I'm so sorry. I didn't realize. Your brother never—"

"It's okay."

"He's a tough nut to crack, you know?"

"Marcel? I guess."

"I understand his girlfriend died in the accident?"

"Uh—" I don't know how to explain their relationship. "She was a friend, yes."

"I'm sure that has a lot to do with it. We have a psychologist—"

"I can tell you right now, my brother won't go for that. I'll mention it, though."

The corners of her mouth lift into a friendly smile.

"What'd she want?" Marcel asks when I return to his room.

"Just to talk."

"About me?"

"No, about a sale at the mall. Yes, about you. She says you're improving a lot."

Marcel grunts and arranges himself in his bed, then asks Blake to hand Alexa to him.

"She probably likes you and thought she'd butter up your sister,"

Blake says and winks at me.

My brother doesn't find that funny and mutters "fuck off" under his breath.

"Watch your mouth around my daughter."

"Oh, please. You have a dirty mouth to rival any of us," Marcel says.

"I do not."

The three of us joke around that way for a while and it almost feels…normal.

"What else do you have planned today?" Blake asks on our way home.

"Um, nothing really."

"Mind stopping at the home store with me? Wrath asked me to pick something up."

"No. Not at all."

Wrath apparently sent pictures of what he needs, so while we're wandering through the bathroom fixtures, Blake has to consult his phone a bunch of times to make sure we have the right stuff. "All this shit looks the same," he grumbles. "I'm buying one of each. He can bring back whatever he doesn't need."

"Is it weird with Rock out of the clubhouse, and now Wrath's building a house and planning to move out, too? Are you guys excited you can party it up more?"

He gives me an odd look. "No. I've been— No. I understand why they want to be away from it. If I had…" He looks away. "If I was with someone, I'd want to be in my own place, too."

"I guess I never thought about the guys actually settling down."

Suddenly, this conversation seems really awkward.

"Think Rock and Hope will have kids?" I ask.

"Don't know what their plans are."

"God, can you see Wrath with a kid? He'd murder anyone who looked at her wrong."

He laughs, but it's an uncomfortable laugh. "We'd all do that."

"Yeah, you're right."

Wrath's waiting in front of the clubhouse when we get back. "Thanks for doing that. I was gonna flip my shit if I had to run down there again," he says as he takes the bags from Murphy. "Sorry, Heidi, I didn't realize you were out with him."

"It's okay. Gave me all sorts of ideas about what I want in a house."

He laughs, but Blake gives me another one of those strange looks. "Come on, I'll walk you back."

We say goodbye to Wrath and head to the path that takes us to Rock and Hope's house. Alexa's cranky and fussy. "I think she wants a real nap. Lights off, in her crib, with her music on, you know?"

He chuckles and settles his hand on my back, guiding me through the woods. The house is empty when we walk in. I take Alexa into our room, change her and set her in her crib, watching her until she falls asleep—which doesn't take long.

I wander into the bathroom, running my fingers through my heavy hair, pulling it up into a quick ponytail. I really need to get a trim but haven't had the time or energy.

When I finally return to the living room, Murphy's still there. "Oh, shoot. I'm sorry. I figured you—never mind."

"Hungry?"

"Now that you mention it, yeah. Hope took chicken out of the freezer. I was going to make dinner so she doesn't have to do it when she gets home."

"I'll help."

My face must have a trace of skepticism on it, because he throws his hands up. "I can cook."

"Okay, okay."

Hope keeps a bunch of fresh herbs in pots on the windowsill. I pluck what I want and chop them while Murphy watches. "Okay, maybe I can't cook like *that*."

I point to a pile of potatoes. "You can wash and cube those for me."

I'm not sure if Blake appreciates me giving him directions, but he does it. While we prep and cook, he tells me stories about working at Furious.

"Every Sunday afternoon these two ladies come in, reeking of alcohol."

"College girls?"

"No. They have to be mid-thirties."

"That's kinda pathetic."

He grunts in agreement. "You could light the place on fire from the fumes coming out of their pores."

I chuckle, throw the chicken in the oven, and set the timer. "Yuck. Isn't that dangerous?"

His shoulders lift. "They don't do much. Mostly lay around on the mats and gossip. They told me the other day they mix their meal replacement shakes with vodka before a night of going out."

"That's gross."

"Whatever. I told them that was clever and sold them another tub. Nothing I say will fix that kind of stupid."

I flick a dishtowel at his side. "You're terrible."

"They're more entertaining than the high school girls who come in and stand around the machines gossiping and getting in everyone's way."

"They're probably there to stare at you, just hoping you'll notice them."

"Oh, I notice them all right. They're a pain in the ass. We make Twitch deal with 'em."

"So, you really like working with Wrath? I always figured he'd be hard to work for."

"He is. He's very exact and doesn't tolerate slackers."

Actually, the two of them working together doesn't surprise me all that much. "You've never been a slacker."

"Nope. Born hustler, baby," he says with an exaggerated wink.

"Born *criminal*. My brother told me how you two used to jack baby formula."

He laughs. "Only for you. I got caught once." He rubs his hand over his stomach. "Told the manager I was trying to lose weight."

"By drinking baby formula?"

"Yeah. He felt bad for me and let me go without calling the cops."

It's such a ridiculous story, I can't stop laughing. It feels good to laugh after so much extended sadness. "It's a miracle I survived."

"I'd do anything for you, Heidi."

I *would do* not I *would have done*. My brain picks up that subtle difference and wonders if Murphy said it intentionally.

"Dinner's almost done. Let me go check on Alexa."

She's still out cold and I decide to let her rest.

When I return to the kitchen, Blake's pulling the chicken out of the oven. "Is it done?"

"I think so."

Hope and Rock still aren't home, so we have a quiet dinner together. I can't remember the last time we just hung out like this, without things being awkward or uncomfortable.

"This is nice."

"It is." He places his hand over mine. "How are you? Be honest."

I hold his gaze for a moment, before turning away. "Eventually, I need to figure out what the hell to do with myself."

"You're here to stay, right?"

"I never wanted to leave in the first place." He seems so relieved, guilt slides over my skin.

"You want to go back to school?"

"I really do. I can't live off Hope and Rock forever. There's supposed to be life insurance from Axel's company, but they're dragging their feet paying it out."

"Why?"

"Something about him not being vested in the company long enough to collect the money? I don't really understand all of it."

"Can Hope help you?"

"I don't think she knows a lot about insurance, but she said she'd find me an attorney who can help if they keep jerking me around."

"Good. That isn't right." He has a look on his face that says he has a way to deal with the problem in mind—and it doesn't involve lawyers.

"I know. I need to figure out how to support myself and Alexa. But I want to help my brother, too. He's taken care of me my whole life. I want to be there for him now."

"You are."

"Violet said he's gotten better since Alexa and I have been back?"

"He has. No doubt. Violet's good at her job, too. Puts up with a ton of shit from your brother, but she never gets flustered."

"Poor woman. She seems so nice."

Blake takes a sip of his drink and shrugs.

"Did you ever find the guys who did it?"

His face hardens for the first time tonight and he turns away. "You know I can't talk to you about that."

"So, it *was* club related."

"You're really too smart for your own good." He takes my chin between his fingers, forcing me to look at him. "You need to watch that around people who aren't me."

His touch feels more tender than harsh, and I'm not insulted by the warning. I've been told my whole life to forget anything I hear around the club. Blake's words almost sound like the kind of warning one of the guys would give his ol' lady. "What about my brother?" I ask after we stare at each other for a few seconds without speaking.

He drops his hand from my face and stares at his plate. "He prefers to think you're blissfully ignorant."

"Are we safe?" I think he understands I mean "we" as in the whole club, extended family and all.

"Yeah."

He helps me clear the table and put things away. I wrap a plate for both Hope and Rock, not sure if they'll want dinner when they come home.

"Do you want to watch a movie or something?" he asks after we've put everything away.

"Are you sure you don't have other stuff to do? I'm fine on my own, I swear." It's a lie, but I can't stand the thought of him being here with me out of pity.

"Is it really so unbelievable that I want to spend time with you?"

"No. I just meant if you'd rather hang at the clubhouse, I won't be offended."

"I don't think the clubhouse is a good place for the baby."

"I meant, you know, *without* me."

"Why would I want to be without you?" The words aren't said in an innocent, questioning way. He says it more like a challenge.

Unsure of what he's looking for, I struggle to answer, "I…I don't know."

He slips his arms around my shoulders. "You think too much. Always worried about the wrong things."

"What should I worry about?"

"Picking out a movie for us to watch."

The Fast and the Furious seems like a safe choice. Man candy for me, fast cars for him. He snorts when the movie starts but doesn't comment on my pick. "Why're you all the way over there?"

"I don't know."

He pats the cushion next to him, and I move a little closer. "What's gotten into you? You used to sit in my lap, or on my shoulders, or on my feet when we watched movies. Couldn't keep you off me."

"Yeah, when I was a kid. You don't want me hanging all over you now."

He chuckles, but his voice is soft, almost soothing. "You don't know jack about what I want."

I slide over a few more inches and he wraps his arm around me, pulling me to his side. "I'm cold."

He whips the blanket off the back of the couch and arranges it over me. "Better?"

I murmur a yes and settle my head against his shoulder. One of his hands strokes over my hair, lulling me half to sleep.

"You falling asleep on me?" he asks in a low voice.

"Mmmhhmm."

He shifts and my eyes pop open to find him staring at me.

"What's wrong?"

One of his large hands cups my face. "Nothing. I like looking at you." His intense gaze tells me there's so much more to his words. I'm lost in the tingling sensation of his palm against my skin. His forehead touches mine, and he inhales heavily. "You know how much I love you?"

I pull in a deep breath and stare into his familiar green eyes, watching me with so much love. "I love you, too." The words pop out with no thought on my part. I've loved him my entire life.

His lips smooth over mine, eliciting a gasp of surprise. He uses it to slide his tongue against mine, so soft, warm, and sweet. His hand slips into my hair, holding my head, so he can take our kiss deeper.

My head swims in confusion and excitement.

Blake keeps kissing me with all the passion of a man who knows exactly what he wants. He nips at my bottom lip, presses his tongue against mine, and groans into my mouth. His hand drops to my waist, tugging at me. The position is awkward, and I think I know what he wants. I sit up, not breaking our kiss, tossing off the blanket and throw my leg over him. His hands move to my hips, making me straddle his lap. He adjusts his position, sliding down a bit. The movement pushes what has to be a very large erection against me, and I moan. All control leaves my mind, and I rock against him.

His hands slide up my thighs, to my back and under my shirt. His warm, rough hands on my skin leave goose bumps. I rub myself against him even harder, and his kisses become more urgent. His breathing grows harsher.

Alexa screams bloody murder, yanking us out of the moment.

I groan in disappointment as I pull away. "I'm sorry."

"It's okay," he answers in a hoarse voice.

"I'll be right back," I promise.

"I'll be here."

MURPHY

I groan as I watch Heidi hurry away.

My mouth still burns from her sweet kisses. Part of me still can't believe I finally had her in my arms.

The guilt I expected doesn't come. Lord knows, if Heidi didn't want to be kissed, she'd let me know. Considering how much and for how long I've wanted her, I'm surprisingly calm. I do have to sit up and adjust myself, though, then stop myself from following her into the bedroom and finishing what we started.

If I want to be with her—and who am I kidding, there's no *if* about it—I better get used to interruptions like this.

She walks down the hallway, carrying a teary-faced, pissed-off Alexa, who's still screaming and waving her fists. "I know, baby. I know." Heidi shushes and coos at her daughter, while taking her into the kitchen. Since most of Hope and Rock's downstairs is an open floor plan, I track Heidi as she goes from the refrigerator to the counter. "Do you need help?" I call out.

"Nope. I got it. I'll be right there. Do you need anything while I'm out here?"

Yeah, 'cause she needs to be fetching shit for me while she's taking care of her baby. "I'm fine."

Alexa's eager to be fed when Heidi returns to the living room and finally calms down when the bottle touches her lips.

"Someone was hungry," I say, watching the two of them.

"I know. I probably should have woken her up to eat before, but she looked so peaceful," she whispers. Her eyes never leave Alexa's face while she feeds her. And my eyes never leave Heidi.

"You can put the movie back on," Heidi suggests.

"Nah, I'm fine." The two of them seem to light up my whole world, and I don't want to look away.

Heidi pops the bottle out of Alexa's mouth and shifts her so she can pat her back.

"So, anyone can feed her now?" I ask.

She raises an eyebrow. "What do you mean?"

"The bottle?" I wave my hand in the air, because I really don't know what I'm asking.

Pink spreads over her cheeks. "Yes, it's formula."

She goes back to feeding the baby, and when they're finished, Heidi hesitates. "Do you want me to take her?" I ask.

"Do you mind? I want to toss this in the dishwasher and change my shirt."

"Yeah, hand her over."

Alexa squeals and claps her little hands on either side of my face. "Got a full belly now, baby?" I ask and she makes the funniest shriek-giggling noises in response, so I ask her more questions.

"She likes when you talk to her," Heidi says quietly as she sits back down next to us.

"You always did, too. I'd come over after school and tell you all about my day. Best part was you couldn't share my secrets with anyone." I said it as a joke, but Heidi doesn't laugh.

"What's wrong?" I ask, settling Alexa against my chest. She coos in my ear and drools on my neck. Heidi apologizes and hands me a cloth.

"I can take her now if you want," she says after I adjust Alexa in my arms.

"I'm fine. What's wrong? You seem upset."

"We almost…was that okay?"

"It was better than okay." I watch Heidi for a few seconds, taking in her pink cheeks, dark brown eyes, and the way she can't keep her hands still. Reaching over, I cover her hands with mine. "There's absolutely nothing to be sorry about. I meant what I said."

She stares at me as if trying to remember my words, so I help her out. "I love you."

"How?"

"I never stopped."

"Even when I was…When I was so…far away?"

I'd do anything to ease the pain shimmering in her eyes. Will my words will help or make it worse? "Even then. It's going to take more than a few miles between us for me to stop loving you."

"Murphy." She sighs.

"Don't do that."

"Do what?"

"Don't distance yourself by using my road name. Not now."

Her eyes widen as if it never occurred to her that's what she was doing. "I'm sorry."

I hold my free arm up for her to curl under and she does. I flip the television back on low, and after a while, I realize she's fallen asleep.

In my arms I have everything I've ever wanted and a feeling of peace settles over me. If this is the reward, I can wait as long as she needs me to.

My thumb rubs over her cheek. "We'll finish that kiss later."

Sometime after the movie ends, the door opens and Hope breezes into the house. "Oh," she whispers loudly. "I didn't realize you were here, Murphy." Rock follows, stripping off her coat and hanging it in the closet.

"Everything okay?" she asks, approaching us with a smile on her face.

I wiggle the arm holding Alexa. "My arm might have fallen asleep."

She smiles when she sees Heidi's face pressed against my leg. "Long day?"

I run my hand over her hair, brushing it off her cheek. "Yeah, we spent time with Marcel."

Rock joins us and gently lifts Alexa from me. "I'll stick her in her crib."

"Where you two been?" I ask Hope.

"Rock picked me up from my office and took me out."

"Heidi made dinner. It's in the fridge for you guys."

Hope nods but doesn't move. "She's getting antsy about doing more stuff around here."

"You guys still okay with her being here?"

Hope frowns at me. I don't think she appreciated the question. "Of course we are. She can stay here as long as she wants. When she's ready to go back to school, we'll work something out for Alexa."

"Thanks."

She sits back in her chair, lacing her fingers over her stomach. "What are *your* plans?"

"What do you think?"

The corners of her mouth curl into a smile.

"Unless you think it's too soon?" I know when Hope's first husband passed away, Rock forced himself to wait a respectable amount of time before pursuing her, so I'm genuinely curious about her opinion.

"It's really up to her," she says.

Rock joins us, moving Hope and sitting back down, pulling her into his lap. "Anyway," she says, tapping Rock's arm. "You two have known each other your whole lives, so—"

"Christ, I don't want to be her option B because she's comfortable and being with me is the easy thing to do." Actually, as I say it, I realize, I don't care.

"Murphy," Hope says and I sense the hurt in her voice immediately. "That's not what I meant at all. And I don't think she would ever feel that way about you. I meant, no one would question it if you got together now or a few months from now or whatever."

I jerk my chin at Rock. "You're awfully quiet, prez."

"You want relationship advice from me? Follow her lead."

"I feel like if I wasn't here, your advice would be different," Hope teases.

He snakes his arms around her tighter, kissing her cheek. "Yeah? Sometimes a man has to do what a man has to do when he's got a stubborn woman. That what you meant?"

She snort-giggles and Heidi stirs.

"Stop, you're going to wake her up," Hope scolds Rock, who ignores her protests and kisses her neck.

"I'm awake," Heidi mumbles.

I raise an eyebrow at Hope. How much of our conversation did Heidi overhear?

She sits up slow and blinks a few times. Her gaze settles on me and she smiles, like she's happy to find me still here.

"Hey," she says.

"How was your brother when you saw him?" Rock asks.

Heidi gives him the details and after we talk some more, Hope and Rock go upstairs, leaving us alone on the couch together.

I want nothing more than to finish our kiss, but I think right now, it's better to give her some space. "Walk me out?" I ask, standing and holding my hand out to her.

"I'm sorry I fell asleep on you," she says as she follows me to the front door.

"It's okay."

"Blake?"

I turn and face her.

"Did you mean it?"

I don't need to ask. "Yeah, beautiful. I meant it. Your little fingerprints have been all over my heart since the day we met."

Her jaw drops.

I lean over and give her a kiss on the forehead. "It's late. Get some rest. I'll see you tomorrow."

Forty-Four

Heidi

I have all night to think over the bit of conversation I overheard. Blake thinks he's second best? That I'd settle for him? When he's the best person in my life and I don't deserve him?

It hurts.

It hurts that I've hurt him.

The truth is ugly. The truth is that I never stopped loving him. If I'm going to be brutally honest with myself, Axel and I probably wouldn't have made it together another year. The few sweet moments we had here and there don't change the fact that I made a mistake marrying Axel when he clearly wasn't happy about being a father.

I didn't know him as well as I thought I did. We didn't have as much in common as I always assumed we did.

Those are my truths. And they hurt. They're unfair because Axel's not here to dispute any of them.

None of that stops me from feeling guilty about kissing Blake last night.

No, not guilty about kissing him. Guilty about how much I *liked* kissing him. Overhearing the advice Hope gave him relieved a tiny portion of the guilt.

Confused and anxious, I wake early and dress Alexa to go visit my brother.

I find Hope awake in the kitchen. She's really the only person I can talk to about all of this stuff. She lost her first husband young, too, so I know she understands.

"It's not quite the same, honey. I didn't have such a close-knit family or a daughter to pull me out of my grief," she says when I attempt to explain my conflicted feelings.

She also wasn't considering leaving her husband when he died. That's the main reason I feel so guilty.

"Gettin' ready to see that brother of yours, Heidi-girl?" Rock asks, joining us.

"Yup."

"I'll be down later this afternoon."

"Thank you, Rock. Thanks for everything you do for him. And for me." I get the words out without being all weepy.

Rock seems flustered by the thanks and Hope pats his arm. "We love you, Heidi," she says.

I attempt a smile and a joke. "Even though I've always been a brat, Uncle Rock?"

His mouth pulls into a half-smirk. "Yeah, Heidi-girl. You were always a loveable little snot."

Warmth fills my chest. While life may have handed me a shitty set of parents, I've been blessed with a wonderful brother and club family.

That warmth lessens as I hurry over to the clubhouse and buckle Alexa into her car seat. Guilt follows me as I sneak my car down the driveway. I can't help it, though. I need time alone to think on the drive to Sunnyview.

"Where's Murphy?" my brother asks when I enter his room.

"Home, I guess. I can't keep bugging him."

"I doubt you bug him." He holds his hands out for Alexa. "Hi, baby," he sing-songs to her. It's funny to see my gloomy brother so head over heels for his niece.

Wrath and Trinity show up next. "You're here early," Wrath comments.

"Couldn't sleep."

While we're hanging out, one of my brother's doctors and the occupational therapist stop by. There's still a number of things my brother needs help with, but since he's been progressing well, they're ready to let him go home by the end of the week. "If there are no stairs."

Marcel starts shaking his head before the woman even finishes. "Nope. My room's on the second floor."

Wrath and Trinity share a look. "You can have our room. We'll move back into Wyatt's old room until the house is finished," Trinity says. Wrath squeezes her hand, and I wonder if they discussed this ahead of time.

"Nah, it's too isolated down there," Marcel says.

The doctor seems annoyed my brother isn't more thrilled about going home. "Well, there's always a Stairlift, but they're expensive—"

"Doesn't matter what the cost is, we just want him home if he can be home," Wrath says. My brother shoots a glare Wrath's way but doesn't contradict him.

Violet takes Marcel down to the physical therapy room while the three of us hang back.

"I wish Rock would get his ass down here. He's good at choking some sense into your hard-headed brother," Wrath grumbles.

"I think you did okay," I tease. "He just doesn't want to look weak in front of everyone."

"It's a miracle the fucker's alive after that accident. Weak isn't how I'd describe him. Pain in the ass—"

Trinity smacks Wrath's arm.

"What?"

Blake shows up while we're waiting for my brother to come back. He nods at Wrath and Trinity, then lifts his chin at me. "Why'd you come by yourself?"

My shoulders lift and my gaze darts to Wrath and Trinity, who are pretending not to listen to our conversation. "I was up early."

"So?"

I shrug again.

"Let's go check on welterweight," Wrath says, yanking Trinity up and out of the room.

"They think Marcel can come home at the end of the week. But he's being difficult."

"What's new?" He takes a seat and pulls it around, so he can face me when he sits. "What's going on?"

"Nothing."

His fingers gently grip my chin and turn me to meet his gaze. "Are you upset about last night?"

"No." *Lie.* "Not exactly."

"What does that mean?"

"I don't know how much I can give you right now, Blake."

"I'm not going anywhere."

"Come on."

"Heidi, I'm done. I'm done with any other girl but you. I know you've been through hell, so I'm not expecting anything. I'm leaving it up to you. When you're ready, we'll be together."

A sigh of relief leaves me. "What if I—"

"You're here!" Marcel shouts from the doorway. "Doc says I can go home at the end of the week."

Murphy's eyes close briefly, then he plasters a smile on and turns to face my brother. "That's awesome, brother. Can't wait."

MURPHY

"What are you up to now?" I ask as I catch up to Heidi out in the parking lot.

"Home?"

"Want to stop for lunch somewhere?"

It makes me real happy when she answers, "Okay" without even hesitating.

She follows me out of Empire to Hog Heaven. I know how much she loves this place. It looks like a shithole from the outside, but the chef is from some culinary school and he serves hearty gourmet food that comes from local farms and stuff. It's the closest decent restaurant to the clubhouse, so the guys end up here a lot.

"Is this okay?" I ask once we're settled in a booth in the back. Alexa's in her carrier next to Heidi, checking out her surroundings. Heidi's stirring her coffee in an endless circle.

She glances up at me. "It is. Thank you. I don't deserve you."

"What are you talking about?"

Her spoon clatters on the table, and she puts her head in her hands. "I don't know."

"Heidi, talk to me."

"What are we doing, Blake?" she mumbles.

"What?"

She tips her head to the side so she can see me. "What are we doing?"

"Having a late lunch?"

She doesn't laugh.

"I don't know what you want me to say. I want to take care of you."

"Why?"

"Because I love you." I'll never get tired of saying that to her. "That's what people in love do—take care of each other."

A brief smile lights up her face before her eyes darken with worry. "What do you expect from me?"

"Nothing. I know it's too soon."

"How long are you willing to wait?"

Forever. "I love you. Take your time. I'm not going anywhere."

She shakes her head. "I don't deserve you."

"What does that even fucking mean?"

Leaning forward, she drills me with a fierce stare. "It *means*, I screwed up my entire life, and you're going to help me put it back together? How is that fair to you?"

"Heidi." I grab both her hands, holding her tight. "You didn't screw anything up. None of it matters anyway. All we can do is go from here. I don't want to be without you any longer. That's a fact. It won't change."

I expect her to move away, to put some distance between us. But she uncurls her fingers and wraps them around my hands. "I feel awful. Axel doesn't get the same chance," she whispers. "But it was his choice to take that job, and I feel guilty for even thinking that way."

I don't know what to say, so I just keep holding her hands and let her talk. "From the second I found out I was pregnant, I kept trying to do the *right* thing, even though deep down I knew it was wrong in my heart."

"Like what?"

"Don't make me say it."

For a minute, she scared me. I thought she meant Alexa was the mistake. But she means getting married. I won't make her say it and I won't agree with her either. I'll just keep holding on to her.

"Now, I plan to do what's best for Alexa and whatever makes me happy."

"Do I make you happy?"

"I don't know yet."

Her answer doesn't upset me at all. I run the back of my hand over her cheek, and she peers up at me. "From now on, I want complete honesty from you, Heidi."

"I haven't lied to you."

I cock my head to the side and she glances away. "Maybe not. But I think sometimes you hide the truth when you don't want to bother someone."

Her eyes widen, like she never realized that's what she does or she's surprised I got her figured out. I'm not sure. "Maybe," she mumbles. Then she fixes her dark brown eyes on me. "You're also real quick to assume stuff, you know," she accuses.

"Oh, yeah? Like what?"

"Like when you showed up on my birthday and assumed I'd hop into bed with you."

I grin because even though that night ended up being a clusterfuck, it was still pretty fucking awesome.

"Why are you laughing?"

"I'm not laughing at all." I pull one of her hands up to my mouth and kiss the back. "It's one of my favorite memories."

She snorts and pulls her hand away. "Yeah, right. I'm sure the epic case of blue balls was very memorable."

I burst out laughing and she glares at me. "What I mean is, you assumed my eighteenth birthday meant I was yours. You didn't ask me what I wanted."

My laughter dies down. She's right. "What did you want?"

"I don't know."

"What do you want now?"

"I don't know," she answers, a little more unsure this time.

"You want me to back off?"

Her mouth curves into a soft smile. "No."

My heart stops its mad gallop at that one simple word. Especially the way Heidi doesn't have to think it over. I think she knows what she wants and she's afraid to admit it. And I'm okay with that.

"But I can't promise anything, yet," she warns.

"Take your time, beautiful."

Forty-Five

MURPHY

I've been reduced to an eleven-year-old boy again. I could go downstairs almost any night of the week and have my pick of hot girls eager to please me. Instead, I'm dick-in-hand, jerking off in the shower every morning. Frustrated doesn't begin to cover it.

When I told Heidi the next move was hers, I didn't consider that we see each other almost every day. Even when we don't see each other, I know she's a quick walk through the woods away.

Since our talk, we've settled into a new normal. Grudgingly, I have to admit, some of the things she accused me of were true. I have always taken her—taken us—for granted. There are a lot of little things about her I don't know because I've always just assumed.

I'm trying to give her space to figure out what she wants. She needs to push past her guilt, her grief, and everything else holding her back and make the decision when she's ready. I won't repeat past mistakes and try to force it. I *will* be her friend and help her with Alexa when she needs it, though. No matter what, there will always be a connection holding us together that I can't ignore.

After finishing my solo shower, I rush to get dressed. Since Marcel moved back into the clubhouse, Heidi's been trying to put her life back in motion. One of those things was to meet with her adviser and get back into school.

Yesterday, I promised to watch Alexa, so Heidi could go to her appointment. Hope has to be in court and Trinity is at the gym with

Wrath.

First, I pop over to see Marcel.

"Need anything, bro?"

He glares at me. "Where you headed off to?"

"I'm gonna go grab Alexa and watch her for the afternoon, so Heidi can go to campus and meet with her adviser."

He sighs and shakes his head. "Christ, would you stop using my niece to get into my sister's pants?"

His words hit me with the force of a tire iron to the chest. "What? How can you even say that?"

"Come on. Babysitting? All this other shit you do for her—"

"I'm trying to be her friend. It's Heidi. Of course I'm gonna help her out when she needs it."

"Yeah, because you want her to jump into bed with you."

"Fuck you." If he wasn't still so mangled from the accident, I'd throat punch him right now. "That's not why. Even if it was, so what? Why does the thought of us together bug you so much?"

He sighs and looks away. "I don't fuckin' know."

I might as well just say it. "Because of all the chicks we used to fuck around with to—"

"Yeah. Probably."

"If I'd known it was gonna cause me this much fuckin' trouble, I never woulda done any of it."

He turns and stares at me for a few beats before speaking. "Heidi's probably given you a ton of grief, hasn't she? Making you work for it?" He grins and I'm itching to punch him again.

"What do you think?" I ask in my best *are you stupid?* voice.

"Fuck it. I'm sorry. No one else in the world would treat her better. And Alexa. That's all that matters. Any douchewit she hooks up with is gonna be in Alexa's life, too."

"Good. Then the douchewit should be me, because you know damn well I love them both."

Laughter rumbles out of him, and it's the best fuckin' sound in the world. Teller's been *dark* since he got home. This might be as close to a blessing to date his sister as I ever get.

Date. We're way past dating.

"Yeah. God help you." He motions me closer and I lean over to give him a hug. "Bring Alexa over?"

"I will."

"Thanks. That kid's the only damn thing that keeps me from putting a bullet in my head."

"Seriously? Your sister, me, the club, everyone loves you. Don't say shit like that."

He nods and waves me out the door. I go, but we're not done with that conversation. Not at all.

Heidi said ten a.m. but I want to spend some time with her before she rushes out the door. I show up at nine and plan to pretend I got the time wrong.

I feel like an asshole when she opens the door looking stressed and rumpled. "Why are you here so early?"

"I thought we said nine?"

"No. Oh. I'm so messed up, maybe I did." She opens the door wider. "Uh, I already fed her. She's napping, but she'll be up soon." Heidi hurries into the kitchen and opens the refrigerator. "She'll want to eat when she gets up and probably every couple hours. There's enough in here."

"Okay. Sleeping, eating."

"And pooping. Lots of pooping."

"Awesome. Can't wait."

She chuckles. "You can stay here with her."

"I promised I'd bring her over to see your brother."

"Oh, good." She hesitates and glances down. "Shit, I need to get dressed."

"Did you eat yet?"

"No."

"Go do what you need to do. I'll make you something."

Since I'm here so early, we have extra time to have breakfast together. "You keep feeding me. Are you trying to fatten me up?" she asks after I stick a plate of eggs in front of her.

"No. You're perfect the way you are."

She glances down. "I'm definitely different than I was before Alexa."

I snort because all the changes look good to me.

"Hey, after my meeting, I'm going to swing by the hospital. Lucas sent me a text. He's back and up at Empire Med."

"Okay."

"He wanted to see Alexa, but I don't really want to take her there right now, you know?"

"I understand."

Should I be rattled that she's going off to visit some other guy? No. Am I?

Not really.

Heidi

My morning with Blake was a nice surprise. He's been living up to his promise of being my friend and giving me time. I know how busy he is between the club and working at Furious, but he makes time to see me and Alexa every day. Nothing big. He doesn't bring flowers or make grand declarations of love. That's not his style. He's practical. Quietly showing me every day that he's here for me.

Like he's always been.

My meeting went better than I expected. I have to wait until fall to re-enroll, but otherwise, I'm all set.

Walking through campus, I'm assaulted with a hundred different memories of Axel and me here. I can even see our old apartment building from my adviser's office.

I didn't think this through.

How can I ever spend time here again, in a place with so many memories?

There are enough colleges in and around the Capital Region that I might have to look for somewhere else to finish my program.

At least I have a few months to think it over.

Lucas looks a hundred times better than he did when I saw him in Alaska, and it's the first thing I say to him.

"Thanks, I still feel like shit. Where's the kid?"

"Home. My brother's finally home now." I don't mention Murphy because I'm not sure how much Axel told Lucas about our relationship.

"Where you living now?"

"With my uncle and aunt. They've been a big help."

"Axel's parents aren't helping you out?"

"Fuck no. His mom was a raging bitch at the funeral."

He looks so stricken, I almost regret my harsh honesty. "I'm sorry. He never talked about his parents much, so I figured something was off there."

"They're not the warmest people."

We talk about a lot of stuff and it's nice to catch up.

A nurse finally chases me out at dinnertime. I didn't realize how late it was. I send Blake a text to let him know I'm heading home.

"Helga Dunning. My husband, Nick, is supposed to be on this floor."

My head snaps up at the name. Not the last name, which I don't recognize. The first name. There just aren't a lot of Helgas around here.

The woman's hair is dark like mine, but that doesn't mean anything.

"Turn around," I mutter. As if she heard me, she does, and I suck in a hit of air. She could be my mother. She looks like an older, poorly preserved version of the image I see every morning in the mirror.

"Mom?"

Naturally, she doesn't look my way. Why would she? She relinquished the title of "mom" more than a decade ago.

"Helga Whelan?" I call out a little louder. This time she does turn. What the fuck do I do now?

Her gaze lands on me and she tilts her head to the side. "Do I know you?" she asks walking closer.

"Heidi? Remember me? Your daughter?"

MURPHY

I wasn't jealous about Heidi visiting her friend.

Eight hours ago.

She texted me when she left school. Then again when she was leaving the hospital.

She spent an awful long time there

"Stop being an asshole," I grumble to myself.

Alexa chortle-giggles and waves her fists. We've had a pretty good day together. She's a good baby. Easy to care for. She sure as hell cheered Teller right the fuck up.

Another hour later and I'm ready to freak the fuck out that Heidi still isn't back. It's not jealousy this time, it's worry.

I'm hanging with the baby in front of the clubhouse so that I'll be sure to see Heidi as soon as she drives up.

Instead, Z joins me. "Pretty soon we'll need to get you one of those kangaroo pouches so you can just carry her around."

"Fuck off."

He laughs like an idiot and Alexa laughs with him. "See, she thinks you're a moron, too," I say.

"You're awfully bitchy today. What's wrong?" he asks.

I give him a look to see if he really wants me to answer or if he's still being a jerk. He's busy tickling Alexa's feet, so I answer honestly. "Worried about Heidi. She should have been home a few hours ago."

"Shit. You call her?"

"Yeah, but I don't want to keep blowing up her phone and distract her if she's driving, you know?"

That's when we hear the crunch of gravel under tires coming up the driveway. "That sounds like her." I let out a relieved breath before the warring sensations of worry and jealousy stir up. By the time she parks and gets out, I'm not sure how I feel.

"Hey, Heidi-girl. Your man was startin' to worry about you," Z says, jerking a thumb in my direction.

This is the first time anyone's acknowledged what is pretty obvious. "Asshole," I growl under my breath. The fucker laughs at me. Heidi didn't seem to hear him at all.

"What's wrong, Heidi?"

Her gaze darts between Z and Alexa, ignoring me completely. "Hey, baby," she says, holding out her arms. I hand Alexa over and watch her carefully for a minute.

"I'll see you two at the party later?" I shake my head and Z makes a "call me" gesture then says goodbye to both of us.

When she raises her gaze to mine, her eyes are wet. "How was Lucas?" I ask, hating that I was jealous for even a second.

"Better. He looked much better than before."

"That why you took so long?" *Why?* Why did I say that?

Her face hardens. "What's that supposed to mean?"

"Nothing."

"You're jealous of my injured, bedridden friend?"

"No."

She leans in and kisses my cheek. "Thanks for watching Alexa, Murphy. I'll talk to you later."

"Heidi, wait."

"No."

I watch her go, hating myself for picking a fight over nothing. We're not actually together. But we're as together as we've ever been. In my head she's mine.

Fuck.

Heidi

I'm so tied up in knots on the way home. Mad at myself for attempting to talk to my useless mother, like some pathetic, needy child. Mad at shutting Blake down when he was probably just worried about me. Just pissed at the world in general.

After spending those awful few minutes with my mother, I *needed* to feel my daughter in my arms. Couldn't wait to get to her. I'm not a bad mother. I'm not. Nothing could ever make me abandon Alexa the way my mother abandoned me.

"Are you okay, Heidi?" Hope asks when I shut the door behind me.

"No."

"What's wrong?"

That's when I burst into tears. Alexa mimics me and screams her head off. Hope hurries over, taking Alexa and wrapping her arm around my shoulder.

"Come here. What happened? Did you have a fight with Murphy?"

"No. Not really."

Now that I have a chance to think about it, I'm surprised he didn't follow me over here and demand an explanation. Maybe he's finally had enough of my back and forth moodiness.

The thought makes me cry even harder.

Hope works hard to balance rocking Alexa so she stops crying and rubbing my back to calm me down.

"Tell me what happened, honey."

"I…I went to school, to talk about re-enrolling for fall semester and things went great. Then, I started remembering all the different things Axel and I had done there, and I felt awful. How can I go on with my life and finish school when he's just *gone*?"

"I wish you hadn't gone alone. Do any other schools have that program?"

"I don't know."

"Are they bad memories?"

"No. Not really."

"Well, you know he'd want you to finish school—"

"No." I cut her off because this has also been bothering me. "I don't know that. He gave me such a hard time about finishing. Every time I brought it up, he had an excuse."

Her face screws into a scowl, but she still tries to defend Axel, which I love her for. "Maybe he was worried about Alexa. Daycare is so expensive—"

"Yeah. That's what he said. But, shit Hope. Please don't tell anyone this."

"What, honey?"

"You know how he promised me we would only be in Alaska for one year?"

"Yes."

"Right before he…died. The morning I drove him to work, he let me know he was considering a promotion that would take us to Indonesia. Either that or he wanted to sign up for another year in Alaska."

"Oh. Oh, wow."

"Yeah. We had just spent two weeks together. I was trying so hard to work on things, like you and I talked about, and it was rough at first but then got better. But he was lying to me the whole time. I must have mentioned how much I wanted to come home or finish school about a dozen times, and he never said a word."

"Maybe he wasn't sure."

"I don't know. He seemed pretty sure about it to me. He knew I'd be pissed. That's why he waited until the last minute."

"I'm so sorry, Heidi."

"I knew after that we weren't going to make it. How could we, when he didn't even consult me on major stuff like that? Or try to discuss it with me?"

"I don't know."

"And I feel like shit for thinking all these things, because now he's gone and Alexa will grow up without her father, and it's all his fucking fault! I'm so mad at him, but I can't be mad at him because he's *dead*." There. I finally said it.

A fresh wave of tears and frustration flows out of me, and Hope hugs me tighter. "It's okay to have these feelings, Heidi. You have a right to them. What you can't do is bottle them up and make yourself miserable."

"That's not the worst of it."

"Oh, dear," she mutters. "What else?"

I sit up straighter and throw myself against the back of the couch. Alexa's watching me and I hold my arms out. Hope hands Alexa over and I cuddle her close before giving Hope the next part of my day. "I ran into my mother."

"What? Oh my gosh. Where?"

"At the hospital. My friend Lucas just got transferred down here. She said her name and I took a chance. It was her."

"Okay."

I'm so embarrassed, I don't know how to put the encounter into words. "I was so pathetic, Hope. I thought I got over this years ago. She abandoned me at my grandmother's. Why did I think she'd give a shit now? Did I think she'd see me and immediately regret her mistakes and welcome me into her loving arms or something?"

"Oh, honey." Hope's voice breaks as she wraps me up in another hug. "She's your mother. There's nothing wrong with any of those feelings, either."

"Yes, there is. I know better. It was so stupid. She didn't care, Hope. I tried to tell her about Gram, about Marcel, about Alexa. She wasn't interested in any of it." I nuzzle my nose against Alexa's head, inhaling her sweet baby scent. "Why'd I do that?" I mumble.

"Heidi, there's still that little girl inside of you who misses her mom. That's okay. It doesn't make you stupid. It makes you human. Your mother's the idiot. From the first time I met you, I thought your mother was a fool for not being involved in your life. You were such a sweet young lady."

"Everyone thought I was a brat."

"You were…spirited."

Her delicate description makes me laugh.

"I think I understand now. You didn't have it easy at your grandmother's?"

"No. My mother had to know how abusive her mother was. Why'd she leave me there?"

"Maybe she didn't treat your mom like that. Or maybe your mother thought she wouldn't hurt you, Heidi. I don't know."

"Maybe she didn't care. Maybe she thought I deserved it."

"Oh, Heidi. No child deserves to be hurt or feel unloved." She pauses and flicks her gaze across the room before asking her next question. "Why didn't you ever say anything during the custody dispute?"

"I was afraid. It wasn't as bad by that point. I mean, if she started in, I was old enough to take off. And I didn't say anything after she died because I didn't want Marcel to feel bad."

She seems to think that over and in hindsight, I wish I'd told someone. Anyone.

"How did you leave it with your mother?"

"I don't know. She gave me a hug and said it was nice to see me. Like we were old classmates or something instead of mother and daughter."

"I'm sorry."

I glance down at Alexa, who's busy tugging on strands of my hair. "I could never just leave her somewhere and not come back. I miss her when I'm gone for a few *hours*."

"You're a good mother, Heidi. You know sometimes, my clients, the ones who came from the worst families, end up being the best parents. It was like they had lived through all the examples of what *not* to do, and it taught them how to do everything right."

Even though her words are serious, laughter bursts out of me. "That was our motto growing up. Marcel and I. 'What would Mom do?' Then let's do the opposite."

She laughs with me. "See?"

An extremely unpleasant smell interrupts us. "She must need her diaper changed. God only knows what Murphy fed her today."

Hope follows me into the bedroom. "Oh, where is he?"

"Uh"—I slide a guilty look her way—"I might have been a little snippy. He was waiting outside for me and I don't know. He sort of implied he was jealous about me visiting Lucas, and after everything, I couldn't deal with it."

"Aww, poor Murphy," she says, not really making me feel better about my behavior. "You should have told him, honey. He would have understood."

"I know."

The corner of her mouth quirks up. "Now that you've changed her, why don't I watch Alexa and you go over and talk to him."

I laugh because Hope is unapologetic about avoiding diaper changes whenever possible.

"Okay. Let me clean up and change. I feel gross."

Half an hour later, I'm on the path to the clubhouse. It's dusk, but I can make out all the extra cars and hear the music all the way out in the woods. Z mentioned a party. Fantastic. At least I bothered to fix myself up.

I wonder how my brother feels about the party. He's avoided all this stuff since he got home. Even the celebration thrown in his honor for his homecoming.

Twitch greets me at the front door. I've met him at Wrath's gym before but didn't realize he's now an official prospect and allowed up at the clubhouse. "Big step up, Twitch." I nod at his Prospect cut. The sight of it makes my stomach flutter. I'd been so excited and proud when Axel was given one.

I was an idiot.

I realize I'm still an idiot when I spot Murphy in the back corner chatting up a familiar blonde. Serena's friend, Amanda. Great, Serena's probably lurking somewhere, too. Why did I believe his "Take your time. There's no one else" speeches?

Amanda runs her fingers over Murphy's arm and I want to slap her, shove her, anything to get her away from him.

Instead, I turn, bumping into Twitch, who followed me inside.

Grabbing his arm, I pull him to the middle of the floor. "Do you dance?"

Forty-Six

MURPHY

I could kill Wrath right now. Twitch is a prospect Wrath brought in. So I blame him for my current predicament. Somehow, Twitch knows Serena's friend Amanda and brought her up to the clubhouse tonight.

Amanda zeroed in on me as soon as she got here and won't go away. "Serena asks about you all the time," Amanda says.

"That's nice. She doin' okay?"

"Didn't you hear what I said? She moved down to Maryland. Got into school down there."

"Oh, good for her."

She runs her finger down my arm and tilts her head in a coy way, which in reality is ugly. "She always said you were a lot of fun."

I hate myself for not going after Heidi earlier. I don't have any excuse except that I was hurt and pissed by her attitude.

But not talking to her kills me.

So does seeing her dancing with Twitch.

Hellfuckingno.

I stare for a good minute, trying to figure out if I'm seeing what I think I'm seeing. I leave Amanda with no explanation. Nope, I'm too busy stomping across the room, shoving people out of my way to get to Heidi.

My hand wraps around her upper arm, and she stares at me in shock. "What do you think you're doing?" I growl at her.

Before she has a chance to open her mouth, I turn my pissed-off face to Twitch. "She's mine and off-limits. Touch her again, fuck, you even look at her again, I'll bury you."

He doesn't answer, but he doesn't look at Heidi before he takes off, either.

I'm expecting her to be spitting fire, but when I face her, she's laughing.

Her mouth twists into a teasing grin that makes me want to kiss her and spank her at the same time. "You're so predictable."

"So are you, brat."

"Your girlfriend looks upset," she says, pointing to Amanda.

"She's *not* my girlfriend." I lean in close. "The only girl *I* want is seriously testing my patience lately, and I don't understand why."

We stare at each other for a second, then I drop my shoulder and flip her over it. "You know what? I'm tired of your bullshit," I say, giving her ass a smack. She squeals and kicks, but I've got a good grip on her legs. She's not going anywhere.

My eyes dart around the crowded clubhouse. Upstairs? My room? Or outside? I catch Wrath watching us and he flashes me a thumbs up. He points to the stairs and shakes his head. Yeah, Teller's up there.

Outside it is.

Heidi hasn't bothered with crap like "put me down." She knows that ain't happening. Instead, my little brat slides her hands over my ass. Tries to get them under my pants.

"Are you trying to distract me into dropping you?" I ask when we're finally outside.

"You better not drop me."

I'm not crazy about navigating the woods out to Rock's house with her over my shoulder like this. Too many chances for her to get hurt. "If I set you down, will you behave?"

"Depends."

Christ, she's a pain.

"On what?"

"What do you consider behaving?"

"Fine. You get a branch to the face, don't blame me." I head straight for the woods.

"Okay. Okay. Set me down."

I lean over until her feet hit the ground but keep an arm wrapped around her.

"What are we doing?" she asks.

"I'm taking you home."

"I was having fun."

Her mouth might be protesting, but her hand slips into mine and she follows me into the woods.

"No, you weren't. You were trying to piss me off. You succeeded and now you're gonna pay for it."

"Oh, embarrassing me wasn't enough?"

"Nope."

She's quiet after that.

"We need to talk. I'm tired of hanging around, waiting for you to figure shit out." My words might be unfair, but she pushed me too far tonight.

"What happened to 'take your time' and 'I'm here for you'?"

"I'm still here for you. But you've had enough time. Now it's time we try something else." I hate being mean to Heidi. She's driving me nuts, though.

Hope's up reading when we walk into the house. She smiles when she sees us together.

"Rock home?" I ask.

"Not yet."

"Is Alexa okay?" Heidi asks, shaking loose from my grasp.

"She's fine, honey." Hope picks up the baby monitor and waves at us. "Sound asleep."

Heidi glances at me. "Let me check on her?"

"Yeah. Go ahead." I'm in awe of the way she can go from pain in my ass to responsible mother in the blink of an eye.

Once she's gone, Hope gives me a knowing grin. I hook my thumbs in my pockets and make my way over to her.

"What's up?" she asks with a smug smile.

"Nothing. Why?"

"Oh, I don't know. Trinity sent me this." Giggling like a nut, she whips her cell phone out and shoves it in my face. The screen's taken up by a picture of me carrying Heidi out of the clubhouse.

My shoulders lift. I'm not embarrassed at all. "Man's gotta do what a man's gotta do."

Her mouth tips up into a grin. "Rock will be so proud." It looks like she's struggling not to laugh.

"You're not mad?"

The laughter disappears. "No." She glances down the hallway. "But she had a rough day, so be kind to her."

"I'm always—well, I try to be. She makes me a little nuts. What happened?"

"I think it's better if she tells you."

Why are women so damn frustrating?

"In fact," She stands. "I'm going to run over to the clubhouse to talk to Trinity."

Bullshit. This is her subtle way of giving Heidi and me some alone time. I feel like an ass for chasing her out of her own house. Rock moved her out here to get her *away* from all the shit going down in the clubhouse, now here I am chasing her back.

"You don't have to do that. There's a party going on," I warn her.

"Nothing I haven't seen before," she says with an eye-roll. "I'll text Rock and tell him to meet me there."

Great. Rock's gonna *love* that. This must be what it feels like to date someone who lives at home with their parents. An experience I never had.

Heidi and I somehow skipped over that fun, innocent, dating stage of things and went right into family mode. Although, to be honest, we've been doing the family thing our whole lives. It's just different now.

Hope leans over and kisses the top of my head. "Be good."

"I'll do my best."

She laughs and musses my hair before leaving.

Heidi still hasn't returned. That's cute that she thinks hiding out will save her from the discussion we're about to have.

Except, when I find her, she's passed out on the bed. Feet on the floor. Clothes still on, one sneaker off. Shaking my head, I peek at Alexa—also sound asleep.

Heidi doesn't stir when I pull her other sneaker off. I work her jeans down her legs but leave everything else on. That's not what this is about. Shit, I'm so busy being driven crazy by her when she's awake, I hadn't noticed the dark circles under her eyes. What the hell happened to her today, and why wouldn't she talk to me about it?

Because you acted like a crazed caveman when she got home.

I snap the light off and Alexa's nightlight throws off enough of a glow for me to see where I'm going.

Gathering her in my arms, I shift her to the other side of the bed and crawl in next to her. It's only a double bed, so it's a good excuse to keep her snuggled up against me.

I plan to be here when she wakes up, because one way or another, we're having our talk.

Heidi

I've got a screeching headache when I wake up.

No wait.

The screeching is Alexa.

I turn but collide with a hard, warm, wall of…muscle. "Murphy, move."

I'm not even shocked to find him in my bed. For some reason, it feels right.

He grumbles and then comes to, jumping out of bed. Before I make sense of anything, Alexa stops crying. Blake's holding her, quietly rocking her from side to side. I hold my arms out. "She needs to be changed."

"I can do it."

A head tilt expresses my disbelief better than words will at this hour.

"I figured it out yesterday, remember?"

Yesterday. Right. When he watched my daughter and then when I got home, I thanked him by being a brat.

"Ugh, did I dance with Twitch last night?"

"Yes," he says in a low, angry voice.

"I came over to talk to *you.*"

When he's finished, he turns to face me. "Should I feed her?"

"There's bottles in the fridge, I'll—"

He holds a hand out, stopping me. "Stay put."

When he returns, Alexa's happily sucking on her bottle. "Did you make sure—"

"Yes," he answers. "Now, what did you want to talk about last night?"

"I don't remember."

The sharp stare he fixes on me makes me fidget. "You were busy talking to Amanda."

"Yeah, Twitch brought her up."

"Oh."

"You know, the world is full of women. Sometimes I have to talk to them. Doesn't mean anything else is happening."

"That's not how it looked. Besides, I know you have history with her."

"History?" He raises an eyebrow. "No, actually I don't. Maybe next time, you march right up to me and let me introduce you as my girlfriend"—my head snaps up at that word, but he continues right along—"instead of trying to make me jealous. We're getting kind of old for that bullshit, don't you think?"

"Maybe *you* are," I grumble. "Seems like acceptable nineteen-year-old behavior to me."

He throws his head back and laughs. Alexa smiles around her

bottle and chortles along with him. "You've been older than your age as long as I've known you," he says. Still sounding too chipper for this hour and at my expense.

"Well, you keep pushing me away."

"Bullshit. Because I told you I wanted to give you time to figure things out?"

Alexa coughs and spits up all over him. "Oh, shit. I'm sorry. Did I do something wrong, Heidi?"

He looks so panicked, I can't even tell him he should have stopped to burp her. I should have been paying better attention. "No. She's fine. It happens."

I take her from him and clean her up, while he whips his shirt up and wipes himself off.

"Oh." It's hard to ignore the tingle in my girly bits at the sight of his bare chest, ink, and muscles. Wow. "It's way too early for that," I mutter, setting Alexa back in her crib.

"What?" He catches the appreciative way I'm staring at him and grins. "See something you like?"

"Good God, yes." What's wrong with me?

He grins even harder and steps up behind me. "I like that," he whispers in my ear.

"What?"

"That you like looking at me."

"I've been drooling over you since I was twelve. This isn't news."

"It is to me." His arms wrap around me and he runs his nose over my cheek, barely touching me but leaving goosebumps anyway. "You're sweet."

"Yeah, it was your personality that made me love you but your hot bod that made me thank God we weren't actually related." It's an overly silly thing to say. And it oversimplifies how I really feel about him, but he laughs, his chest rumbling against my back.

My hands open and close, remembering all the times he hurt me in the past. "I hated all those girls who had your attention."

He stops laughing.

"Hated the things you did with them."

"Did you hate me too?"

"No. I wanted to. But no. I loved you too much."

"I never, ever wanted to hurt you," he admits. His voice comes out so raw, I know he means every word.

"I know that now. Then, it hurt."

"I'm sorry." He kisses the top of my head. "You're all I want."

My stomach makes this inhuman rumbling noise and he rubs his hands over my belly. "Maybe I should feed you, and then we talk?"

"Okay."

He pushes me toward the bed. "Don't move. I'll be right back."

"I'll be here."

MURPHY

The weight of Rock's gaze settles on my shoulders before he even announces his presence. I turn away from the stove and find him leaning on the counter, arms over his chest.

"Bet you never expected to wake up and find me in your kitchen."

He fights back a smile. "No. I didn't."

"Sorry."

"Hope gave me a heads-up last night."

"We didn't—it wasn't—"

"Simmer down. You don't have to explain anything to me."

"She passed out last night. I just stayed so we could talk this morning."

He tilts his head, taking a glance down the hallway—I guess to see if Heidi will overhear our conversation. He's definitely here for a reason. Might as well get it out in the open.

"What's on your mind, prez?"

"Known both of you a long time."

"Yeah. You've been—" He holds up a hand and I try not to laugh.

I know how much he hates when any of us say he's like a father to us.

"Anyway. Love both of you."

"I know."

"But you need to understand, it's not only about her anymore. It's about that baby girl, too."

"I know that, prez. I can take care of them both. I'm—"

His mouth tips up in a smile. "If she lets you."

"Well, yeah."

"And if I'm gonna be finding you in my kitchen every morning, will you at least put on a shirt?"

I glance down. "Sorry. Alexa spit up on—"

"Take what you need out of the laundry room." He nods down the hall.

"Thanks."

"Oh my. How'd I get so lucky?" Hope's soft, teasing voice snaps my head up. While she might have been cracking a joke about finding me half-dressed in her kitchen, her eyes are focused on her husband. He wraps her up in his arms and kisses the top of her head.

"Why you up, Baby Doll?"

"Oh, I'm sorry. Did you need more time to terrorize Murphy?"

I burst out laughing and Rock gives her a squeeze.

"Morning." The three of us turn. Heidi's carrying Alexa, who starts giggling when she sees Hope. Heidi glances at me. "I thought you—"

"Sorry, Heidi-girl. I interrupted him," Rock says smoothly, holding out his arms for Alexa. "Morning, baby." Hope joins him in fussing over the baby, and Heidi shrugs at me. If I make a single grandparent joke, Hope will probably murder me, so I don't.

"Miss me?" I ask Heidi, low so I'm not overheard. She nods and gives me a shy hip-bump. We fix breakfast for everyone together. When we're done, Hope and Rock head downstairs.

"I'm afraid to ask what's down there," Heidi jokes.

"I don't think you want to know. It's one of those childhood-ruining moments you can't un-know."

Heidi laughs so hard, she has trouble catching her breath. I love making her laugh, but I haven't forgotten about the talk we need to have.

"So, you want to tell me what last night was all about?"

She glances away. "Nothing."

"Heidi."

"You hurt my feelings. Lucas really is just a friend."

"More than anything, I was worried about you," I say gently. Part of me wants to point out she acted just as jealous when she saw me talking to that girl last night, but we already covered it in the bedroom, so I don't bring it up again.

"I'm sorry. I should have called you."

I know something else is bothering her, because Hope told me Heidi had a shitty day. "What happened yesterday?"

She squirms and gets up to clear the table, but I hook my finger in one of her belt loops and yank her closer. "Don't ignore me."

"I ran into my mother at the hospital."

Holy shit. No one has seen or heard from that bitch in at least twelve years. "Seriously?"

"Yup."

I don't need to ask. If it had been some loving family reunion, Heidi would have come home in a much different mood yesterday. Instead, I pull her down onto my lap and wait for her to tell me what happened. "I'm here for you, beautiful."

"I guess she's remarried. She was visiting him. It was awful, weird, and awkward, like she didn't feel bad or guilty or even care."

I hug her a little tighter and see if she wants to continue.

"Why did I even bother? What did I think would happen? We'd have some sappy TV movie reunion where she'd beg me to forgive her?"

"She's your mother."

"Please. Hope's more of a mother to me than Helga ever was. I hate myself for even bothering. I tried telling her about Alexa, Marcel, her mother dying...she didn't care about any of it."

"You have so many people who love you. It doesn't matter."

"I know. I *know* it. I knew it when I opened my big, stupid mouth."

"Please don't do this to yourself. You're so sweet and full of love. Why wouldn't you expect your mother to be, too? It's not your fault."

She tips her head up but doesn't look at me. "Should I even tell my brother?"

The only thing that will upset Marcel is that Heidi was hurt. He gave up on his mother a long time ago. "Yes, but maybe wait until you're not so upset."

She turns and stares at me. Then, she kisses my cheek. Soft and sweet. So perfectly Heidi.

"Thank you, Blake."

"I was worried about you."

"I'm sorry. I just wanted to get home." She ducks her head. "I wanted to see you and hold Alexa."

For a second, I can't say anything. My throat's too tight. "Then I acted like a jealous jerk?"

"Yeah, and I was too frazzled to deal with it."

"I'm sorry."

"Me, too." She presses her forehead to mine and I tip her head back to kiss her. She shakes out of my hold. "What are we?"

"Did you ignore everything I said before?"

"No."

I grasp her hip with one hand, keeping her in place. "You're mine. I'm yours. End of story. Boom—there it is. Is that better?"

"Don't make fun of me."

"I'm not. I'm explaining where we are."

"How are we…? After everything? If I hadn't been so stubborn. We should have—"

I sense what she's about to say and stop her. It's bad enough she has these *thoughts*. If she voices them? It will give her something else to feel guilty about later.

"Hey, then you wouldn't have that beautiful baby girl."

She blinks at me.

"Any waiting was worth it to have her. Yeah?"

She nods.

"No more guilty *what-ifs*. It's time to focus on the road ahead of us, not behind."

"Okay."

"I'm here for you. Whatever you need, whenever you're ready. You know where to find me."

Forty-Seven

Heidi

I can't sleep. All day my conversation with Blake has replayed in my head. Over and over until it's a heavy feeling lingering in my chest.

It's still hours from sunrise and I'm restless. I get up and check on Alexa, because that's what I do when I can't sleep. Sit, watch her, and hope I'm making the right decisions for her.

Memories of how much I resented my mother every time she got involved with a new man won't stop haunting me.

But, I'm not my mother. And Blake isn't some random dude I picked up in a bar.

He broke younger Heidi's heart many times. But that's all childish and rather insignificant compared to what I've been through since then. I mean, *boo-hoo*, the boy I had a crush on when I was twelve had some girlfriends. Big deal.

He's the same guy who made sure I was never alone on my birthdays. Who went out of his way to make me feel special. He's the man who's here for me now, helping me take care of a child that isn't his, without me even asking.

The tightness in my chest still won't go away.

Blake said I could always call him.

I send a text instead.

Are you up?

What's wrong?

Everything. Nothing. I can't sleep. I miss him.

I need you.

I didn't mean to send that. But it's out now.

Checking on Alexa one more time, I grab her baby monitor, my phone, and a sweatshirt. Outside, the moon shines through the trees. Bright enough to make out my surroundings. I drop down onto the first step and wait.

A few minutes later, crunching leaves and breaking branches tell me Blake's almost here. Either that or I'm about to be eaten by a bear. My heart kicks up, confident it's Blake.

"Heidi, what's wrong?" he calls out in a harsh whisper.

Leaving everything on the porch, I hop down the stairs and run to him, almost knocking him over.

"Whoa, what's the matter?"

No matter how much I want to, I won't cry. "I missed you. I'm sorry. I love you."

His arms tighten around me, and he moves us so we're up against the side of the house, covered by shadows.

"Say it again."

"Which part?"

Instead of answering me, he lowers his head. I'm not sure what I expect, but I love the way his lips touch mine. Soft at first, but not hesitant. Sweet and hot. He licks my lower lip and presses his mouth against mine harder.

I pull away and continue as if he hadn't interrupted me. "I've always loved you. But this…this is different."

A slow smile spreads over his face. "How?"

"Bigger. More. I don't know. Harder."

"It's real." He traces a finger over my cheek.

Yes. It's not a crush. It doesn't hurt. It doesn't feel one-sided. I want to make him happy as much as I want him to make me happy. I don't want to hurt him anymore and I trust him not to hurt me.

"What happened?" he asks.

"Nothing. I couldn't stop thinking about you. I mean, I'm always thinking about you, but I needed to see you. I'm sorry it's so late."

"Heidi, you can see me whenever you want," he says in a solemn, raspy voice.

"What if I want to see you all the time?"

He yanks me tighter against him, a happy manly-growly noise works out of his throat, and he leans down to kiss my cheek and whisper in my ear, "That's what I've been waiting for."

He's so riled up and I love it. His hands are everywhere, at my hips, trailing up the sides of my body, over my shoulders, gently touching my face. A little less gentle as his lips find mine again. His tongue brushes against mine. It's a kiss infused with longing and love.

As if I can't tell how much he wants me from his kisses, he slips one hand under my sweatshirt, stroking my skin but not moving higher. He pushes his hips forward, and he's so hard against me. If I wiggle a little bit—

"Heidi?"

"Yes?"

"Is this what you want?"

"I want you."

"Are you sure you're ready?" The sweet concern laced in his words intensifies my need.

"Yes."

His hand disappears from my skin and he backs away. "This shouldn't be here."

"What? Why'd you stop? Keep kissing me."

"Heidi, I want to do a hell of a lot more than kiss you. But it should be special."

I can't help the smile that spreads over my face. "Single-mother-sex doesn't get to be *special*. It has to be *fast*." I rush to add, "From what I hear."

He rolls his eyes and shakes his head. "You're everything. And our first time should be special."

I roll my lip, sinking my teeth in while I consider his words. "When?"

"Now."

"It's the middle of the night."

His teasing smile relaxes me. "I'll ask Hope in the morning if she minds watching Alexa over the weekend. But, I can't pawn Alexa off on her whenever—"

"Hey." His hand brushes against my face again. "I'm not asking you to."

"I don't want to be my mother. Dumping my kid somewhere so I can go get laid."

"Heidi. You're nothing like your mother at all."

Something still stops me.

"Next time, we'll take Alexa with us. Family trip. I promise."

My breath catches. I blink a few times, unable to form any words. "Next time?" I finally say.

He wraps his arms around my waist, lifting me up and nuzzling my neck. "Yeah, next time. I want to take lots and lots of trips together."

I wrap my arms around his neck and kiss his cheek. "I'd love that."

Reluctantly, he lets me slide down his body until my toes touch the ground. "It might be time for me to find my own place. I've probably way overextended my stay at Casa North."

Blake snorts. "I doubt it. But yeah, we'll talk about it."

"Talk about what?"

"Our living arrangements."

"Our?"

"Yes, *our*. You think I'm letting my girls move somewhere alone, you're nuts."

I suppose some women might be offended by a bunch of the words in that sentence. Not me. All I heard was him referring to my daughter and me as "his girls."

"Okay," I answer. "We can talk about it."

A relieved smile brightens his serious face, as if he'd been expecting me to argue. But I'm done fussing over stupid things. I've wasted enough time being stubborn and childish.

"Do you want to come in?" I ask.

"That's not a good idea."

We're entering a new part of our relationship. One where I feel comfortable pressing my hand against the front of his pants, rubbing firm strokes over the hardness underneath. He sucks in a hiss of air. "Don't."

"But—"

"If you keep it up, I'm going to pin you to the wall and fuck you hard and fast, and that's not what I want for our first time."

"What about what I want?"

He cocks his head to the side. "What do you want?"

I think over his words. About our first time being special. We have our whole lives for down-and-dirty-in-the-woods sex.

"I don't want mosquito bites on my butt."

Laughter rumbles out of him and he shifts away from my touch. "Call me as soon as you talk to Hope."

MURPHY

You'd think that lengthy conversation about the logistics of *doing it* would be a boner-killer. You'd be wrong. Nope. My dick's so hard I can barely walk back to the clubhouse.

I don't know where to take her. I'm a little frantic because one, I can't remember the last time I went this long without sex, and two, I can't remember ever wanting anyone more.

After a little research, I catch a few hours of sleep. First thing in the morning, I place a call to a lodge in the Adirondacks that looks nice. More upscale than either of us are probably used to, but Heidi deserves the best. They even have the room I want available for two nights. I'm not sure if we'll be able to stay the second night, but I book it anyway.

I hate imposing on Hope, too, but I think she'll understand.

As I'm finishing the reservations and having a few extras added to the room, Heidi texts me.

Good to go. When do you want to leave?

I fire back: *Now.*

Like, right the fuck now.

I run around my room like a crazed man throwing stuff in a bag, grab one very important piece of paper, shove it in my pocket and I'm ready to go.

My hand's on the railing, and I'm about to head downstairs, when I realize I need to check in with Teller. Not to inform him I'm finally going to bang his sister—I'm not that crass. I just want to let him know I'll be gone for a few days.

I slip my phone out and tap out another text to Heidi.

Give me a few minutes.

I knock before pushing open the door.

"I didn't say come in," he bitches when he sees me.

"Yeah, but since when do I wait around for an invitation?"

"True."

"How you doin'?"

"Fine. Why?"

"I, uh, I'm taking off for a few days."

I'm a little surprised he doesn't ask where. For a few seconds, I wrestle with whether I should tell him Heidi's coming with me, but I finally decide against it.

"Go," he says, waving his hand at the door. "I have Wrath, Z, and Trinity up my ass twenty-four-seven, I'll be fine."

"Murphy?" he calls out as I'm about to shut the door.

"Yeah?"

"Please don't knock my sister up."

"Asshole." I flip him off, but there's a big part of me that's relieved. And an even bigger part of me is happy he's back to joking around here and there.

I stop in the kitchen and throw some bottles of water, sodas, and iced tea in a cooler. Excitement's buzzing through me when I get to my truck and load it up.

"Where you headed?" Wrath asks.

"Shit!" My elbow slams into the door. "How can someone your size be such a stealthy motherfucker?"

Because it's Wrath, he takes that as a compliment.

"I'm taking Heidi away for a few days."

He raises an eyebrow, folds his arms against his chest, and leans on the side of my truck. "Really? I'm not sure how I feel about this."

"Good thing no one asked your opinion."

"Ballsy, that's good."

I gesture for him to move so I can open the back door, then freeze when I see Alexa's car seat.

"What's wrong?" he asks.

"Nothing. Hope's watching the baby for the weekend and I feel bad leaving her."

He stares at me.

"What? It's not weird, right? Parents go away together for weekends, don't they?"

"You realize what you just said, right?"

"What? Going away together?"

He slaps the side of my arm. Hard. "Never mind. I take it back. I feel good about the two of you together."

Forty-Eight

Somewhere with you

Heidi

While Blake might have been eager to finally have sex, he still takes his sweet time. First, there's the three-hour drive up the Northway. Then another half an hour finding the place.

It's amazing, though. A huge, elegant lodge nestled in the mountains behind a glittering lake.

Not even the snooty old man who checks us into the hotel snuffs out my excitement. I'm so wound up—thrilled, throbbing with anticipation—that I'm afraid I'll explode in the lobby.

When we're finally inside our room, the door closes and I jump him. My arms wind around his neck and I press a kiss to his mouth. He kisses me back, quick. "Whoa. Slow down."

"Slow? Really?"

He drops the bags to the floor and wraps both arms around my waist, keeping me still. "Yeah. Let's take our time."

Crap. That makes me feel slutty. Tears cloud my vision and I push past him to go to the bathroom.

"Hey, what's wrong?"

"Nothing." I'm being silly. I know that's not what he meant.

"Heidi?" His serious tone makes me stop. "Talk to me."

I open my mouth, but I don't know how to explain the awful feelings welling up inside. "You make me feel like I'm being too eager," I whisper finally. It doesn't make a lot of sense, but it's the best I can do.

He brushes the hair out of my eyes. "I'm thrilled. I've just been waiting so long. I want to do everything right. Want this to be perfect for you."

Each word is filled with so much emotion, it drives the doubt out of my chest. He's overthinking this as much as I am. "It will be perfect because it's you. Because it's us."

"Yeah," he agrees.

Feeling better, I rock to my tiptoes and kiss his cheek. "Thank you."

His gaze darts around the room, and I take a second to appreciate it, too. "Wow. Fancy, Blake."

He chuckles and moves to the small bar area on the far wall. I follow him over and gasp when I see the box of plump chocolate covered strawberries. Blake knows they're my favorite.

"How?"

"I asked for them to be in the room, along with the flowers." He nods at the vase on the table at the foot of the bed.

I'd been so focused on him, I missed the flowers. I slip my hand into his. "That was so sweet, thank you." He places a kiss on my forehead. "We should probably move the flowers, though. Things are going to get wild on that bed, and I don't want to accidentally break the vase."

His eyes widen before he bursts out laughing. "Damn right they are."

Turning, he plucks one of the strawberries out of the box and holds it for me to take a bite. Strawberry juice and chocolate end up all over my face and they're so good, I don't even care.

Blake lowers his head, kissing me soft and slow. I sway and steady myself by holding on to him. His kiss grows more urgent and he presses is body against me. Years of wanting each other seem to shape our kiss. We're finally together. Alone together. Able to learn everything about each other.

"Love you, Heidi," he murmurs as he ends our kiss, searching my face as if he wants to memorize this moment.

Pulling away, I lean over to pick up my bag. "Give me a second. I want to change."

He lifts an eyebrow but lets me go.

I take my time, stripping down, rubbing coconut oil into my skin until I'm soft and smooth all over. It takes a second of rummaging through my bag to find the black and green lace bralette and panty set I brought with me. I bought it with Murphy in mind. How long ago I won't say. It's a sheer, black, fishnet material with green lace. The top has stretchy fishnet cups with a keyhole cutout. Useless for support. Perfect for sexiness. There are a bunch of straps that wind down and around my ribcage. The panties are full bikini panties—no thongs for me. The material of both pieces is so sheer, everything is visible. It's a little bit sweet and a little bit slutty.

Of course, Blakes's seen way hotter girls in way tinier outfits for years at the strip club and at the clubhouse.

The thought is like a bucket of ice water over my head.

"Heidi?" He taps on the door.

The concern in his voice helps me forget about the thoughts that should stay in the past. I whip my hair into a long, messy braid over one shoulder and open the door.

"Holy. Fuck. Wow," Blake stammers while backing up a few steps to take all of me in. "That's so fucking hot. Turn around."

Bracing myself on the doorframe, I spin and slowly wiggle my butt. I peek over my shoulder and find him staring, running his hand over his beard, possibly drooling. "Is this okay?" I ask.

"Yes." In a few smooth, measured steps, he's pressed up against my back, winding an arm around my middle and pulling me against him. "You're every fantasy I've ever had and finally in my arms," he whispers against my neck.

My breath catches.

"But now I'm worried."

"About what?"

The arm around my middle flexes, squeezing me tighter, while he wraps his free hand up in my braid and gives it a gentle tug. "I'm worried," he says in between tiny kisses along my shoulder. "That I'm so worked up, I won't be able to be sweet and gentle."

"I don't want gentle. I want you."

His hands drop to my hips and he turns me so I'm facing him. I reach up, looping my arms around his neck. "I want you the way you are. Just you and me. No pretending we're anything other than who we are."

"I love you, Heidi. You understand that, right?"

I can't find any words, so I nod instead.

"I've always loved you, but like you said, this is different."

"This is forever?"

He was wrong. He can be gentle, because he places the softest kiss on my forehead and says, "Exactly."

MURPHY

As soon as I have all of her, I know that'll be it for me. She's all I want, all I've wanted for way too long.

Those few moments together on her eighteenth birthday—Heidi riding my fingers, exploding for me—was the hottest thing I've ever seen. I had the worst case of blue balls after, but it was still the best sexual experience of my life. Doesn't matter how many girls I've been with or how many filthy things I've done. That small taste of her fucked me up permanently—the way I always knew it would. I tried living without her and it's impossible.

My lips move from her forehead to her mouth. One of my hands slides into her hair to hold her still. My other hand squeezes her hip. The solid feel of her against my body beats out every fantasy I've had.

Against my mouth, she makes these eager sounds and her body

melts into mine. Her hips arch toward me, and I slide my hand from her hip to grab her ass. She moans into my mouth again and drags her fingers from the back of my neck to my scalp. The shivery sensation from her nails on my skin feels so good, I lean into it, silently asking for more.

I'm so hard. Too hard. Afraid-I-might-hurt-her hard. I couldn't stop if I wanted to, so I remind myself to be gentle. We're so close. She's in this sexy see-through, lacy outfit and I can't resist. Her body tightens as I slide my hand down the front of the tiny scrap of lace between her legs. Heat pours off her. Slick, wet heat. She jumps and lets out a little cry when I graze her skin. I use that gasp to push my tongue into her mouth. She tastes as sweet as I remember. My lips slide to her jaw and I nudge her toward the bed, still kissing my way down her neck.

The back of her legs hit the bed and she lets out a surprised *oh* sound. My fingers brush against her inner thigh and she shudders. "Get on the bed," I whisper against her ear.

She does something so perfectly Heidi, I'm rocked to my core. She turns and jumps on the bed, scooting all the way to the top and landing in the pile of pillows. Sweet, eager, not meant to be seductive—but it is. Then she does something completely unexpected, by patting the bed and wiggling her eyebrows. "Come get me," she taunts.

"Wait," I say.

She drops the cute *come-to-me* look. "What?"

"Here." I slip the paper out of my pocket and toss it onto the nightstand.

"What's this?" she asks as she reaches over and picks it up. She has some medical training, right? She'll figure it out. Her gaze flicks up after she finishes reviewing it. "An STD test result sheet? Is this supposed to be romantic? Because I'm not feeling it."

She's teasing, and I let out a short laugh. "I'm trying to be an adult here."

"Well," she says, glancing down at the results one more time—*surprised I'm clean, perhaps*—and shaking her head. "I don't have one for you."

"I don't need one from you."

Her big brown eyes stay focused on me as if she's waiting for more information. Shit. Why is this so fucking awkward? Because it's Heidi and I'm trying to do everything right, but instead, I feel like I'm screwing everything up. I reach up and rub my hand over the back of my head while I figure out how to explain I've never gone bare with anyone else, and I don't want there to be anything between us. "Are you on the pill?"

"Oh." She averts her eyes and nods, as if my question finally helped all the pieces click into place. "Uh…" Her forehead wrinkles and she tucks a piece of hair behind her ear. "Well, no. I was breast-feeding and then, you know, there didn't seem like much point." Her cheeks are bright red now, and I feel like an asshole for putting her on the spot.

Call me twisted, but I'm also harder than a motherfuckin' hammer. Not because she's embarrassed—I'm not that much of a dick.

"Anyway, I should warn you that Alexa happened while I was on the pill, so…" she trails off.

"Really?"

Her eyes snap to mine. "It happens."

I hold up my hands. "I wasn't—"

"I know." She huffs out a breath. "So, now that you've pretty much killed my lady boner, what should we do?"

How can I not burst out laughing? "Mine's fine."

Her eyes immediately zero in on my dick, which only makes things more uncomfortable behind my zipper.

"How nice for you," she says with a sly smile.

I slip my shirt up and over my head, since she seemed to enjoy checking out my upper body before.

She still likes it, because she takes in a sharp breath, kneels up, and runs her hands over my chest. I take one of her hands and drag it lower. She gives my dick a squeeze through my jeans, and I almost come in my pants. I really should get one out of the way so I can calm down.

"Do you want that?" I ask, as she strokes me even harder.

"Yes."

"Want to kiss it first?"

She pulls away and gives me strange look. I feel dangerously close to begging her to suck my dick. A new experience and not one I'm currently enjoying.

"No?" I ask.

"Not yet. You need to give head to get it."

What the what?

I can't come up with a response. My experiences with *that* haven't been positive. Girls I've been with either didn't want it or were only looking to please me, so they never asked, which was fine, because I don't enjoy doing things I'm not good at.

But this is Heidi. Not a club girl or random chick I don't care about. There's nothing I won't do for her.

Why am I still thinking about this?

Get your face between her legs, idiot!

I work a cocky grin onto my face and rub my hand over my chin. "All you had to do was ask, sweetheart. Lie back."

She narrows her eyes—seeing right through my cocky bullshit, I'm sure—but does as I ask.

"Spread those legs for me."

Almost shyly, she does it. For someone who boldly told me what she wanted five seconds ago, the shyness is funny.

"Why're you laughing at me?" she asks.

"I'm not," I answer as I slide onto my belly and grip her thighs with my hands. I glance up at her. "You've got a pretty pussy, baby." My eyebrows wiggle, and she laughs so hard her legs shake.

"Touch me," she whispers.

How can I say no? I push the thin strip of lace out of my way and trace my fingers over her smooth skin.

"Use your tongue."

"Calm down, bossy. I'm getting there."

She screws her face into this pissy expression that's both unexpected and cute.

"Keep it up." I slap her pussy lightly and she gasps.

"Did you just spank my pussy?"

"Yup."

She laughs and her knees fall together, so I wedge my shoulders against her legs. "You want me to kiss you here, keep your legs open."

I'm watching her face closely for every reaction. Her breathing picks up. She likes when I tell her what to do. Good.

Hooking my fingers into her panties, I drag them down her legs. "These are pretty, but they've got to go."

She laughs softly.

"Did you buy them for me?"

"Yup."

"Thank you."

I can't get over how pretty she is. All pink and glistening.

All mine.

I place little kisses against her inner thigh. Slowly working my way up. I take a slow lick and she makes the sweetest gasping-moaning noise, arching her hips up.

"Do you like that?"

"Yes. More."

"So demanding," I tease. I trace a few more long, slow licks over her wet flesh. I can't get enough of her. My hands dig into her hips, pulling her to my mouth, so I can run my tongue up her center over and over.

Her hands grip my hair, and she lets out a bunch of stunned little cries and gasps.

"You like that, Heidi? Tell me. Talk to me."

"Uh…ah…yes. More."

I lick and suck and tease her with my tongue and fingers until she's trembling. I want to make her come on my tongue more than anything else I've ever wanted.

A few seconds later, she does.

"Oh, Blake, please." She draws the words out until they're a high-pitched moan.

Kiss and nip my way up her body, stopping to play with her breasts, which are still covered in the black lacy top.

I keep kissing, softer as I reach her neck. "Did you like that?" I whisper.

"Oh my God, yes."

I can't help smiling, pleased with myself. "You sound surprised."

She opens one eye and the opposite corner of her mouth quirks up. "Well, I figured with all those girls willing to do whatever you asked, you might be lazy in bed."

"Wow," I say, drawing out the word and laughing at the same time, because secretly to myself, I'm laughing at how well she has me pegged. "I did not see this coming."

"What's that?"

"You being such a brat."

She covers her mouth and giggles. "Sure you did."

Grabbing her hand, I bring it to my mouth and kiss her fingers. "I love that you always say what you're thinking instead of what you think I want to hear."

"Lucky for you that I'm full of opinions."

"Yeah, I am lucky." I trace my finger over her cheek. "But you know what, beautiful?" My voice comes out lower. Rougher. And the smile fades from her face.

"What?"

I've never been with a woman who challenges me the way Heidi does. Tease and flirt, sure, had plenty of that. But challenge me until all my instincts are riled up? Nope.

From Heidi, I love it. Gets me hotter than anything. I want to please her more than I want a quick release. She also pushes me to discover what *I* really want.

She's watching me with expectant eyes, her chest rising and falling rapidly, waiting for my answer. "The punishment for that bratty mouth of yours is that I'm going to fuck you so thoroughly, you won't be able to walk straight. Have fun explaining that when we get home."

Heidi

"Is that a promise or threat? Because it kind of sounds like fun."

Blake growls against my throat and places rough kisses all over my neck and shoulders, making me laugh and then moan.

This…I didn't expect sex to be so much *fun* with Blake.

"Why are your jeans still on?"

He looks down. "Help me get them off."

I'm eager to help him with that and work his belt loose. Popping the button on his jeans is harder and working his zipper down impossible.

"It's stuck."

"No kidding. You might need to cut me out of them." He sits up and then stands, working his pants off. I sit up and tease my fingers around the edge of his boxer-briefs. The sight of him turns my body to fire.

He takes my face between his hands, tilting my head back for a kiss. We fall back against the bed together. I work my hands into his underwear, dragging them down. He finally helps me kick them off. Then we're warm skin on skin, parts rubbing against each other. It feels natural and wonderful and a little bit scary.

He's so hard and heavy, almost dangerous against me. Will this hurt? He said he might have trouble with gentle. Was that all talk?

Will he tear me apart with all the feelings I've nailed down for so long, or will he tear me apart with pleasure?

His hand moves from the back of my neck to my shoulder, sliding the skinny strap down. His mouth follows his hand, placing gentle kisses along the way. The coolness of the air disappears under the wet warmth of his mouth over my nipple. A little bird-type cry escapes me, and he smiles against my skin.

The longing in the pit of my stomach isn't new. But the tingles racing over my skin, the tightening of my breasts, the burning flush moving over my skin—I haven't felt any of those things in a very long time.

His hand covers my other breast, his rough skin deliciously wicked against my softer skin. I can't stop stroking my hands over his body. Down his back, up his sides. "Blake," I whisper.

He lifts his head. The need in his eyes painfully clear. "Are you ready?"

I reach down, wrapping my hand around him. He inhales sharply and closes his eyes. Slowly, I slide my hand up and down his hard length, savoring the smooth skin. He keeps watching as I stare at every inch of his body. I stroke a little harder and he inhales sharply. "Stop, beautiful. Give me a second."

I still my movements but don't take my hands away. There's nothing in this world that could make me stop touching him. He leans over, reaching for the nightstand, slides open the drawer and grabs a few items, scattering them on the top of the nightstand. I don't even bother looking, because it doesn't matter. I trust him and want everything he wants.

He rips into a condom, and I move my hands to his stomach while he slides it on.

"Was the hotel stocked with condoms, too?" I tease.

"No, while you were changing, I put some things away."

"Ooh, what else did you bring?"

"You'll see. Now, quiet." He runs his hands up my body, stopping to pull the lace cups of my bra all the way down. I'm a little anxious about the stretch marks on the sides of my breasts, but he doesn't seem to notice. Instead, he gently brushes his thumbs over my nipples, then lowers his head to suck one in his mouth. His beard softly scratches my skin, intensifying every nip and lick. Even though I'm watching every move he makes, I let out a startled gasp when his teeth gently graze over my sensitized nipple, and I shiver with pleasure. Cold air teases my skin as he moves to the other breast and teases me at the same pace.

Heat pulses between my legs, growing hotter with every touch. I want his hands all over me. I need him inside of me. But he seems content to tease and torture me. And from the seductive smirk he's wearing, he knows what he's doing to me and loves every minute of it.

"Blake, please." I'm so excited. Ready to jump out of my skin. I try to guide him to me, but he brushes my hand away.

"Not yet."

I groan and he chuckles. "I'm torturing myself too, you know."

"Then *fuck* me."

The tip of his cock deliberately grazes my wet skin and I arch my hips up. *Almost there.*

He pulls back. His face is a mixture of concentrated control and raw need.

"Stop teasing me."

His fingers brush over my cheek and he stares into my eyes. "I've been waiting for this a long time, Heidi. I want to remember every second of our first time."

My heart flutters and I reach up, pulling him down for a kiss. While he claims my mouth, his cock brushes against my entrance and I tilt my hips up. This time he doesn't tease me. He slips in, not enough to quench my burning need, but oh, *fuck* does it feel good.

He breaks our kiss. Our eyes lock and he thrusts. Entering me with excruciating slowness. I need the extra time to relax and adjust to the size of him.

My eyes close, then open, I want to see every reaction on his face. My breath hitches. He's so big, pulsing against me. I lift my legs, wrapping them around his hips. Letting him know I'm ready for anything he wants to unleash. His hands shift, gripping, pulling me closer as he shoves himself deeper inside me.

So good.

Incredible. Better than I ever imagined. Worth every second he's made me wait.

"Blake." It's the only word that makes any sense. He pulls out, pushes in deeper. Our lips meet and he moves faster, pumping his hips against me, driving inside me harder and harder.

"Heidi." His voice is rough, strained.

"More."

"I'll give you more. You feel so fucking good."

"So do you."

He leans down and presses a kiss to my lips. Next to me, his arms shake with the pressure of holding himself up and maybe holding himself back.

"Don't hold back. I want you. Give me everything. I can take it."

He silences me with a searing kiss, covering me with his body, wrapping his arms under me, holding me tight. When he lifts his mouth from mine, I'm breathless and panting. He sits up a little, hooking my legs over his arms, spreading me wide, thrusting into me even harder.

Soft *oh, oh, oh* noises pop out of me. Everything feels so good, I'm overwhelmed.

MURPHY

I'm so fucking close, but I don't think she's anywhere near where she needs to be. My hands slide under her ass, pulling her up, changing the angle. She moans and twists under me.

"Good?"

"Mmmhmm."

"Are you close?"

"Feels good," she answers without opening her eyes.

"That's not what I asked."

Her eyes snap open. "No. But—"

Fuck. My thrusts stall. I nip and kiss my way to her ear. "Tell me what you need."

She bumps her hips up against me and lets out a frustrated little noise that almost makes me lose it completely. I count back from five. "I need you to not stop."

Chuckling softly, I wrap my arms around her and roll us so she's on top. "Sit up. Show me what you like."

"Oh. Oh. *Ow.*"

I chuckle and she smacks my chest. "Figures you're huge *everywhere.*" She takes a second to sink down, and I run my hands up her thighs to her hips. "You're so fucking beautiful up there."

Her face goes soft and she smiles. Her breasts are free from the skimpy top and she takes a second to slip her arms out of the slim straps. Somehow, leaving it on even though it's not covering a damn thing, is dirtier, hotter than if she were completely naked.

My hands tighten on her hips, urging her to move. She gasps and moans. I tilt my head up so I can watch my cock disappear into her. Pretty soon, she's grinding down on me hard. "That's it. All the way," I encourage.

"Oh. There. Fuck." She clenches me so tight, I barely hang on. But I so badly want her to finish before I get off.

"You feel so good. You have no idea."

She goes liquid at those words, moaning louder. Her eyes close and her head falls back.

"That's it."

Fuck, I'm buried so deep in her, I can't hold on much longer. My fingers brush against her nipples and she lets out another moan, completely lost. I move my hands back to her hips, helping her movements. She rides me faster and faster, beautiful breasts bouncing. Breasts I want my mouth on. I sit up a little, changing the angle and she presses against me harder. I'm hitting her so deep and she keeps trying to get more. It's fucking amazing.

"Fuck," I pant through gritted teeth. "I'm really close, Heidi. But you feel so good. Don't stop."

She grunts in response, so tight and tense, ready to explode. *So close.* "Ah. Oh. Blake. There. There."

"Thank fuck." I grip her hips, holding her down on me tightly as she shudders through her orgasm. Her hips keep moving, grinding her pelvis against mine. "Fuck," she whispers, drawing the word out until it's unbelievably sexy coming from her lips.

I'm done. I'm pulsing inside her, groaning hard through my own orgasm. My hands squeeze her hips so tight I know I'll leave marks, but I can't let go. We're both shaking, both orgasms blending together, so that I can't tell if the flutters of pleasure racing over me are from her or me.

It takes several seconds for the pleasure to fade to where I can catch my breath or open my eyes. She slumps down over my chest, and I have enough of my brain left to wrap my arms around her. When I'm a little more with it, I graze my lips over her forehead and hold her tight, loving the way we're still melding together.

She picks her head up and traces her finger over my mouth. "That was fucking amazing."

"Yes, it was."

Soft laughter eases out of her, contracting her muscles around me, making me groan. "Christ, I hope I can get it up again. We need to do that twenty more times."

She gently rolls off me, curling up against my side. "I have faith in you."

I turn and tap my finger against the tip of her nose. "Give me one second."

My legs barely carry me into the bathroom to dispose of the condom and clean myself up.

When I return, she's stripped off the lacy top that had barely been hanging on anyway. She's lying on her side, facing me, head propped up on her hand.

I stop dead so I can stare at every bare inch of her. "Do you have any idea how sexy you are?"

She extends her hand, inviting me to join her. "No. Come show me."

Forty-Nine

MURPHY

Much, much later we're wrapped up together the way I've always wanted to be with Heidi. Not just the naked, worn out from too much sex part, but the part where my arm's holding her close and her head's resting on my chest. It's just us. Quiet. Peaceful. Her soft fingers absently trace feather-light hearts over my heart.

"Who was your first?"

Okay, that question was *not* a part of this fantasy.

"Why are you asking?"

Against me her shoulder jerks. "Just curious."

"Heidi—"

Her fingers stop their tracing and tap my chest. "Come on. You know *everything* about me."

I'm not sure if that's true, but there's no way I'm bringing up anything remotely related to her dead husband in this moment.

"Some girl from school I was friendly with," I finally answer.

She picks her head up and stares at me. "Not a club girl?"

My whole body's on alert. This conversation feels dangerously close to stomping through a minefield. "No."

"How old were you?"

"Sixteen? I don't know. She was tutoring me in English." I tip my head down so I can see her better. "You realize you were eight then, right?"

"I know." She's quiet for a second and my entire body tenses, waiting to see what she says next. "How many others?"

Fuck me. I don't want to answer that. This conversation is bound to tear open old wounds and here she is holding a saltshaker. "What are you asking? You want a number, Heidi?"

"I guess."

My gaze runs over her face, but she's calm. I try to think it through but keep coming up blank. She's waiting with a curious expression, but her body's relaxed against me. It's the reason I answer such a dangerous question. Never mind that I can't lie to Heidi any more than I can lie to myself. "I don't know."

She doesn't snort in disgust, pull away, or judge me. I trace my finger over her lips. "It doesn't matter. You're my last."

Her mouth turns up slightly and she kisses my hand. "Did you love any of them?"

That I can answer easily. "No."

"Not one?"

"No."

I hesitated that last time and she picks her head up again. "I won't be mad. I thought this was what adults in new relationships do."

Her earnest words make me chuckle, and I lean over to kiss the top of her head. "You want the truth? I only seriously *cared* about one—Trinity." She opens her mouth to say something then closes it. "Not the way you think. You remember what a chubby, awkward kid I was?"

"No. I don't remember you that way at all."

The quick, honest way she says it is so sweet, I lean in and give her another kiss. "Thank you. But I always felt that way about myself. She was genuinely nice to me. She helped me find my place in the club, encouraged me to run for Road Captain when they needed me. Besides your brother, she's the only one I talked to about my mom dying." She murmurs my name against my skin, and I squeeze her a little tighter. "But as far as wanna-marry, spend-my-life, have-children-with love, there's only one. You."

She rubs her leg against mine, sliding over me, shifting her body, so she's lying on top of me. Her forehead touches mine for a second, then she plants a soft kiss on my lips. "Thank you for being honest."

"I'll never lie to you."

"I know."

"You're part of me, so lying to you is lying to myself."

She kisses me again, longer this time. One of her hands moves up, running through my hair. "I know. I feel the same way."

Heidi

That conversation wasn't as icky as I thought it would be.

I'm not *thrilled* the man I plan to spend the rest of my life with has been with so many women he's lost count.

But, it took a lot for him to be honest with me.

"You were my first love," I whisper.

"I know."

"You were the first to break my heart, too."

"I never meant to."

"Are you mad I didn't wait for you? That you weren't *my* first?"

"No." He traces his fingers over my cheek. "I could never be mad at you for anything, Heidi. I may not have been your first, but I'll be your last."

Fifty

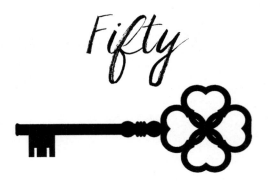

Heidi

Waking up next to Blake makes me happier than I ever imagined. I have time to study the ink on his chest and arms. But, because I can't help touching, I end up waking him.

"What're you doing?"

"Memorizing every inch of you."

"Hmm, I like that." He leans over to kiss my forehead. We're quiet together, touching each other. Tracing our fingers over every inch of one another as if we're both trying to commit every plane and angle to memory.

He brushes his finger down between my breasts, settling his hand on my belly.

"Do you think Alexa'd like a little brother or sister?" he asks, breaking our silence.

Two kids before twenty? But there's a skip in my heart, a flutter in my belly, at the thought of having a child with Blake. But, the question also unnerves me for reasons that leave me unsettled and defensive.

"I don't know. Why, you feeling like you need to have your own kid with me?"

"No." He rolls us so he's on top of me but holds himself up so he can stare at my face. "I'll never lie to her about who her father is, but she's *mine*, Heidi. She's mine as much as any other kids we'll have." Every word is full of such fierce passion, I regret my words. He's been good to Alexa since day one, and I don't doubt him for a second. He rolls back to his side of the bed and stares at the ceiling. "I just thought maybe it'd be nicer to have them closer in age or something. I don't know."

"Okay," I whisper.

He turns his head. Guess he wasn't expecting that answer.

"Yeah?"

"Well, not right this second."

"No. You need to finish school. And I need to get busy building us a house."

"Really?"

"Fuck, yeah."

"How many bedrooms is this house going to have?"

The corner of his mouth pulls up into a devilish smile. "How many do you want it to have?"

"I hope if we have daughters they have your red hair."

"Why, so they can get teased in school?"

"As if you'd ever let anyone pick on your kid."

"True." He reaches over to the nightstand and I fake-groan.

"I don't think my pussy can take any more, Blake."

He laughs so hard, shaking the bed as he keeps reaching for whatever he wants. I tilt my head but just end up with my nose in his armpit.

"What are you doing?" he asks and I nip him. "Ow. I was going to give you something. Now I don't know if you deserve it."

"More orgasms? Because I definitely think I've earned them."

He slips his hand between my legs, gently stroking. "Thought you couldn't take any more?" His thumb brushes over my clit and my head falls back against the bed.

"Oh, fuck," I murmur. "I was so, so wrong."

A shudder ripples through my body and my back arches. Blake's hot, wet mouth closes over one nipple, while he pushes a finger inside me. My eyes pop open and his eyes burn into mine while he lazily pumps his finger in and out. I roll my hips against his hand, and he lets out a harsh breath.

"That's good. Do that again, beautiful," he demands.

Lifting my arms over my head, I brace my hands on the head-board and roll my hips again.

"Fuck, that's hot."

One finger becomes two inside me.

"Open your eyes, Heidi," he commands in a rough voice. "Watch."

My first thought is *no*. I don't want to look. But as my hips rock against him faster, I'm curious. My gaze slides down, watching his fingers reappear, shiny and slick from me. I watch as he slides them inside me and brushes his thumb over my clit. My hips buck harder against his hand and my orgasm sweeps over me. Before I can scream, his mouth covers mine, sucking down all the moans and cries that rush out.

Blake pulls back, breaking our kiss, removing his fingers from me.

"Fuck, I could do that all day."

Wrung out, I make a moaning sound of agreement.

"But, I wanted to give you something besides an orgasm this morning."

I flick my gaze in his direction and he hands me a small white box. Eager to see what it is, I sit up. "Can I open it?"

"Yeah. Don't freak out. It's not a ring. Not yet, anyway."

I glance up at him, the box forgotten.

"What?"

He slides his right hand over his left ring finger. "Ring. Engagement. Married. That's part of the whole 'you're mine and I'm yours' thing."

"Oh. I just wanted you so bad, I didn't think about all that other stuff."

My words seem to stun him, which is only fair, since he shocked me. He recovers quicker than I do. "Gonna patch your ass, too."

"Ha. Good luck with that. My brother's never going to vote yes."

"He might surprise you."

Blake's delusional, but I'll let him live in fantasy land a little longer. "You think I'm ol' lady material?"

"Fuck, yes. You know how to keep your mouth shut, well, unless you're around me."

"Sorry."

He gently squeezes my chin between his fingers. "I love your mouth. Yes, you're ol' lady material. You love the club as much as I do."

"True."

"And you never talk about the club with outsiders."

He's not asking. He knows me too well. But I answer anyway. "Nope."

"Okay then."

"That's your call. But I'd proudly wear your patch, Blake."

"Thank you. Now, will you please open your present?"

I flip the lid off the box and find a lovely, shiny pendant in the shape of a key nestled inside. The bow of the key is shaped like a four-leaf clover. It's simple, elegant, and the prettiest thing anyone's ever given me. It also has a little weight to it. Not something cheap he picked up on a whim.

"Blake, it's so beautiful."

He motions for me to hand it to him and I turn, lifting my hair out of his way.

"You've held the key to my heart from day one, Heidi."

MURPHY

I'm embarrassed to say when I had the necklace made for Heidi. Let's just say, I never expected to be able to give it to her. After I latch it around her neck, she jumps off the bed and runs to the mirror to check it out.

Having a naked Heidi running around the room makes me feel like I'm the luckiest fucker on the planet.

"It's beautiful. What's the stone in the middle?"

"Green tourmaline."

"It's almost the color of your eyes. I love it so much. Thank you."

While admiring her ass from across the room is nice, I'd rather have my hands on her. Stepping behind her, I cup her hips and pull her to me. Her fingers dance over the delicate white gold chain. "This looks so fragile. I'm afraid Alexa will break it. She likes to yank on anything she can wrap her fingers around lately."

"I'll find you a sturdier leather cord for it, and when she's older, you can put it back on this chain."

She turns and throws her arms around my neck. "Thank you." This is what's always been nice about giving Heidi gifts. No matter how big or small, she always genuinely appreciates everything.

"Do you want to get dressed and look around the grounds? There's supposed to be hiking trails, and we can kayak on the lake if you want."

"When do we leave?"

"Tomorrow afternoon."

She lowers her eyes and trails her fingers over my abs right down to my dick. "I'm having more fun here."

Even though her touch is light, it's intense and I groan. "I—" Her fingers wrap around my cock and I totally lose what I wanted to say. I lean forward, placing my hands on the mirror on either side of her head. "I don't want you to think this is all…we're all about sex. Or that's all I want." Wow, that was a difficult sentence to get out while her fingers squeeze and rub me smooth and steady.

"Blake, I would never think that about you. We have so much more between us. But this has been a really long time coming, so I'd like to spend the weekend *coming* with you." She snickers at her little joke and rubs her thumb over the tip of my dick, smearing pre-cum over me.

I huff out a bit of laugh, then hiss as she drops to her knees, raking her nails lightly down my thighs as she goes.

"What're you doing?"

"Well, I'm not down here to give you a pedicure. I'd like to give you a blowjob."

"Fuck," I groan. Life with Heidi will never be boring. "That's the funniest and hottest thing I've ever heard."

"I think most guys would find that hot."

"No. It's hot because it's you, and I've probably been fantasizing about this long enough that my ass should be in jail."

"Oh, really?" She draws the word out and grins. And her hand's still lazily rubbing up and down my dick.

"Harder, Heidi." She licks her lips, and it's possible I'm going to come before she gets her mouth near me. She shifts and the movement pulls me out of my lust fog. "Come here." I grab her hand and pull her up off the floor.

"What's wrong?"

"You shouldn't be on the floor."

"You don't want your blowjob?"

"Oh, I want it. And I'm going to get it." I lead her over to the bed and tumble down, bringing her with me. She squints at me, and I cup her face in my hand. "This is better."

She gives me another suspicious look and kneels up next to me.

"This is better." I reach out to stoke my thumb over her cheek.

First, she turns and kisses the hand rubbing her face, then she lowers her head. When her tongue drags along my shaft, from base to tip, I'm done. Gone. Her mouth closes over my dick and I groan. My hand moves to her hair, pulling it up into a rough ponytail. "Fuck, that's so good, Heidi."

Her answer is to wrap her fist around my cock and take me deeper. She grips me harder, jacking me off slow and then taking me all the way to the back of her throat. "Heidi." I whisper her name like a prayer and she looks up at me. She smiles, then devours me. She takes every inch and what she lacks in experience, she makes up for with enthusiasm.

"Heidi, I can't. I'm gonna—" She takes her mouth off me with a soft pop, but her hand keeps working me. "Get on. Get on top of me."

"But I'm not done."

I open my eyes and hers are shining with mischief. While I'm definitely enjoying bratty Heidi, it's time to explain who's in charge. I point to the nightstand. "Grab a condom, roll it on me, and get on my dick."

Her lips curl into a smirk, but she bends backward and grasps a condom. The movement puts her gorgeous tits on display, and I cover one with my hand, lightly pinching her nipple.

"Oh, fuck."

I pinch a little harder and she moans.

She's taking too long. I need to be inside her. Plucking the condom out of her hand, I rip it open and roll it on. I pull her up and over me. "Ride me. I want to watch you take me the way you want, until you get what you need, then I'll decide how we finish."

Her lips part in surprise. "I want to be offended," she says, lifting herself up. "But that's really fucking hot." The last part of her words are lost in a moan as she sinks down, taking me inch by inch into her body. She takes a few seconds to adjust, then she works herself up and down. "Hands," she whispers and I lace my fingers with hers, helping her steady her movements.

"That's it. Keep going."

She smiles and I know she's thinking of something smart to say back, but she's too blindsided with bliss to get the words out.

I watch every bit of pleasure that plays out over her face. As she gets into it, her necklace bounces, catching my attention. "You're so pretty, Heidi."

She hits the right spot and keeps hitting it until she freezes, tenses up all over.

"Oh. Blake, I'm so, I'm gonna—"

"Yeah, you are. Give it to me."

I let her ride it out for a few seconds then grip her hips and roll us.

"Can you take more?"

"Yes."

That's all I need to hear. I slip a few pillows under her ass, tilting her at the perfect angle to slide in deep.

"Oh my God. I can't."

"Am I hurting you?"

"No. It's good. So good."

Finally, she opens her eyes and stares at me in wonder. Her breath hitches and her body jerks under me. The soft moans and curses coming from her mouth trigger me, and I come so hard, for a moment I can't see or hear anything.

Breathless, I fall down next to her, and she hooks her arm around my neck, rolling into me for a kiss. After a second, I pull back. "Let me clean up."

I'm so out of it, I don't realize she followed me into the bathroom until I catch her reflection in the mirror. "What's wrong?"

"Nothing." Her lips quirk up and her eyes dart to the shower.

I take a step closer, brushing the back of my hand over her nipples. "Want me to clean you up?"

"Yes," she whispers.

The shower's large. A big, square box with multiple sprays coming from two sides. Once we're closed inside, she uses her smaller body to nudge me backward until my back's against the wall. "Stay still," she says, grabbing a small bottle of bodywash and pouring it into her hands.

She washes me with a serious expression. When she's finished, she places a gentle kiss over my heart. Her fingers trace the tattoo of a shamrock with the Lost Kings MC skull and crown in the middle that takes up most of my chest. "I've never gotten to see this up close."

"I know."

She takes a slow route to my arms, tracing different lines of ink. "I remember when you got the first one. I thought you were so cool."

"Yeah? I didn't give it as much thought as I should have."

Her mouth turns up as she keeps tracing my arms. "Did you cover it up?"

"Yeah."

"Hmmm," she hums, and her hands return to the shamrock.

"I need to get this touched up," I say absently, brushing my hand over my chest.

She presses close again, kissing my chest. Her teeth graze over my nipple, making me jolt and groan at the same time. I'm so focused on what her mouth's doing, I don't notice where her hands are until she wraps one around my dick.

A hiss of pleasure eases out of me as she slides her hand up and down.

"You know what your next tat should be?"

"Huh?" I've been struck stupid by her hands on my dick.

"I think you should have *Property of Heidi,* tattooed right here." She squeezes me a little harder so I know exactly where she's talking about.

I laugh—an awkward sound because she's still slowly jerking me off. "Even I'm not that adventurous." I brush my hand over a spot a little north of where she's playing. "Maybe here."

She raises an eyebrow. "I was only teasing."

"I'm not." My hands close over her face. "What do you want?"

"Shower sex with you. That's one of *my* fantasies."

Fuck. The direct thing totally works for me. My dick's very excited about the idea of picking her up, pinning her to the wall, and fucking her while the water pours over us.

"Give me a second." I hop out of the shower and grab a condom from one of my bags on the counter. She's waiting, wet and eager when

I step back inside. "How do you want it?"

One of her shoulders lifts and she does the shy-lip-biting thing that also turns my crank. "However you want to give it to me."

Christ, that's fucking hot. My hands grab her slick, wet ass and she loops her arms around my neck. It's not as easy as I thought with the slippery tile surrounding us. But I manage to pick her up, pin her to the wall, and slide into her without falling.

Steam and our combined groans fill the room.

Property of Heidi. Sounds right to me.

Fifty-One

Heidi

"How do you feel about getting out of this room for a few?" Blake asks as we're having another hazy, post-sex nap. We've pretty much gone at each other for twenty-four hours straight at this point. Only stopping to shower, nap, or order room service.

"Mmm." I yawn and stretch. "What did you have in mind?"

"Taking you to dinner someplace nice. The room service is fine, but I want to take you out."

"Like a date?"

He chuckles, jostling me around until I sit up and face him. "Yeah, Heidi. Like a date."

"Okay. I even brought a date dress."

His mouth turns up in an appreciative grin. "For me?"

"Yup."

He follows me into the shower, so it ends up being another hour until I shove him out of the bathroom and get ready. The dress is sophisticated, but that's why I liked it. I feel more grown up. Like it makes sense for me to hold Blake's hand. We may have spent the last twenty-four hours in bed, but I want to make sure any lingering "little sister" type feelings are completely obliterated. The dress is a black, clingy fabric that skims my curves and ends at my knees. It's held up by one wide strap over my shoulder, leaving my arms bare. Plain, but pretty and sexy.

Blake must agree because he sucks in a deep breath when he sees me. "Wow. I feel underdressed now," he says, pointing to his jeans and plain T-shirt. "You're fucking beautiful."

My cheeks warm. No matter how many times he tells me I'm beautiful, I still tingle all over when I hear those words from him.

His gaze slides down to my feet. "Those are sexy." He holds out his hand. "Come on. If we don't leave right now, we're going to be back in bed."

My free hand flies to my mouth to hide my laughter.

"You have such a pretty smile. Don't cover it up."

"Sorry. Grams always told me that gap in my front teeth made me look like a rabbit—"

He turns and stares at me. "What gap?"

"Uh, the one I've had forever?" I flash a smile at him and he stares at me. Having him study my flaws so seriously freaks me out, and I swipe my hand over my mouth again.

"Heidi, your grandmother was a bitch. All I see is pretty. Now, knock it off."

"Hmm," I grumble as he pulls me into the elevator. "I know I'm not your usual type."

"My usual what?"

"You know, tall, skinny, pretty blondes."

He shakes his head and I think maybe mutters a prayer for strength. "You're nuts." He fits his hands over my hips. "I'm only interested in one gorgeous girl who fits in my hands just right and has pretty long, *brown* hair."

"Me?" I tease.

"Only you."

The rough catch in his voice melts me and I feel a little bad for teasing him. "I love you, Blake. You're everything to me."

He doesn't answer with words. But no words are needed. His hands slide from my hips to the small of my back, and he pulls me up and into his body. Lowering his head, he takes a soft kiss. I'm the one who pushes up on tiptoes to make the kiss last longer. It's as if something snaps inside him and he presses me up against the wall of the elevator, deepening our kiss. I'm lost in his arms wrapped tight around me, his mouth against mine, his heat searing my skin. So lost, I don't even notice the elevator jerk to a stop, or the doors slide open.

Someone clears their throat and Murphy finally pulls away. An older couple stands in the doorway, horrified expressions in place. Completely unconcerned, he takes my hand and pulls me into the hallway.

I giggle as he tugs me forward and run a few steps to catch up to him. "That was awkward."

"Fuck it." He turns and grins at me.

"What made you pick this place? It's kind of stuffy. I think we're the youngest people here."

He slows down and wraps his hand around my waist, tugging me closer. "I don't know. I wanted to take you someplace really nice. Special. Plus, it was the only nice hotel that had a room on short notice."

"I'm sorry. I wasn't complaining. It's beautiful here. I just feel a little out of place."

He leans over and kisses my cheek. "You're beautiful and you're never out of place."

A few seconds later, we learn that's not exactly true.

MURPHY

"Sir, the young lady isn't old enough to dine here. There's an age restriction," the snobby old fuck at the door explains as we cross the threshold to the hotel's restaurant.

Heidi tugs at my hand. "Let's go. We can do room service again."

"No. Stay here."

I crook my finger at the guy and take him aside.

In my calmest, lowest voice, I explain how the next few minutes are going to play out. "Listen, I'm paying an obscene amount of money to stay in your uptight hotel. My girlfriend's nineteen. Neither of us are planning to drink. If you say one more word that upsets her, I'll break every bone in your botoxed face."

He stares at me. "Well, ah, your attire is also a problem," he says nodding at my jeans.

I continue glaring at him, and he finally comes to the conclusion that my threat is a promise if he doesn't do as I asked.

"Very well, sir. I'll find a table."

I slip a twenty into his hand. "A quiet table by the window, please."

He leaves without another word.

"What did you say?" Heidi asks, rushing up next to me and taking my hand.

"Nothing. Slipped him some money and asked him to find us a table."

She twists her mouth and narrows her eyes in an *I-don't-believe-you* expression. I lean over and kiss her forehead. "Don't worry about it."

The old guy returns. "Right this way."

As instructed, he leads us to a quiet corner table. He pulls Heidi's chair out and fusses over her so much, she blushes. One hard look from me and he disappears.

Heidi's gaze drifts to the window. "Oh, look how pretty the lake is at night."

I can't look at anything but her.

"Blake," she whispers after staring at the menu for five seconds. "Everything's so expensive."

"It doesn't matter. Get whatever you want."

She opens her mouth, hesitates, and bites her lip. All of it adorable. All of it distracting me from finding something on the menu for myself.

"What?" I ask.

"I want to try the scallops."

"Then do it. Whatever you want."

The waiter pours our water and I give him our order.

I hate taking my eyes off her for even a second. My hand slides over hers. "You're beautiful."

"You make me feel beautiful."

"Hey, you never told me how it went at school."

She gives me an uncertain look. "Okay. I feel bad I didn't let my brother know I was going away," she says, completely changing the topic.

"Uh, I told him I was going away for a few days, and he pretty much figured it out."

She laughs softly. "Really?"

"Yeah. I think he's made his peace with you and me being together."

"At least you won't drag me to Alaska," she says.

I'm not sure how to respond, so I don't. Our food arrives and she spends a lot of time checking it out before she takes a bite.

My steak is perfect, so I ask her if she wants to trade.

"No. I'm good."

She finally dives in and hums with pleasure.

"Good?"

"Yes."

After dinner, we order coffee and she asks for chocolate mousse. When the waiter leaves, I lean over the table. "Now I want to smear chocolate mousse all over you and lick it off."

She doesn't laugh—probably because she senses how serious I am—but she turns sideways and crosses her legs. My eyes are immediately drawn to her sexy, fucking green high heels. There's a strap across the front, letting her toes peek out and another strap around her ankle that finishes in a bow, making them a wicked combination of sexy and cute. Shoes aren't usually something I pay a lot of attention to on a woman, but I can't stop staring at Heidi's long, sleek legs or her perfectly painted pink toenails. She runs her hand down her leg and slowly drags it back up. I can't tell if it's a nervous gesture or if she's trying to drive me nuts.

"What's wrong?" she asks.

"Nothing. I really like what you're wearing."

Her cheeks turn pink and she lowers her gaze to the table. "I wanted to, you know, look like we belong together," she says, twirling the spoon round and round in her coffee.

I snort. "You're way too pretty to be with me."

"I meant look older."

"I know what you meant."

Her dessert's dropped off and she spends so much time licking and savoring the fluffy chocolate, I end up counting back from one hundred. The thing is, she's not doing it to torture me or give me a painful erection I can't do anything about at the moment.

But that's why it's so damn hot.

"Are you trying to kill me?" I ask mid-lick,

She hesitates, then nudges her bowl to me. "Try it."

"That's not what I meant."

When she's finished, I take her hand and lead her outside. There's another restaurant and bar at the other end of the lodge. The bar looks more relaxed. "I should have brought you here," I say.

"Doubt they had scallops."

"You're probably right."

There's a patio outside and even though it's still cool out, a few couples are outside dancing. "Oh, I love this song," she says, dragging me outside.

"I don't dance, Heidi."

"I know," she says, wrapping her arms around me and swaying from side to side, until it's impossible not to follow her. "I remember that was your excuse for not taking me to my junior-high dance."

Yeah, that and I didn't want to get arrested.

The memory's bitter-sweet, because I know I probably hurt her feelings when I explained I would not be escorting her to any school dances. I hold her a little tighter, happy that part of our lives is behind us.

"We definitely couldn't have done this," I murmur into her hair.

"No." She tilts her head back staring into my eyes. The heels put her at the perfect height for easy kisses, and I take a few. She tastes like chocolate.

"I'm really liking the shoes," I say when we part.

She places kisses along my jaw and whispers in my ear, "I have a secret."

"What's that, beautiful?"

"My underwear matches the shoes."

It takes a second for her words to sink in. I'm not quite used to this grown-up, confident sex-kitten version of Heidi. She's a lot of fuckin' fun, though.

"Prove it."

Her brows draw down. "What?"

"Give 'em to me."

"Now?"

I stare at her, explaining without words, that yes, I mean *now.*

The corners of her mouth quirk up. A sexy little smile that says she's considering it. Her gaze darts around the patio, finally landing on a dark corner. She drags me over to it, tucking herself between the low stone wall and my body to wiggle the panties down her legs. This may have started out as a teasing challenge, but she has my full attention as she balls them up and slaps the underwear in my open palm.

"Green. See?" She smiles with satisfaction, but I feel like the winner of our little game. I confirm the colors match and tuck them in my pocket.

"Hey, give them back," she protests.

I grab her hips, sandwiching her between my body and the wall behind her. "You won't be needing them."

She slides her hands through my hair, pulling me in for a kiss. Kissing for so long, I forget where we are. My hands fist in the material of her dress, tugging it up. She breaks the kiss, laughing softly. "There are people here."

No one's paying attention to us, but I'd rather be alone with her than risk getting caught. "Come on," I say, grabbing her hand.

"What, no midnight kayak ride?" she teases and I stop.

I turn, wanting to give her anything and everything she wants. "We can do that."

She wraps her arms around my waist, clinging to me. Her happy face tips up, her brown eyes finding mine. "I'm kidding. Take me to our room."

Heidi

We're barely inside the door, and he has me pinned against it. Rough hands skim over my legs, under my dress, gripping my thighs. I slide my hands through his hair, pulling him in for a kiss. Deep, long kisses that make it easy to forget where I end and he begins. I have no idea what time it is or of anything outside this moment. Cool air touches my skin as he pushes my dress up around my waist. His lips trail down, kissing and licking my neck.

"I can't get enough of you."

"Good."

"I mean it. I've never wanted anything more than you," he says against my lips.

"Me, too." Warmth spreads over my skin. His hands tighten on my hips and he turns me to face the door. Big, warm hands slide over my ass and upper thighs. Next, he works the zipper down, peeling the dress from my body. He leans in and presses a kiss to my shoulder. "You looked beautiful tonight. Will you wear this for me again?" he asks in a low, husky voice.

"Any time you want." I answer, stepping out of the dress.

He makes a growly noise that sounds a little like thank you and keeps kissing my shoulder, up to my neck. "Hmm. This is green too," he says, running his finger over the back of my bra. "So much attention to detail."

"Only for you." I barely get the words out. The roughness of his clothes pressed up against my bare skin leaves me quivering, aching to find out what he plans to do to me. From the moment he asked me to hand my panties over downstairs, my body's been pushed to the edge. I'm so worked up I might explode. "You need something?" he asks with a rough chuckle.

I flatten my palms on the door and push back against him, arching my back. His hands slide down my body, encircling my waist, pulling me into him. One hand drops, his finger finding my clit, massaging, circling until I moan. Finally, *ohmygod*, finally he slides a finger lower, pushing in and slowly pulling out. I shudder, trembling as my orgasm builds. "Please, don't stop."

He kisses my cheek. "No plans to stop, beautiful. I want you to come for me over and over tonight."

The promise of more to come combined with his steady touch sets off flashes of white light behind my eyes, and an orgasm ripples through my body. My brain's unaware of anything but the pleasure of Blake's hands.

"Turn around," he says against my ear.

Slowly, I gather control of my body and turn, my skin rubbing against the soft fabric of his shirt.

"Take my shirt off," he demands.

"My pleasure."

He lets out a soft, rumbling laugh that turns to a groan when I slip my hands under his T-shirt. Stripping the shirt off, I drop it on the floor with my dress. I look up at him through my lashes, while running my hands over his exposed skin, enjoying the hard muscles of his chest and abs.

His next movements are so quick, I barely know what's happening. He pins me to the door with his hips, while his hands drop to his belt and he works his jeans open. The clink and drop of his belt sends shivers through me. Anticipation flutters over every inch of my skin as he pulls a condom from his pocket and smooths it on. He steps closer, gripping my ass and lifting, pressing my shoulder blades into the door. "Wrap your legs around me, beautiful." His husky whisper has me eager to do anything he asks.

I'm so frantic to have him inside me, I wriggle, digging my hands into his shoulders. "Easy, I got you." Then he's pushing forward and it's so, so good. I pull his head to me and kiss him. "Fuck, you're perfect. We fit so right." Both of us look down to where we're connected, watching as he pulls out and pushes back inside.

I'm so overcome with feelings of belonging to Blake. Wanting him to be mine. "You're mine." My words come out in a hard whisper, but he understands them fine.

"*Hellfuckingyes* I am."

A second orgasm washes over me. Heavy breathing fills the air. My mouth closes over his skin, my teeth grazing, tongue tasting. He grinds his hips into me and comes with my name on his lips.

Slowly, he lets go of my hips and I unwind my legs from his body. My legs are trembling so hard, I can't hold myself up. He picks me up, carrying me across the room. Shuffling because his pants are somewhere around his knees. Gently setting me on the bed, he drops a kiss on my forehead. "Be right back."

I stretch out, throwing my arms over my head.

"Even after fucking me dry, seeing you like that goes straight to my dick." Despite his crude words, he gently traces his finger down my leg, landing on my foot. "Want me to take these off for you?"

"Please?" I ask, holding my foot up.

He gently works both shoes off, then climbs into bed, hovering over me, lowering his head to kiss me. "Now that's what you call dessert."

He settles next to me, snuggling me close.

"Better than chocolate mousse?" I tease.

His warm laughter rumbles right through me. One of his hands cups my cheek, and I stare into his green eyes until I'm lost. "I want to learn everything about you, Heidi. Every little thing that makes you tick. What turns you on. Everything you enjoy."

I tilt my head, kissing his hand. "We have our whole lives ahead of us."

Fifty-Two

MURPHY

Our trip home goes by way too fast. I'm happy we took my truck instead of the bike. This way I can hold her hand, and enjoy her recap of our weekend and all the other things she has to say. As we drive up to the clubhouse she grows quiet.

"What's wrong?" I ask.

"Nothing. I can't wait to see Alexa. I miss her."

I reach over and take her hand, giving her a gentle squeeze.

I can't say goodbye to her yet, so I walk her over to Rock and Hope's. Plus, I want to see the baby, too.

Rock and Hope are in the living room with Alexa.

"How was your trip?" Hope asks as she rushes over to hug both of us.

Heidi's blushing like crazy, so I answer for her. "Fun. Peaceful."

A knowing smile slides over Rock's face as he joins us and hands Heidi's daughter over. "She missed you," he says to Heidi.

Heidi's gone. Lost in making baby noises and cooing at her daughter. I think it's the sweetest thing I've ever seen. I can't believe how much I love this woman.

It's a little awkward with all of us standing in the entryway. Hope finally has us move to the kitchen. I feel like I'm overstaying my welcome, but I can't find it in me to say goodbye to Heidi.

While the girls catch up on everything Alexa did while we were away, I ask Rock if I can measure a piece of property to start building a house. The corner of his mouth pulls into a lazy smile. "You know you can. The property belongs to the club. Figure out where you want to build, and I'll help you anyway I can. We should probably think about extending the driveway from the clubhouse out here or putting in one from the other access road."

We've never had more than one entry point at the club property, so that's a big undertaking and also a security issue.

"I think the driveway from the clubhouse should be enough. Maybe we can do a circular thing that loops around."

He nods. "We'll ask Wrath what he thinks."

"I can tell you right now what he's going to say: 'stay the fuck away from my house.'"

Rock laughs. "Yeah, probably." His gaze strays to Heidi and Alexa. Then he gives Hope a look and tilts his head. Finally, he turns to me. "You can stay here with them if you want."

I can't tell if they discussed this ahead of time or if Rock just came up with the idea. Hope excitedly picks up his thought. "I never use my home office. We can move Alexa's things in there for now, so you two can have privacy."

I'm so stunned by the offer, I can't answer them. Heidi keeps blushing and won't meet my eyes.

"Are you sure? I don't want to be in the way here."

"Well"—Rock nods at Heidi—"they can't be over at the club-house all the time. Alexa will be miserable listening to all that noise."

I huff out a laugh. "You sure it won't be weird for you two? I mean, you moved out here to get away from the clubhouse, not have extended guests."

"Family's always welcome," Hope assures me.

My gaze swings to Heidi again. This time she's watching me with a hopeful expression. "That okay with you?"

"Yes," she whispers. "I'd like that."

"Okay then."

Heidi

Rock and Murphy spent the afternoon rearranging Hope's office and then moving Alexa's crib and other stuff into the cleared space. It's not ideal, but it's nice to have a room to myself again.

A room that includes Blake.

"Is this weird? It's weird, right?" I ask before settling down for the night.

"It'd be weirder if I was over at the clubhouse and you were here."

"True."

"I don't want to spend another night of my life without you next to me."

His words stir up so much happiness inside me. I don't want to spend another night without him, either.

"Kiss me," I whisper.

He glances over and a playful naughtiness enters his eyes. "Where, beautiful?"

"Anywhere you want."

The naughty gleam is replaced by warmth and sweetness as he shifts to kiss my lips, my cheek, my forehead, and back to my mouth.

I can't stop touching him. His warm skin revealed from the waist up. I stop at the drawstring of his flannel pants.

"Wow, first night under Mom and Dad's roof and you're already going for a quickie," he whispers against my ear, teasing me.

"They're all the way upstairs."

He rocks his hips against my hand. "Keep going," he whispers, his lips skimming my neck.

My fingers trail a little lower, resting against the soft flannel and the hard bulge behind it. A little pressure and he groans, squeezing his eyes tight. "Not yet. This is about you."

Hmm…I like that, but I'm also frustrated, wanting to explore every inch of him.

"Take your shirt off," he growls in my ear. Low and demanding. I can't get my shirt off fast enough. Or wriggle out of my shorts.

His hands cup my breasts, squeezing enough to thrill. He runs his thumbs lightly over my hard nipples, and I gasp.

"Do you like that?"

"Yes."

"Tell me what you like. I love hearing you say it." His mouth trails down my collarbone, finally replacing his thumb. He lingers on each nipple until I'm squirming beneath him.

Excitement builds as he throws the covers back and trails lower, over my stomach, nipping at my skin. He doesn't yank my underwear off. No, he drives me nuts first, nibbling at the small scrap of fabric covering me. My hands settle on his shoulders—to push him away or pull him closer, I'm not sure. I'm trembling everywhere, little noises coming out of my mouth. I'm barely aware of when he slips his hands under the straps at my hips and eases the cotton panties down my legs. Then his mouth is on me, touching me, kissing me. His hands hold my thighs apart to give him access. His tongue traces over me, feather-light, slowly building pressure. Then the pressure stops.

"Is that good?" he asks.

I groan in frustration. "Don't stop." Tipping my head up, I find him grinning. "Don't be a jerk." He laughs even harder, then abruptly licks me again, sending my hips shooting off the bed.

After that bit of teasing, he's all focus, making me forget everything. Where we are, who we are, nothing but his tongue, lips, mouth, teeth on me matters. Pressure builds as he pleasures me with so much care and focus, that any doubts I have melt away. My body responds, *reaching, reaching, reaching* for something, just beyond my grasp. When it hits, every muscle in my body tightens as the shock wave of pleasure crashes over me.

When I finally open my eyes, he's kissing his way up my body. I reach down and brush my hand over his cheek, and he turns to kiss my fingers. "That was amazing," he says.

"Yes."

He settles next to me, pulling me into his arms so we're pressed together so tight I can feel his heartbeat, rapid like mine. He kisses me over and over. "I want to do that a hundred more times."

My laughter seems loud in the quiet surrounding us. "I won't say no."

Fifty-Three

Heidi

The warmth of Blake's protection and love surrounds me so tight, I'm smiling before I'm even fully awake the next morning.

"Hey, beautiful," he murmurs at me. Turning over, he pulls me closer, sealing his mouth over mine.

A sort of grunt bursts out of me and I push him away. "Don't. I'm all morning breath stinky."

He tips his head back and laughs.

"You're all minty fresh, though. How long have you been up?"

"A while. Now shut up and kiss me." He rolls me under him, and we spend a lot of time teasing and tasting each other. I shift, spreading my legs and bumping my hips up to meet his hardness.

"Blake," I whisper. "I need—"

Screaming interrupts my words. "Alexa's up," I groan.

Blake's up and out of bed. "Stay there. I'll grab her."

Ugh, this is awful. I don't think he realizes the fun we had over the weekend won't happen on a regular basis. Those days are over for me and for him, if he wants to be with me.

I'm a puddle of mush as I watch him saunter back into the room, swaying Alexa in his big arms until she settles down. She wraps one tiny fist around his beard and yanks hard.

"That's her new favorite thing."

"I noticed."

He hands me a bottle and as she settles into my arms for her morning feeding, Blake sits on the edge of the bed, watching us with a smile.

"I'm sorry," I say. "Are you sure you've thought about this? I'm… being with me means not having any time to ourselves. Are you ready to have your life turned upside down?"

He reaches out and brushes his hand over mine. "You're what I want. Don't ever doubt it."

I don't know why I feel compelled to warn him. He's spent enough time with Alexa and me over the last few months to know what he's getting into. "Being with me will change everything for you. Your life won't be the same."

He shifts and runs his hand over Alexa's head. "I know what I'm taking on. I'm ready for it, beautiful."

"Well, you *are* so much older than me," I tease to break up the heaviness settling over us.

Instead of laughing, he smiles. "Thanks for reminding me that I'm a big perv."

"I didn't mean it like that."

"I know."

He's quiet for a while, watching us.

When Alexa's settled back down, I slip across the hall and tuck her back in her crib, then duck into the bathroom. As soon as I step back in the bedroom, Blake's hands are on my hips, yanking me against him. "Where were we?"

Laughter dies on his lips as he takes in my expression. "What's wrong?"

"You said you're ready for it. But, what about those cross-country trips you love taking? I can't go with you."

His brow wrinkles. "So, we'll take my truck. We should wait until Alexa's older so she can remember the trip."

"What?"

"She's too young—"

"No, I got that part."

"The truck?"

"I thought the whole point was to do it on the bike? Wind in your face and all that." I poke my finger in his chest where his flash would be if he were wearing his cut. "Mr. Road Captain."

"So, we'll do that when the kids are older."

Whoa. What? "Kids? Plural?" I glance down and run my hand over my belly. "Do you know something I don't know?"

His mouth slides into a wide grin. "You know what I mean. We talked about this."

"Uh, I guess."

"I feel like you're overthinking things again. Let me worry about road trips and stuff."

"Okay."

"You know what we do need to worry about?"

When I can't come up with anything, he laughs. "Your brother."

"Oh."

"I'd like to officially tell him."

I slap my hand over my chest. "You mean you didn't ask for his permission before you defiled me?"

I get a smack on my butt that ends in an ass-grab. When I wiggle my hips, he slaps my ass again. "Watch it, Heidi, I can spend all day spanking your ass."

"You wouldn't dare," I taunt, just to see the look on his face.

I get more than I bargained for. He puts me over his shoulder and tosses me on the bed. After a flurry of kisses, he sits up. "Come on, get dressed. I can't enjoy this knowing I haven't told him yet."

I'm touched by how much he cares about my brother. But also *frustrated*.

Love for Blake and my brother wins out, and I slip into a pair of jeans and one of Blake's LOKI T-shirts. Alexa's squealing and kicking in her crib when we check on her. I dress her, and then we walk over to the clubhouse.

Hand in hand.

Blake carries Alexa and she baby-babbles the entire way. She's been putting some sounds together like "buh" and "gah" lately. But her favorite thing is blowing raspberries and yelling. She loves the sound of her voice.

"Maybe she'll be a singer," Blake says after a particularly ear-splitting screech.

"Maybe."

I'm not expecting my brother to be downstairs, but he's in the living room. So he, along with Wrath, Trinity, Ravage, and Sparky, see us come in the house holding hands.

"Finally!" Ravage shouts, and gets a smack from my brother. Everyone else laughs.

Marcel holds his hands out for Alexa and spends a few minutes cooing and playing with her before turning his big brother face on Blake. "Have fun deflowering my sister?" Marcel asks as we settle into the couch across from him.

I point to Alexa. "I have a baby. How exactly could he have deflowered me?"

Wrath turns his head and cough-laughs.

Marcel grumbles at us but holds his hand out to Blake. When Blake slaps his open palm, Marcel tugs him forward. "You better marry her."

"Planning on it."

"And I want a nephew, so get on that, too."

"Oh my God! What is wrong with you?" I snap, while Trinity howls with laughter.

Actually, everyone's laughing, except me.

"I'm just messing with you, little sister." He gives Blake a sharp look. "But not about the marriage part."

"I'm working on it. I want to start on a house first."

Wrath raises an eyebrow. "All right, little brother. I can help with that."

"Rock and I were talking about what to do with the driveway."

While they talk about that stuff, I reach over and tap Marcel's hand. "Are you okay?"

"Yeah, there's no one in the world who will treat you two better than fuckface will."

"Hey," Murphy growls.

"I meant how do *you* feel? Are you getting around okay?"

He scowls at the question. "I'm down here, aren't I?"

"Pain in the ass," I mutter under my breath.

"So, where are you going to stay?" Trinity asks.

"Casa North, where else?" I answer.

Trinity answers with an "Aww."

My brother raises his eyebrows. "You're staying there, too?" he asks Blake.

Warmth spreads over my cheeks. This is awkward. But, Blake wraps his arm around my shoulder and answers with a simple, "Yes." That leaves no room for discussion.

MURPHY

Since making our announcement to Teller went over better than I expected, I take Heidi and Alexa out to celebrate. I figure it will also give Rock and Hope some alone time in their own house. I really am worried they'll eventually regret having us there.

"Would you rather rent an apartment near school while we're building the house?" I ask.

She looks completely stricken at the thought.

"Move away from the club? No."

"Okay. It was just a thought."

She ducks her head and plays with her fork. "I'm not sure if I'm going back to Hudson Valley."

"What? Why?"

"I just don't want to," she says more forcefully, tipping her head up and glaring at me. "Stop trying to push me into stuff all the time. You and Marcel both are always trying to tell me what to do. Stop."

What the fuck? Where is this even coming from?

As if she senses the tension at the table, Alexa bursts into tears and Heidi scoops her up to comfort her.

Reaching over, I tickle Alexa's little hand until she grips my finger and stops bawling.

For now, I drop the school discussion. But we're definitely coming back to it later.

The rest of our time out is tense, annoying the shit out of me, since this was supposed to be a happy outing.

When we return to the house, Hope's in the living room. Knitting of all things. Heidi takes Alexa into her room, and I join Hope.

"I never pictured you knitting," I say with a chuckle. The first time I've felt like laughing all night.

"No? Tawny taught me." She gets her yarn and needles all mixed up and throws it down in disgust. "I suck at it, though. What's up? You two look tense."

I do a quick scan of the hallway. "Now Heidi says she doesn't want to go back to school."

"Back to school or back to Hudson Valley?"

I frown, thinking over our conversation. "What's the difference?"

"Oh, she didn't tell you, I bet."

"Tell me what?"

Hope lowers her voice. "She had a hard time being on campus the day she went. A lot of memories of Axel…"

"Oh. Fuck me." Why the fuck hadn't that occurred to me?

"She told me she was going to look for the same program at another school around here."

"That makes more sense. I asked her about finding an apartment near school, and she shut down."

She tilts her head, pinning me with a genuinely confused look. "Why would you look for an apartment?"

Shit. Hope's voice almost seems hurt. I'm trying to do the right thing here, not seem like an ungrateful dick. "I don't want to…overstay or cause problems or bother you guys. It's a lot of extra people to have in your house."

Shaking her head, she reaches over and takes my hand. "Murphy. It really is fine. We don't mind. You're more than welcome to stay here as long as you need to. I mean it."

"Okay. Thank you."

She nods at the hallway. "Go talk to her."

I'm not sure if she's in Alexa's room or ours, so I try the baby's first. She's in her crib sound asleep, and Heidi's curled up on the floor watching her daughter.

"Honey, why are you on the floor?"

She turns and sits up. "I don't know. When I was in Alaska, I'd sleep in her room a lot when Axel was away. Feels weird having her over here, I guess."

Something about her answer doesn't feel right to me. Squatting down next to her, I slip my hands under her legs and back and pick her up off the floor. She places her hand on my chest. "You're so strong."

That's not true. She alone has the power to break me. Like right now. The lost expression on her face tears me apart. "Come on. You're not alone any more. I'm here. We're right across the hall if she needs you."

In our room, I set her on the bed. "Tell me what's going on."

She gives me a curious look as if she has no clue what I'm referring to. "Okay. I'll start. Hope told me you had a hard time when you went to campus the other day."

"She did?" A flash of anger crosses her face.

"Don't be mad at her. *You* should have told me."

Her face takes on that lost expression again. The one that hurts all the way down to my soul. Especially when she can't meet my eyes. "After seeing my mother, I forgot until you said something. Then it hit me. Hard. I'm so sorry."

"Why?"

"That I'm...that it upset me."

Her need to apologize to *me* makes me feel like such a failure. "Jesus Christ, Heidi. Am I that much of a jerk that you think I wouldn't understand?" No matter my personal feelings, he *was* her husband and the father of her child. I know she loved him. It's barely been a few *months*. Of course something like that would upset her.

Her coffee-brown eyes finally meet mine, full of surprise. "You're not mad at me?"

"Fuck no. No wait, I *am* mad you didn't just tell me what was bothering you at dinner."

"I—"

I hold up my hand, stopping her. "I get why you think I wouldn't want to hear about it. I do. But I'm telling you, it will *not* upset me or hurt my feelings or anything else if you want to talk about it with me." I stop and think how to express myself so she gets it. Placing my hand on her cheek, I gently turn her face to mine. "I might be your *boy-friend* now, or your future-husband," Yeah, that sounds much better. "But most of all, I'll always be your friend. You can tell me anything."

She throws herself against me and I wrap her up in my arms tight. "Thank you," she murmurs against my chest.

"Heidi, this is real now. We're in this together. I'm always here for you."

Fifty-Four

Heidi

Clearing the air with Blake lifted so much of the gloom that settled in my head and heart. I'm so used to choking on the things I think will upset people, I didn't know how to explain it to him.

I should know him better by now. He's always wanted to fix what's broken in my life and take care of me.

He's been spending so much time with me, cementing our relationship I think, that he's taken a lot of time off from Furious. So today he had to go in, and I promised him I'd look into what other local schools I could transfer to. When I get a call from an unknown number, I almost don't pick it up, except I know the gym has a few different lines, and I don't want to miss a call from Blake.

"Heidi? It's your mother."

I freeze, then pull the phone away from my face and stare at it for a few seconds.

"How did you get my number?" I finally ask.

"The boy you were visiting in the hospital? He gave it to me."

"Why?"

"I told him you were my—"

"No, why did you want my number? You didn't seem all that interested in talking to me."

"Honey, I was worried about my husband. I'm sorry. Why don't we meet up for lunch and catch up?"

It's a terrible idea.

A really terrible idea.

"Where?"

She names a place near the hospital, and we plan for a late lunch.

My brother's been doing a lot better and getting around more. Since I don't want to subject my daughter to my mother yet, I ask if he'll watch Alexa, giving him some vague school excuse. He's just so damn happy I'm going back to school, he says yes without further details. I feel like a shitty sister for lying to him.

My mother looks a lot more bedraggled than the last time I saw her, and not to be shallow, but that raises a red flag for me, right away.

Even though she made these lunch plans, my mother "forgot" her wallet, so I end up paying for lunch. Turns out it's a good way to remind me that, except for the joint account with my brother, I don't exactly have much money. Axel's life insurance *still* hasn't paid out. I need to set my feelings aside and get that straightened out soon. If not for me, for Alexa.

My mother must have been listening the other day. I briefly mentioned Alexa's father had died in a work accident in Alaska.

The woman I haven't seen in over ten years has the nerve to ask about Axel's life insurance.

"You should make sure they pay it for your little girl."

"Yeah," I answer with as much disinterest as I can come up with. I want to tell her to fuck off and mind her own damn business.

"So, you said Ma kicked the bucket?"

"Yes. I would have told you but I didn't know where to find you."

Her shoulders twitch. "What happened to the house?"

"Marcel sold it and put the money in a trust for me. I can't touch it until I'm twenty-five, though." I don't tell her that Grams set the trust up to specifically make sure my mother didn't get a penny of her money.

Honestly, that she left it to *me* was a surprise.

"Can't you get that money for emergencies or school or something? Seems like being a widow with a kid, you might need it. Where are you living?"

Oh, she'll love this. "You remember Uncle Rock, right? He's President of Marcel's MC now and I'm staying with—"

"Christ, Heidi, wasn't he close to my age?" I know exactly what she's implying, and it pisses me off.

"Uh, no. And he's like a dad to me, so *ew*." She has the nerve to roll her eyes at that. When Rock's done more for me in a week than this woman ever did in my entire life. "I'm staying with him and his wife."

"What about your brother?"

"He lives at the clubhouse."

"What's he doing?"

"I don't know. Maybe you should ask him yourself." Besides his role as Treasurer of the Lost Kings MC, I don't know exactly what my brother does, nor do I ask questions. Just like I don't ask Murphy what he does for the club beyond his Road Captain duties.

"So, Rock and his ol' lady have their own kids?"

"Not yet. They just got married, like last year."

"So, why don't you leave your daughter with them? They'd probably be thrilled."

Rage bubbles up inside me, but I keep my voice as even as possible. "Is that your answer to everything? Dump your kid somewhere?"

"How are you ever going to find another husband? No man wants to take on some dead guy's kid—"

A band of blind fury tightens around my head. I reach up and rub my temples before speaking. "Then that's not the kind of man I want in my life or my daughter's life." What was I thinking? This woman doesn't give a shit about me. Never has. Never will. "Let me guess, you need money. Is that why you're suddenly interested in my life?"

I try sipping my coffee to calm myself, but my hands continue to shake with anger.

"Well, Nick owes these people—"

"Nope." I slam my mug on the table. "I'm out. Have a nice life, Helga. Lose my number."

I push out of my chair, grab my purse, and power-walk the fuck away from that crazy bitch.

Ugh, how could I let that woman fool me? Again. But as I shut myself inside my car, my rage subsides, giving way to the familiar ache of abandonment. Vividly, I picture myself as a broken little girl running to look out the window every time she heard a car, hoping it was her mom.

All the ugly memories and feelings threaten to drown me.

I'm better than this. I'm over it.

I'm a mother now. Not a broken, abandoned little girl. Not anymore. I love Alexa, and I'd do anything for her. *Die* before I abandoned her.

Drying my tears, I'm overwhelmed with the need to see Blake. I'm torn between not wanting to bother him at work and needing to see him.

"We're in this together. I'm always here for you."

Choosing to trust his words, I point my car in the direction of Furious Fitness.

MURPHY

"Heidi, what are you doing here?"

Right away, I know something's off. My girl's eyes are red and puffy.

"Jake, can you take over for me?"

"Yeah, man."

Since Wrath isn't here, I usher Heidi into his office and close the door behind us. "What's wrong?"

"I'm sorry. I know you're working. I needed to see you, though."

"It's okay. Tell me what happened? Is Alexa okay?"

She gives me half a smile. "Yes. She's with Marcel. But I did something really stupid."

I lean against Wrath's desk and pull her into my arms, kissing her cheek. "I doubt that, beautiful. You're the smartest girl I know," I murmur against her ear.

"My mother called." My jaw tightens. This won't be good. Heidi gives me the rundown of lunch with her mother and I'm ready to find the woman and choke the life out of her selfish ass.

"I don't know why I thought she'd be different. All she wanted to do was find out if I had any money to give her."

"Fuck that."

"That's pretty much what I said."

"Good."

"I made it out of there without crying, but I lost it once I got to my car."

"And you came here to see me?" I ask, so damn happy that she finally understands she can come to me when she's hurting instead of bottling it up.

She sniffles and nods. My arms wrap tighter around her, and I press more kisses to her cheek. "I love you, Heidi."

"I love you, too."

After Heidi calms down, I talk her into sticking around. I need to have her close and I don't want her driving home alone when she's upset. She calls her brother to let him know where she is, and he's more than happy to have extra time with the baby.

"I have to tell him about seeing Mom. Warn him. Don't you think?"

"We'll do it tomorrow." Teller will probably hunt the woman down and kill her for upsetting his sister.

"We?"

"Yes, we."

She grins and kisses my cheek before grabbing a bottle of Windex and a rag and cleaning the mirrors that line the gym walls.

"You don't have to do that," I say, placing my hand on her arm.

"If I'm hanging out here, I might as well be useful."

How can I not kiss her again? "Thank you."

"She okay?" Jake asks when I return to the front counter. I know he's got a reputation as the *panty-whisperer* or some shit, but he seems to be genuinely worried about Heidi.

"Yeah, just family stuff."

"She's a sweet girl. If someone needs an ass kicking, let me know."

My mouth quirks up. "Will do. Thanks, bro."

He finishes up his work and leaves, locking the door behind him.

Heidi's cleaning the last mirror when I walk up behind her and grab her by the hips. "Hey, pretty girl. All done?"

She leans back against me. "Mmhmm."

Gently taking the cleaning supplies out of her hands, I set them on the weight bench next to us. "You know what I spend a lot of time thinking about in here?" I whisper against her ear, pulling her against my body.

She shivers and stares at my reflection. "No, what?"

I keep one arm wrapped around her waist and slip the other one under her breasts. "Bending you over something."

Her breath hitches. "And?"

"Fucking you." I take her earlobe between my teeth, grazing it enough to make her shiver.

"What?"

"Anything. Desk, front counter, this weight bench we're standing next to. Actually, I can lie on it and you can straddle me—" My hand skims down her body, stopping to rub right between her legs. Even through the soft, thin sweatpants she's wearing, her heat sears my fingers.

"Ah. Oh…Blake, every light in the place is on." As she says it, though, she reaches back, curling her fingers around my dick, softly stroking me through my shorts.

"Good point." My other hand slides up her ribcage, gently kneading her breasts until her head falls back. "You're all mine."

She makes a soft humming noise in the back of her throat.

"We should shut the lights off," she says, with a soft, husky laugh that fires me up even more.

"I don't want to take my hands off you."

"Do it," she whispers.

Heidi

I can't believe I let Blake talk me into this.

Who am I kidding? I didn't need a lot of convincing. The minute he put his hands on me, I was ready to rip my clothes off.

I turn as he flicks the light switch. The overhead safety lights come on, throwing off enough illumination to see him clearly. "Maybe we should—"

My blood freezes as a red dot bounces up and down on the wall, next to Blake's head.

"Down!" I scream, as I dive toward him. He drops to the ground, as I crash into him. A second later, a bullet slams into the plaster above us.

"Holy fuck! Baby, are you hurt?" he asks, placing his hands on either side of my face.

I whisper, "No." As another bullet punches through the wall.

Lower than the first one.

My heart's pounding so hard, I hardly hear him urging me, "Move. Stay low. Wrath's office." He points down the hall, and I crouch-run my way there, stopping once to make sure he's behind me. We close the door behind us as quietly as we can. "Wrath has a Glock Forty-Three and a Sig in the bottom left drawer. Both 9mm. There should be ammo in there, too. There's a vest in the closet, put it on."

"What about you?"

He lifts his head and glares at me.

"Okay, okay."

I have to shuffle through a few books and papers before I find the small metal box at the bottom of the drawer that I assume holds the guns.

Wrath's trained me on the Glock before, so I load that one and hold on to it. Murphy will have to handle the Sig.

I scurry over to the closet and find not one, but two Kevlar vests. Jackpot. I throw the larger one at Blake and slip into the other one.

"Wrath's on his way," Blake says, when I crouch down next to him.

"Do you see anyone?"

"No, they could have been shooting from the other side of the road." He glances down at the gun in my hand. "You okay?"

"Yeah, Wrath's had me shoot this one before."

"Thank fuck." He glances at me again. "You did good, babe. If you hadn't warned me—" I let out a sob and he squeezes my hand.

"Do you think the cops are coming?"

"Don't know. Notice we didn't hear much? Had to be using a silencer. A rifle with a silencer isn't easy to come by."

I don't for a second think this is anything other than club business, and I'm scared about what Wrath might be driving into.

Murphy gives me a tired smile when I voice my fears. "He knows what he's doing."

It feels like hours before we hear someone at the back door. "Stay down," Murphy orders as he runs over and peeks out the side window. "It's Wrath and Rock."

They push into the office and the four of us huddle behind Wrath's desk. Murphy explains what happened and the guys all tell me what a good job I did. I don't even realize I'm still gripping the Glock, until Wrath pries it out of my hands.

He pushes his keys at Murphy. "We're parked down behind the bakery. Get her home."

"No," I whisper in a frantic hush. "Don't stay, please. Come with us."

"Heidi-girl, someone shot at my gym." His gaze darts between

Blake and me. "They could've hurt you. I want to find the fuckers."

"Please. I don't want anything to happen to you," I plead, close to tears.

Murphy shakes his head. "I'm pretty sure the shot came from across the road. They could be long gone."

Wrath grits his teeth. His gaze strays to the front window and back to us. "Your truck's in back, Murphy?"

"Yeah."

"Take Heidi out that way." He points to the side. "Just in case, I want you to drive through the parking lots until you get to route fifty-five. None of them have dividers more than a couple inches. Your truck can handle them."

"Okay."

"We'll be right behind you."

I finally let out a breath.

"In the morning, we need to check that spot out," Wrath says to Rock.

"Yeah, you might want to call Whisper in on this, too."

Murphy leads me out the way Wrath told him to, and we drive home in silence.

Fifty-Five

MURPHY

There will be an emergency meeting as soon as everyone's at the clubhouse. Right now, I need to get Heidi home safe. I want her far away from bullets and crazy-ass mothers.

Everyone's buzzing with news of the shooting when we walk into the clubhouse. Marcel freaks out when he sees Heidi and hugs her to him until she can't get a breath.

"I'm okay, Marcel, I swear." She grabs Alexa and immediately buries her face against her, running her hand over Alexa's curly brown hair.

"I'm going to walk them home and I'll be back."

Marcel shakes his head. "Hope's upstairs. Might as well stay here. The guys moved Alexa's other crib into your old room, Heidi."

"Thanks."

Z points to the war room. "Church as soon as Rock and Wrath get here."

I walk Heidi to the staircase. But before she takes the baby upstairs, I give her a kiss. "You did great tonight. Fuckin' proud of you."

"We're finally together. There is no way I'm losing you."

I touch my forehead to hers, and she runs her hand over my cheek. "Try to get some sleep. I'll be up as soon as I can."

Rock and Wrath come in a few minutes later. Dex and Bricks right behind them.

The entire club's seated at the table within minutes.

Rock points to me to start the meeting. "Tell us what happened."

Leaving out the part about how I was about to molest the fuck out of Heidi over one of Wrath's gym benches, I explain how we were closing up and she saw the red dot and yelled for me to get down. It's then that it comes rushing back how she *dove* for me, too. *Shit.*

I wrap up my story with, "Two shots. I hustled her in the office and sent Wrath my 911."

"Christ, Murphy. They were aiming for your fuckin' head. Who'd you piss off lately?" Z asks.

I glance to my right. "You mad about me and Heidi, bro?" I ask Marcel. A small joke to lighten everyone up.

He barely cracks a smile. "Ain't funny, fuckface. She could've been hurt."

"Sounds like she kicked ass to me," Bricks says.

"What do we know?" Rock asks.

Wrath shakes his head. "Nothing. We're good with the Wolf Knights. Whisper's too greedy to fire at the gym he owns a piece of. I've been in talks with the owners of the salon next door to buy that piece of property, but no one else should know about it."

Z lifts his chin in Wrath's direction. "Could it have something to do with Dylan?"

"I doubt it." Wrath shakes his head. "He's not involved with his dad's club. Seems pointless to target him."

Dex raises his hand. "Loco came by Crystal Ball earlier. Said there was a Ransom sighting and he had one of his guys running it down."

"Christ," Rock grumbles.

Wrath nods. "Makes sense. Ransom's the only Viper we haven't exterminated yet. Bold fuckin' move for him to be up in our territory, taking shots at our businesses, though. Never mind us. That could have brought Empire heat. Stupid risk. Even for a Viper."

Dex signals Rock and gets the nod to speak. "We shut Crystal Ball down and sent everyone home as soon as we got the call."

"Thank you." Rock sits back and runs his hand over his chin. "What about the trouble we've had taking over Ironworks? Do we think it could be one of the crews pushing in from Vermont?"

"Anything's possible. Loco swore he had it covered," Z says.

I meet Wrath's eyes across the table. He forces a quick smile. "We'll find 'em."

Feeling like somehow I let him down, I drop my gaze.

The guys keep discussing scenarios, but Wrath's low voice snaps my head up. "Murphy?"

"Yeah?"

"It's just a building, bro. I'm more pissed you two coulda been hurt."

"Yeah," Teller slaps my arm. "Why was she there, anyway?"

Glancing around the table, I decide it's not time to bring the reappearance of Heidi's mother to the club yet. "I'll tell you later."

"Aww! Someone was gonna get some nookie at work," Ravage shouts, making everyone except Teller laugh.

"Knock it off, cocksucker. That's my sister."

I'm laughing too hard to confirm or deny.

"Just stay off my desk," Wrath warns.

"All right. Get some sleep. We'll meet again in the morning." Rock dismisses everyone and I head straight upstairs to Heidi.

Except she's not in my room.

I find her in her room with Alexa.

I hate to wake her up, but there's only a twin bed in here. "Baby, come on. Let's go to my room," I say, pushing her hair off her face.

"I'm not comfortable in there."

I think I understand why. And since she's pretty much forgiven and forgotten my former manwhorin' ways, I crawl into bed behind her and pull her to me.

Of course, that means we're pressed up tight against each other. My hand strays to her legs. Bare. She's wearing tiny cotton shorts and, from the feel of it, a tank top.

Five seconds after that, she has my very hard dick poking her in the ass. I shift backward, but she moans and turns over, grabbing the back of my head, pulling me to her for a kiss.

"Heidi? You awake?"

She reaches down and squeezes me through my shorts. "I am now."

Fuck, the entire night slams into me and I surge upwards, pinning her under me, taking her mouth, yanking the straps of her top down, kissing my way down her neck.

"Blake, please—"

"No condoms in here, baby."

"I…I don't care."

My brain and my dick have completely different reactions. I still her movements and take her chin between my fingers. "You think we're ready for another kid? Or you saying that because you're rattled from earlier?"

"What?"

My dick's not amused. But, one of us needs to have a clear head.

"Come on, get her monitor, and let's go down to my room." I tug her out of bed, give her enough time to check on Alexa and grab the baby monitor, then I take her hand and we race down the hall to my room.

As soon as we're inside, I pin her to the door and strip her shorts off, flinging them over my shoulder. Our kisses are quick and desperate. Desire for her pulses through my veins.

We part long enough for me to drag her to the bed. I fumble with a giant box of condoms in my nightstand drawer.

"What'd you do, buy them in bulk?" she asks. There's more annoyance than amusement in her voice.

"Yeah. I bought this box thinking of the many, many positions and places I plan to fuck *you* in, brat."

I finally get the fucker open and spill a bunch of them on the nightstand, grab one, and dive for her. Her loud giggles echo through the room as I wrap my arms around her. "Shhh…your brother's right next door."

"Oh. Sorry." She laughs even harder.

I want to turn those laughs into moans. I kiss her from mouth to neck. "I lose my mind around you." She tastes so sweet, my tongue traces a path to her breast, rolling her nipple with my tongue.

Her back arches.

"Like that?"

"God, yes. Would you fuck me already?"

"Wow. I'm thinking I should gag you when we're in here," I barely get the words out as I squeeze into the rubber and clutch her hips.

I love teasing her. Making her moan. But I really need to be inside her. I thrust in slow, and she gasps.

"Good?"

"So good."

I keep moving slow at first, but that only lasts for so long. I let loose and she wraps her legs around me, grabs my hair, and tries not to make too much noise. Just the sight of her fighting to be quiet while she tips over the edge is enough to make me come.

Later—after Marcel threw a number of things at the wall and told us to knock it off—I wrap my arms around her tight. "You scared me tonight."

She picks her head up, staring at me in the dark. "When? How?"

"Diving in front of that bullet. Don't ever do that again."

Her hand settles on my chest as she pushes herself up. "It was instinct, Blake. I didn't think about it."

I don't know what to say.

"Besides, I really hope we're not going to be shot at again," she says, settling back down in my arms.

"Me, too."

Fifty-Six

MURPHY

We get nowhere on the shooting.

A few afternoons later, Jake and I are down at Furious helping Wrath replace the front windows with bulletproof glass and tinting.

It never got reported, so there's no impact on business, but we're still a little jumpy.

"That should do it," Jake says. Wrath informed Jake and Whisper of the shooting, otherwise no one outside of the club knows.

Jake tilts his head at me and quirks an eyebrow, silently asking Wrath what I have no idea.

"What's up?" I ask after Jake leaves.

"You've been busting your ass here for over a year now."

"Yeah?"

"This is probably a shitty time to ask since the place just got shot up and all, but I swear I was planning to ask before."

"What? Are you proposing? Because I'm really planning to marry Heidi."

The corners of his mouth lift. "Very funny, little brother. No. I still want to go through with the expansion and want you to buy in as a partner."

I don't have any words at first. "Really?"

"Fuck yeah."

We spend some time going over business stuff—honestly, I'm still too shocked to process the whole thing—before heading to the club-house for church.

We drove down together in his truck since he had a cargo bed full of material for the gym repairs. "You ever planning to patch Heidi?" he asks me.

"Christ, we just figured shit out. I was giving her brother some time to adjust."

His loud, rumbling laughter fills the cab. "Fuck him. He's had enough time to adjust." He glances over. "Besides, he might surprise you."

"I was thinking of throwing it out there today."

He nods. "About time."

Feeling encouraged from Wrath's words, I can't wipe the grin off my face as we sit at the table. Rock knows I'm up to something and keeps an eye on me. As soon as regular business finishes, I raise my hand.

"I'm claiming Heidi." I turn and look at my best friend. "Anyone who has an issue with that should say so now."

He stares at me, a slow smirk forming at the corner of his mouth. Like an absolute asshole, he grumbles, "About fucking time."

"Dick." I reach over and slap him and he grins at me.

"Since it looks like big brother isn't going to have a meltdown, should we take a vote?" Rock asks.

Usually a vote on an ol' lady is just the officers. Rock doesn't ask the rest of the guys to leave this time.

"She knows better than anyone to keep her mouth shut," Z says. "She's a little badass. Knows how to shoot. Never asks questions. Young, but good ol' lady material."

That's a lot of stuff in Heidi's favor, and I can't help feelin' proud that Z feels that way about my girl.

Wrath grins. "She was ready to take a bullet for you, Murphy. I don't think you'll do any better than that."

Teller adds, "She loves the club as much as any of us." Which I guess is his way of saying yes.

Rock stares at me thoughtfully for a few minutes before giving his okay. "She understands the life. She'll be an asset to the club as an ol' lady."

His endorsement leaves a lump in my throat. "Feelin' old, prez?" I ask to shake it off.

"Yes." He shakes his head, but he's smiling. "Love both of you. You certainly took the longest route possible to get here."

"Thanks a lot." I can't stop grinning though, so he knows I'm not too pissed.

Z stands and leans over the back of his chair. "When do you want to do it?" he asks with a sly smile.

"Don't know. Haven't talked to her about it recently. Soon."

"Please tell me you didn't knock my sister up?" Teller asks.

"No, you dick." Then, because I feel like being an asshole after that question, I add, "Not that I haven't been trying."

Yeah, it was a dick thing to say, but he had it coming. Everyone laughs.

Except Teller.

He punches me in the arm. "Fuck you," he grumbles.

Z walks over to our side of the table and drapes a leather vest in front of me.

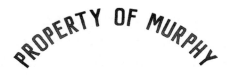

All the officers' patches are already sewn on the side. My four-leaf clover's right up front on the left.

My jaw drops. "Holy shit." I glance up, looking over each of my brothers. "When did you do this?"

Z's gaze slides away. "When she moved back. Figured one way or another, you'd *finally* claim her ass. Didn't want you to have to wait."

Wrath points to Rock and then himself. "We had to wait forever for ours. Be thankful we broke him in for you."

"That sounded really gay," Z snarks back.

"You wish."

I can't wait another second.

"All right, fucksticks. I'm out."

Z holds his hand out, but I pull him in for a hug. "Thanks for doing this, brother. I really appreciate it."

"Bonfire later," Wrath says, slapping my open palm. "Trin bought this little tent thing, so you can bring the baby."

"Thanks."

Everyone else congratulates me on the way out. I stuff her vest back into the plain brown package and head to Rock's house.

Heidi's playing on the floor with Alexa but jumps up when she sees me. "How was church?"

"Good. Feel like going for a walk with me?"

"Sure."

We haven't built a driveway out here yet, but Z and I have been working on smoothing out some of the paths, so it's easier to use Alexa's stroller. Turns out strollers are like fucking cars, and I ended up finding a Sport Utility Stroller with three sixteen-inch wheels, a hand brake, and a footbrake. It's badass, and Alexa loves being in it. Which is good, because today she's in for a long ride.

Heidi glances at the package in my hands but doesn't say anything. Part of me thinks she already suspects what's about to happen.

Doesn't dim my enthusiasm one bit.

We take the loop that passes Wrath and Trinity's house—which is *finally* finished and keep going. Heidi gives Alexa a running commentary of everything we pass, and I never get tired of listening to her.

We finally stop at the place we're planning to build our house. Heidi's giddy and rattles off a long list of stuff she wants the house to include.

I can't wait to give her anything and everything she wants.

When she winds down, I motion her over. "You know you're already my ol' lady, right?"

"I guess," she teases.

"Brat."

She grins even bigger.

"You know what's in here, don't you?"

She points to the address on the front of the package. "Patty's Patches."

"Fuckin' Z," I grumble.

Heidi

Until Hope, there hadn't been any ol' ladies in the club since I was a kid. Even so, I remember how much I wanted one of those vests when I grew up.

No, not *one* of those. Murphy's.

To finally, officially, belong to him.

I can't stop the fluttering in my belly or the blood racing through my veins. I'm well aware of what people outside the club would think about a patch declaring me "property of" and don't care one bit.

I know without a doubt I own Blake's heart as much as he owns mine.

He shakes the vest out, setting the empty package in one of the stroller compartments. Alexa squees and claps her little hands, as if she knows what a big occasion this is.

I'd spied the officers' patches on Hope's vest and Trinity's vest but wasn't sure they'd end up on mine.

"My brother really voted me in?" I ask running my fingers over the familiar dollar sign patch.

"Hell yeah, he did." He helps me put it on and zips it up, adjusting the buckles on the side. "The assholes must have done it a while ago, too, because Z had it ready and waiting for me."

"Really?"

"Yup. Z called you a little badass."

Knowing the men I've looked up to since I was little, and consider my uncles, think I'm worthy of being part of the club in this way steals my breath.

When he's finished, I throw myself against him, and he holds me for a long time. Neither of us saying a word.

Blake moves first, kissing my cheek. "Love you so much, beautiful."

"Me, too."

Before I get weepy or something, he turns me to face the woods. "So, is this the spot? You're sure?"

"Yes. I love it."

"Good."

We take the long way back to Rock and Hope's house. "Bonfire tonight to celebrate," he says as we get closer.

"Alexa—" I'm worried about mosquitos and bonfire smoke in her eyes, which he apparently realizes.

"Wrath said Trinity has it covered."

"Oh my gosh!" Hope yells from the porch, rushing down the stairs to meet us. "Rock told me you voted today." She grins at Murphy and pulls me in for a hug.

And just like that, I'm officially an ol' lady of the Lost Kings MC.

Fifty-Seven

MURPHY

Nothing beats being surrounded by family and having your girl in your arms. My girl wearing my patch.

She turns, feeding me a sticky, messy s'more. I end up licking most of it off her fingers, which makes her squeal and laugh. "That tickles."

She turns and pushes me until I'm flat on my back in the cool, wet grass. My hand cups the back of her head, holding her still for a long, lingering kiss.

"For fuck's sake!"

Something hard thumps my leg, and I break away from Heidi's sweet mouth. "Ow."

Marcel's towering over us, waving his cane in my face. "Have some respect, would ya? Just because I voted her in doesn't mean I want to watch you violate my sister all night long," he grouches, dropping into the grass next to us.

"Then don't look," Heidi sasses back.

He pokes her in the side and she slaps his hand away. I sit up, pulling her with me. "What's up?"

"Rock wants to see you."

I look out over the field bathed in the orange glow from the fire and clouds of smoke. "Where is he?"

Teller points to the left of the fire, where I just make out the silhouettes of what can only be Wrath, Z, and Rock.

"You know what it's about?"

"Sounds like you're headed to Sway's tomorrow."

"Fuck that." No way am I leaving Heidi alone for a single night. Not this soon.

She seems to sense my resistance. "Go on. See what Rock needs."

"You sure you're okay, babe?" I ask, kissing her cheek and she nods.

"She's fine," Teller snaps.

"You're begging for an ass kicking, you know that?" I warn.

He lets me pull him up off the ground with minimal complaining.

"You know, if she's gonna be an ol' lady, she has to get used to you being away sometimes," he advises on our way over.

"Maybe it's *me* who doesn't want to be away from her. Ever consider that?"

His hand clamps down over my arm, stopping me. I face him, bracing myself for the *you're such a pussy* insults he's probably planning. His jaw works for a second—and holy shit, is my best friend actually speechless? Finally, he loosens his grip and continues walking as if nothing happened.

Heidi

As I watch Blake and my brother walk away, Alexa lets out a flurry of fussy noises. Sitting up, I poke my head in the little tent Trinity set up for us and do a quick diaper change.

"How is she?"

"Oh, shit!" Startled and feeling foolish, I back out of the tent to find Trinity smiling down at me.

"Sorry, didn't mean to scare you."

Brushing grass off my pants, I stand. "Thank you so much for doing that." I gesture lamely at the tent.

"No problem. I didn't want you to feel...left out when we do stuff like this."

Before I can thank her, she nods at my vest. "Congratulations."

My cheeks warm and I glance away. "I think I'm still in shock."

Her lips slide into a sympathetic smile. "Long time coming."

"True." A bunch of things I've wanted to say for a while come to mind. "Trinity, I'm sorry I was so mean—"

"Don't. We're fine. I understand." She lowers her gaze to the grass for a few seconds before continuing. "I would have...I would have felt the same way." She stares in the direction of the guys, who appear to be having a heated conversation. "He loves you."

"I know."

"We're only friends."

Embarrassment for starting this whole uncomfortable conversation warms my cheeks but I smile anyway. "Please. I only have to be around you and Uncle Wrath for five seconds to know there's no one else for you."

She snorts and bumps me with her shoulder. We both sit down on the blanket Blake brought with us.

I'm not sure why, but I still feel like there's more to say. "Murphy told me...he told me you were there for him when his mom died."

She blinks a few times before answering. "That was a rough time."

"I know I met her once or twice, when I was little, but I barely remember her."

"Hey, Trin," my brother says, interrupting the supremely awkward talk Trinity and are weaving through.

"Where's Blake?" I ask.

"Christ, you *can* be apart for five seconds, right?"

"No. Not really." I stick my tongue out at him, because well, he's my big brother.

Next to me, Trinity shakes with laughter. "Young love."

A flash of pain freezes my brother's face for a second. Whether it's physical pain from the accident or something else, I'm not sure. "Hey." I lean forward and tap his hand. "I never got to tell you about running into Mom."

His blond eyebrows shoot up and his jaw drops. He'd look less surprised if I'd smacked him upside the head with a branch. "What? When?"

For the next few minutes, I recount my two recent encounters with our long lost mother.

"What a bitch," he mutters.

"Pretty much," I agree.

Trinity nods at Blake and Wrath, who are making their way over to us. "Jeez, the four of us could form a 'shitty mothers club.'"

It's an awful thing to laugh about, but that doesn't stop us.

My brother grabs my hand, giving it a quick squeeze to get my attention. "I want you to stay away from her."

"No problem there."

"I'm serious, Heidi. She's bad news. If she calls you again, let me know."

Marcel's gradually eased up on the overprotective big brother antics over the last few months, so I take his warning seriously. "Okay. I will."

"What's going on?" Wrath asks as he sits next to Trinity and pulls her into his lap.

"You tell us." I glance up at Blake. "Are you taking off?"

He runs his hand over his beard before settling down next to me. "Not tonight. Tomorrow."

I wait for more information, but instead he asks about Alexa.

"She's fine."

Rock and Hope wander over. Hope waits patiently while Rock smooths out a blanket next to ours.

After they're sitting, Rock lifts his chin in Blake's direction. "Ol' ladies were invited down, too. If that makes it easier."

"Fuck that," my brother snaps.

Blake ignores Marcel's outburst. "I know Tawny said it would be family friendly, but I don't want Alexa down there."

Part of me is a little annoyed Blake's making this decision without asking me. In some ways, I'd very much like to go to the downstate club and have Blake introduce me to everyone as his ol' lady. But the responsible mother part of me knows he's right.

"Um." Hope waves her hand in the air. "I'd rather stay here and help Heidi with the baby."

My heart skips. I was worried I'd be the only one staying behind.

Trinity turns to Wrath. "Are you running down, too?"

Wrath shoots a glare at Rock. "Apparently."

"I volunteer for baby duty, too," Trinity says, making Wrath chuckle.

I lean over and whisper, "Thank you."

She flashes a quick smile and mouths, "No problem."

My brother falls back in the grass. "I'm out. Still can't ride."

"You can always sit in the van, ya fuck," Blake says, leaning over and smacking my brother's arm. He turns to Rock. "Sway gonna be pissed if no ol' ladies come down?"

Rock lifts his shoulders. "Fuck him if he is."

Later, when everyone has drifted off to…do their own thing, Blake turns to me with uncertainty brewing in his eyes. "Are you mad about not going?"

"No." I've been working hard on being truthful with Blake no matter what. The way he asked me to. "I'd really like to have you"—I feel childish admitting this—"you know, tell everyone I'm yours. That you're with me. But you're right, it's not a good idea to bring Alexa down there, and I can't ask Hope to watch my daughter all the time. So, no. I'm not mad."

His mouth slides into a hint of a smile, but his eyes still seem troubled. His words are strong, though. "Believe me, Heidi, I'm yours. I'm not going down there to… I meant it when I said there was no one else for me."

"I'm not worried about *that*. I trust you."

He covers my hand with his. As always, his touch is gentle as he picks my hand up, dipping his head to kiss my open palm. "Thank you."

Fifty-Eight

MURPHY

"I'm fine, I swear," Heidi says for the tenth time this morning. Even though I've asked her ten times, there's no exasperation in her voice. Nope. She wraps her arms around me, kissing my jaw.

"I haven't spent enough time with you." I lower my voice, my mouth hovering over hers. "I don't want to spend a night away from you." I squeeze her a little tighter against me.

She makes a sweet "aww" sound and presses her lips to mine.

"For fuck's sake," Z groans from a couple feet away. "We won't even be gone for forty-eight hours, Murphy. You'll survive."

"Jealousy's an ugly color on you, Uncle Z," Heidi teases, making him smirk.

Z kisses Alexa's cheek and adjusts her in his arms. "Your mom's got a smart mouth on her, baby girl. You're gonna be just like her, aren't ya?"

Laughing, because that's probably true, I let go of Heidi, but sling an arm over her shoulders. "Where's prez?"

Z cocks his head to the side. "Where do you think? Having a goodbye slamfest, no doubt."

Heidi slaps her hands over her ears. "Ew! Why would you say that in front of me?"

Z and I chuckle at her expense, and my reward is her hand slapping my chest.

She stomps over to Z with her arms out. "Give me my daughter back. I don't want her first word to be *slamfest*."

"Could be worse." Z chuckles as he hands Alexa over.

Our attention's pulled toward crunching leaves and snapping twigs in the woods. A few seconds later Rock and Hope come strolling out.

"About time," Z grumbles.

"Sorry." Hope giggles, not looking one bit sorry.

Behind us, the front door slams open. "Are we going or not?" Wrath bitches. Trinity laughs and nudges him down the front steps.

We circle around Rock. My hand's tight around Heidi's waist. I don't want to let her go until the very last second. We discuss the route we're taking and when we plan to return tomorrow.

Then, it's time to go.

I take Alexa out of Heidi's arms and cuddle her against me. "Be good, baby."

"Da!" she yells, slapping my cheeks. A burst of high-pitched baby giggles spill out of her, and my reluctance to leave grows even stronger.

Rock kills the moment a few seconds later when he kicks his bike over. The rumble startles Alexa and she wails, tears sliding down her red cheeks. "Shh. It's okay." But Alexa's not having it. I hand her back to Heidi. "Better take her inside."

Heidi gives me one last quick kiss. "Love you. Be safe."

"I'll be thinking of you the entire time."

She gives me a soft smile in return. "Me, too."

Heidi

I'm surprised at how calm I am as I watch the guys take off from inside the clubhouse.

Last night I meant it when I told Murphy I trust him. I don't feel abandoned either.

Hope steps next to me. "They'll be back before we know it."

"I know."

Fifty-Nine

MURPHY

The back county roads we take down to Sway's place instead of the Thruway are slow. For the first time in my life, I'm not enjoying the wind in my face.

Something's missing and I know exactly what it is. Heidi at my back.

Wrath's crankier than I am about the trip and has been giving Rock shit every chance he gets for forcing him to come along.

Z's amused by all of it.

Rock signals for us to pull over about twenty minutes from Sway's compound. "Are you two done sulking?" he asks, pointing at Wrath and then me.

"I'm cool, prez," I answer.

Wrath just folds his arms over his chest.

"He'll have church first thing tomorrow morning, and we'll head home after."

"I might stick around," Z says.

Rock tosses him a look. "That's fine."

When we finally arrive, Sway's place is quieter than usual. Only a few bikes in the front parking lot. "Where is everyone?" I ask Rock.

"On a run. Just supposed to be Sway, his VP and new SAA. Rest of the guys will be back for church in the morning."

"Fan-fucking-tastic," Wrath grumbles.

Sway greets us right inside the clubhouse doors. "Hey, motherfuckers. Took ya long enough."

He gives Wrath a hard handshake. "You haven't been here in forever."

"I know."

Tawny sets us up in rooms, and Sway asks us to meet him in their chapel.

Surprisingly, he sweeps us for bugs before letting us into the room. That's new.

"What's going on?" Rock asks.

"Listen," he says, his gaze straying to me. "I need to come clean with you."

An unease spreads through my gut.

Sway focuses on me. "The case on Bull's been closed. You're fully clear."

I hadn't given that much thought in a few months. But, it's good to know. Wrath sits forward and pins Sway with a hard stare. "What aren't you saying, brother?"

Sway's gaze flicks from Wrath to me to Rock. "Bull was a snitch."

"Fuck me," Z says letting out a low whistle.

"I'm sorry you got caught up in it," Sway says to me. "From what we were able to tell, the morning after the fight, he went in to meet with his handler, so that's how they knew about you."

"It's all good," I answer. Because fuck, what the hell else am I going to say? Our club's been airtight for years. *Years.* Bull had less time in the club than me, but he'd still been in long enough that finding out he was a rat is a huge blow.

I imagine it's killing Sway to admit this.

"What can we do?" Rock asks.

One corner of Sway's mouth lifts. "It's handled. Your boy Loco helped us with Bull. We had one other brother who was compromised. That's being taken care of tonight."

Jesus Christ. Sway's telling us he let one of Loco's guys take Bull out? A snitch? Someone who betrayed the entire brotherhood? That shit's usually handled by the club, not passed to an outsider.

This whole situation is pretty fucked up.

"Besides you four, only my VP and SAA know about Bull, so I'd like to keep it that way. I don't need brothers turning on each other."

"Yeah. Okay," Rock says, sounding preoccupied.

Sway slaps his hand on the table. "Go. Enjoy yourselves."

The four of us hit the bar and just stare at each other. Z mouths a "what the fuck?" at me and I shake my head.

"That is beyond fucked," Wrath mumbles. "Bull was an asshole, but a snitch?"

Rock's still quiet.

"What's wrong, prez?"

He shakes his head. "Later."

Sway slaps my back and pulls me in for a side-hug. "Serena's supposed to be stopping by later."

"Uh. Not interested. I'm with someone."

"So?"

Z snorts into his glass.

Sway eyes Wrath, Rock, and me with a teasing look of disgust. "Seriously? Your gals make you wear like metal cages on your dicks or something?"

Wrath moves to unbuckle his belt. "Yeah, wanna see?"

It's such a funny, unexpected thing for Wrath to do, it breaks all the tension of the night.

The front door slams open. A bunch of Sway's guys and a small army of club girls spill inside.

The only thing I feel is how much I miss Heidi.

"Rock, you need me?" I ask.

"Nah. Go ahead." He finishes his drink. "Actually, I'll go with you," he says, eyeing the growing crowd.

"I want to call Heidi before she goes to sleep," I explain on the way down the hall.

Rock's mouth turns up in a smile. "Figured."

Wrath catches up to us, almost knocking me over. "Fuck this," he grumbles. "I'm fuckin' out of here after church."

"Right behind you, brother."

We have to do the whole breakfast thing the next morning before we can get down to business.

Sway wands everyone for bugs again as we enter the chapel.

"So, let's start with the reason I dragged you guys down here," Sway shouts after slamming his gavel down. "The whole barn arson thing from last time y'all were down here has been closed. Permanently."

Rock sits forward. "How?"

"You really don't want to know," Sway answers. "Moving on. Remember the deal I told you we were working on with Stella?"

Sway's guys make a bunch of lewd noises, but the four of us are blank.

"The porn star?" Sway prompts.

Rock nods and gives an exasperated, "Yeah."

"She's scheduling some film dates in your area next year. Would you or your guys be up for providing security?"

"Fuck yeah," Z offers.

Rock glares at him.

"What? Dex and I will do it."

"I need at least four guys on it," Sway says.

"Four guys for one girl?" Rock asks not bothering to keep the irritation out of his voice.

Sway shrugs. "Can't be too careful."

"We'll work something out," Rock says. "Just give me a head's up."

"No problem."

They move on to club matters specific to their own charter that don't have a lot to do with us.

Couple hours later, I'm back on the road, headed home to my girls.

Sixty

The hardest roads lead to the most beautiful destinations.

Heidi

"Guys are home!" Trinity yells.

When they've all parked and shut the bikes down, I grab Alexa and head outside. My eyes lock on Blake, and I can't get to him fast enough. He meets me halfway, crushing us in a big hug. Alexa squeals and puts her hands on his chest, pushing him away.

"Uh oh. You mad at me, baby?" he asks her.

She ducks her head against my neck, hiding. Blake looks so upset. I shouldn't laugh, but can't help it. "Give her a minute."

He leans down and gives me a quick kiss. "Missed you."

"We missed you, too."

"Did you miss me, baby?" he asks Alexa. A few belly tickles finally convince her to turn his way and giggle. She holds out her arms and he takes her.

"How was it?" I ask.

"Nothing exciting."

With one arm carrying Alexa and the other around my shoulders, we follow everyone inside for dinner.

"How was your trip?" Hope asks after we're all seated.

The guys give the predictable vague answers.

Wrath takes Trinity's hand, whispering in her ear.

"You two ready for the wedding?" Z asks.

"Fuck yeah. Christ, it's taken forever," Wrath says with a grin. "First, we're taking a pre-wedding trip."

"Who the fuck goes on a pre-wedding vacation?" Teller asks.

"*We* do. Shut the fuck up," Wrath answers. He closes his hand over Trinity's. "She's been doing a lot of planning and shit, and I want to take her away for a few days." He lifts his chin at Blake. "I gave Dylan some extra hours so you're not shorthanded at the gym. You should be all set."

"I'll take care of it."

"Do you have a final guest list?" Hope asks.

Trinity whips out her ever-present pink wedding binder. "Lilly's invite got returned. Do you have a current address for her?"

Z's head snaps up. "You invited Lilly?"

Blake leans over. "Wanna go on a date tonight?"

The minute his shoulder brushes against mine, I lose track of the conversation going on around me. "Where?"

"You'll see."

"What about Alexa?"

"She's invited, too."

"Oh. Then, yes."

He pushes his chair out. "Later. We're headed out," he announces.

Sparky grins at us and flashes Blake a thumbs up.

We say goodnight. Blake takes Alexa from me and carries her back to the house.

"You don't want to hang out at the clubhouse a little longer?"

"Nope. Want to be alone with my girls," he says, taking my hand.

We stop at Rock and Hope's. I watch with a mix of curiosity and amusement as Blake packs a backpack for us and a bag for Alexa.

"What are you up to?" I ask.

"You'll see."

Outside, we pop Alexa in her stroller and Blake leads us into the woods.

We reach the building site for our house, and I gasp. "What is this?"

It takes me a second to take everything in. There's a large tent, fire pit, chairs, a cooler, and sleeping bags set up outside.

"Oh my God. How did you…? You were away."

Blake grins, clearly pleased that he managed to surprise me. "Sparky set it up for me."

Intrigued, I unzip the tent and stick my head inside. "Roomy." I wiggle my eyebrows at him and he laughs.

MURPHY

Later that night, after Alexa's safely tucked into her little travel crib inside the tent, Heidi and I are lying back on the sleeping bags, staring up at the stars.

"This is so beautiful. Maybe we don't even need to build a house," Heidi whispers.

I tuck her against my side by wrapping my arm around her. "I'll put skylights in the bedroom."

"Okay."

A buzz of adrenaline zips through me from what I'm about to do. I shift so I can see her better. She's still stargazing. "Heidi?"

Her curious eyes meet mine. "Yes."

"You gonna marry me?"

She sits up and stares at me. Between the light from the moon and the fire, I can make out all her beautiful features. "Are you asking for real?"

I can't keep the grin off my face, and I shouldn't tease her. I sit up and take her hand. "I'm asking for real."

Slipping my hand inside my cut, I pull out the tiny box I've been hiding all night.

"Heidi, will you marry me? Will you and Alexa always be my girls?"

She doesn't even look at the ring I slip on her finger. "Yes, yes, yes!" Her words come out in a rush and she knocks me backward, peppering my face with kisses.

After a few more kisses, she scrambles closer to the fire to look at the ring. "It's so beautiful. When did you buy this?"

"Don't worry about it."

"I love you, Blake," she says, returning to me. This time, I sit in one of the chairs and pull her into my lap.

"No more hard roads, beautiful. You and me. Together. I want to make you happy for the rest of our lives."

Her mouth curves into a sweet smile, and she places her hand on the side of my face. "But, those hard roads take us to the most beautiful places. Isn't that what you've always told me?"

Staring up at the stars, then back at her, I answer. "It's true."

The End.

Epilogue

Somewhere down the road...

MURPHY

"What's wrong, beautiful?" Heidi's been quiet all morning, but now she looks almost scared.

As her nervous brown eyes meet mine, her bottom lip trembles further setting off warning bells in my head.

"Nothing."

"What's behind your back?"

Slowly, she pulls her hand from behind her and waves a small white stick at me. "I'm pregnant," she says softly.

"Holy shit! Really?" My heart thuds with excitement. "Oh my God, this is awesome!"

I yank her into my arms, hugging her so hard she gasps.

She ducks out of my hold. "I'm sorry. I know we weren't—you're happy, right?" Her fingers twist her wedding rings round and round. The worst is how she won't meet my eyes.

I tuck my hand under her chin, lifting her face to look at me. "Heidi, I'm thrilled."

Finally, she relaxes a bit and gives me a hint of a smile. "I still need to go to the doctor to be sure."

"Okay. Tell me when so I can go with you."

"You'll do that?"

"Of course I will. I can't wait."

The last bit of fear or tension seems to flow out of her and she wraps her arms around my middle, resting her cheek on my chest. "I love you, Blake."

My hand runs up and down her back and I hug her tight to me. "Love you, too."

Alexa toddles over, wrapping her little arms around my leg. "Up," she demands.

With one final kiss on Heidi's forehead, I let her go. Leaning over, I pick up Alexa, lifting her high in the air until she squeals and giggles. "You ready to be a big sister, baby?" I ask.

Her eyes light up and she claps her hands.

"She's already a good big sister to Grace," Heidi points out.

I tuck Alexa against my side and she twists and turns. "Gracie?"

"Not yet, baby. They'll be over later."

"I hope it's a boy," I say. Heidi rolls her eyes. "Poor Chance is already outnumbered as it is."

"Please. He'll be thrilled when he's older."

I groan. Alexa needs a brother to help me beat Chance, and any other boys, off her when she's older. *Please, let it be a boy.*

"Can we keep it a secret?" Heidi asks. "Just until we know for sure?"

"Absolutely." On second thought. "Make the appointment soon. I'm way too excited to keep my lips sealed for long."

"Baby," Alexa says.

"Uh-oh." Heidi laughs and places a finger over her lips. "Shh. Secret."

"Secret baby," Alexa repeats in her sweet toddler lisp.

I doubt it will be a secret much longer.

Notes From the Author

Well, I hope you don't hate me too much. *More Than Miles* was quite a journey. It wasn't as painful or difficult an experience as I had with *Tattered on My Sleeve*, but I definitely stressed about how my readers would feel about certain things.

The story evolved over a long time. When I initially introduced Axel, in *Corrupting Cinderella*, I fully intended for Heidi to end up with him (I have two hundred #TeamAxel bracelets to back me up on this!) When I got to know her a little better in *Three Kings, One Night*, I thought she might want a life outside the club—I knew Axel would never patch in to the Lost Kings. Then through *Strength From Loyalty* and *White Heat*, I got to know her better, I realized how important the club and family was to her and knew taking her away from that would be the worst thing you could do to Heidi.

I knew Heidi wouldn't be a virgin—I hate stories where the hero has bedded anything on two legs, but the heroine's been saving herself for him all along. Heidi was not the type of girl to tolerate that. You might be interested to know that I fully intended for Murphy and Heidi to have sex in that opening scene. However, when it came time to write it, Heidi said, *fuck no* and the phone rang.

Some authors claim their characters do not influence the story, that they, the author, direct every action their character makes. I am not one of those. Any time I've tried to force events, it comes out flat and stilted. My characters frequently decide to do whatever the fuck they want no matter what vague outline I've sketched out. That's part of what makes this fun for me. It's the same reason I stopped worrying about molding my writing to the romance "norm" of a rising conflict, black moment at the seventy-five percent mark, etc. I don't write that way. It's boring to me. I finally stopped trying (in fact I recently walked out of a workshop on conflict, because it was doing me no good. Life is too short to feel bad about myself.) A lot of you love my books for my characters. Some readers seem confused/disappointed by my lack of conflict. That's okay. I have enough people at this point who have told me they've read the entire series over the course of a week to be comfortable with my style.

I enjoy the developing background MC story. Yes, I focus on the romance, but I also enjoy the MC culture and even though it is romanticized, I hope I do it justice. I had the opportunity to sit down with a few bikers recently and felt pretty confident that my series is more realistic than people think in *certain* respects. Highly romanticized in others.

I had fun with *More Than Miles*. *Tattered* stressed me out greatly, because it was difficult to write. I agonized over and wrote from scratch every piece that was included in *Tattered* only to be accused of "copy and pasting" from the first three books. My readers who "got" *Tattered* and loved Wrath and Trinity—thank you! I absolutely loved *White Heat*, even though I knew it probably wouldn't sell well, because I believed in the story and felt it needed to be told. That my readers seemed to love *White Heat* as much as I did helped make up for the lack of sales.

Knowing how much pressure those two books put on me for their individual reasons, Mr. Lake asked me to slow down and take my time writing More Than Miles. He knew what a long, complicated story it was turning into. He wanted me to go back to when I started working on Slow Burn, and it was just pure fun for me. Unfortunately, because I am also a horrible procrastinator, I do have to set a firm deadline at some point. I enjoyed my time with Murphy. I even wrote an epilogue! Something I swore I'd never write (sorry, Vanessa!) because I normally don't like reading them in other books.

At one point, I thought about scrapping Alaska all together, making it a simpler story, but I knew I'd hate myself if I took the easy way out.

The story evolved from many conversations with my crit partners. Hours of discussion with Mr. Lake (who was #TeamAxel from the beginning and not happy about Axel's demise.)I knew Axel wasn't patching into the club, but how or why? Some people suggested he could be a traitor working for a rival MC, but that felt too cliche. And although he wasn't right for Heidi, deep down he wasn't a disloyal person.

Axel and Heidi just weren't right for each other. They made mistakes that I think many young couples make, especially when they have poor role models. I could have gone the route that Axel was abusive, and at a certain point, I realized I might be sending that signal (although that wasn't my intention.) Two people can grow apart or just not be right for each other without either of them having to be the "bad guy." I don't think it was wrong for Axel to not want to be a father at twenty years old. He tried to step up, but he also wanted to follow his dreams. Both of them kept trying to do the right thing because neither wanted to admit they weren't right for each other.

Did Axel *have* to die? Some of my followers may have noticed I backed off the #TeamMurphy/#TeamAxel thing at a certain point. It just seemed cruel once I knew he wasn't going to survive the book. I worried about his death seeming like a cop-out and discussed alternatives at length with…just about everyone. In the end, I felt it would really suck if Heidi and Murphy went through all of that just to have Axel lingering in the background. He'd always be in their lives because of Alexa, and I didn't think that was fair to Heidi and Murphy. Honestly, I also loved the irony of him being killed by the job he loved more than his family. It just felt "right" to have him go. Sorry, Axel. I think it was clear, Heidi and Murphy would have ended up together whether Axel lived or died. It's why I chose not to "show" any sex between Heidi/Axel or Murphy/anyone else. I already did it in Tattered, and it didn't feel necessary here.

I jokingly called this the "murder book" at one point. Bull died…I wasn't planning on that. Mariella…*poor Mariella*. I swear my intention was never to fridge her. There was a point that I planned for her to end up with Teller, but like I said, when I make plans, my characters rebel.

At a certain point, I realized this was really Murphy's book. He spoke to me the loudest. He was so conflicted, so much softer at heart than I realized. I love him dearly and boy did he make me cry at times.

I cried for the lonely little boy who thought no girl would ever like him, to the teenager and young man who ended up with more girls than he knew what to do with, to the man who was convinced there was only one girl he ever wanted. I loved his surprise at not knowing who Heidi really was. He loved her. He'd been there for her since she was little. But at a certain point, he had to keep his distance, so it meant he missed knowing who she was a person. Once he figures it out he loves her even more. As it should be. His unconditional love and acceptance of her daughter was also one of my favorite pieces of his personality.

Another favorite part of mine was Heidi's bossiness in bed. I realize that some people will take Murphy's reaction/thoughts as "un-alpha" or something stupid like that. But his reaction made sense. I hate books where the manwhoring hero is some sex expert (Except for Wrath, because it was a point of pride for him) and the girl comes in 5.2 seconds of him getting near her. I think the more likely scenario when a guy has girls willing to service him whenever/however, is that he takes and doesn't bother to give back (feel free to send me your differing opinions on this). Plus, Murphy's still young and has never had a serious relationship. Of course, he rises to the occasion, and revels in figuring Heidi out (a very alpha thing to do in my opinion) otherwise he wouldn't be a romance hero.

I loved Heidi's growth throughout the whole series. I knew she had a bad background. She was bratty but not for the reasons people assumed. I loved seeing her go from insecure to confident. As my crit partners, Kari, and Virginia assured me "nothing makes you grow up faster than having children." I think Heidi turned out okay. I loved how she grew to realize what mattered and what didn't. Some people won't agree with her mending fences with Trinity, but I thought it was the logical, mature thing to do.

Those of you who have asked for more Hope and Rock, I hope you loved seeing them in More Than Miles. I knew they'd be a big part of it because Heidi would go to them when she had nowhere else.

Next, I plan for Wrath and Trinity to have their wedding. Someone shot at his gym, after all, so you *know* Wrath has some thoughts on that. I then planned for Z's book to be next, but during More Than Miles, Teller became such a strong character, my betas were dying for his story. I *think* I know who he ends up with. You've actually met this person in previous books.

If you read *Between Embers*, you realize I'm very aware of what all my secondary characters are up to. Maybe *too* aware you might think. What the heck was Z up to? *I* know what he's been up to. Are you wondering who Grace and Chance are? Will it surprise you if I say I know? What was Rock so distracted about at the end? Now *that* I don't know. Rock was tight-lipped through this book. My crit partner, Kari says it's because he's an uber-alpha and didn't like the story not being about him. I think I agree with her assessment.

I've been lucky enough to meet a few of my long-time readers this year. I've enjoyed meeting new readers as well and hope to make it to more signings and events in the future. Thank you to the readers who grilled me about who Heidi would end up with, it felt surreal to meet people who care about my characters as much as I do.

While writing More Than Miles was fun, as some of you know, at the start of the editing process, my beloved Pug passed away. It was unexpected and absolutely shattered me. Mr. Lake and I have a lot of people in our lives of the "it's just a dog, get over it" variety. The love and sympathy that friends and strangers expressed during this time meant a lot.

Thank you.
Much love.
Autumn

Also by

AUTUMN JONES LAKE

To be notified when new books are available for pre-order; Sign up for my newsletter, http://eepurl.com/bTSNkn.

Follow me on Book Bub. https://www.bookbub.com/authors/autumn-jones-lake

SLOW BURN (Lost Kings MC, Book #1)

Forced to represent an outlaw biker, a married attorney must come to terms with her feelings for her client while avoiding the danger he brings into her sedate life.

CORRUPTING CINDERELLA (Lost Kings MC, Book #2)

Love is the ultimate outlaw.

Although widowed attorney Hope Kendall cares deeply for President of the Lost Kings MC, Rochlan "Rock" North, the truth is they come from completely different worlds. Add to that the fact that they are also both headstrong people, and they have a very rough road ahead of them.

Real love isn't a fairy tale.

For Rock, that means introducing Hope to what it really means to be part of his brutal and shady world, where the Lost Kings Motorcycle Club is his main focus. For Hope, it means accepting the things she can't change, and understanding that Rock is a man who will do anything to keep her safe.

Love doesn't follow any rules.

As Rock continues to draw Hope deeper into his world, painful misunderstandings, past relationships, and opposition from the members of his club will threaten to drive them apart.

How do a lawyer and a badass biker with a heart of gold keep their love alive while their opposing worlds collide?

THREE KINGS, ONE NIGHT (Lost Kings MC #2.5)

A collection of three short holiday stories set in the Lost Kings MC world.
Heidi and Murphy.
Wrath and Trinity.
Z and Lilly.

STRENGTH FROM LOYALTY (Lost Kings MC, Book #3)

As a dark cloud descends over Hope and Rock's already precarious future, will a long-hidden secret push them both past the point of no return?

TATTERED ON MY SLEEVE (Lost Kings MC #4)

Wrath & Trinity
I had her first.
I fell in love with her.
Then we fucked everything up.

Warning: *Tattered on My Sleeve* is not a "typical" romance. It's not even a typical MC Romance.

Lust.

Eight years ago, the Lost Kings, MC was recovering from turmoil within the club Wrath and Trinity met. Their connection was instant and explosive.

Fury.

Wrath and Trinity's story is a heart-breaking, soul-crushing, tear-your-heart-into-pieces story. The way they hurt each other over the years is intense, raw, frustrating and sometimes dark.

Forgiveness.

Can they move past their horrible pasts to become better people and ultimately forgive each other?

They've wasted too many years. Once Wrath learns the dark secret that's been fueling Trinity for years, he'll stop at nothing to prove they're meant to be together and that she's worthy of the love she keeps denying.

*While there is technically no cheating in Tattered on my Sleeve, Wrath and Trinity's journey to love takes a much different route than Rock and Hope's.

WHITE HEAT (Lost Kings MC #5)

Rock & Hope, Wrath & Trinity

The queen always protects her king.

For straight-laced attorney, Hope Kendall, loving an outlaw has never been easy. New challenges test her loyalty as she discovers how far she's willing to go to protect her man.

If you have hope, you have everything.

MC President, Rochlan "Rock" North finally has everything he's ever wanted. Hope as his ol' lady and his MC earning money while staying out of trouble. The only thing left is to make Hope his wife. But as their wedding day nears, an old adversary threatens Rock's freedom, the wedding, and throws the Lost Kings MC into chaos.

Love makes the ride worthwhile.

While the club waits for Rock's fate to be decided, Wrath has to balance solidifying his new relationship with Trinity and fulfilling his president's orders.

Loyalty gives an outlaw strength.

Threats from unexpected places will challenge every member, but in the Lost Kings MC, brotherhood isn't about the blood you share. It's about those who are willing to bleed for you.

BETWEEN EMBERS (Lost Kings MC #5.5)

This collection of short stories is intended to be a fun, companion to White Heat. If you were wondering what the other guys were up to during Rock and Hope's wedding, here's your chance to find out.

Short stories include:

Teller

Murphy

Z

MORE THAN MILES (Lost Kings MC #6)

Sometimes the road you fear the most is the one that leads you home.

Blake "Murphy" O'Callaghan, Road Captain of the Lost Kings MC, has the world by the balls. Money. Women. The wide-open road. It's all his, everything he wants…except the one girl he loves, the one girl who's off limits. His best friend's little sister, Heidi.

Abandoned by her mother when she was only eight, Heidi Whelan's familiar with heartbreak. Especially the heartbreak of falling in love with her big brother's best friend. When Murphy pushed her away, it broke her heart. Now, on her eighteenth birthday, he claims he loves her? Growing up around the Lost Kings MC, Heidi's witnessed his manwhoring ways. He'll never give that up for her. Besides, he's too late: Heidi's in love with her high-school boyfriend Axel.

Axel Ryan loves two things—motorcycles and Heidi. He signed up to be a prospect for the Lost Kings MC because it seemed like a fun way to get closer to her. Now that he's gotten a taste of MC life, he's not so sure this is where he belongs. He's confident Heidi shares his dreams for the future, so even if he chooses another road, their relationship will survive the detour.

With more than miles between them, will the deceptions they've lived with for so long be too much to overcome? Can Murphy convince Heidi that the hard roads they've traveled will lead to the most beautiful destination of all, or is he destined to ride the open road alone?

KICKSTART MY HEART (MC Meets Mob #1)

Included in the 80's Mix Tape anthology
Setting: Los Angeles, 1989
A fledgling actress and the son of an MC President who wants to be a rock star.
Little do either of them know how much they actually have in common.
*Has a slight connection to The Lost Kings MC Series.

Coming Soon

Objection

White Knuckles (Lost Kings MC #6.5)

Teller's Book (not yet titled) (Lost Kings MC #7)

After Burn (Lost Kings MC #7.5)

Zero Tolerance (Lost Kings MC #8)

Author Bio

Autumn prefers to write her romances on the classy side of dirty, and she's a sucker for a filthy-talking, demanding alpha male hero. The bigger the better. She believes true love stories never end.

Her past lives include baking cookies, slinging shoes, and practicing law. She's an active member of her local chapter of Romance Writers of America.

Autumn was born and raised in upstate New York. She still enjoys all four seasons there with her very own alpha hero and their dogs.

You can easily find Autumn on Facebook, but she also always loves to hear from readers at:

AutumnJLake@gmail.com.

Sign-up for her newsletter here: eepurl.com/bTSNkn

Visit Autumn here:
www.autumnjoneslake.com
Facebook: facebook.com/AutumnJonesLake

VEXED

If you're interested in learning more about Romeo, the president at the club Murphy and Dex visited, here is an excerpt of his story, *Vexed* (Iron Bulls MC #4) by Phoenyx Slaughter.

About *Vexed* (Iron Bulls MC #4)
by Phoenyx Slaughter
Falling in love will only leave you vexed.

Recent high school graduate, Athena Vale, might seem bubbly and uncomplicated, but she has big plans and even bigger dreams, she's only ever shared with her best friend, Karina. Athena's strict upbringing has left her curious about taking a walk on the wild side—just once. And she knows exactly who she wants to go wild with.

President of the Iron Bulls MC, Reed "Romeo" Crownover has no shortage of women willing to entertain him. But these days, there's only one girl on his mind—Athena. When she shows up at his clubhouse on the night of her eighteenth birthday, he decides it's time to work her out of his system.

But one night turns into two, two turns into three, and soon the no-strings fun turns into something more passionate than either of them expected. An intense romance neither of them have ever experienced or knew they wanted.

She's half his age.
He doesn't fit in her world.
She's leaving for Los Angeles to start a new life in a few days.
Their connection was vexed from the start.

VEXED
adjective: vexed
verb: vex

1.(of a problem or issue) difficult and much debated; problematic.
synonyms:disputed, in dispute, contested, in contention, contentious, debated, at issue, controversial.
1.annoyed, frustrated, or worried.
synonyms:annoyed, irritated, exasperated, irked, piqued, nettled, displeased, put out, disgruntled; informal aggravated, peeved, miffed, riled, hacked off, hot under the collar, teed off, ticked off, sore, bent out of shape.

CHAPTER ONE
Romeo

HOW CAN I STILL BE fucked up over one little girl?
Athena.
That sweet little bitch has had me acting stupid since the day her sassy ass showed up at my clubhouse.

It's Dante's fault. My Sergeant-at-Arms found himself a girl, Karina. Hot, smart, and down for about anything. Stare at her for longer than two seconds and you're asking for an up close and painful introduction to Dante's fists. My stone-faced-killer friend doesn't fuck around when it comes to his girl. It's *her* best friend I haven't been able to stop thinking about.

Tagging along with Dante to the girls' graduation yesterday didn't help. That's *high school* graduation, mind you. All I thought about was how today she'd be turning eighteen. Not even running into her uptight, upscale, bitch-faced parents had settled my dick down.

Like fuck do I plan to chase after her. Not my style. Besides, there's enough willing girls trolling my clubhouse who've been legal longer than five seconds. Any one of them will be thrilled to service me, then go away. The way I prefer my relationships. Quick and uncomplicated.

Unfortunately, my dick isn't interested in any of them. No matter how hard the girls have tried to get my attention tonight.

Spotting Dante and Karina walk in the front of door, I glance behind them. No Athena.

I'm capable of casually asking about her without sounding like a complete creep, right?

Then she stumbles in the door. With her scared little Goldilocks expression, she looks like she's about to meet up with the biggest, baddest wolf.

Me.

Dante's wearing his *I need to choke someone face.* Hooking my thumbs in my pockets, I approach the trio slowly.

"What's up?" I ask Dante, who rolls his eyes at me. He's not fooled one bit by my laid back act.

"Hi, Romeo," Karina says shyly. I still can't get over how a scary motherfucker like Dante managed to snag such a beautiful and soft-spoken chick. "Um, Athena and I spent the day with her family for her *birthday*, and she asked if she could join us tonight. I hope that's okay." I appreciate the emphasis Karina puts on the word birthday. What a nice, subtle hint that her friend's now fair game.

Finally.

"Is it your birthday, sweetheart?" I ask Athena. When I put all my attention on her, she blushes and glances at the floor. A much different reaction than I expected, considering how tough she usually acts.

"Yes."

Dante sighs and steps away from the girls. Karina leads her friend to the bar and I ain't happy about not being able to say more than a few words to the girl who's taken over my every wank fantasy for weeks now.

Taking me by the arm, Dante pulls me a few steps away. "Listen, I ain't got no say over what you do with your dick, brother. But I feel responsible for her, being she's Karina's friend and all. Treat her with care, please."

It's a lot for my Sergeant-at-Arms to say. There aren't many females he gives two fucks about. And I sure as fuck don't remember the last time I heard *please* come out of his mouth. For once, I set my sarcasm aside. "Yeah. She'll be okay with me. I won't let her out of my sight."

Dante searches my face and must finally decide I'm sincere, because he nods. We join the girls at the bar. Dante immediately pulls his girl to his side.

"Athena, we'll be upstairs. You need anything, call your girl." He tilts his head toward Karina, then drags her upstairs. Not that she protests.

Athena watches them leave, but I can't take my eyes off her. She pushes her shoulders back and slowly swivels her bar stool toward me. "Am I finally allowed to have a tour of your clubhouse, Mr. President?" she asks in a low, husky voice I don't expect from someone her age.

Seems Miss Goldilocks isn't so scared anymore.

"Come here, you," I say as I pull her closer. I spin her seat, so her back's to the bar and she has to tip her head back to see my face. Staring down into her bold, steel-blue eyes unbalances me. "Did you have a good birthday?"

"Not really. I think you can make it better, though."

I can make it better, or I can make it the biggest mistake of her young life. I shouldn't mess around with this girl. She deserves a nice guy, who isn't almost twice her age.

Except, I've wanted her from the second we met. And now there's no reason I can't have her.

Athena

All day I begged Karina to let me tag along to her boyfriend's motorcycle club, but now that I'm here, I'm terrified.

The reality is so much scarier than all the things I've fantasized about since the first time I visited the Iron Bulls MC's clubhouse.

A few weeks ago, I'd dropped Karina off to visit her boyfriend. I hadn't expected the president of the club to take an interest me. The intensity of his deep blue eyes tied my tongue in knots and I made a fool of myself. That had been during the middle of the day. Things were relatively calm.

Tonight, the clubhouse is in the middle of a big celebration, and I've never seen some of the sex acts being done around me. Not even on those five-minute Pornhub clips I've snuck a peek at once or twice when I found my way around my parents' firewall.

My best friend has been keeping serious secrets. It blows my mind Karina hangs out around this erotic mayhem and never told me. I'm utterly shocked and throbbing with curiosity about everything I see.

You're a whore just like your friend.

I give myself a shake, hoping to silent my parents' ever-present criticism and focus. I swore if I had another chance to talk to Romeo, I wouldn't embarrass myself. Yet here I am, gawking like a scared little girl.

This is the scene Romeo's used to. The kind of behavior he expects. Sexy, confident girls. Not virgins who have no idea what they're doing.

Well, some idea.

But my ex-boyfriend, Bobby, might as well have been an armadillo for all the similarity he has to Romeo.

The arrogance of having a road name like Romeo. Either he's really good in the sack or has a micro penis.

God, I hope it's not a micro penis.

The way he's staring at me and running his hand over a chin full of scruff, I think I'm about to find out.

"Did you have a good birthday?" he asks while watching me as if I'm the only person in the room.

Because he wants to get in your panties, idiot.

He doesn't even pretend he's not checking me out. His deep sapphire eyes gleam with sex and mischief while they appreciate my long, bare legs, covered by a short, frilly skirt. I practically feel the weight of his gaze as it moves up my body, over my hips, and over the swells of my breasts, barely concealed by the flimsy fabric of my camisole.

"Not really. I think you can make it better, though." Where the hell did I find the lady balls to say *that?*

Romeo likes my forwardness. A feral smile lights up his face. Hell help me, this man's insanely hot. The beard scruff doesn't hide the hard angles of his jaw. The fitted T-shirt he's wearing under his leather vest hints at the rock-hard body underneath. Tattoos peek out from every available inch of skin. His thick, dark hair seems too wild to be contained and falls over his forehead in a way that declares *badass.* Every inch of him screams reckless, gruff, crude, dirty, dangerous, and utterly irresistible.

I'm so in over my head with this guy…this man.

And I can't wait to see what happens next.

Printed in Great Britain
by Amazon

82912132R00281